Wives & Other Women

(Philip II of Spain)

Linda Carlino

VeritasPublishing
8 Vane Road Barnard Castle
County Durham DL12 8AQ
England

First published in 2008
Revised and reprinted in 2009
Revised, reformatted, and reprinted in 2009

Family trees: Linda Carlino
Cover: *Venus & Adonis*, Titian, Museo del Prado
Photographs: Museo del Prado

ISBN: 978-0-9555980-2-9

Printed and bound by
BookPrintingUK.com
Peterborough, England

www.VeritasPublishing.co.uk

Philip II of Spain

At a time when men, especially kings, were expected to produce male heirs Philip embarked on several dynastic marriages but was always disappointed and frustrated.

Wives & Other Women focuses on these loveless marriages — and his compulsive pursuit of other women.

With a background of family turmoil and a court plagued by intrigue and treachery, the result is a fascinating and very lively story.

Acknowledgements

I would like to extend my heartfelt thanks to all my friends in England and in Spain for their continued support and encouragement.

Words could never express my indebtedness to my dear husband for the countless hours he has devoted to all the unseen background work necessary to bring the trilogy* into being. It has been a long, challenging, but rewarding journey for us lasting several years. Together we have made a dream become a reality.

*That Other Juana
*A Matter of Pride
*Wives & Other Women

Contents

Spain

1554

Maria Manuela

Wives of Philip II

1543

Maria Manuela
(cousin)

|

Carlos

1

Isabel drew her long, thin fingers through the damp curls still clinging to her temples, releasing them to let them fall amongst the golden tangle of tresses on the pillow. Next she pulled the sheet over her nakedness tucking it under her arms, knowing how her lover enjoyed this vision of her after their lovemaking, insisting it made her a study in unalloyed purity.

'I shall miss you so much,' the words escaped on a sigh as she gazed at the embroidered coat of arms on the canopy above her.

'Not nearly so much as I shall miss you.' Prince Philip of Spain turned, propped himself up on one elbow and smiled down on his mistress, his love for almost twelve years since he was but a youth of sixteen. 'You are the only one I have ever loved, the only one I could ever love. If ever there was an ideal wife for me it is you my Isabel de Osorio.'

Still concentrating on the coat of arms, the quartered shield of lions, castles, the vertical red and gold bands of Aragón, she announced, 'I shall retire to a nunnery.' She confirmed the decision with several decisive nods.

Philip howled with laughter, kissed her sensual lips always so incredibly inviting. He rolled onto his back, 'That has to be the most absurd suggestion I have ever heard. You, a *nun*? Unimaginable! The Church would never survive! I see it now; 1554 will go down in history as the year Isabel de Osorio brought about the downfall of a convent in Spain.'

'How unfair of you to laugh; you know full well that that is what widows do. I am about to become a widow, therefore I must do as other widows.'

'But I am not going to die. Sadly my leaving puts an end to our life together, but there is no need for you to say farewell to the world. And, you have our children to raise.'

'My brother could so easily do that for me; I think I will not have the heart to. I would be far better employed praying for you and I could do that best if I were in a convent.' She sighed again, 'It was all so different with your last marriage; we would be together whenever you wished.' And, she added to herself, they could still be together had he gone ahead with the Portuguese contract to marry this other cousin of his; but no, instead of marrying the princess and bringing her to Spain to live he was going far away to marry the English queen.

For an instant she wanted to wound him in retaliation for the hurt she felt at being abandoned; a dismissal similar to that of his cousin in Portugal, a woman the same age as her, not that much older than Philip. They were to be set aside for an old lady. Everyone was gossiping about how his father had reneged on the Portuguese agreement at the last minute because England offered better pickings, and that there had been no resistance on Philip's part.

'This bride is your ancient crabby old aunt Mary ... and England no more than ... and what of the feelings of the spurned princess?'

'Go no further! Do not speak of matters forbidden to you! Keep to your own affairs!' He leapt up, throwing off the bed coverings, snatching up his quilted robe.

She had nettled his conscience and she had no business to. Political marriages were complicated, and as a prince he fully understood the rules and the breaking of them when it suited; but her words had caught him unprepared, had stung him; had planted his own questionable behaviour firmly before him. The letter he had written to his father was there again; ... *your suggestion comes at a timely moment inasmuch as King John of Portugal, the wealthiest of all kings, has chosen not to be as liberal as he originally intended and is now suggesting a mean and paltry dowry. The English match, therefore sounds more advantageous.*

Isabel threw a robe about her shoulders and followed him from the bed, deserting their recent love nest. 'Oh, dear God, what have I said? I beg your forgiveness, my lord; it was my selfishness speaking. I should have held my tongue. To think I could have uttered such dreadful things; and to you, the most wonderful of men. You will leave me now with such hatred in your heart.'

He turned to fold her into his arms, his anger banished. 'No. The fault is all mine; insisting we spend this one final night together. I should have realised how difficult it could be.'

'You will forgive and forget?'

On this occasion he would forgive and forget; a rare if not singular decision. She was probably the only one to be so favoured.

'All is forgiven.' He helped her into her robe teasing free the golden curls trapped beneath its collar. He smiled at his darling Isabel de Osorio. This was the woman who had filled his heart with love after almost three years of loneliness and grief following the death of that other beloved Isabel, his mother.

They bathed with lavender perfumed water from a large bowl near the fire; he helped dry her, wiping away the remaining tears from her petal-soft cheek.

'Now, some wine; and it is time for giving and receiving gifts.'

'But Philip I have none. I had no idea.'

'Hush, hush; leave everything to me, my sweet darling.'

She followed him to a small table cluttered with papers, boxes, a wine jug and two glasses then watched as he poured the rich, dark liquid into the waiting Venetian glasses already splendid enough in their majestic colours and gold stems.

'To my true bride, my real wife,' he touched his glass against hers and sipped.

She looked deep into his pale blue eyes, drinking more deeply from them than the glass clasped in her hands. Those eyes which had sparkled and laughed his joy in her company from the moment he had first seen her, in his sister Juana's court all those years ago. They were not, as so many insisted, piercing cold, making you look away. Far from it, they were kind eyes, and what people didn't understand was that Philip was shy. It was all the fault of his father; yes, he had much to answer for.

Philip set the glasses down. From amongst the chaos on the table he chose a folded piece of paper carefully secured with a red ribbon and handed it to Isabel standing back to watch and laugh, as her struggling hands shook, making the untying almost impossible.

'How foolish! I am all fingers and thumbs.'

The paper was finally opened to reveal a ring and a message in Philip's dreadful untidy scrawl, '*A wedding ring for my true love and bride,*' she read, '*with my undying love and affection, Philip.*'

'Let me put it on your finger. There, this puts the seal on the old priest's blessing when he made you my bride.'

Isabel could do no more than stare at the exquisitely designed ruby and diamond ring. After an eternity, or so it seemed, she kissed Philip, stammering, 'What can I say?'

'For the first time you are speechless. Amazing; my Isabel is speechless. I hope you can make those lovely blue eyes look at something else, for a little while at least. I am impatient to show you my gift to myself.'

Philip congratulated himself for having made the right choice in selecting the ruby ring from the many he had taken from his grandmother's jewellery caskets. And grandmother would be none the wiser living as she did in her world of semi-madness.

'This will travel with me to the icy northern land of England.'

The heavy curtain along one wall was drawn aside revealing a huge canvas.

'Oh, my goodness!' Isabel's hands rushed to her cheeks to cover her blushes, 'I recognise the man for that certainly is you; but, the lady surely cannot be ...' she hid her eyes. 'Can it be? Is it?'

Philip was behind her, hugging her shoulders, kissing her golden head, 'Yes, my love, there we are, two Greek gods. *Venus and Adonis*. I had Titian paint it for me.'

His eyes greedily devoured once again this painting of the young god, hunter turned shepherd, his bow and arrows hanging unwanted on a tree. He delighted in his image as the young Adonis preparing to leave with his dogs. He indulged himself, his gaze first fixing on the handsome and muscular god before moving to the voluptuous Venus reaching out to detain Adonis, the sensuality of her outstretched arms encircling the god's body seeming to burn into his own flesh, arousing him.

'Adonis must leave, must go to Persephone as Zeus has ordered, despite the pleas of Venus. Zeus commands; they obey.'

Isabel peeked between her fingers at the figures, speaking to him over her shoulder, 'I see it all. How clever of you. You are my Adonis and your father is Zeus; and you will still have my arms about you, however far away,' she turned and playfully threw her arms around him before pushing him away. 'But how wicked of you! At least someone had the decency to save me from the embarrassment of being identified. Gracious me, all that nakedness for everyone to see; thank goodness my body is pressed against yours and only my bare behind is on view. What would people think?'

'As I said, this is for my eyes only. When I retire to my apartments on cold English nights, having fulfilled my duties to my lady wife, I shall feast my eyes and heart on this reminder of our wonderful times together. And if perchance anyone else should see it, I shall merely remind them of the legend and inform them of the increasing popularity of such works of art.'

'Excuses, excuses. I know how you enjoy the role of voyeur; watching, examining; and unobserved if possible.'

She was right, of course; and he wondered if she knew of the other paintings in his possession, and that this was an addition, a most prized addition, to his growing private collection. He had commissioned a total of six canvases of erotic paintings by Titian; all mythological paintings or poems as the master referred to them.

'This is the final gift.' He pulled the curtain back across the canvas returned to the table and picked up a long slender box that had lain hidden amongst the disordered papers.

'I have no need for more jewels,' she cried inviting him to join her in admiring the betrothal ring with its flame-red stone flashing in the candlelight.

'I have never heard a lady say that before. However, you will find that this is not a piece of jewellery.'

'What then?'

'Open the box.'

She took it from him, intrigued by its weight. Her mind raced. So, it wasn't jewellery, but what could he have decided to give her that was so heavy? Scissors? No, needlework he knew was not one of her pleasures and scissors would not be so heavy. An ink pot with matching sander? No, the box was too shallow.

She raised the lid. Lying on a bed of crimson velvet lay an enormous key.

'A key?'

'How clever of you. Yes, it is a key. But a key to what?'

'The key to your heart?'

'You silly, you have always had that.'

'Then is it a key to a chest containing ... ? No, I cannot think. You must tell me; no more teasing.'

'This is the key to the mansion of Saldañuela, which is yours along with the rents of all the surrounding lands; a suitable home for a mother and her children; my children.'

She squealed her delight, 'Saldañuela! You know how I adore it. We had such wonderful times there. Oh, those deliciously cool patios, the galleries to catch the winter's sun, the logia overlooking the rolling plains; everything. I cannot believe it. You are too generous. I do not deserve such a gift.'

'Would that I could give you more.'

He kissed her and led her by the hand to the fire, inviting her to join him on the cushions scattered on the floor. The logs smouldered and pulsed their scarlet heat despite the grey ash gathering at their edges. He tossed on more wood sending sparks shooting and crackling before hungry flames licked and curled themselves about them.

'Ten wonderful years, Isabel.'

'And I thought I had lost you within the first when Princess Maria, your pretty Portuguese bride, arrived.'

'A disastrous marriage'

'It started well enough; your romantic meeting.'

Lying on the cushions, his head resting on Isabel's lap, he recalled those early days.

'It was October. At the suggestion of the Duque de Alba I stayed at his home near the small town of Aldeanueva. The princess's cortege was to pass that way the following day.' He smiled, 'Gómez and I and a few other so-called hunters went there and mingled with the crowds. We felt sufficiently disguised wearing very rustic looking brown leather jerkins and thigh boots. Our huge hats were pulled well down over our ears, and we had thick scarves about our mouths.'

'All the same the crowds could not help but be curious.'

'Possibly; but I think everyone was too excited, anticipating the royal procession. Then at last it was there after an interminable wait as hundreds of pack mules and ox carts lumbered their way past. It seemed that the princess had brought half of Portugal with her.'

'We all know how rich the Portuguese are. They would never miss all the gold and silver plate, the fine materials, the jewels. I think they have long been the envy of ...'

'My story. The first to appear through the townsfolk's triumphal arch of branches, leaves, and fruits was a group of six Indian musicians; they were followed by the Archbishop of Lisbon; the Duque de Medina Sidonia came next. At last my bride arrived; in a curtained litter. Imagine my disappointment; I was sixteen, I had waited for hours in the October cold to see a curtained litter.'

'At least the locals were left with something to excite them. A mule had shed one of its shoes and someone raced to return it to one of Sidonia's servants. The servant turned his nose up at it saying his master had no need for it and that the mayor could put it to the use of the community. A gold horse shoe; I wonder what it was worth.'

'To return to my story, Alba said we were to wait in an upstairs room of an inn at the next village. He would say that the litter required some repairs and hoped that the princess would travel the few miles by mule. It was an easy journey and she would not be inconvenienced; and the Spanish people would be overjoyed to see her.'

'We ladies could talk of nothing else for days; we were most envious. Princess Maria wore a dress of white silk slashed with gold, a purple velvet cape, a purple bonnet with an enormous white feather. The mule was caparisoned in red brocade and the saddle was of silver ...'

'I insist this is my story. Gómez and I waited an eternity then she was there. She stopped to arrange the gold hairnet beneath her bonnet ...'

'She removed her gloves.'

'Isabel you are incorrigible. She did indeed remove her gloves. Then she happened to glance up in our direction. Gómez beamed at me, "My lord, I congratulate you on your good fortune, a pretty Portuguese princess." "Perhaps plump?" I replied. "Perfectly proportioned," he insisted. "Passable." I clasped his shoulders and we laughed with relief; you know how different the real thing can be from the flattering miniature portraits.'

Philip lapsed into silence.

Isabel sighed, 'As I said, I thought I had lost you. The stories that arrived ahead of you were as nothing to seeing you together at your wedding. You were such a handsome couple. It was almost too much for me to bear. Yet it was not too long before you returned to my side, to my bed.'

'And you know the reason for that. Poor, sad Maria. I felt sorry for her, but ... Had it not been for you ...'

'We all saw what was happening to her but could do nothing to help. She resorted to eating to comfort herself; four huge meals a day with cakes and biscuits in between. She grew fatter and fatter in her melancholy. And whose fault was it that she got into that state?'

'I hope I do not stand accused.'

'Initially no. Speaking plainly, your father's demands were absurd, far too demanding. When he was your age he made his own decisions, and I believe that you had every right to do the same; and especially with regard to how much time you spent in bed with your wife. And then there was that awful tutor or governor, or whatever his title was, who carried out your father's instructions to the letter, he was obviously thoroughly enjoying his role treating you like erring children. The embarrassment of having the bed curtains drawn aside while you and Maria were ... No wonder your times together were fraught with inhibition, repression, distress. And now I come to you; yes it is disappointing that you did not tell him to go to Hell. On the other hand ...'

'On the other hand I was free to come to you as often as I wished and you would banish all the misery.'

She stroked the fair hair about his temples, pleased that the reminiscing was now focussing upon her. 'I remember our first dance. I confess I had even prayed to God, begging Him to make you choose me as a partner. I had watched you so many times and was desperate to join you. And you did invite me. I could scarcely breathe.'

'I offered you one corner of my handkerchief; I held the other.'

'Our hands had barely touched, but I began to tingle. When you turned to me to bow a flame shot along the handkerchief searing every part of me.'

'And you faltered, losing your step.'

'I thought I surely would fall, my legs and feet were no longer part of me. You gave me such an icy stare, angry that I was spoiling your otherwise perfect allemande. You gave the handkerchief the fiercest of tugs. Such a warning!'

'My anger was short lived. How could it have been otherwise when you arched your darling little eyebrows and your beautiful white teeth bit down on that perfect lower lip begging my pardon; I was yours.'

'And that night you came to my bed,' she whispered.

'And that night I came to your bed. It was your turn to show perfection, to lead in the dance, and such a merry dance. You were unashamed of your nakedness, uninhibited in your love making.'

'You so very quickly overcame your prince-like reserve, discovering emotions and sensations that until that moment you never knew existed.'

He nodded; smiling. 'One moment,' he sat up, kissed her then went to fetch their barely touched wine. 'A toast to our dancing days.'

'Our dancing days.'

Philip became pensive, 'If only you had been my wife instead of Maria. You would be my queen and I would have two fine heirs. I would not be going to England. I would not have Carlos for a son; a nine-year-old sickly child, weak in mind and body. Oh, Isabel, if only you had been born a princess and not a duchess.'

Isabel placed a finger gently over his lips, 'I have enjoyed the privileged life of your mistress. The entire court treats me with deference; my brother basks in my status. I am free to come and go as I please. Now, why would I want to exchange any of that for the life of a queen? It would be nothing short of imprisonment, an unspeakably dull and lonely life restricted mostly to my apartments, nervously waiting for you to come to officially bed me as some part of an agenda, not to make love to me because that was what you desired. Were I your wife I would also be surrounded by doctors laying down the law about what I may or may not do once I was with child.'

She remembered how it had been a death sentence for Maria, a protracted death sentence lasting the eighteen months of her marriage. The doctors, in their wisdom, had bled her to induce a pregnancy, had bled her constantly throughout her pregnancy because she was always unwell. Then they bled her after a complicated birthing because she was suffering from puerperal fever denying her any remaining strength to fight the infection and blood poisoning that they themselves had caused when they tore the child from her womb. And look what they did to the child in the process; Carlos will bear the scars of their ignorance for the rest of his life. It was such a shame, and she had great sympathy for Carlos; a mother's sympathy. But the spectres of Carlos and Maria must be banished.

'Oh no,' she concluded, 'I thank God I am a duchess and a mistress and not a princess born to be the bride of a prince. Fortune, if not God himself, has smiled on me.'

'Such a lecture! But I would have you know I am more than a prince, I am now a king; King Philip of Naples.'

Emperor Charles V, Philip's father, an ever absent father, the father he barely knew, known mainly through his letters, had decided that it was only fitting that Queen Mary of England marry a king. Therefore he had decided to bestow the kingdom of Naples on his son. It was not a big country, admittedly, but the title lent dignity.

'Then enough of all this tiresome idle chatter. Let me be the first to enjoy the bed of this new king.' She dipped her finger into her wine, traced it along his lips then greedily licked away the glistening droplets. He cupped her face with his hands taking delight for the last time in her smooth skin as his tongue eagerly sought hers.

England

1554

Mary Tudor

Wives of Philip II

1543	1554
Maria Manuela (cousin)	Mary Tudor (aunt)
|	
Carlos	

2

Mary Tudor, queen of England, bustled up and down the Long Gallery of Winchester Palace with four of her ladies following in close attendance. The dreary wet grey of a summer's day was disappearing fast, giving way to a pewter dusk pressing heavily against the many windows taking up much of the southern wall. A scurry of servants lit candles and soon pools of warm yellow began to appear in clusters, the waxed wooden floor echoing their comfort.

The queen's pace increased betraying her excitement, the hopes and fears of what was about to unfold. At last, following more than four months of inexplicable delays, her future husband had arrived in England. He was about to enter through that very doorway at the gallery's far end, the doorway to a small private staircase leading down to the garden. Across that garden, in his apartments, Philip would be preparing for this, their first meeting. She would soon be with the prince whose portrait she had carried with her everywhere since their marriage contract had been finalised so many, far too many, months ago.

'Tell me ladies, how do I look?' She stopped to ask them, halting what had become an agitated stride. Mary's voice, as dark and luxuriously velvet as her dress, was to some too deep and forceful for a lady, especially one so small and weak.

Her four attendants searched for any negligent omission on their part. Everything appeared to be perfect: the black French hood with its trim of diamonds and gold-set rubies that sat neatly over her auburn hair and framed her face; the black velvet dress over a frosted silver-white panel of underskirt; the collar of jewels nestling amongst delicate white lace at her throat; a pearl, *La Perla Peregrina,* gift of the Emperor Charles, at her breast; the jewelled girdle resting on her hips. Everything was as it should be.

'Ladies, ladies, I know you would not have erred in my dressing. I asked you rather your opinion regarding my image.'

Nor did she seek that. She was begging for compliments, flattery, lies, anything to boost her confidence. Philip was at last here. Unfortunately, those added months of delay, those months of increasing anxieties, had done little to help the already engraved evidence of the preceding thirty-eight years of unhappiness and terror. And there was no escaping the cruel fact that she was eleven years older than him. How would Philip react to what he saw?

She chose not to wait for their responses but hurried on, 'I think we all look very well. Here we are in our velvets, silks, and satins, ribbons and bows; butterflies finally emerging from our dull chrysalises, and such pretty butterflies, too. Hush, I will not hear a word to the contrary. Oh, ladies, I shall never forget your devotion both to myself and to my mother, Lady Katherine, the queen. May God rest her soul.' She made the sign of the cross. 'But now is the time to celebrate.'

And yet she was not ready to celebrate, she was still tormented by the past. For thirty lonely and loveless years she had been virtually a prisoner. At one point her father, King Henry VIII, had demanded the removal of her household and threatened them with imprisonment if they so much as referred to her as *the Princess Mary*. Not only had she been called *bastard* but there had been loud and malicious gossip that she might not even have been the king's bastard. Eventually she had had to capitulate, submitting to forces too great for her. She had dipped the pen in the ink then signed a document declaring her mother's marriage to the king as incestuous and unlawful. What choice had there been when the alternative was physical violence? One of the threats still haunted her; the harsh voice spitting out those terrifying words, *Beat her head against a wall until it is as soft as a baked apple, then she'll sign.* Yes, with her enemies closing in on her she had finally denied her own birthright, forsworn her beloved mother's marriage, making her blameless mother no better than a whore.

'No one will ever understand how it felt to be so utterly alone, without my mother, without a single friend to speak for me, with no one to defend me. If only my Cousin Charles could have been near to help. But I had no one, I was alone, forced to be on my own. You were all taken from me.'

She turned to Strelly, her oldest and most loved lady, 'Oh, Strelly, I signed three times on that confession: that the king my father was the Head of the Church; that the Pope be denied his pretended authority; that the marriage of my mother was by God's law, incestuous.' Mary began to weep.

Strelly beckoned for handkerchiefs. 'My lady; that has all

been put behind you, now is not the time for weeping. Take this; allow me to help. Tears and reddened eyes are hardly in keeping with meeting your betrothed for the first time.'

Jane, the youngest of her ladies at just sixteen, smiled, her own eyes twinkling, 'Far rather think of our adventure that almost was.' She giggled.

'Yes,' Strelly joined in, 'Your bid for freedom that never came to pass!'

Mary dabbed at her cheeks with the silk handkerchief. 'Excitement indeed; and all because when I asked permission to celebrate the Roman Catholic Mass my brother, King Edward, refused and my life was threatened by those around him, especially the Protector.'

'Yes, my lady,' Jane was eager to continue, 'but I was thinking of that night at Maldon; the unannounced arrival of the gentleman from Flanders. He had come from your cousin to help us escape. His ship had anchored just off the mouth of the estuary, and a handful of men had rowed upriver.'

Mary nodded, 'Ah, just so, the corn merchant; supposedly come to do business in the local town.'

Jane was thoroughly enjoying recounting the story, 'And you sent me amongst the menservants to discover who had second suits of the right size and shape. I insisted on seeing them all because I needed three outfits, and all quite different.'

It was Strelly's turn, 'Meanwhile, my lady, you tried to reason with the foreign stranger that you would need at least two days to arrange the packing of some of your favourite dresses and personal items ...'

'And he all the while becoming more and more impatient, reminding me I was seeking to flee the country, not idly contemplating moving on to another of my houses. He insisted I travel light; that once across the water and safe in Brussels I would want for nothing. We were asked to be ready within the hour to be rowed downstream to board the waiting ship.'

'Then Jane returned with the news that she had the three suits.'

Jane pouted a little, 'And I was disappointed to find you still undecided whether or not we should go, my lady.'

'My steward had made the decision for me.'

'By telling lies!' Jane was still furious with the man.

'Just so,' sighed Mary. 'But it was enough. When he told us that the bailiff and his men were already on their way to arrest the crew of the boat and that at the next tide he intended to seize the waiting ship in the name of the king, what could I do other than forget the whole enterprise?'

'So that was that.' Jane shrugged, 'But how I would have enjoyed dressing in doublet and hose, slapping my thighs, sounding all hale and hearty, clapping Strelly on the back like a well-seasoned sailor ... and spitting.'

Mary laughed. 'Bless you dear Jane; three fine men of the sea we would have made. Like as not we would all have been sick within minutes of our setting sail. And let us not forget that had we sailed we would not be here to greet Philip.'

'My lady, how wonderful to see you restored to such good cheer.' Strelly turned to Jane, 'Your diversion was most timely.'

'And you see, Jane, everything has turned out for the best. We await the arrival of my betrothed. He is a prince of my own choosing, a Catholic prince, a Spanish prince from my mother's family, and I am the happiest of women. I tell you ladies that now, at long last, I do have a family; people I can trust, confide in. I am to have a husband at my side, and my Cousin Charles the Emperor ready to advise. It is with God's good grace we have been guided to this day.' She grasped their hands inviting them to share her joy.

The door, that very door, at the end of the gallery was opened. The moment had arrived. A thundering in Mary's chest, in her throat, in her ears, seized her, suffocating her.

'His Royal Highness, Prince Philip.'

A gentleman of slight, though reasonably well-proportioned stature stepped forward. He removed his cap to execute a deep sweeping bow, his two fellow countrymen, his friends and confidants, following suit. He approached Mary, his *dear and well-beloved aunt*, as he laughingly called her when he was with those who might share any of his confidences.

She screwed up her eyes the better to see him, her eyesight was not so good these days, and gasped. Here was the prince of her dreams. The portrait had not lied. He was elegant with a handsome face and glorious golden hair; decidedly perfect. And had he purposefully set out to discover what she would be wearing this evening or was it a happy coincidence that he was similarly attired in black and white?

'*Sois le bienvenue,*' she muttered shakily, her voice nonetheless surprising in its depth and tension.

22

'Gracias, vuestra majestad.' There would be no French from him, or Latin. Philip was determined to speak the only language he was comfortable with; misunderstandings had to be avoided at all costs. Mary would have to speak Spanish too, like it or not. There could be no excuse; after all she must have learned it at her mother's knee.

'Querido primo mío,' she smiled him her tacit understanding of the situation. He was about to become her husband, her lord and master, she would not permit even the merest hint of any friction whatsoever.

Mary kissed her hand before offering it to Philip. He bowed over it, kissed the royal ring, then raised his head to plant a kiss on her lips. Someone had told him about this quaint English custom of kissing virtual strangers, and it was one he considered most acceptable, perhaps not at this very moment, but which he intended to put to better use elsewhere.

Mary's cheeks burned, every part of her burned, she trembled. She was thirty-eight and this was her first kiss. It was a gentleman's kiss; it was a lover's kiss.

Philip escorted her, like no other possibly could, to the two chairs under the royal canopy. She sat down welcoming the opportunity to control her breathing, rest her quaking limbs, assure herself this was no idle dream. The courtiers gathered nearby in two groups: ladies and gentlemen; English and Spanish.

'At last, my lord, I have you safely by my side,' the deep, heavy tones so incongruous with so small a frame continued to surprise Philip and his gentlemen.

'Dear lady,' Philip studied the lined face, the myopic grey eyes, the nervously twitching mouth, wondering if she were to smile more would she not look quite so time-ravaged. He would soon see.

'Dear lady, this evening I have done no more than, warrior-like, pass unscathed through your garden encountering fearlessly and with inestimable courage the dangers of perfumed flowers, playing fountains and mysterious arbours.'

She giggled and spluttered; one hand to her mouth. 'Oh, goodness me, I referred rather to your journeys beforehand.'

Philip would rather not be reminded of his six days of wretched seasickness crossing the Bay of Biscay. He turned her attention instead to the English weather, having heard how much the English enjoyed discussing it. In this instance it would certainly be most relevant considering his recent mud-caked travels through the countless quagmires of the country lanes.

'I submit that when Englishmen remove their buskins and hose it must be to reveal webbed feet. I have never known such rains in summer; day after day of unremitting downpours. What must it be like in winter?'

Again she giggled, a hand brought to her mouth again lest Philip notice the absence of several teeth. It was an absurd, foolish young girl's chuckle bordering on the ridiculous, so unbecoming in someone so old, and which Philip was already beginning to find an irksome alternative to the dour countenance.

'My lord, our summer rains become chilled autumn inundations before eventually turning into cold, winter snows. In this way we know which season we are in.' Mary burst into laughter, clapping her hands in triumph at her quick humour. She had never been so happy. Still chortling she continued, 'I am reminded of how just this last winter some of our discontents found the snow a useful weapon. They threw snowballs at your envoy! Fortunately balls of snow do little damage, rarely anything more than the hurting of one's pride. Goodness me, how often in the past have I had to pay for someone to play at snowball fighting and here was entertainment free of charge. Most obliging.'

'Just so,' Philip, not wishing to discuss anything political, changed the subject, 'I have been watching your fluttering hands. They are like two beautiful butterflies flashing in the Castilian sun.' He caught them to arrest their nervous flight.

This drew forth more of Mary's titters, 'I remarked to my ladies only moments before you came that we were all like butterflies; such an amazing coincidence.' Her eyes rested lovingly on her ring, 'This ring, my lord, is so beautiful,' she brought it close to her eyes that she might enjoy its splendour all the more. 'How touching to choose for me a ring with petals so red set about a splendid diamond. A perfect Tudor rose. It may be worth a fortune, but I tell you my lord, for me the far greater value is the thought.'

'It is a most special ring to be offered to only the most deserving of ladies. Years ago it was a gift from my father to my mother, and now it is my gift to you.'

Despite harbouring a lifelong dislike for the theatre he had to acknowledge his own talents as a rather fine actor. The ring had cost nothing from the outset. His father had stolen it along with many other items from grandmother, Queen Juana, always an excellent source of exquisite jewellery. Also, it was his father who had sent it to Mary for he himself had found it impossible to raise the enthusiasm for such gift-giving. He was following his father's instructions to marry this person; that was enough.

More recently he had visited his grandmother, so securely locked away in her place of *retirement*, to say his farewells before coming to England; and while he was there he too had happily plundered the precious hoard. Mary and her ladies were the lucky beneficiaries of his largesse; each one wearing the rings, buttons and clips he had carried away. And then, of course, there was that other ruby and diamond ring he had selected for his beloved Isabel.

Mary blushed a little and hesitated, 'I think the court should withdraw a little now to offer us some privacy. Would you not agree?'

Gómez and Feria bowed and retired.

These two men were so different in every way and yet both had been chosen as close advisers to Philip.

Gómez was a tall, handsome thirty-eight-year-old Portuguese with an olive complexion and dark hair and dark well-trimmed short beard. He had come from Portugal many years ago to be pageboy to the young Prince Philip. Since then he had forged his way to his present position using every devious trick available, and he now gloried in his hard-earned status with its financial rewards. Philip naturally benefited from this master of intrigue and therefore valued him highly.

Feria was not so tall and was some years younger. He was as fair as Gómez was dark. Feria had not had to seek his fortune for he came from one of the richest and oldest of Spanish noble families. His blue eyes revealed his complete honesty. Philip wanted him close for precisely that reason; that, along with the fact that he was no drain on the exchequer.

This evening both men had dressed in dark colours according to Philip's wishes; he wanted no suggestion of frivolity at this serious initial encounter of the two nations.

As they walked down the gallery Gómez was first to speak, 'By God, but she's a lot older than we understood, and nothing like her portrait. I am shocked. God knows what she looks like in daylight. Where is the beauty everyone was impressed with? Long gone if, indeed, it ever existed. More likely those damned

Venetian ambassadors have been exaggerating again. And what do you think of the voice and that ridiculous laugh?'

Feria nodded, 'However, she is on the small side and Philip does not take kindly to a lady being taller than him. Perhaps too you are uncharitable when you say she is not good looking. Something tells me that she has been a beauty but that the worries and hardships over the years have furrowed her brow, have pinched her mouth. And as for the giggling, I would suggest she is no different to any young maiden in love for the first time. Forgive her, rejoice for her.'

'You are kindness itself. If only the emperor had chosen to marry her there probably would have been fewer problems. For a start it is preferable for the husband to be older; but more importantly the English regard him as a friendly Netherlander and not a sinister Spanish Catholic.'

'There would have been difficulties enough with Charles; we both know he is, well, often a bit wanting these days,' Feria mouthed the words, tapping at his temple with a forefinger.

They, as well as many another, knew there was no future for this marriage. Philip was perceived as nothing more than a Spanish prince come to England to further the Spanish cause. From the moment the contract was signed the undisguised hatred towards him was becoming more venomous and violent.

Mary had only gained Parliament's approval for the marriage by swearing that Philip would never interfere with the government of her people, would not deploy Spanish troops in English garrisons, would not seek English support against the French, nor would he ask for English money to be sent abroad to assist Spain in her political ambitions.

Philip, for his part felt absurdly fettered with all these constraints. He had gone so far as to swear to God on the Holy Bible that he had only agreed to such outrageous proscriptions in order to proceed with this wedding.

Gómez stroked and tugged at the dark curls of his beard. 'Philip still hopes to become king of England. For my part I cannot see that happening. So, is he brave, or misguided; or simply being a dutiful son following his father's commands in order to extend the power of the Hapsburgs?'

A young lady of remarkable beauty approached them, 'Sirs, Mistress Jane Dormer at your service.' She bobbed a curtsey, 'Her majesty invites you to take some refreshment; if you will kindly follow me.'

'Damn my eyes, Gómez, I would be pleased to follow that

sweet young thing to the ends of the earth; such grace, charm, beauty. I tell you I might agree to anything if by doing so it would make her mine. I have found it difficult to look at anything or anyone else all evening. I wonder ...'

'Such haste my friend; how quickly you have been pierced by Cupid's arrow. But you are right, she is most agreeable. A veritable English rose amongst a thicket of thorns. But what of your family? I understood you were soon to be betrothed.'

'I would not be the first to renege on a marriage arrangement; look no further than Philip and his Portuguese cousin. But let me remind you that since my brother's death I am now in the position to decide my own future, and this fair damsel is far more to my liking than the child of twelve my mother has chosen. If I do decide to wed this Mistress Jane and have the consent of Philip and that of Queen Mary then neither my mother nor anyone else would dare complain.'

'Let me wish you God speed in the chase! It could well be that you take an English bride to the altar long before I have the chance to return to Spain to wed my Ana.' He opened the locket bearing the image of the beautiful and bewitching Ana de Mendoza y de la Cerda.

Gómez shrugged away the thought of the years he might still have to wait. 'And now to indulge ourselves in horse piss; I do beg your pardon Feria, I should have said excellent English ale. The things one does for one's master! I pray to God it tastes better than the last lot.' He glanced at the queen, 'You could be right, she may have been good looking once; do you suppose that if she were to dress in the Spanish fashion she might appear younger?'

'You do see there is hope, then, for this saintly virgin who may have been misguided in her choice of gowns?'

They held their goblets in readiness. Queen Mary raised her glass, impatient to broadcast the news, 'A toast to the king of Naples. The queen welcomes a king not a prince; an equal, nay more than an equal. Parliament must take note; this is most gratifying. To King Philip of Naples.'

'King Philip of Naples!'

She drank to Philip, more in love with him than any poet could find words to pen. Until today, for the most part, her emotions had never reached beyond comfort with her few ladies and distrust for everyone else; she had occasionally been allowed to love and be loved by her mother, but she had certainly never known the love of a man. Her eyes sought out

27

Philip's that he should see this loving wife before him. But it was not to be, Philip was a reserved young man and there were very few with whom he felt sufficiently confident for prolonged eye contact; his mistress Isabel and some intimate friends being the few exceptions.

'My lady, the rules of etiquette require we leave you now. Nor would I wish to tire you further this evening. I am afraid I must tear myself away from your delightful company. Would you be so gracious as to tell me what I should say as I leave?'

Mary's world of bliss crumbled. She was bitterly disappointed that the evening was to end so abruptly, but had to admit that her darling Philip was correct about the etiquette.

'The evening has passed far too quickly. But you are right, you must go, and as you leave you must say, *goodnight, ladies.*'

He kissed each lady as he passed, happy to put the newfound custom into practice so soon, *goode nahit, laydeez.*'

When the gentlemen had gone the ladies laughed and giggled with delight at the evening's entertainment and with the excitement of more to come.

Mary clapped her hands and turned a dizzy full circle, 'God has been most good to me, to send me such a husband and a father for the next king of England. Oh, Philip is so handsome, so charming, so dignified, so distinguished, so – so royal!'

3

There was no other way to describe it, it was a din: astonishing; uncouth; unacceptable. Mary, heady with so many glorious emotions, was blissfully unaware of Philip's discomfort.

It was a royal wedding feast the like of which had not been witnessed for many a year. The bride and groom wore white satin with sleeves paned with cloth of silver beaded with pearls and diamonds. A broad gold chain resplendent with rubies and emeralds reached from Mary's shoulders down to her waist. Philip also wore a gold chain bearing a gold pendent lamb, the Golden Fleece, the insignia of the knights of Flanders.

English noblemen supported the canopy over the royal couple. Philip had insisted that the honour would be theirs alone and not to be shared with the Spaniards, another of his several attempts to charm the hostile natives.

Seated at the two long tables stretching away from their high table down the entire length of the hall were the many guests, each and every one of them having laid out a small fortune to provide themselves with the best of satins, brocades and damasks of every hue.

The hall with its vaulted ceiling, flags, and banners recording campaigns and deeds of chivalry, and with, until today, an overwhelming aura of chill austerity, was a riot of colours and noises: reds, greens, blues, gold, fought for attention; laughter and raucous voices battled for supremacy; musicians with lutes, virginals, viols, sackbuts seemed but to entertain themselves in the midst of the uproar.

But this uproar, this pandemonium, was alien to Spanish royalty, where the etiquette of meals demanded more formality. For Philip even that held no appeal and, given the opportunity, would always prefer to dine alone. His finer sensitivities were being tested. Today was further proof, if further proof were needed, of his conviction that the English were barbarians.

Mary touched his hand reminding him of her presence. His eyes met hers then moved quickly to rest on her blushing cheeks, experiencing for a moment a wave of sympathy for his bride, this gauche sixteen-approaching-forty-year-old queen of England; his *dear and well-beloved aunt*.

The tables with their snow-white damask covers and set with gold and silver plate groaned under a vast array of culinary wonders, the pride of several cooks hired for the occasion.

'We cannot tempt you to one of the fish dishes, my lord? Haddock in ale, or perhaps this cold pike in gelatine? Both are truly delicious, or perhaps some ... ?'

'My lady I never, ever, eat fish,' nor, he told himself, did he wish to discuss his dietary predilections.

'But on Fridays and fast days?'

'His Holiness the Pope has granted me dispensation,' he expected that to put an end to the topic.

The dishes and their leftovers were removed and the stained table covers replaced in readiness for the next course as pastry coats of arms, sugar crowns and other spectacular subtleties for their entertainment were brought in; each one receiving rapturous applause.

Philip turned away from the commotion determined not to criticise. 'You looked quite charming in church with your hair tumbling like a bronze river over your shoulders.' What he had seen was, in fact, a vision of his beloved Isabel's wonderful curls cascading over her naked shoulders, arms, and breasts. He closed his eyes the more to savour the image once again.

'Oh, my lord, had I thought for a single moment you were watching me, why I would have been quite overcome.' She reddened, giggled before hastily looking away, her wrinkled hand held to her mouth hiding those dreaded gaps.

He rejoined her, reluctantly torn from his reverie, 'You were too intent on your prayers to be aware of my attentions.' He considered he had given the words a touching degree of tenderness for this sad creature at his side.

'My lord, I have so many reasons for giving my thanks to God. He directed the Holy Father to forgive me for my grievous faults: denying my mother's marriage; declaring that I was no more than a bastard; acknowledging that he, the Pope, had no authority and was no better than a pretender. Oh, Philip, I signed three times on that detestable document. Three times I betrayed everything most dear to me; three times I denied the truth.'

Philip had had to listen patiently to this *crie de coeur* every time they had met, 'Dear lady, everyone knows you to be entirely innocent in this. You were alone and afraid. But you should not dwell on such thoughts, especially not today. I will not have those pretty cheeks drained of their glorious colour, nor will I have a trace of a frown on so delicate a brow.'

Mary's heart leapt. His voice was the music, his words the psalms her soul had so longed for. 'And I also had to offer my thanks to God for granting me such a husband. I had prayed to Him for someone from my Spanish family; had thought it would be my cousin, then your dear name was mentioned. You can have no idea how my spirits were dashed when I was told you were already wed. Then my joy was rekindled discovering that the contract had not been completed. Today I gave thanks for you as my husband, coming to me with your support and bringing that of Spain. My lord, my heart no longer thunders with anxiety, but with a joy it has never known.'

'And all bound by this simple gold band.'

'Such has been the custom of all English maidens, great or small, when they marry; and before God I am no better than any of them.'

'An endearing sentiment.' He gave her hand a paternal pat of blessing.

'And your gift to me of three handfuls of gold.'

'We Spanish have customs, too. The *arras,* those gold coins are my pledge that I will hold and keep you secure.'

'I almost laughed when Strelly opened her purse and hurriedly scooped it in, fearing for some reason you might want it back; we had been so poor for so long.' Mary chuckled happily; remembering Strelly's faux pas. 'I swear I do not know if it is the wine, of which only a drop has passed my lips, but my cheeks burn so ...'

'And most charmingly. What have we here?' He released her fingers to watch the arrival of roast quail, larks, and many another tiny bird. These were followed by chickens, ducks, and finally swans, magnificently displayed on their silver and gold salvers. Next came venison, lamb, beef, all on enormous chargers borne shoulder high. Loud cheering saluted every marvel as it appeared.

Philip winced, allowed a few more drops of ale to be poured into his goblet, regretting he had forgone the pleasure of wine but rather hoping that his choice had been noticed by the critics about him.

He added this further self-denial to his mental list of sacrifices: there wasn't one soldier accompanying him, excepting the many in the guise of servants, and not one of his company was part of the official entourage; since their arrival in this barbaric land he and his courtiers had eaten and drunk the disgusting fare that had been served up on every occasion; they had all adapted to life without the traditional afternoon siesta and to retiring early at night; he had even permitted the Anglicising of his name. All this was to win the hearts of Englishmen and ensure that one day the English crown would sit on his head. He would not complain. It was his duty as his father's son to make England a firm ally; to bring it back to the True Faith; and, of course, to extend the power of the Hapsburgs.

'The cooks are to be commended for their imagination,' he dipped his greasy fingertips in the lemon-water and dried them on the proffered towel.

The table coverings were removed once again. A fanfare introduced quite a different subtlety this time. Four tumblers dressed as royal pages leapt, rolled, somersaulted their way to the centre of the floor, two, who were dwarves, via the lower tables cartwheeling along them managing to snatch up titbits on the way. Their routine completed they threw themselves down on bended knee to receive their *royal bride*.

'Why, it is Little Jane, Jane the Fool!' Mary laughed and chuckled at her dwarf, the small, plump woman who had come waddling into their midst, her painted red cheeks shining like two rosy apples. The auburn wig was outrageously large and almost fell over her eyes. The chaplet of white flowers set askew minded one of an inebriate as did her hauling in of her wedding veil, done with about as much ceremony as a fisherman with his nets. Everyone laughed.

Little Jane and the wig with its chaplet and veil were for a moment separated revealing a newly shaven head; they were then reunited causing even greater laughter. She responded by throwing her bouquet over her shoulder vaguely in the direction of one of the tables. Now she looked about her, put her hands on her hips and scowled.

'Where's my Felleepay? Felleepay, where are you? You must be here somewhere.'

She went about the room followed by hoots of laughter as she inspected the gentlemen, grabbing them by the chin, tugging at their beards, twisting their heads close to hers, peering at them closely before pushing them aside in mock disgust, making indistinct but obviously bawdy comments on the gentlemen's physiques.

She and her coarse cackling approached Philip and Mary. She stopped in mock amazement. There was total silence. Her screech of horror at finding her husband Felleepay sat next to the queen sent the whole audience into gales of laughter.

Now the furious miniature bride hurried her wobbling bundle of flesh to Mary's side demanding this impostor remove herself immediately, insisting she should think a thousand shames for having usurped the position of such a one as she. The noise found a new level.

Philip made an excellent attempt at laughter but resolved there and then to write to his sister Juana asking her to give him her dwarf, Magdalena Ruiz. She would have played this role to perfection; very drunk but no bawdy jokes as she searched for her groom, instead a fury flying like arrows from her sharp tongue; and if that didn't intimidate and entertain then her two fierce little marmoset monkeys certainly would. Now he did laugh remembering her tantrum when he told her everyone was going hunting at El Pardo when she wanted to go to Aranjuez. All three feet of her barred his way and she declared he would have to kill her in order to pass.

Still laughing Philip joined with the rest in tossing coins to the entertainers.

Desserts were served; fig and raisin tarts, cherry potage, fruits from the countryside.

Later came the dancing, the floor rapidly filling with other dancers, amongst them Feria and Mistress Jane Dormer; the Spanish duke had rushed to her side intent on being the first to ask.

Philip invited Mary to join him in a saraband. Her feet floated above the oaken boards, her head in clouds of happiness. She glanced at the young man at her side, delighting in those pale blue eyes, that fair complexion, those lips so full and ... this was the husband who had come to love and protect her, to make those decisions she had found too difficult to make on her own, to win back for her the hearts of her people. God had granted her an added favour; He had given her a man to love, to awaken in her such passions that in the cold and bitter world of her past had never existed.

In a few hours time, as soon as darkness fell, Philip would come to her bedchamber.

4

The bridal bed with royal canopy and curtains of green velvet had been blessed by bishops. Mary had been disrobed and was now in her nightshift, the lace collar drawn closely about her neck by its white satin ribbon, the cuffs buttoned securely at her wrists, and a white broderie anglaise bonnet tied beneath her chin.

She lay cushioned amongst her many pillows; waiting, waiting nervously for Philip, the green bedcover almost up to her chin, awaiting this part of marriage about which she at almost forty knew nothing and on which some of her ladies had tried to instruct her using an embarrassed confusion of intimations. All that she could be certain of was that she was experiencing new and exciting sensations awakened by the presence of her Philip, her husband. Until a few days ago she had never known lovers' passions, sensual pleasures. They were so exquisitely disturbing she was convinced they must be sinful.

And of her wifely promises made that day? She had vowed to God she would be in every way a dutiful wife to Philip, would love and obey him, would do anything, everything that was expected of her. At the very beginning, in those early days of the negotiations, she had had doubts about this, concerned that he might prove too young and she too ... she cast aside the word old substituting it with mature. All her worries had disappeared as quickly as melting snow when she discovered in him a man of experience, someone who could exercise considered judgement and with wisdom sufficient for them both. All her fears had been unfounded; the difference in their ages was irrelevant. He, not she, was the mature one.

She must write to her cousin the Emperor Charles, thanking him once more for his assistance in arranging this marriage. In her letter she would list all Philip's perfections, confess her unworthiness, concluding by telling him she was the happiest, although the least deserving, bride in all Christendom.

And tonight Philip would lie with her and sire a child: an heir for England's throne, an heir for the Netherlands; a grandson for Katherine of Aragón, the mother she had betrayed and for which she would carry the burden of guilt for the rest of her days. The gift of a son would show God's absolution. This child would also be a half-brother to Philip's other son, Prince Carlos. She had heard rumours that he was deformed in mind and body, an ugly person in every way. God in His mercy would surely grant her a boy, a healthy boy. But what if her baby was a girl? She had experience enough of the severe disappointment when the offspring of a king was a girl. Her own life would have been quite different had she been a boy. When she was young hadn't her father recognised his bastard son, created him Duke of Richmond and Somerset and then suggest he be made heir, while she was shunned then her royal title removed? God must surely grant her a boy.

The door to her chamber opened, the flames of the many candles drawing back in deference, bowing their reverence to the one who had entered. Soft footfalls approached her bed but she did not look in their direction. It was time. The great unknown was about to become known.

Philip removed his robe lifted the bedcover and slipped between the sheets. He was beside her. She was conscious that he looked at her but she didn't move, she could not, dared not remove her gaze from her firmly entwined fingers.

'My lord,' the words struggled their frightened way into existence, 'I do not know what is expected of me, what I must do. My ladies, my doctors, they all say so many ...'

'Hush, dear lady,' there was no time for diversions such as talking. 'We are together that we might provide God and England with a new Catholic soul. Do not concern yourself. I know what is necessary.' He kissed her gently, mechanically: once on her forehead; once on her cheeks; once on her mouth. He raised her head to take away the pillows to lay her flat. His hand found the skirts of her nightshift and pulled them up and over her knees, higher still until the hem had reached her hips. As he did so his fingers brushed against her thighs starting up fires within her, terrifying her with their ferocity, suppressing the urge to protect herself from this brutal attack against her modesty. She swallowed hard, shook, freed her hands from the bedcover to grab at the sheet she lay on. At the same time Philip moved swiftly onto her, pushing her thighs apart. She was terrified. Yet she remained unresisting as her ladies had advised. He was touching her in a place so private. He was searching then finding a way to enter her. The pain was excruciating. He was hurting her! Did he not realise? There were no words of apology, of explanation, of excuse, from her dear love. He had become as a stranger attacking her in some kind of frenzy. She bit her lip so as not to howl. He pushed and lunged. A scream of pain had to be stopped; she would allow only a strangled groan to break free. Perhaps if she could ease her legs further apart it would make the tearing inside her less agonising. If she were to give him more room might that help? But there was no need to do anything for after a mighty thrust and groan Philip collapsed on her then rolled aside.

They lay on their backs in silence.

She wondered if she ought not for the sake of decency push her shift back down over her knees. There had never been any threat of her nakedness being revealed, not even to her husband, but she still felt it unseemly that her lower body was uncovered.

Although quite shaken she was proud to have accomplished her painful duty. She had survived the ordeal and knew she could endure this experience again when necessary; for God and for England.

'I told you all would be well, did I not?' Philip sat up and leaned over her to stroke her temples, grateful that he had completed his mission and could now retire. He reached for his robe.

'My lord?' Mary stopped; Philip was leaving, but she must not question this lack of courtesy. Nor would she admit to herself that he had been the cause of a most unnerving and harrowing experience; that too would be to criticise her Philip. If he would only stay by her side for a few moments, hold her hand, offer some gentle and encouraging words, all would be forgiven. On the other hand God knew how she was hurting and how desperate she was to hug her torn and battered body. She suspected her private parts were bleeding and she might require medical attention; her ladies would know. 'My lord,' she began again, 'now we shall have a son, a future king. He will grow up to be like you, a defender of the realm, against France, against Scotland.'

'Indeed. But now it is time for both of us to rest. It has been a long and busy day. I shall see you tomorrow.'

'You will come to my chamber tomorrow?'

'Just as you wish. I had thought, rather, we would meet after luncheon.'

'Ah no, my lord, it is the custom that I should not appear in public so soon after we have ... we have ...' she blushed.

'Then it will be my pleasure to come to you tomorrow

36

evening,' his lips brushed her cheek. He pulled on his robe and left the room his thoughts turning to a pretty young thing he had noticed earlier that day.

5

'My lord,' Gómez rose quickly, throwing down his pen onto a mountain of papers. Philip strode towards him, elegant in dark blue velvet doublet and matching hose another of Mary's many gifts.

'Good morning. Feria not here?'

'Having a final word or two with a young lady. He will be most concerned to learn he was not here to greet you, sire. We both thought you would be with the queen some while yet.'

'You jest. Do I not play the gallant enough as it is? The dear old aunt has been bedded, you would surely not ask more of me? But listen to this for fortune; the custom here is that the lady shall not appear in public following her deflowering, or should I say the consummation of the marriage. Gómez, I am free for some time.'

'You were in my thoughts last night, and if I may say so, I marvel at you, my lord. Such fortitude; I swear that this is a chalice that Christ himself would find difficult to raise to His lips. When I consider my own complaints about this country, so trivial by comparison, I hang my head in shame at my weakness. It proves that kings are made of much sterner stuff than we poor wretches.'

Philip answered from the window where he stood eyes fixed on something below in the garden, something which demanded his attention. 'Not an easy lesson to learn, but I have been an exemplary student. In a nutshell, God and the Hapsburgs come before any personal feelings. But, and you know this well, once business has been attended to, I turn my mind and body to the pleasures that life does offer. It is simply a matter of moving from one mode to another.'

'Exactly; but what strength, what discipline is demanded.'

'I have my memories, images, and, on this occasion, something else. Come here, tell me what you see.'

Gómez came to his side; followed his gaze. Three young ladies had found what they thought to be the seclusion of an arbour. They were huddled together sharing something secret and amusing.

'Could you perhaps be interested, my lord?'

'Could be? Am! That is what I call intriguing. See, the lady in lemon and black. How prettily her head moves when she laughs. And such a trim little waist, so damned intoxicating. Gómez, you will discover who she is and where she lodges. I want no delays.'

Feria rushed in, flustered and full of apologies. Philip took him by the shoulders, 'Do not concern yourself, we have spent our time wisely. We have been observing some English ladies; all to deepen our understanding of this nation, naturally. But to business. Have you arranged for Paget to come? He is the one we decided upon, am I right?'

'The very one, the one who is a total stranger to scruples; he awaits your pleasure.'

'Then show him in, there is much to be done.'

Mary's adviser, Paget, privileged at this time to have her full confidence, entered and bowed.

'Good morning, your majesty, I hope I find you and the queen both well.'

'We are. She is keeping well and busy. At the moment I believe she is fully occupied in trying on new dresses, especially those my sister sent as a wedding gift; and when she tires of that she will probably discuss the weather at length with the Duquesa de Alba who, by the way, wishes it to be known that she takes great offence at being kissed on the lips by strangers. Do be seated.'

They moved to chairs set around a bare table. Pens and paper had been deliberately denied; there would be no note-taking at this meeting.

'Speak,' Philip commanded without raising his eyes from the floor.

'Unfortunately, your majesty, to add to the dislike of all things Spanish harboured by some of my countrymen, gossip is now being spread that King Edward, her majesty's late brother, is not in fact dead but lives and is being held prisoner. I believe that Courtenay is at the root of this, and it is not the first time he has meddled.'

'Who is this Courtenay?'

'A nuisance of the first order; and frivolous too. It has been noted that while he pursues the Mistress Jane Dormer, he also has the Princess Elizabeth under consideration. However, I have him under constant observation.'

Feria shot a hurried glance of alarm at Gómez.

Philip continued, 'Courtenay and Elizabeth, we shall come back to them. Moving on to more important business, tell me what is to be done about gaining the trust of the queen's council?' He studied the lines swirling about a knot in the oak flooring.

Disconcerted at having to address nothing more than Philip's profile Paget continued somewhat hesitantly, 'Ah, yes indeed, my lord; once you have that the queen will support you in any demands you make of it.' Paget continued speaking to the side of Philip's head. 'I would say you should reduce the size of the council and have it consist of only those you are convinced will support you or who would take little persuasion.'

Gómez snorted and raised his eyebrows, 'Pure daydreaming! The chancellor has half the council under his thumb. You mean to get rid of all those men?'

Paget reddened, his mouth twitching in anger at the criticism, 'It will not be difficult. I assure you the chancellor has had his day. He has upset the queen once too often. The sun is beginning to set on his dominion.'

Philip shifted his gaze from the floor to the toe of his blue velvet shoe. 'In that case Paget, you will furnish me with the names of those of the council in whom I can place my trust; I shall then discuss the matter with Queen Mary.'

He must not delay his start towards gaining the crown; being a mere consort was unacceptable. He turned to Gómez and Feria, 'You will work with Paget to uncover all you can about this gentleman named Courtenay; and about Princess Elizabeth, too. This is to be done with some urgency. I think both of them could be dangerous. I need enough information to present to the queen that she may follow my advice without question. Paget you may go.'

Feria waited until the door closed behind him.

'Sire, if I may,' he leaned across the table. 'This may not appear relevant, but bear with me. Paget mentioned Miss Jane Dormer when he was speaking of Courtenay; well, I request your permission to seek her hand.'

'A clever move, and most timely,' Gómez congratulated him. 'I think this is more than a competition to win a fair maid. I never thought of you as a schemer.'

'And you know full well that I am not. Your majesty must understand that I have formed a great admiration for the lady on many counts.'

'And she is a young beauty; even has this Courtenay chasing her,' laughed Gómez.

Philip straightened his back, his anger flooding the space

between them, 'We are here to determine policy not discuss a lover's dilemma. So you wish to marry this Mistress Dormer and not the child bride in Spain? Very well; and you would go against your mother's wishes?'

'A mother's wishes are not set against those of the king.'

'And how can this be of any interest to me?'

'Jane is one of the queen's closest ladies. For some years she was a friend to the late King Edward. She had been brought to the palace to be one of the young courtiers, a playmate. She danced and sang for him, even read to him. She will know quite a lot about events and occurrences in the court of King Henry during his last few years and thereafter in young King Edward's. That should prove useful. Jane's loyalty to the queen is beyond doubt; she would do anything to ensure her happiness, but as my wife she would provide even greater service, both to her majesty and to yourself; perhaps by privately reinforcing your wishes in the queen's ear?'

'As you said, Gómez, a clever move. No need to scowl, Feria, you have my blessing. I shall see to it personally that your suit is successful. Which reminds me Gómez, you must not neglect that other little matter we discussed.'

6

Here was yet another perfect day. October had known no other. The gold of the sun and the bronze and copper leaves spread autumn's remaining warmth across gardens and through parks.

Of equal delight were the echoing autumnal hues of the brocades, satin, and velvet skirts as they rustled and swirled across the floor. The Duque de Feria and Mistress Jane Dormer led the others in a pavan. Music and laughter filled the room and the hearts of the dancers. In these heady days there was no tiring of pavans, galliards, sarabands, although there were still some who preferred to idle away the moments in lighthearted gossip or games of chance.

Queen Mary, transformed from faded bloom to youthful blossom, took her pleasure basking in the sights and sounds of her merry court. Gone were the almost constant headaches; not once had she had to summon her dentist to deal with a chronic toothache. She was reborn.

Gómez, standing to one side observing, reflected on how Philip would soon change all that. As the outgoing tide leaves deep ridges on the pale sands, so would the deep furrows rapidly reappear on her pallid cheeks. At the moment there was no way of the queen suspecting that her high spirits were destined to be crushed. But that was life; he looked away to dismiss the inevitable sadness of it all and came almost face to face with Philip who had made an unnoticed and decidedly hurried entry.

Gómez hazarded a guess that the heightened colour about his lord's face told something of a very recent rendezvous with a certain young beauty, the Viscountess Montague, the lady of the pretty head, the trim little waist; both so damned intoxicating.

Philip paused, assumed his more formal stance, making the most of every inch of his paltry height, before walking with all the dignity of a king towards his wife.

'You are not dancing, my lady,' Philip feigned disappointment as first he kissed the royal ring then her fingertips.

'I was determined to wait for you my love, my life,' she beamed, reaching to stroke the fair cheek which today had a much rosier bloom, to touch those full lips. 'There is no one in the world can transport me ...'

'Would that you had had other dancing partners for now is

not the time for such diversions. I must speak with you, immediately. Shall we retire?' A smile belied his urgency.

'This very moment, my lord?'

Without replying he led her to the antechamber inviting her to sit by the window.

He took her hand and began, 'You know that beyond these walls there is still much ill feeling towards me and my countrymen; and that Parliament remains divided.'

'Yes, but, that is only a matter of time, I think.'

'I do not wait for time to solve my problems; I attend to them myself, immediately.' This was far from the truth, he hated making decisions. First he had to seek advice from all those he knew would have strong but different opinions. He would then ponder long and hard on their observations until finally forced into making a judgement. What he should have said was that he was frustrated beyond measure and was not of a mind to sit twiddling his thumbs while Parliament continued to procrastinate about his future. He would follow Gómez's suggestion to put a considerable distance between him and this inhospitable, intolerable country. He continued, 'I have decided that it would be best for me to go to Brussels for a short while. I can use this opportunity to visit my father.'

Mary's heart sank. This could not be. After so few weeks of happiness, after so little time to love and be loved, to have this snatched away so suddenly. She prayed this could not be. She wept knowing it could.

'My lord, I beg you not to go. This is too sudden. Why must you go? I cannot bear it. If you were to leave my side I would die.'

If she were to tell him she was with child then he would not go. But neither she nor her doctors were certain, and she could not talk about something that could turn out to be false. It was true there had been no sign of her menses for almost three months; but in all honesty that was not unusual for her. The doctors were reluctant to try any medications because they might make the babe come before its time.

Philip kissed the ugly, wet wrinkles about her eyes. He opted for a softer tone; it would be irritating beyond words to have a lengthy tearful scene. 'My reasoning is this, my dear. By removing myself for a while it would allow the tempers of some Englishmen to cool, to regard the situation more dispassionately. I will require only the smallest of armies, say five hundred horse, two thousand foot, no more.'

'But the promise we made never to ask the council for armed support?'

'I would never break that. My lady; it hurts me to think that you should have such suspicions.'

'I would not, it is just that it might appear ...'

He hushed her with his finger on her lips, 'I would merely have them for my own protection, travelling so close to France; and I am certain you cannot have forgotten I came here without any troops of my own, bowing to your Parliament's wishes. Nor would it be wise to have France consider us weak. No, my dear, armies speak of strength. And what would Scotland think, discovering England chooses not to provide me with arms? Exactly; it would be an invitation to meddle in England's affairs! My lady, I want everyone to know that wherever I am I will be ready to protect you and your land.'

'It is true, I do worry about the union of Scotland and France; but I doubt if I could persuade ... if you leave I will be on my own ... I am unable to govern without you ... who is there to trust amongst my counsellors? I would be too afraid to make a decision. The only decision I ever made, was forced to make, on my own was to sign that piece of paper denying the legality of my mother's marriage and ...' Apprehension crowded in, fear began to suffocate her. She would be plunged once more into those terrifying days of the past. More tears began to flow.

He became paternal, 'Dear soul, it is not a question of my leaving England, but of my visiting Flanders. You must realise God imposes heavy burdens on those He has appointed as monarchs. Look no further than my father and mother who were separated for years because of God's demands.' He raised her head to look into her eyes for a moment, just a moment; smiling, cajoling, 'And we shall be apart for only a few weeks.'

'You swear?'

'Of course; you need me at your side to help with matters of importance. I know how little you care for decision making.'

That was enough to bring about a fresh flood of tears. 'I only made one decision, and I will regret it for the rest of my life. I knew it was wrong of me to besmirch the good name of my mother, yet I did, and the same with the Holy Father.'

Philip swallowed his impatience at the aggravating repetition. He became the father confessor. 'You have been forgiven. How long will it take to convince you of your innocence?' He soothed the wet cheeks with the gentlest of strokes. 'As for my going to Brussels, I would never contemplate going without first dealing with some important matters that will set your heart at ease during my absence. My departure depends entirely on the knowledge that you will be free of all concerns. If you promise to smile I shall tell you all.'

How could she do otherwise? He had such winning ways and she was only too ready to comply, to accede to his every desire. She looked up at him doing her utmost to summon a smile to her trembling lips.

'That is so much better, my lady. Perhaps some refreshment to restore your spirits then we can begin?'

'My lady, you spoke of who is to be trusted on your council. I have decided to rid it of those who are not sympathetic to your wishes: Walgrave, Southwell ...' He listed them all.

'They are all Gardiner's men, those who sought to have me marry Courtenay, and he no better than a vassal! How could I possibly marry one of my own subjects? They are the very ones who would not give their blessing to my decision to marry you. And now you would dismiss them! Can this be true? I can scarce believe my ears. Oh, my lord, my husband, my friend, my sword and shield.' Gone were the tears, her eyes shining instead with admiration for her saviour.

'You speak of Courtenay,' Philip was pleased she had introduced the name, 'Courtenay; a Plantagenet, am I not right? And is he not the man you chose to make the Earl of Devon?' He had memorised every word of Paget's dossier.

The criticism hurt her, he was being unfair, yet she sought to apologise. 'He is nothing; a nobody. I did it as a favour to his mother, a dear friend of mine. He had, after all, spent his entire youth in the Tower through no fault of his own determined to stay by his mother's side. When I had them released I could not give him back his youth but at least creating him earl offered some compensation. I am convinced he will feel forever indebted to me.'

'He poses a threat.'

'I think not, my lord. He is no more than a frivolous, vain, stupid ...'

Her naivety was infuriating. 'And therefore so easy a tool in the hands of those who would remind him of his royal blood.'

'Never, my lord!'

She had interrupted, further annoying him, but he would

45

show who was master. He would frighten her, it was the best way. 'Let me suggest something for your consideration. What if Parliament proposes his marriage with your half-sister Elizabeth?'

'They would not!' She was shaken, 'Would they?'

He watched as this new fear began to take hold. Now was the moment to strike home his advantage. It was for her own good. 'I am certain they will, and Edward Courtenay will take little persuading; as you say he is vain, and ambitious too according to many. Vanity; ambition? I might add that it would be a marriage of immense appeal to the heretics. They would have Elizabeth Tudor with Edward Courtenay as the Plantagenet husband for the throne of England. The question of Elizabeth's legitimacy as the daughter of Ann Boleyn would no longer be of significance, Courtenay has all the royal blood necessary.'

After allowing her a few moments of reflection and panic he comforted her. 'I have the perfect solution. First, you send Courtenay abroad on some pretext; why not with letters for the emperor in Brussels. His return could be delayed for as long as you wish, he could be detained at my father's pleasure. Then, more importantly, you will have Elizabeth marry my Cousin Savoy. This accomplished, the danger will be gone.'

'Would Parliament accept? But then perhaps I must be insistent? But, would I not be publicly recognising her rights to the succession if I were to promote the marriage?'

This was no time for that kind of wavering; he had to ensure she would abide by his decisions. 'Give it some thought. She will be marrying a Catholic, will bear Catholic children … But, goodness me yes, there is also something which may possibly have slipped your mind. Is it not a fact that the princess has been, shall we say, fruitful?'

Paget had done his research with thoroughness and now Philip delivered the information with a skill worthy of Gómez.

He waited.

Mary was overwhelmed by a battle of emotions. Her half-sister had had a child. Was that what Philip was telling her? Moral indignation, fury, jealousy, fear, they all fought for precedence.

'I cannot believe it! I know nothing of this. Elizabeth has lain with a man?' Envy prevailed; she, whose womb cried out to be home to the future king of England, an heir sired by Philip, had just been dealt a shattering blow. Her sister had been with a man and had already given birth. The sensations she had felt in her womb were probably nothing more than a cruel fancy, a daydream come to mock. Envy turned to hurt and anger. 'Elizabeth is a harlot. Like mother, like daughter; Boleyn was a whore, so is she. I should have known.'

Fury turned to fear, personal injury had to be set aside. Elizabeth and this child were a threat to the throne, to the True Faith, to her own life. 'And who is the father? Is he not a danger too? Philip I am afraid. I thank God that you are here to help me through this tangle of evil thorns that beset me. Tell me; I must know everything then you can advise me what to do before it becomes common knowledge.'

With Mary now no more than a bundle of worries and completely at his mercy, he could afford to be gentle. 'I am reliably informed the father was the Admiral, Lord Seymour.'

'Praise be to God he is dead, sent to the block by his own brother the Lord Protector.' She crossed herself, 'I cared little for either of them. It was said that the admiral had letters hidden in his boots, letters urging Elizabeth and me to oppose the Lord Protector; and all the while he was ...'

'But you interrupted. Seemingly the affair began when she was a child of thirteen. It continued even after his wife had discovered them in bed together.'

'And he was the man who with such indecent haste took my stepmother for wife; my father not cold in his grave ...'

'Be that as it may, at some point a midwife was sent for and a child was delivered.'

'Where is this child now?' And if she knew, what would she do about it?

'Patience, dear lady,' how grateful he was for additional information received from Feria. 'Mistress Jane Dormer told Feria how the midwife was blindfolded and brought to the house. A child was delivered of a very fair young lady, but then was miserably destroyed.

'Jane is not one for gossip. She would only report it if it were true.'

'And the reason she told Feria was because she knew we were seeking to verify events and she could swear to the reliability of the informant.'

'My poor Jane, she is too young and innocent to know of such things.'

'If you will allow; the midwife never knew whose child it was. She had been handsomely paid for her services, though obviously not quite enough to keep her mouth shut. The infant is dead, the father is dead; there remains only Elizabeth.'

'A tiny babe destroyed like an unwanted pup. How dared they offend God in such a way?' She cupped her hands about her belly to protect the unborn child should he be there. 'And that Lord Seymour, our uncle, was its father! Dear God the world is so full of sin; and that there should be so many sinners in my own family. May God forgive the remaining one; the whore.'

'With God's help you will also forgive. You are the kindest of mortals, showing compassion for everyone, from the highest to the lowest. Nor would you wish Elizabeth's error to be a cause of dangerous conflict to upset your plans. I am here to help you be strong and resolute.' He took her hands. 'I must emphasise, my dear lady, that you follow my advice apropos the Duke of Savoy. Far better to have Elizabeth marry a good Catholic and bear Catholic children than to have her remain here with the possibility of some further liaison; for example a marriage with Courtenay.'

'A quick decision is called for, you are so right.'

'Courtenay will be despatched abroad. Elizabeth must be brought to you to swear her allegiance to you as her sovereign, and to seek reconciliation with the Catholic Church. Have her come here. You will have to be strong; remember you are the queen; you are the one with the power.'

'Yes, I must be strong. I shall be strong; but oh ...' Mary's hands began to shake, her body tremble.

Philip was exasperated with her obvious weakening. 'I shall be at hand. I shall be your witness. That tapestry will be perfect; I shall conceal myself behind it and hear every word. Then, if you need me, I can slip through the door that lies behind it to take the brief walk down the corridor and make an unannounced entrance.'

She clasped his hands to her breast in gratitude, 'All the while you will be my hidden strength. Hidden strength; hidden, do you see?' She giggled nervously.

He set her hands down in her lap, angered by the allusion to his penchant for spying and eavesdropping. 'I will also be your strength when Cardinal Pole returns.'

'I shall need it. It is as if my Cousin Pole is my conscience: he always writes such critical words, always taking me to task over my omissions, reminding me of my shortcomings, my tardiness in returning the English flock to the fold.' Some of his letters had quite terrified her with their accusations and threats of God's punishments. He was also annoyed that she had gone ahead with this marriage when he had advocated she remain single.

'This then should please you. I have promised Parliament on his behalf that he, as Papal Legate, will never ever seek for the return of lands to the Church, and that he will not exceed our directives.'

'My dearest Philip, I cannot believe my fortune in having such a husband, you relieve me of all concerns, you are my strength. And to have the additional support of my cousin Emperor Charles; I have never known until now the joy that comes from a family that cares, that loves me. But wait. I must show you this.'

Mary hurried to a table eagerly snatching up a sheet of paper. She had dismissed or forgotten his decision to leave as soon as possible. 'See, Philip, what I have written to the Emperor Charles about my wise, prudent, intelligent husband.'

'Dear lady. This is all in Spanish. That I should have such a clever bride. Ah, but see here, this is an error, and here yet another.' He returned with the letter to the table and taking up a pen proceeded to correct and amend mistakes, making notes on the errors in the margins.

Mary was crestfallen, 'I shall rewrite the letter. It looks so untidy, ugly.'

'No, no; do you not see it represents a combined effort; a partnership, if you will? It emphasises our determination to work together. This will be the first of the letters Courtenay will carry to Brussels.' He examined the letter once more and finding everything to his satisfaction replaced the pen in its stand. 'And now shall we join the others?'

'You go my dear. I wish to pray for a few moments. My mind is such a confusion of thoughts.'

'As you wish, I shall await you with impatience,' he kissed her finger tips congratulating himself on yet another magnificent performance; the ease and manner with which the correct words had tripped from his tongue.

He bowed and strode swiftly to the door.

Philip made straight for Gómez wondering if he should or could renew his efforts to seduce the young viscountess. Her reaction to his latest attempt had been a shock to his ego.

'Am I permitted to ask about this afternoon, my lord?

Philip ignored the wry smile. 'The first part was easy, I

followed your directions to the person's apartments, and unbelievably a window had been left open. I thought it a positive invitation; but how wrong I was.'

'How wrong were you?'

'I might just as well tell all. It took little effort to clamber inside. I was there for only a moment or two before the person entered the room. She was not pleased to see me there, but Gómez her anger made her lovelier than ever. I pleaded with her to accept my apologies; insisting my presence there was a huge mistake; that I had intended visiting one of my courtiers but had taken a wrong turn along the gallery.'

'Rather weak and lame.'

'The person thought so too. When I tried to kiss her hand by way of apology she drew away and made for the fireplace and took up one of the fire irons.'

'And you left swiftly which accounted for the rosy hue about your cheeks when you arrived here.'

'The point is this, Gómez; the person is taking far more wooing than I thought. Should I continue the pursuit, or should I not waste any more time on a lost cause? Is the answer to look elsewhere?'

'The latter, my lord, there are others who I think you will find more willing. Shall we take a stroll about the room and study the possibilities?

7

'We seem to have been here for ever.' Jane Dormer sighed the heaviest of sighs. Unbelievably no more than a few weeks had passed since Queen Mary had retreated from the world and its diseases. With a greatly increased court of ladies she had come to Hampton Court to await the birth of the heir to the throne of England.

Jane moved away from the window, away from the beckoning May sunshine warming the garden with its emerald lawns and bobbing springtime flowers. The air in the room was heavy, the sound of the two lutes too melancholic, the voices of the singers too sad.

Strelly Frideswell watched the young woman as she came towards her, looking so pretty in her claret coloured gown with its embroidered cream stomacher. She set her needlework aside and rose to take her hands. 'My poor Jane, betrothed for so short a time and now wrenched away from your handsome duke's side. I do sympathise but you are not alone in pining for a loved one, many wives have been plucked from every part of the land and brought here to idly waste away their days in futile waiting.'

'How can you say that? How can you be so negative?'

Strelly stole a sympathetic glance over her shoulder at her mistress slumped in her chair and looking so old, bloated, tired, and very ill. 'Our lady queen is not with child. She clings to the delusion, but I am convinced she knows full well there is no child. It is no more than a dream.'

'But she is great with child; that is for all to see. Her breasts are swollen with milk.'

'Oh, Jane, dear innocent one, there is more to carrying a child than what you see. You will understand when your turn comes. But let me just say that because the queen's desire is so strong she seems to have succeeded in tricking nature itself into believing. Unless, and I fear this more, her body suffers from the dropsy.'

'Then why are the doctors not recommending hyssop?'

'Because they have no wish to dash my lady's hopes, perhaps?'

'But Strelly on that day when she met her cousin Cardinal Pole, did she not feel the child quicken?'

'Yes, dear Jane; that is what our queen said.'

Jane looked questioningly at the other ladies, 'And are there many who think like you?'

Strelly nodded.

'But this is too awful to be true.' Jane bit at the back of her hand, 'I thought our misery was because we longed for the freedom of the garden instead of being cooped up. No, I will not have it Strelly! Two weeks more and you will see.' She ran her fingers over the waiting cradle with its freshly painted coat of arms, the quilted red satin lining, the fringes of gold, 'You will soon hold a baby, hopefully a boy.' Her lips quivered, she brushed away a tear, 'And we will all be with our men folk once more!'

'That will be the only happy event in this whole sorry business.'

Jane returned to the window. She pictured herself on the arm of Suarez de Figueroa, Duque de Feria; just repeating his wonderful name made her pulse race. She imagined strolling over those lawns, the sweet smelling herbs springing delightful scents of summer's beginnings from beneath their feet. One day she would walk with him in the grounds of his palace in Spain; pass under his coat of arms, the five fig leaves, set above a grand entrance. True, there was the challenge of an unhappy mother-in-law, nursing a grievance that her wishes for the choice of bride had been denied; but then again her handsome betrothed had assured her that his mother would instantly recognise her virtues and see in her the perfect wife for her son. She reached for her rosary to pray, to seek forgiveness for having indulged herself in so many private fancies when all might not be well with her mistress. The death's head at the end of the beads added its admonition.

Queen Mary heaved her weary bulk from her seat and moved slowly towards her ladies. As she walked her hands cradled the heavy belly that pushed aside her dress revealing more than the usual show of embroidered forepart panel. Her fingers caressed the swelling then she joined them in prayer begging God to grant her the gift of a child.

'I know what you are all thinking.' She tried to sound cheerful, wagging a finger, 'You feel it is too beautiful a day to be shut away in here with me. And you, Jane,' she squinted the better to study this beautiful girl, this young lady, who had

52

charmed her from the start when still a child, with her looks, gentle manner and unshakeable adherence to the True Faith, 'dearest Jane, with those stray tears, are feeling just a trifle cross that you cannot be with Feria. My dear it will not be for much longer. Tomorrow I start my lying-in, and then, why, it will be but a matter of days.'

Never, no, not for one moment did Mary allow her eyes to meet those of Strelly. She had to avoid the grave doubts that lay there. 'I have only one more duty to attend to, and then I am free of government for some time to come, free to give all my attention to the new child. God granted me such a husband in Philip, ladies, and now He is about to grant me Philip's son.'

Strelly seized the opportunity to speak of something other than this phantom child and gladly added her praises to those of her mistress, 'King Philip is so intelligent, wise, prudent, and as handsome as anyone could wish for. The love he has for you shines from his eyes.'

'And yet, perhaps he, too, is growing tired of this waiting Strelly?'

'My lady, every husband finds his wife's childbearing tiresome. But the moment the child is in his arms, my goodness, his chest puffs out with pride, he struts and strides; but ...' She had rushed into replying and had fallen into the trap of talking about the impossible. 'Would you care to take a turn about the room? It may help pass the time until his majesty arrives.'

Jane arranged the folds of her mistress's dress, the fall of the sleeves with the red bows set here and there, 'I think it such a charming idea to have these amulets to keep you and the infant from harm.'

Her words sailed by unnoticed. Mary was much too preoccupied with Strelly's words. She had stopped short again, hadn't she? Why did she have to be so certain that she was not with child? Dear God, if only Strelly, just for this once, was mistaken. But when she had given her reasons she had chosen such gentle, honest words and they had come from a truthful, guileless, utterly trustworthy heart. If only the circumstances could be different and Strelly were able to speak of happier events; if only. Yet Strelly might still be wrong.

And Philip; when, how, was she going to admit to him her own doubts? As soon as she did she knew he would leave for Brussels with not a moment's hesitation. He had only delayed his departure because of her pregnancy, and oh, how angry he had been when granted nothing more than the powers of regent in the event of her death in childbirth and the survival of this heir; she cupped her hands about her distended belly. That had been a bitter blow to his pride. She had promised further attempts to have Parliament reconsider its decision, but he had shrugged and walked away telling her not to give it any further consideration.

Why was life so unfair? After surviving all those years of suffering and victimisation, she had been granted a husband to love; a consort more than worthy of the role; a wise and prudent leader whose every action was for the good of her people, including the salvation of their souls. Why then was there still this reluctance to recognise his merits? Almost a year had passed, a year of Philip's constant efforts to build bridges across chasms of suspicion; to demonstrate goodwill. And still no progress had been made. Indeed, if she were honest, the situation had worsened.

But despite all these setbacks he remained faultless in his attentions towards her. Beneath the surface she knew there lingered hot passions carefully concealed. He was, after all, a young man. Yet he loved her, of this she was certain, not in the way she loved him, with the whole of herself; of course not, but still he loved. If only God would grant her this child then everything would change. Her council, Parliament, her people, all England would rejoice and Philip would be accepted unreservedly. She reached for the rosary hanging at her waist to add to the many prayers already offered to the Holy Virgin to intercede for her. Should she not be with child she would be failing in her duty to her people, to the Hapsburg dynasty, to God; but more importantly, to Philip. The pain, the shame, the humiliation would be unbearable.

A little while ago when her cousin Cardinal Pole had come to see her, to bring her some good news she had been the happiest of beings. England had been reconciled with the Pope. Her own soul and those of her people had been saved from eternal damnation. It was then that she had realised she was with child. There had been no doubts about the baby then; it had moved. It had shared her delight! Since then her womb had filled; but later on there was no more movement. Then Strelly had said ... she refused to allow herself to remember just what it was that Strelly had said.

The door opened. She turned to greet her beloved, her sadness melting away. He was the sun come to kiss awake the sleeping morning rose. She opened her arms to him, just as petals welcomed the warmth.

Philip needed additional fortitude today. Following his many setbacks in this insufferable country he now had to make his way through air laden with heat and a suffocating reek of women's stale sweat and dried piss. It reminded him of the stench that had emanated from his grandmother on his last visit. Holding his perfumed handkerchief to his nose he made his way to Mary.

Strelly ushered the ladies away, many to look longingly once more through windows holding them prisoner, taunting them with the views of glorious spring beyond their reach.

Mary called to them, 'I would be obliged if you would continue the music. It brings great calm and consolation. My lord, at last you are here. I have spent so many days, and such long days too, without you. But why in black?'

'Nothing that will distress you, have no fear. My grandmother has died.'

Queen Juana, the almost immortal grandmother was, thankfully, at long last dead. The news had just arrived from Spain that she was no more. For the last fifty years she had clung to life with an infuriating determination. He made the sign of the cross, 'May her soul rest in peace.'

At last his father, Charles I of Spain, could abdicate, retire from all government, knowing that there was no longer any possibility of supporters rallying to her cause and threatening civil war as had happened once before. The Spanish crown would pass from his father to him and Spain was the largest, richest, and most important kingdom in all of Europe. Let England take note of that! Visions of fortunes reminded him that he must write soon to his sister telling her to take into her safe keeping any of grandmother's remaining jewels.

'May God rest her soul. My aunt, Queen Juana, dead; I can recall when I was a child my mother telling me of Queen Juana's decision to withdraw from the world when she was widowed. I find it strange for one only in her twenties to turn her back on so many pleasures that life still had to offer, why, if I at that age had been offered the opportunity to be a part of the outside world instead of being confined, I would have grasped it with both hands.'

'It is an old Spanish custom, dear lady, for a widow to retire to a convent.' But not, as in his grandmother's case, to a remote palace to be kept behind locked doors, and with guards set about the place that no one might enter. 'Enough of that, we do not want any sad thought that might furrow your brow. I hope I find you well.'

Unfortunately there was no bloom of the mother-to-be about her cheeks, no added sparkle and depth to the eyes. He remembered his beloved Isabel when she was with child, and longed so much for the return of those days, instead Mary looked ill.

'I am well, my lord, although a little tired carrying this joyous weight.' She kept her eyes averted.

Philip accompanied her to her chair, she leaning all the while on his arm.

He knew she was not pregnant. And if she were, he lamented, what good would it do? The whole situation was, he admitted frankly, a mess. Everything about this marriage was an unmitigated disaster. His countrymen were still attacked. There was continued religious dissent. Only the other day he had been sickened by the sight of a dead cat nailed to a church door. Someone had dressed it as a priest, shaved the crown of its head like a tonsure. A wafer had been fastened to its paws.

His opinions on the nauseating barbarity of the English had been further reinforced.

Then, too, there were those notices found fastened to doors, or blowing about the streets, some even discovered in the royal palaces; and all declaring obscenities suggesting that if Mary was pregnant it would be with either a Spanish dog or a monkey!

The refusal of the council to have him crowned had been the final straw. Enough was enough. He would wait until this farce of a pregnancy was concluded and then he would leave. He had done everything possible for Mary and her English savages. He could travel to Brussels with a clear conscience.

'I am pleased that you are well. The Princess Elizabeth still awaits your pleasure. I hope you are strong enough for the audience, my dear. This business really must be dealt with. Already there has been too much delay; months of delay. And, as promised, I will be quite close.'

'Forgive me, Philip, I have been reluctant to receive her; as you know I am afraid that in doing so I would be acknowledging the possibility of her being heir to the throne. Oh dear, I have disappointed you with my weakness.'

He would say no more, he was impatient to have this other ridiculous piece of theatre over and done with too.

She reached for his hands. 'Knowing you are nearby will

give me strength. It is a clever idea of yours to hide.'

Philip bristled, 'I believe I said I would take up a strategic position concealed behind the tapestry, not hide. And remember I do it in order to be of assistance.'

'My lord, forgive my careless choice of words,' she sought those beautiful blue eyes that he might see her contrition, but he was angry and would not look at her.

He brightened as his thoughts turned to the Princess Elizabeth. She had been waiting for weeks to be admitted to Mary's presence, so he had taken the opportunity to visit her and had found her to be a most interesting young lady.

'Philip, the Princess Elizabeth may be informed that I will grant her an audience later today.' It had taken an enormous effort to sound strong but she had no idea from where, or if, she could summon sufficient confidence to see her through this interview with her half-sister.

8

The room was unchanged from earlier in the day, but now soft candlelight replaced the May sun. Queen Mary's ladies stood in the shadows, their conversations hushed, Strelly's eyes and ears ever attentive lest her mistress should need her. She watched Philip as he kissed the queen's hand to take his leave of her.

'Remember, dear lady, I can be at your side in less than a moment.' Philip bowed then strode towards the tapestry covering a door to a corridor. He pulled aside the heavy cloth with its scene of leafy oak woods, a lady about to release her falcon to seek its prey amongst the twisting branches and dense foliage. He wondered if Mary would have as much resolve against her own quarry or would she prove to be no different than the unsuspecting rabbits.

Princess Elizabeth attended by Jane and her cousin entered the room and approached Mary.

She had taken great care in her choice of dress for this audience, wishing neither to offend nor invite criticism. Her dress was of russet brocade, she wore only a few jewels, and her French hood was trimmed with two simple rows of tiny pearls.

'Your majesty.' The twenty-year-old Princess Elizabeth, tall, slender, and beautiful, moved gracefully across the room, making three deep and elegant curtsies as she did so.

Mary offered her hand that Elizabeth might kiss the queen of England's ring.

'I am honoured to be welcomed to your court. I trust I find you well, your majesty.'

'A little tired, perhaps,' and weighed down by so many doubts she could have added. 'And you are recovered? We were most concerned for your health; and this for the second time.'

Elizabeth smiled at the sarcasm. She knew that everyone had suspected her of feigning illness rather than come to face Mary; indeed she had been virtually dragged here. On that other occasion when she had been summoned from Woodstock she had ended up in the Tower; she was determined it should not happen a second time. 'I am now quite well. I thank you for your interest in my wellbeing.'

Mary peered at her, examining every detail of her face: the striking eyes, the olive complexion, the golden hair. How she envied her. Elizabeth had all the looks that she herself once had but then had lost so very quickly to life's cruel blows. This young woman had also borne a child. There was no comfort to be found in being offended by the immorality of the situation; Elizabeth had accomplished something she could probably only dream of.

She must start, soon; but where to start?

When she had inherited the throne she had had Elizabeth imprisoned in the Tower and subjected to rigorous questioning over a period of some months because of her involvement with Courtenay and, thankfully, the dead traitor Wyatt. The only evidence that had been found was Wyatt's letter to Elizabeth urging her to put a greater distance between herself and London that she might be safe. Other than that there was nothing to reveal where her true sympathies lay. Her avowal of innocence had remained unbroken.

Recently, following Philip's advice, Courtenay had been sent abroad bearing letters to the Emperor Charles V, King Charles I of Spain. These letters were, in fact, of no consequence but at least Courtenay was no longer in the country thereby removing one danger. Elizabeth had been removed into the country, away from London and any possible conspirators. All that was needed now was for her to declare her allegiance to the throne and to the True Faith.

'My lady queen, I have come on bended knee to beg you to believe I am as true a subject as anyone in this land.' Elizabeth threw herself to her knees before her sovereign.

Mary was speechless. This was all too sudden; as yet no questions had been asked, no answers demanded. These must come first. She prayed to God that He would give her guidance and Philip would give her the strength.

'Princess; for months you have claimed to be innocent of all treason, yet have continually refused to prove it to us.'

'My lady, I am here at your request, a much longed-for request, to swear my allegiance.'

Philip listened to the words coming from that most exquisite of rosebud mouths with lips this evening drawn tight in determination; pictured those delightful eyes imploring forgiveness; saw that pretty little head, one moment held low in penitence, then raised radiating humility and innocence to her queen; all the while determined to outwit her.

He had been quite taken aback when he met her some days ago. Naturally her beauty had been described to him many times, but he was no fool when it came to praises sung by ambassadors and flattering portraits. However, not only was she surprisingly good looking but she was vivacious, intelligent, and had a ready wit. It was unfortunate, on the other hand, that she stood a few inches taller than he, and perhaps was more intelligent than he; but there were often drawbacks to any relationship.

He closed his eyes and listened, and imagined, and relished his pleasure.

Mary was determined to have a straight answer. 'I ask you, how is it possible for you to swear allegiance without first opening your heart to speak honestly? Is it because you have no conscience?'

'My conscience is clear. I stand firmly, as I always have, by the truth.'

'I pray your truth is judged by God as being the truth.' Mary was getting nowhere but she would keep trying. 'And the letters from Wyatt, you continue to deny receiving them?'

'My lady, Wyatt swore before his death that we had never written to each other.'

'But that was a lie. There was at least one letter, its existence was well known. Allow me to remind you of its contents; it spoke of his earnest wish that you remove to a place of safety.' Mary's heart was pounding as though she were the guilty one.

'My lady I never received such a letter from Wyatt; how could I since someone else appears to have intercepted it.'

Wyatt had confessed to that letter, but there must have been others about which he lied in order to protect Elizabeth. 'So you continue to deny all contact?

'My lady, with respect, I can only continue to protest my innocence. I had not thought to find there would still be lingering doubts.' Elizabeth's eyes opened wide in apparent disbelief.

Mary's heart beat faster than ever. This woman was getting the better of her, but then she would, with the cunning of the guilty to support her. She leaned over the still kneeling princess. 'Tell me, what is meant by the rhyme you engraved on your prison window in the Tower?

Much suspected of me
Nothing proved can be.

Does it declare your innocence; or more likely, does it refer to a lack of evidence?'

Elizabeth still refused to answer directly, 'That was nothing other than my angry reaction to such severe punishment. And I do confess to my remaining angry.'

'And you still think your punishment was unwarranted?' Mary thought she was getting somewhere at last.

'If I were to say yes, it would offend you.'

'Ah, but I suspect you would willingly tell your tale of wrongful accusations to many a sympathetic listener.'

'Never, my lady; I have never complained, nor will I complain openly about my detention in the Tower, although those who caused it with their vile insinuations, their false accusations should look to their consciences.' She bowed her head, 'But it was your will, and I accepted it without question.'

'Enough,' Mary's deep voice growled her frustration. Elizabeth sounded for all the world like some saint beyond all reproach who had been injured by injustice. Not once had she accepted any guilt, any wrongdoing or deception.

'My lady, my queen, on bended knee I swear that nothing can be proved against me. I seek your good opinion. I swear lifelong allegiance. Ma'am, you see before you a humble, true subject for as long as I have breath in my body.'

Philip, still behind the tapestry, shook his head grinning, thinking how bold the lady was; far too bold. Something would have to be done about that. It was, however, reassuring that she had shown herself capable of submitting to authority.

His next thought was that this daring, this audacity, added to her amorous experiences would make her an excellent bedfellow. It could well be that Courtenay and the Admiral Seymour had been of great service to him, while he would magnanimously overlook that unfortunate pregnancy. Yes, all things considered, should Mary die in childbirth or, more realistically, from whatever ailed her, Elizabeth would make a most welcome bride. That would make a fitting reward for the recent onerous duties placed on him by God and his father. And should that come to nought, a close relationship with the lady would ensure his safety in this land of savages when she became their queen; she would also appreciate him as an ally against that other Mary, the queen of Scotland, and her husband the dauphin of France.

'Rise, Elizabeth.' The audience had faltered, had staggered lamely to an end. Mary offered her hand. 'You may go back to

Woodstock. Arrangements will be made for your full household to be returned to you.'

'I am more than grateful for your understanding and generosity of spirit.'

Mary was standing by a window trying to make sense of what had taken place. She had to fight her misgivings on having so readily offered freedom to this woman whom she knew to be guilty of every crime levelled against her. She fretted that she had been careless in showing such lenience. Might Elizabeth, given an opportunity, become involved in yet another struggle for the throne?

Philip's footsteps caused her to turn. She reached out to him, 'I was not very good, was I?'

'Dear lady, you have shown Elizabeth that you know all about the conspiracy, whatever she may say, and that you forgive her.'

'I have? I certainly have shown clemency where others might not have done quite so readily.'

'She will feel beholden to you. The issue has been dealt with to our satisfaction. There is no need for further discussion. There is, however, one other matter. Ah no, wait until I have finished,' he raised his hand to halt any interruption. 'Following the burning of that heretic Latimer I have written on your behalf to insist that the other bishops bestir themselves to put all heretics to the fire. Not enough is being done to show God how serious is our intent.'

'But Philip this is breaking my heart. These are my own people.'

'What does your cousin, the cardinal, say?'

'Why, nothing.'

'There you have it then, it shows he concurs with our strategies.'

Cardinal Pole had insisted time and again that he did not agree with these policies and had told Philip he would not be party to such Draconian measures. Fortunately the cardinal had decided for some reason not to share his sentiments with Mary, so Philip's hands were free.

'Dear lady allow me to be your conscience in this matter.'

This was the moment to hold her hands as he made his farewell, to allow himself to look kindly into her eyes. 'I really must go now leaving you and your ladies to womanly affairs.

But, dear lady, I must chide you for one grave omission.' He was impressed by his gentleness. 'You did forget to tell Elizabeth about our plans for her marriage. I feel we must write to Savoy very soon. I could do this if you wish.'

'You are so right. I did forget to ask.'

'A queen never asks, she demands!' His voice was too harsh. He would be more patient. 'She is a subject, and one who could at any time constitute a danger. We want her married and out of the country.

'I cannot bring myself to do that.'

'Dear God in Heaven!' How quickly he had forgotten his resolve to be patient.

She began to cry, 'Forgive me my lord for my weakness, but I am afraid to recognise her as heir to the throne which I surely must do if she is to be wed.'

'She will never inherit the throne,' he assured her, knowing full well it was only a matter of time before she did, 'the child in your womb is your heir. I should not have raised the issue, forgive me.'

'My Philip I would forgive you anything.'

'Then I shall be on my way,' he raised her chin with the crook of his finger and planted a kiss on her cheek, wondering how much longer must this ridiculous farce of a marriage continue.

He thanked God for the benefits of Hampton Court; the excellent hunting both in the field and with the ladies. He was already anticipating more sport later in the day. Meanwhile he would talk to Gómez about making ready for Flanders and the exciting city of Brussels.

9

'My lady, the woman is here and ready. If it pleases you, ma'am, shall she be brought in?' Jane hurried to Mary's chair bobbing quick curtsies.

'You are excited Jane. Will it be worth our while, do you think?' Anything would be worthwhile, anything that might bring encouragement. 'So,' she enquired of Strelly, 'shall we see this woman?'

Strelly had followed Jane, making a slower, more measured, entrance. 'My lady, I am sure you will find delight in receiving her.'

'Then we shall wait no longer, have her brought to me. But this is to remain our secret. No one must know other than we few ladies that we have allowed a stranger into our midst. We might well be courting the risk of some disease. I am certain it would be considered reckless.'

An elderly soul in an equally ancient garment of varying shades of grey, with hands and face freshly scrubbed and gleaming was ushered into the room. The door closed behind her. She stopped, rooted to the spot, open mouthed and wide-eyed. As if hoping to escape she turned quickly back towards the door to find her way was barred by the group of ladies-in-waiting who had accompanied her, some holding bundles of linen.

'Bring her to me, Strelly.'

Strelly drew the woman by a reluctant elbow across the immensity of space between the door and the dais.

'Good day to you, Mistress … ?' The queen's greeting sent the old woman, completely overwhelmed, to her knees, head in hands. 'Whatever is wrong with the woman? What is your name, dear lady?'

There was no answer.

'Her name is Mistress Smith, your majesty.'

'Do stand and let me look at you, Mistress Smith.' Mary watched the grey heap unfolding to reveal a heavily lined face of someone probably of great age, someone far, far older than she. Could it be possible, then?

'How old are you?'

No response.

'How many years do you carry?'

Not a word.

'How long have you been wed?'

Utter puzzlement set Mistress Smith's wrinkles shifting and deepening.

Mary was at a loss, 'Strelly, I feel we need some help here.'

'My lady, Mistress Smith has grown up children with little ones of their own; boys old enough to run about the town as mischievous boys do. With permission,' she hesitated, 'we estimate that she is about forty years of age, ma'am.'

Mary fought back her horror at this revelation. This old hag, dear and remarkable as she might be, was her age. If only she had a mirror that she might find some flattering reassurance; proof that she looked years younger than this, this wizened old soul.

'How many children do you have, good woman?'

Mistress Smith found her voice. 'They's, let me see, two lads and three lasses all growed up.' She rejoiced in a question she could answer. Now she was on firm ground. 'Others died when they was babbies, so they don't count. Then there's these last 'uns and I can tell you ...'

'I expect it was a surprise to have more babies.'

'Surprise? Why, bless yer, it was a bleedin' shock.' She slapped her soiled grey skirts sending clouds of months' old dust about her. Spittle and burbling wheezes and chuckles escaped through great gaps between yellowing fangs.

Oh, how it offended the senses, Mary thought, hoping that she herself had always taken enough care to ensure that nobody would see that she had lost several teeth.

'Show me the babies.' Mary beckoned the ladies by the door.

They brought her the bundles they cosseted in their arms. The cloths were drawn back. Mary gazed down upon first one, then two, then three tiny miracles of God's creation.

Her ladies watched, some still with hope, praying that this would stir the queen's child lying so still in her womb.

Mary chose one of the bundles, cradling it in her arms, drawing it close to her bosom.

It was a heartbreaking moment for everyone. They all loved her, they knew how much she cherished little children, how she showered her affection on them whenever possible. They had accompanied her times without number when she had gone with village children to help gather flowers to make posies or chaplets, or on frosty days to enjoy games in the snow. How often had they attended her when without any thought for her own health she had insisted on visiting the tiny things when they lay sick in their beds? If anyone deserved a child of their own, then surely it was she.

Their eyes followed her every move as she strolled to and fro her head tilted down to the tiny form in her arms.

With the gentlest of fingertips Mary stroked the delicate skin, gasping with delight when wondrous brown eyes opened or tiny bubbles appeared on cherubic lips. If only she could have a precious mite like this; just one.

'If only God would grant me such a child, Mistress Smith.'

'Why, bless yer, yours is going to be far better 'an that. An' I must say you looks far enough gone for it to be coming pretty soon, you mark my words.'

'Yet I doubt it will ever come into the world.' There. She had said it. Her fears had been made public.

'That's only 'cos, if you don't mind me saying, you's a bit older 'an most. Believe you me I knows that means little ones take longer in coming,' Mistress Smith announced, hands on hips, and with all the assurance of a physician.

Mary smiled. Here was another straw to grasp at, just like the midwife's suggestion of mistaken dates. She handed the child back.

'I thank you for the visit, and wish you and your family well. Ladies see that the good woman is sent home with blankets, linens, food and money.' Her arms were empty and she gazed at their emptiness knowing that they were destined to remain so.

'Oh, Jane, how fortunate she is to have three babies and at her age, too. And I only ask for one.'

'And you will soon be delivered.' Jane willed it so. And if not, then it surely must be possible, as some were already suggesting, that if Mary was unable to have her own child one could be delivered to her childbed by an alternative route. There would be many a mother only too willing to accept a purse of gold in exchange for an unwanted mouth to feed.

A clamour of church bells from spires and steeples shattered their silence. Jane fled the room, calling over her shoulder that she would discover the reason.

'Strelly, is this more trouble? Could it mean an outbreak of plague in London? How foolish I was to allow that woman in here. Could my Philip be in danger? Might Elizabeth have started a rebellion?'

'None of those I am sure, dear lady.' She did her best to sound confident. 'But here is Jane, and not too alarmed, and I do believe the bells are being stopped. What is it, Jane?'

'Oh, it was a mistake, nothing more.' Jane kept her head bowed.

'Look at me Jane. Did they think there had been a calamity, an uprising?' Mary was shaking.

'No, my lady.'

'Jane; I said look at me. Do not be so obstinate. Tell me.'

Jane raised her tearful face to her mistress. 'Oh, my lady, I am so very, very sorry. News was broadcast that you had been delivered of a son, and all the bells of London were ringing out the glad tidings that England had an heir. Someone has been sent post-haste to still them. Ma'am, I am so sorry.'

'Oh Jane; Strelly,' the queen wept, 'who would wish to torment me like this?' She sank down to the floor sobbing uncontrollably, drawing her knees up to her chest, wrapping her arms about them, curling herself into a protective cocoon.

Her two ladies knelt at her side to comfort and to weep. Strelly, her own tears hot and angry, put her arm about Mary's shoulders. She was furious with all those who had continued to insist on building up her mistress's hopes where none should exist. She raged against those who would now taunt her in such an evil way.

10

Almost two years had passed since Mary had given permission for most of her ladies to go home, to return to their families; she had no need for them. Strelly had been right; there was no child.

On this summer's day her few remaining faithful and intimate attendants sat or strolled in the large, impersonal, room at Westminster; and waited. They waited for Mary and Philip to emerge from the Council Chamber.

'It has got to be today,' Strelly and Jane whispered to each other as they walked.

'Oh yes, it must be; we have all prayed for it for so long. And I pray it will bring an end to the evil ridiculing of our beloved queen.'

'That anyone would dare beggars belief. Dear lady, she has known very little joy in her life.'

'At least she has enjoyed some happier days recently.'

'And she was made to wait long enough for those, too. Philip had made so many promises: said he would be away for no more than two weeks; said it would be no longer than two months; said he would return before Christmas; said he would definitely be back in England before Easter. And how long was he away? More than a year, Jane; and what finally brought him to our shores?'

'I see your opinions on King Philip have changed. I recall you singing his praises to her majesty often enough in the past.'

'That was all pretence, I never have cared much for the man but the queen always delighted in his company and does so once again. I would not wish to deny her that for all the world; the Lord knows how old and ill she looked without him, and always in tears. I was very concerned.' Strelly looked about them to make sure there was no one near. 'To be honest with you, I think his charm is nothing but deception; the real man is callous, has no heart. I will never forgive him for that particularly cruel letter he sent her, saying he would never ever set foot in England unless he was made king; do you remember? She was doing everything she could and that was his response! And as for his other letters, when he did make an effort to write, they were all filled with anger. But there, I have had my say. Someone is coming.'

The door to the Council Chamber opened; but it was to allow the French ambassador through; and it was a very annoyed French ambassador.

Jane watched him as he strode furiously back and forth his face as black as thunder, 'Dear Lord but he is an odious man. I wonder if his displeasure means that our prayers have been answered.'

The ambassador halted his to-ing and fro-ing the moment Philip and Mary appeared. He started upbraiding Mary. 'God knows I have done my best to maintain peace between England and France, and what has happened in there? You decided it far better to suckle greedy Spaniards. Oh, but the caricatures and lampoons do not lie!'

Philip was enraged, 'What is this, how dare this man speak to you like this? He is no diplomat, no ambassador!'

Mary, encouraged by Philip's presence, made confident by his supporting arm, replied, 'For more than a year I have had to endure this man's insolence, his evil words, his jibes and taunts, all like poison darts designed to injure. For more than a year I have been aware that he has fed his French master with exaggerated tales of unrest amongst my people. For more than a year I have known of his persistent encouragement of rebels.'

The ambassador's voice for once was stilled, an unacceptable turn of events for one who usually silenced the queen with his intimidating onslaughts.

Mary continued, to the delight of her ladies who had never thought to see such a day, 'But you and your master King Henri of France forgot that however much some of my subjects fear England's alliance with Spain, they also have a great fear of France. And so, Monsieur Ambassador, you went too far, playing into my hands.'

'Untrue, it had nothing to do with King Henri or I, it was a move by disenchanted Englishmen – of whom there are many I might add.'

'They were rebels, rebels who had been succoured for some time, no, what I should say is rebels who had been sent by you to France to be made welcome guests of Henri. No matter, it has served our purposes; you forced the council to side with me. You must get to your desk with all haste, take up pen and paper and inform your king. Ah, and here is Feria I expect with more good news.'

'Your majesties, Gómez has written from Spain telling of his success in raising funds for our armies in the Netherlands. We can now stand in force against France.'

'This is excellent news, Feria, for we now have the additional support of English men and money.' Philip raised his voice that the disappearing ambassador should hear, 'That should make an interesting post script to your letter.'

Mary shook her head and clapped her hands with delight, 'My cousin, the retired emperor seems to conjure up gold whenever necessary. He once sent me a shipment of *ducados* when I was sorely pressed, and now this when Spain has financial problems of her own.'

Philip took the letter from Feria. 'You are so right, my lady,' he scanned the hurried scrawl. 'My father may have retired to a small monastery almost lost to the world; he might be old and ill; but, by God, when set a task he has the enthusiasm of a young lad. I see he has increased the church tithes, is selling a new Papal Bull of Indulgence, and to add to his successes a bullion fleet has arrived in Seville and he has demanded the entire shipment.'

'Oh, Philip, if only I could do the same. For some reason the Pope remains antagonistic towards me and my cousin Cardinal Pole. I cannot understand why he still seeks to chastise us when we have done so much to rid England of heresy, to bring our flock back to the Holy Mother Church. I ordered executions, burnings, and to what end? It pained me to take the lives of my own countrymen, but I thought that God and Pope Paul required it of me. I am a failure in everything I do.' Her high spirits were gone, her head was bowed, her shoulders hunched.

'How did the meeting of the council go, my lord; did the members take much persuading?' Feria asked following an earnest look from Jane Dormer to change the subject.

'Exceedingly well; we said very little, in fact we left it in the council's hands.' The council had been so shaken by the ease and speed with which Stafford and the other rebels had sailed from France, seized an English town and spread their proclamations of their intent to usurp the throne, that they had needed no persuading. The fact that the guilty had all been dealt with by the executioner's axe or rope had not diminished the fear of a French invasion, it was far too real to be ignored.

Mary raised her head and spoke with resolve. 'My lord Philip, I have decided to sell my crown lands, as many as are required to cover any deficit that the council's grant may leave.'

'My lady, you are more than generous,' Philip kissed her hand.

He studied this sad woman at his side, probably the most unfortunate of monarchs. She was virtually penniless. Having inherited an empty exchequer she had endeavoured to pay off her father's and brother's debts from her own meagre income. Parliament had refused her the customary grants because they might find their way into Philip's purse. She was in debt to the German banks having borrowed money to fit out ships which were then kept waiting for months, waiting for Philip to decide to return to England. Now she was prepared to sell her crown lands to help finance the war; but then she would have to since she had restored all rebels' confiscated lands to their families. On the other hand she had given him neither a son nor a crown, had continued to dither about Elizabeth's marriage to Savoy, so she owed him this support at the very least.

'My lady,' he repeated, 'you are more than generous; too generous, generous to a fault; even returning rebels' lands making them comfortable and yourself unnecessarily the poorer.'

'Which reminds me of Courtenay; poor, sad Courtenay dying so soon after I had granted him permission to return to England; he never got to see his home again. Everything turns to failure.'

'I will have none of that. Today marks the beginning of our road to success. England and Spain will show how strong and determined we are in the face of France's aggression. Henri will soon sue for peace, as will the Pope.'

'I think you are right; I am convinced that Henri would prefer to seek increased power by other means than war. But what is this war with the Holy Father? It disturbs me; it grieves me that any monarch should take up arms against him.'

'You know enough of this octogenarian hothead to understand how his hatred for Spain coupled with his desire to make the Kingdom of Naples his would so quickly drive him to war. The Duque de Alba will soon put him in his place and an amicable accord will be reached. As for the war with France, although it would never have come about had your council been stronger and more resolute months ago, we have no other option. But be of good cheer, our generals and our men are of the best and we will have the French pleading terms in next to no time.'

'How my heart lifts to have you by my side, to hear your words. Now it is time for action.' Mary took a deep breath and ordered, 'Bring in the King of Arms.'

The herald entered and knelt before his queen.

'King of Arms, you will go with all speed dressed entirely in black that no one can know your identity to France, to the court of King Henri. When you reach the court you will wear the royal tabard to deliver our declaration of war.'

A heavy silence followed although Strelly and Jane would dearly have liked to applaud, this was vengeance indeed against the French ambassador and all those who harmed or still sought to harm their mistress.

Jane hurriedly whispered, 'This might bring their majesties closer together, do you suppose, a special bond?'

But the answer came from Philip. 'My lady, you have played your part well. Now it is my turn. Preparations must be made for my departure.'

Mary reeled as if struck by some mighty blow. 'Departure?'

Philip explained, 'I must get to Brussels. There is much to be done: to coordinate the deployment of troops from Spain, Germany, the Netherlands, England; armaments need to be organised; provisions sought. There can be no delay.'

She wanted to plead that if he went there would be no one to support her. Where would she find the strength to fight the sniping French ambassador and an often belligerent Parliament? Who was there to help if someone tried once more to steal the few boxes of gold in the exchequer?

He held her hands. 'Cardinal Pole is here to advise, and I will leave Feria with you who you know to be trustworthy and reliable.'

Her voice trembled with fear as she asked the question already knowing its true answer. 'When do you hope to return? You were away so long the last time when you thought it would be only a matter of weeks.'

'I can only say that I will be away for as long as it takes.' That was no lie at all, the war had to be fought and won, after which he really must go to Spain. He had never formally met his subjects since assuming its crown. 'Meanwhile you could attend to the marriage of Elizabeth and Savoy.'

Mary couldn't possibly face that. It was all too complicated; she barely recognised her as her half-sister, and Parliament continued to refuse even contemplating such a marriage. She pushed it to the back of her mind.

More significantly, and she was cheered by the thought, should she tell him, as she had two years ago, that she was with child. This time she was certain because she had definitely felt something there whenever she traced her fingers across her belly. Perhaps now was not the best moment; but when she wrote later to tell him the good news, then he would be at her side in no time.

Brussels

1558

11

Brussels was decidedly the place to be if you enjoyed the social life, and for almost a year there had certainly been plenty of it; almost too much. But no, perhaps there had been just the right amount to distract a person from the many and persistent problems ever present in England.

Philip sat at his desk studying his courtiers, tapping his chin with his idle quill. They, like him, had finally discarded their sullen and weary masks, the legacy of their English sojourn. In their ones and twos he had gradually summoned them all to Flanders; each one impatient for their name to be called.

Of course someone had to be left behind and the lot had fallen to Feria. So there he stayed, alone but for the lovely Jane. Philip hoped these two had by now persuaded Mary to insist upon Elizabeth's marriage with Savoy.

Life would have been so much more pleasant had it not been for the Calais disaster last winter; but then whose fault was that? Suspicious English minds had been at the root of it all. Had they accepted his advice and offers of military help regarding that fort, so severely undermanned and riddled with French agents, its loss would have been avoided. Fortunately no blame could be laid at his door.

Philip dismissed all his frustration with two swift taps of the quill, turning his mind instead to his glorious victory against the French at St. Quentin. That day, 10 August 1557, had been nothing less than spectacular. It could not have been bettered, not even by his father when at the very height of his military prowess. Perhaps the most gratifying part was that it had provided him with the opportunity to show his father his true mettle. Unfortunately, the German soldiers had disappointed him with their brutality; God knew he had tried to prevent them sacking the town, but that was war.

He pictured his father, retired in his small palace in Spain, all too ready to belittle and denigrate, to pour scorn on his triumph; determined that no military action could ever match his own. But there was no possibility of criticism; it could not be denied, he had proven himself, he had earned his spurs. And more recently the French had been dealt a devastating blow at

Gravelines. This second victory ensured that the French would not be harassing his borders again.

However, he was as tired of war as was the whole of Spain. The Spanish purse was empty. Something had to be done. France, too, was in debt so must be of the same opinion. Yes, it was time to think of peace negotiations, and now of course Spain would go to the table with a strong hand. As part of the treaty he might offer his son, Prince Carlos, in marriage to the French king's daughter. He could already envisage how history would applaud him as Philip the Peacemaker. Carlos did have one or two physical and mental shortcomings – he glossed over the truly worrying degree of his son's disabilities – he was nevertheless heir to the powerful throne of Spain.

'Your majesty,' Gómez was hurrying towards him, a knowing smile playing on his lips.

Gómez, his invaluable friend, if kings are allowed friends, continued to serve and smile despite a continued longing to be with his betrothed. Five years had passed since Philip had arranged the contract. Gómez was more than satisfied to be offered such a prize as Ana de Mendoza, an only child, who one day would inherit the titles and wealth of one of the greatest families in Spain. At that time she was still a child, twelve years old, now she was a young woman. Gómez had shown him her recent portrait and, by God, she was a beauty! What was it they were saying all over Spain? Ah, yes, that she was *the envy of all women; and the desire of all men*. Poor Gómez having to tolerate all this waiting. Still, in the meanwhile the good folk of Flanders did their best in providing the diversions required by men with passions.

The quill, having measured languid time, was hastily discarded. Philip was eager for news. 'The envoy?'

'Not long arrived: safe and sound, my lord, and will be with you immediately,' his smile broadened.

'Let us hope for an agreeable report as well as refreshingly good company. Do something with those papers, Gómez. I had already tired of them, and now have no interest whatever. Ignore the pile on the left; they are nothing more than the daily epistles from Mary, repeatedly urging my return. Dear God but she is so wearying. No doubt I shall deal with them; eventually.'

Gómez directed Philip's attention to the silent figure standing in the doorway. He pushed back his chair and rushed towards his envoy, 'You are most welcome.'

The young woman was raised from her curtsey and gathered

into his arms. Philip kissed her fair forehead, her delicious desirable mouth, 'Dearest cousin, I have longed for this moment. You are well, and had a good crossing?'

The courtiers having enjoyed this unexpected diversion retired to discuss this demonstration of something rather more than cousinly affection.

'The crossing was perfect, my lord, and my heart rose with each wave knowing it brought me closer to home.'

'And to me, I hope.'

'And to you, cousin. The Lord knows my bed is always cold without you, and my English bed was chillier still.'

'And what of me? I have been lonely, too. My arms, my bed, have been empty all these months.'

'Not according to what I have heard.' She planted a forgiving peck on his cheek. 'It was common knowledge in Queen Mary's court that the soirees at a certain person's home not so far from here have been particularly successful recently, and I understand that one young lady is soon to retire from society because of her interesting condition.'

'Would you have me sit here all alone awaiting your return with nothing but my own dreary company?'

Christina tut-tutted, 'That was the subject of yet more gossip. You had company enough here in the palace. An English lady, no doubt you will know who I mean, on her arrival in England let it be known that it took her several visits to your bed to ensure that her husband's exile was revoked. So, you were never once without solace and comfort the whole time I was away!' She became serious, 'But are you truly well again? Queen Mary was frantic with worry when she heard you were ill, while all I wanted was to be at your side to bathe your fevered brow. You were always in my prayers.'

'I was ill, but not seriously so, it was over in a few days. Shall we say it did not seriously interfere with my social calendar; my Lady Mary concerns herself too much. But I thank you, dear heart, for your prayers.' He kissed the precious fingertips of the hands that had prayed for him. 'But to business. Shall we take a stroll in the gardens? I feel the need for fresh air.'

'And I thought for a moment that my very presence would be refreshment enough!' She teased, kissing him lightly, holding fast to his hands.

He had almost forgotten how delightfully attractive and enticing the Princess Christina was, even at times like this when dressed in fiercely severe black ambassador's robes.

They walked hand in hand along the corridor, down the stairs and out into the formal garden. Everything was at its best today.

'Cousin, I swear your very presence makes the colours sharper, the perfumes more intense, why, even the bees are busier than ever.'

They strolled along broad flagged paths passing flower beds all arranged with military precision inside huge myrtle-hedged circles and rectangles.

Philip stopped, 'Ah, my fair Christina.' He threw his arms about her, hungry to kiss every part of her face, all the while impatient to race with her to his bed that he might kiss her neck, her shoulders, her ...

'This will not do, my ambassador; to serious matters. What news of a marriage for Elizabeth with Savoy?'

'I doubt it will ever come to pass. I hasten to add that Feria and I tried every argument, all to no avail. Queen Mary refuses to recognise Elizabeth as heir to the throne and therefore cannot be persuaded of the necessity of her marrying a Catholic to ensure a Catholic successor.'

'What damned nonsense is that? Of course Elizabeth is heir. Married to Savoy she would be returned to the True Faith and become a fitting monarch for the English throne. Or would my lady wife rather have Mary of Scotland inherit along with her husband, the future king of France? Would she really prefer to see England under the heel of a French master?'

'We raised that on several occasions. But she says she cannot make a decision without you.'

'There isn't time for such stupidity! Oh, I wash my hands of her! I have done everything I can. Now it's up to her. But a decision must be made soon, time is short. God knows that if only she had moved with greater speed the Calais disaster would have been avoided.'

'The queen remains deeply injured by those events and the burden of that defeat weighs heavily on her. She mourns that when she dies the surgeons will find Calais engraved on her heart. She is hurt and disappointed that you have not found it important to go to comfort her.'

'That is for Feria to attend to.'

'And still you will not go?'

'I will not be persuaded. I have repeatedly told her that I refuse to set foot in that country unless I am promised the crown.'

'I have to report that these days there are too many throughout the length and breadth of the land talking quite openly about seeking Elizabeth's favour, recognising her as future queen. Yet Mary seems incapable of taking any action against them.'

'How can she be so weak!'

'The queen still hopes you will return to sire a child, to prevent Elizabeth from inheriting.'

'Dear God, not that again. I have gone through Mary's sordid pregnancy play-acting twice. Enough is enough. Never again!'

'I wish I could have been the bearer of better tidings.' Christina drew a letter from her purse, 'A letter from her majesty, my lord.'

Philip broke the seal and let his eyes roam over the lines of yet another of his wife's tiresome missives, *My dearest lord and husband, I humbly seek your pardon, but the Lady Elizabeth has refused the offer of marriage. She will not accept Savoy. Believe me I have truly tried both in this and to have her return to the True Faith. I am sorry beyond all measure to upset so wonderful a husband. Please, I beg of you, do not criticise me or say that I cannot expect God's forgiveness if I fail.*

He folded the letter having no interest in finishing it. 'The same old excuses and apologies for lack of resolve. My patience is exhausted.'

'I have a great deal of sympathy for her. Her spirits are very low. We have watched her prepare gifts to send to you every day, and waited with her as she looked eagerly for something from you in return only to have her hopes dashed time and again by your lack of response.'

He bristled, 'Her innermost feelings were best kept private and not a subject for idle gossip.'

'Like as not. You should know, by the way, that she can ill afford all those gifts of jewels and clothes. Queen Mary is deeply in debt.'

'Enough! Tell me instead what she thought of my portrait.' Mary had requested it when in an ecstasy of hero worship; her hero of the battle of St. Quentin. The portrait had disappointed him. He thought it made him look decidedly uncomfortable in his armour. It declared he had not been a soldier, but had been well away from the battlefront dealing with the endless paper work that wars create. In any case he loathed the disorder, the noise, the blood, the filth of it all; it gave him a pounding headache and chronic diarrhoea.

'The queen was overjoyed. She giggled at your apology for appearing before her bareheaded, declaring how much better it was to see your handsome fair head.' She suddenly turned away, cupping some roses in her hands, pretending to drink in their perfume, hoping to conceal her discomfort, her guilt, at the role she had been playing for some time and would now continue to play.

'What is it Christina? Tell me.' He drew her close.

'From the beginning Queen Mary did not take kindly to me as your emissary. She would have preferred a gentleman. There was always an air of unease when I was in the room. Then, when I gave my official farewell, well, I was shocked at what happened. It was all so very, very, sad.'

She would not tell Philip how embarrassing those few moments had been. Mary had turned on Christina, railing about her returning to the side of Philip. She called her Philip's mistress, a whore. She screamed, reminding her exactly whose husband she was hurrying back to; to flirt with, to bed with. She had howled her hatred for Christina's infuriating beauty, intelligence, talents, her vivaciousness and her damned excellent health; jealous that she lacked them all. Tears had flooded from Mary's reddened eyes cascading over puffy cheeks. Dribbles from her nose ran onto her lips. She was so despairingly ugly.

Nor would Philip hear from her that Mary had then taken a pair of scissors to hack and slash at the beloved portrait before collapsing into a sobbing heap. He would never know that her last view of Queen Mary was of her being led gently from the room in the comforting arms of Strelly and Jane.

'What was so very sad?'

'She wept bitterly because I was the one leaving. I was the one soon to see you, while she must remain in England.' This was a truth, of sorts. 'As I said before, her spirits are so very low and she is often overcome by bouts of weeping. It takes her ladies every effort to console her. My lord cousin, I am afraid the queen of England is far from well.'

'You are right, Christina, the queen is unwell. I am quite aware of how ill she is, but we must leave her health in the hands of her doctors. In the meantime she, as with any other royal, must put her country's affairs first before her own wellbeing; and that includes marriage contracts.' Philip would not be moved to sympathy.

Christina laughed mischievously, only too eager to change the subject, 'Like the one your father arranged for me with Henry VIII. Dear God in Heaven! It is as well I refused, or tonight you would be making love to Christina, your widowed mother-in-law, instead of Christina your cousin!'

'If only your father had not had the misfortune to lose the crown of Denmark. You would still be a princess with a fairly handsome dowry, and a perfectly suitable bride for me. I would have been able to extend the Netherlands' trade into the Baltic.'

'You will never change. You and your head and heart forever focussed on politics, power, and religion!'

'Not always. Tonight we shall have a banquet, then dancing, and lastly private celebrations in my apartments. Then, dearest Christina, you shall see what my head and heart are focussed on.'

'That might just be the Philip I know and love, and have missed so much!'

12

'A year almost; and to have it pass with such haste.' Christina looked deep into the eyes of her cousin to hold them with hers.

'But nonetheless a good year, a busy year; and all the while you have been by my side, my mistress and my inspiration for dealing with the French; a novel combination. However, all good things must come to an end.' Philip kissed her and moved to the window stepping into the slanting rays of spring sunlight, disturbing the dancing motes.

After a moment's pause he asked, 'And your opinion on my decision?' He ran his fingers across the border of fruits and flowers on his recent acquisition, a silver-topped side table. They traced over the figure of the dying Adonis, the beautiful Venus rushing to his side her bare feet oblivious to the thorns tearing at her skin.

'How could you possibly go wrong in choosing a wife with the name of Elizabeth. Or should I say Isabel? Our great grandmother, queen of Castile; my mother; your mother the empress; all were called Isabel.'

'And she the best of all. No one could ever begin to compare with my mother. She was perfect: as wife, mother, and sovereign of Spain. She was beautiful, tender, sensitive, yet a woman of courage and steel. Everyone's heart was broken when she died.' He turned to Christina, thinking of yet another Isabel almost as wonderful. 'But this is not the moment for dwelling on the past. It is the future that beckons.'

Christina crossed the small salon to join him, 'I should think so, too!' The silver figures and trees of the table drew her attention, 'The workmanship is of the highest quality, but who in the world would want such a melancholy piece in their home?'

The very Isabel he was thinking of; Isabel de Osorio, never far from his thoughts. He knew she would find great pleasure in this because she would see it as a reminder that she was still his one and only love.

'My lord, you sent for us,' the voice belonged to the Duque de Feria. He and his wife Jane waited at the door.

82

'Come in, come in; welcome to Brussels! Jane, I am sure you will find much to cheer you in this delightful city. May I first say that I appreciate everything you did for Queen Mary; you were a good friend and looked after her well. Now it is our turn to care for you, to bring back the roses to those pale cheeks. You are not ill?'

Jane curtsied but could not bear to look at the man who had been the cause of such pain and heartache for her beloved mistress. She prayed that God would forgive him for all the hurt he had caused, would forgive those cruel letters sent to Mary when she was on her deathbed, letters demanding she redouble her effort to have Elizabeth marry Savoy, accusing her of incompetence, threatening her. How often had she watched her tearful mistress writing to Philip begging him not to be angry with her.

'It is just that I am a little tired, your majesty. The last few months were very difficult, and my lady's passing was not an easy one. The queen suffered dreadful pain from the tumour in her womb and there was little we could do to comfort her, even our prayers went unheeded. The last thing she said to me before drifting into unconsciousness was that I should not weep for her. She told me she had had the sweetest of dreams where she saw herself surrounded by lots of children singing and dancing and playing. Oh, how I remember those wonderful times we used to have in the countryside. She loved to be with the little ones, they were always a joy to her. If only God could have granted her the gift of a child of her own. Now that she is in Heaven perhaps she will find many a baby to cherish, many an infant to play with.'

'Yes, yes indeed. Christina, we cannot have this young bride be so sad. I give you the duty of taking Jane in hand to raise her spirits. And you can begin this very moment; off you go.' Philip was not going to be dragged down into a black morass of useless, sickening female sentimentality.

Feria waited until the ladies were gone, 'Jane was right, it was all very sad, very sad indeed. Mary died lonely and unloved by a nation she had tried so hard to protect from sin and danger. Even as she lay dying there were those determined to mock some even planning the wording on her tomb MARIA RUINA ANGLAE. It was her dying wish that you would include the return of Calais to England as part of your peace treaty with France.'

Philip ignored him, Calais belonged to the past.

Feria handed Philip a small box, 'The Pearl, *La Perla Peregrina*. My condolences.'

'I thank you, a most timely arrival, please keep it for the moment. Well, Feria, last year was quite a year for the grim reaper, first Aunt Leonor, then my father, then Aunt Maria and finally Mary. May God rest all their souls. Can you imagine the expenses incurred with so many funeral honours I have had to hold here in Brussels? But that is over and done with. Tell me of Queen Elizabeth.'

'I was invariably the last to know anything about her thinking or her decisions. I wish the new ambassador better fortune. I repeatedly reminded her that she owes her throne to you, but she would have none of it. I also told her majesty not to forget that Mary of Scotland had every right to challenge her for it and was probably only biding her time. I did my best to impress upon her that you would be prepared to defend her against Mary and France provided she made no moves against the Catholic Church in England.'

'And how did she respond?'

'I cannot be sure. She goes to Mass every day, but I doubt it will last. She is a strong woman and will have her own way. It's quite remarkable, the people see her father in her and I can assure you they fear her in the same way. They would not dare show the disrespect they blatantly poured on Mary.' Feria shook his head, 'I cannot tell you the feeling of relief to be out of that cesspool of ignorance. *Happy Wednesday* is how the English barbarians refer to the day of Mary's death and it would seem that many call her Bloody Mary because of those heretics who perished preferring the stake to repentance.'

'We will focus our thoughts on Elizabeth, God knows Mary was barely capable of doing anything when she was alive, she can certainly be of no significance now she is dead.'

'My lord, I did everything I could. I hope I have not incurred your disfavour.'

'Absolutely not, Feria, she was a lost cause all along. But Elizabeth?'

'Queen Elizabeth is cross with you, she finds you a very poor suitor.' He raised his eyebrows, 'She stamped her foot and pouted, quite put out that you could not wait for her answer; not even for a few months.'

Philip laughed, 'I can imagine it. However, I knew all along she had no intention of accepting, and she was equally aware I truly had no stomach for another English marriage.'

'You will find this interesting. Although she continues to insist that had she ever contemplated marriage it would have been with you and with no other, and that having declined your offer, she vows she will never wed, it would seem that Elizabeth has a lover.'

'He isn't the first, and probably will not be the last. Who is it this time?'

'A certain Lord Dudley, Robert Dudley. He has an interesting family, both his father and grandfather ended up on the scaffold.'

'Because of religion? It is of no consequence; and Dudley himself?'

'An excellent suitor; young, handsome, tall, courtly, excels in jousting. She has made him Master of the Queen's Horse, granting him lodging in the palace. It is no secret that she is greatly interested in him, spends hours in his chambers day and night, to the extent that she is beginning to neglect her duties. The people are talking of nothing else. There is, however, an obstacle.'

'There often is. What is this one?'

'Dudley is married. But, his wife has a serious malady of the breast and cannot last much longer. Apparently, as soon as she is dead Elizabeth and Dudley intend to marry.'

'Marry; that would put a completely different complexion on the religious question. Hopefully she will think most carefully about a decision which could cause a further move away from the True Faith. Our friendly alliance might be rather short-lived after all. It is as well for her that I have other arrangements in place to ensure England's safety. Now let us join Gómez and Alba.'

He picked up a sheaf of papers and set off for the audience chamber wagering with Feria that they would find Alba, the soldier, on one side of the room with his supporters. Gómez with his fellow politicians would have positioned himself on the other as far away as possible. They were firmly at odds with one another; even more so these days.

'Alba is here in Brussels, my lord?'

'Yes, just recently arrived from France.'

CR   SO

There they were, as he had so rightly surmised, separated by the width of the room and an ocean of ill feeling, and he found

85

the situation quite amusing. From the moment he had sent Alba to Italy Gómez's star had been in the ascendancy, with Alba promptly forgotten. No one had been closer than Gómez for three years. Then Alba returned to be lauded as a hero, turning heads and hearts in his direction. It was the time for his star to dominate. Gómez suddenly developed several maladies, enough to prevent him taking any part in the public acclaim. Gómez and Alba, Philip asserted, were no better than overgrown schoolboys.

He called to Alba, 'A moment or two of your time.'

Feria joined Gómez and watched the Gran Duque de Alba, the glorious general, make his way to the king's side looking today every inch the statesman in his burgundy velvet robe. This rival was in his late fifties: tall, thin, and of fiercely proud bearing. The hair and his beard were sparse and greying. His long face was sallow and lined, battered since early youth by a lifetime of devotion to Spain's military campaigns, but his brown eyes had lost none of their youthful sparkle.

'So,' Feria observed, 'the old man refuses to retire. It surprises me that he has enough spirit to live let alone get involved in wars and politics.'

'I wish to God he had retired, the damned nuisance. For the life of me I cannot understand why Philip entrusted him with difficult negotiations. I imagine it was the interfering Christina who persuaded Philip to give him and not me the honour. And why? Because of his success in Italy. Of course he was successful, he is a soldier, damn it! But successful soldiers do not necessarily make successful negotiators. Anyway, I had already shown him my feelings on the so-called Italian triumph; I refused to give him the satisfaction of seeing me at any of his receptions. I said I was ill.'

'Gómez, you disappoint me. You know Philip well enough to see through his little game. He must have felt he was becoming too reliant on you and had to redress the balance; hence Alba. Now tell me the news on the treaty, everything went well?'

'Who knows? Alba is playing tit for tat for my snubbing him and is refusing to give me any details.'

Philip and Alba had concluded their discussion. 'So, gentlemen,' Philip announced, 'we have peace with France. It brings good news for our Cousin Savoy; his lands are returned and he is to marry King Henri's sister'

Sounds of congratulation echoed about the room, for the peace treaty, for Savoy, but even greater emotions were stirred by the thought that they would all soon be returning to their homes in Spain.

'The wedding dowry is perfect too. Whatever we give in jewels for the bride, the French will give ten times the amount in gold. Alba has done well. Preparations can now proceed for him to go to Paris as proxy for my marriage to Princess Isabel de Valois. Feria you may now give Gómez *La Perla Peregrina,* Gómez you will be responsible for its security and that of all the jewels.'

Gómez hissed under his breath, 'Damnation! That man Alba is now going to be the proxy!'

Feria hushed him, whispering, 'That is only of interest to you. I am trying to believe what my ears have apparently just heard. I thought Prince Carlos was to be the groom.'

Philip was happily nodding at his courtiers whose stunned silence had changed to murmurings and then to polite applause, 'It is true that I was at one time considering my son as husband to this daughter of the king of France, but he and the princess are too young. You must understand there would be a danger in a long delay before the consummation of the marriage, and their tender age would cause such a delay. This treaty is a delicate one and there is no room for any complications; my being the groom will ensure there will be neither delay nor complications.'

There was no realistic alternative to his decision. Isabel was thirteen years old and Carlos not much older. Even if Isabel was already a woman, and the French doctors had told Alba she was not, children born of very young parents were usually sickly and unhealthy. Carlos himself was a prime example of that!

The marriage would take place in July despite the fact he had been a widower for only six months. He congratulated himself on the speed and success of the agreement.

'Yes, gentlemen, I am the one who will *bed* France. Alba, you have my promise that as soon as your duties in Paris are complete you may return to your home to attend to your own affairs. Gómez, you have my word that you will be married to your Ana before the year is out; and I will be there to ensure everything goes well.' It would also provide a longed for opportunity to see this captivating and desirable young lady.

'My lord,' Feria knelt before him, 'if I may, I seek your permission to return to my home. I spent almost all my income when in England. It was an honour to serve you, but after five years I need to get my affairs in order or my wife and I will be penniless.'

'Then see to it as fast as you can, for I need you at my court. Although I have my general with his military stratagems, and Gómez alert to intrigue, I need you because you are unbiased as well as honest in everything you do.' Philip clasped him by the shoulders, then turning on his heel, left his courtiers to ponder the news of his impending marriage and, what may be more significant, his son's likely reactions.

They all knew of the prince's violent temper, some had had the misfortune to be on the receiving end of it. Nor was his growing animosity towards his father a secret. What would he do when he discovered that a marriage contract had been signed robbing him of his intended bride, and that the thief was his own father!

France

1559

13

It was the last day of the year and it was cold, bitterly cold; colder than anything Isabel had ever known. And she was still in France. Ahead of her lay her route along the snow-covered pass through the Pyrenees and into Spain. Ahead of her was her new home, the country which had for years been the enemy of France. She felt lonely, homesick, and afraid.

The thirteen-year-old princess made queen by her marriage to Philip II had spent the morning in the small salon waiting, was still waiting, to be told that her litter was ready and the entourage about to set off. Outside the snow fell relentlessly adding to the inches already carpeting the frozen ground. Enormous icicles hung like menacing lances from every eave. Howling winds blew down chimneys and icy draughts forced their way through windows and doorways.

Isabel, like the world outside, was also dressed in white, telling the world she was in mourning for the death of her father, killed so tragically when jousting at her wedding tourney. Her dress was of white velvet over skirts and sleeves of white quilted satin brocade, her raven black hair had been combed back and tucked under a white velvet bonnet with its looped ropes of pearls about its brim. Her Florentine complexion, inherited from her mother, was made more beautiful by her dark hair and eyes.

Four of her closest ladies attended her, all hovering about the fire except for the occasional excursions to the windows to peer down through veils of scurrying snowflakes. Below in the courtyard the few remaining mules with their snow-covered burdens were gradually leaving to join the growing train of sure-footed beasts carrying everything the royal party owned out and away into the mountains.

The room was quiet, the ladies speaking very little, all anxious about an unknown but certainly hazardous journey, fearful of plunging to their deaths or, what might be worse, a highly likely daunting Spanish reception.

The door was thrown open and just as quickly closed by an exceedingly small man with exceptionally bowed legs.

'You sent for me,' the dwarf squeaked his ill-tempered demand for an explanation for his summons.

'I did, Montagne, and you took so long to find.' Isabel smiled at her beloved fool.

'It will take even longer to find me if you insist on us travelling in that weather out there. I tell you the snow is up to my knees already. I warn you; think again.'

'You exaggerate, Montagne.'

He clambered onto a chair by the fire shuffling his way to the back of the seat, his short, stunted, booted legs stuck out before him, his tiny arms locked across his chest intending to demonstrate his defiance.

'Why has it taken such an age to get to the frontier?' His thin, sharp voice cut across the space between them. 'Let me tell you why. It has taken so long because you were indulging yourself being feted at all our stopping places. As a result the weeks have slipped by and you have got us into this intolerable situation. I have grave doubts if I should allow myself to be a part of this insanity.'

Isabel's lips began to tremble, her eyes fill with tears, 'Montagne, you sound so cross.'

'I have every right to be; sending me out into a blizzard! Come to think of it, white is hardly the most suitable colour you have chosen for travelling in these conditions, whose harebrained idea was that?'

'You know I am in mourning for my father. Montagne, I think his death was an omen.'

'Stuff and nonsense. I thought you were too intelligent for superstitious twaddle. And, let me add, your father died in June and it is now one day short of January, your days of mourning are well over.'

'Montagne, I am feeling miserable, and I sent for you to cheer me with your wit and wisdom. You are not being very helpful.'

'Cheer? There is no cheer to be had save for the fire, and we are going to leave that soon enough!' He looked her up and down, 'I think you ought to wear a jolly colour, a yellow or red, that would remind us of a warm and welcoming blaze; and they are the colours for a young girl.'

'Young girl? A few months ago I put aside my school books, said goodbye to my childhood, to become a wife to one who was my father's sworn enemy, to go to live amongst my country's enemies. I am having to grow up very quickly.' Tears weren't far away.

'Stop feeling sorry for yourself. At least you know you can grow, look at me, what growing have I ever done? Do you see me whimpering? And have you spared a thought for your sister-in-law Mary, queen of Scotland and now France? She was but a tender little thing when she had to leave her home.'

'She came to live with friends and family. Another thing, my husband is twenty years my senior, a cold man they say, very religious, too religious. What will he expect of me? I know I will fall foul at every turn.'

'He will expect what every husband expects, obedience, silence, and not too much laughter.' Montagne pushed himself free of the chair, dropping nimbly to his feet. 'For any other information on wives, or other women for that matter, you will have to ask elsewhere; these ladies will know what goes on behind the bed curtains. All I want you to remember is that whatever the situation all you need is confidence. Yes, always remember your self-confidence; that is where the answer lies.'

'You are of no help whatsoever.'

'Well, then,' he turned as if to go, 'continue to wear white and get yourself lost in the snow; perish sooner rather than later.'

'What do you mean? You scare me.'

'Good. I want to shake you from this ridiculous self-pity. I am talking about not being at the mercy of others.' He rubbed at his collar, 'Would you mind sitting down, my neck hurts having to look up all the time.'

Isabel sat in the chair he had so recently vacated.

Montagne puffed out his pigeon chest, 'Listen carefully to your tiny Montagne. I have confidence, and where does it come from?'

'From gifts and bribes, like the jewel in your cap,' Isabel sniffled.

'Not at all, those are the results of my strategies, my wit, or cunning if you prefer. Yes, I have to remember what is important and what is not; remember who is important and who is not; and then summoning up the confidence to proceed. I have nothing else in my favour yet I have succeeded. So it takes confidence, my lady, confidence. If the likes of me can succeed so can you. Let me illustrate this with some comparisons. I am deformed and ugly whereas you are tall and quite, quite, beautiful. I have a foolish waddle; you glide with grace and elegance. You are intelligent and have got your learning from books; I have to rely on information overheard from behind ladies' skirts, going unnoticed in a crowd.'

'And you have done very nicely,' a hint of a smile played on her lips as she thought of his luxurious lifestyle.

'A man has his living to make, and where would I be if I could only count on the pittance you pay me? But we digress. Take my advice, from this moment I want you to always remember who you are and what you are; keep in mind the words *self confidence*; concentrate on your beauty, charm, elegance, your intelligence, your sweet and caring nature ... Shall I go on?'

'That will do perfectly. I confess I had not expected a lecture, but I thank you nonetheless.

'My pleasure. Believe me, my Queen Isabel the Peacemaker, you will have everyone eating out of your hand, including the dour Philip. Now, one final suggestion; rid yourself of that dreadful mourning. Do what you have always done; bring colour and joy into our lives.'

Spain

1560

Isabel de Valois

Wives of Philip II

1543	1554	1560
Maria Manuela (cousin)	Mary Tudor (aunt)	Isabel de Valois
|		|
Carlos		miscariage Isabel Clara Catalina Micaela miscarriage

14

'There she is. That's her.'

'She's beautiful; bless her!'

'And still only a child' … 'Not even fourteen, I heard' … 'Welcome, *Isabel of Peace.*'

Shouts of joy were coming from all directions as Philip and Gómez threaded their way through a crush of courtiers gathered to catch their first glimpse of the French princess, now the queen of Spain.

The crowded patio of the Duque del Infantado's palace offered some protection against the icy January wind, but Philip still pulled his cloak tighter about him holding the large collar firm across the lower part of his face. He squeezed between two gentlemen and a corner pillar stone. This was a perfect vantage point; Isabel would slow down when she reached this part of the arcade. He leaned on Gómez's shoulder trying to secure his footing on the narrow ledge at the pillar's base.

He watched Isabel's progress along the sheltered arcade. The truth was about to be revealed; was she the beauty that Gómez and Alba had promised him? The wind, as if on cue, whipped at Isabel's hood, revealing a perfectly oval shaped face with a complexion neither fair nor dark and with a translucency like the most delicate of porcelains. She had the daintiest of noses and a pretty rosebud mouth; charmingly arched eyebrows were set over the darkest of eyes. She was a joy to behold; and she was his.

He had to fight to quell the unseemly passions that she was stirring within him. It was too good to be true; he couldn't believe his good fortune.

'I grant you she is not bad looking, not bad at all, perhaps too tall and unfortunately with dark hair, but nonetheless quite agreeable.' Philip leaned down whispering into Gómez's ear, 'All in all, I think you may have given me a fair report. She may well measure up to the *Thirty Perfections* required of an ideal woman.'

'I cannot answer for all the requirements, my lord; for example her knees or the colour of her nipples being beyond my remit!'

'And rightly so, you devil! I think Brussels has been your undoing. Yes, this one will do quite nicely. It will be a pleasure to visit her bed.' He jumped down, 'So, back indoors to receive the young lady.'

They pushed their way through a counter flow of those still determined to see Isabel as she passed.

At last Isabel's journey was over and the comparative warmth of the hall, despite its bare tiled floor, was so welcome after the intense cold she had endured for so many weeks. Her thick, fur-lined, travelling cloak was removed and there she was for all to feast their eyes on. Here was a promise, a foretaste of a longed-for summer after far too long a winter. A bonnet of red velvet nestling on dark curls and a red velvet dress with its matching heavily quilted gown emphasised her extraordinary beauty and her delicate frame.

Philip's sister Juana was given the honour of escorting this young stranger to his side. She knelt at Isabel's feet to kiss the hand of the child bride of her brother, the hand of her queen.

'I am Juana, sister of His Majesty King Philip, I bid you welcome, your majesty.'

'I thank you, dear sister.'

Isabel invited Juana to stand. She smiled at this pretty woman in her mid twenties. This was her new sister and, she prayed, soon to become her friend; although the serious eyes and mouth were a little off-putting. But they could be excused; a few years ago hadn't she had to leave her baby son in Portugal to return to Spain? Of course, this was the widowed Juana, the princess who had been married for so short a time. At least her black velvet dress was made to look less austere with the addition of a fine white silk scarf caught at her waist with a diamond brooch, and with the lace ruff at her neck edged with tiny pearls. Her golden curls were partially covered by a white velvet bonnet with a trim of pendent pearls only too ready to dance. Isabel was convinced there was every possibility for a friendship with her Spanish sister.

They began their slow walk Isabel almost gliding with exquisite French elegance and pride, and taking those few moments to study the gentleman who was waiting to receive her.

What did Isabel see? She saw someone old enough to be her father; the monarch whose name was anathema to France; the very person who had been so hated by her father and to this day still loathed by her mother (although continuing to congratulate herself on having made so excellent a match for her daughter). She noted that Philip wasn't very tall, in fact he was rather short; fortunately that was a bonus as tall people intimidated her. Was he angry? He certainly wasn't about to smile, and his pale blue eyes were like ice. The closer she got the older he looked; perhaps the receding hairline was to blame. She wondered if he was still mourning, he had after all been so cruelly widowed twice. Her youth must surely soon reawaken his heart.

'So, my Lady Isabel,' he challenged, 'I see you have given me the most thorough of examinations. What is it that disturbs you most about this ancient person before you, is it his hair? You certainly gave it a great deal of attention, enough to count each and every one of the grey hairs.'

The words were sharp; they cut deep, they devastated, just as they were intended, because he hated any form of scrutiny and he was alarmed that she may have noticed the increasing baldness that he thought his barber had managed to camouflage.

Her confidence, which had been growing with each murmured compliment and with every whispered word of welcome as she passed along the row of gathered courtiers, withered and died. She was at fault for doing no more than what she did with everyone when meeting them for the first time, what she had just done when meeting Juana a few moments ago; wasn't it what one always did, show an interest, begin to form an opinion?   That he should criticise her so cruelly, so publicly was humiliating. What she had said to Montagne about falling foul at every turn could be only too true.

'My lord,' she fought her tears. 'I did not seek to offend,' she humbly offered, earnestly, quietly, and in Spanish. She had understood his words perfectly.

'I only jest,' he turned to the guests in mock appeal, but they all knew he was pretending shock at her reaction; they all knew he had been angered by her examination. 'My Lady Isabel mistakenly supposed I was being serious. As if I would be so churlish! My lady, it was only because you never allowed your eyes to stray from my head that I thought to tease.' She had better learn soon, or be told, that looking at him or seeking out his eyes unasked was absolutely forbidden.

There was a hint of laughter from somewhere, but it was no more than a polite titter and did little to reassure her. She was reminded of her mother's warnings of the sobriety and gravity of the Spanish court. How could someone as lively as herself survive in this schoolroom atmosphere?

'Introductions!' Philip had reverted to being a gentleman of manners. 'The lady on whose arm you are resting is my sister Juana.'

As Juana curtsied once more Isabel redoubled her prayers that despite the ten years difference in their ages she might still find in her a friend and confidante.

'His Excellency Prince Juan.'

She had let herself down again, she was so busy thinking about a friendship with Juana that she had no idea who this handsome youth was. He was about her age and with fair hair and beautiful blue eyes and looking nothing like the portrait of Prince Carlos that she had seen showing him to be far from handsome despite the royal artist's skill and Spanish ambassador's eloquent words to disguise the faults and imperfections. And hadn't she heard that he was probably demented?

'Prince Juan at your service, my lady.'

Of course; this was Juan, Philip's half-brother, the love child of Philip's father, the Emperor Charles V, and a certain lowly German woman. As this was not Philip's son Carlos, where could he be? Were he here protocol would have demanded his introduction before Juan's. Why then, was he not here? Was it because at one time she was betrothed to him, and he had no wish to see her?

Philip interrupted her thoughts, 'My nephew Prince Alessandro di Parma. His mother is currently the governor of the Low Countries.'

Another handsome young man! Alessandro was of the same age as Juan and equally attractive, but his eyes and hair were quite the darkest of browns. Perhaps with the presence of Juan and Alessandro the court might not be so dreary after all.

Gómez and Alba were next to come forward. She beamed at them, 'It is quite like meeting old friends again. How delighted I am to see you!'

'The joy is all ours, ma'am.'

A very old, rotund and most hirsute gentleman, the Duque del Infantado bowed to Isabel, as Philip introduced him, 'This is our host, and this his splendid palace. There could be no place more suitable for our marriage.' And it was also admirably located, just a short ride from the home of Gómez and his exciting wife Ana.

'Welcome, my lady. I am deeply honoured.'

'I thank you, sir, for your hospitality.' Her smile was returned twofold from two merry eyes and from happy lips almost lost in a sea of silver whiskers.

Introductions over, Isabel was accompanied to her apartments by the Spanish ladies who had been chosen by Philip: Princess Juana, the Duquesa de Alba, and Ana de Mendoza the wife of Gómez. These were followed by two of her French ladies, the Countesses Clermont and Montpensier.

Two hours later Juana led Isabel into the family chapel. A widowed Spanish countess carried Isabel's train, much to the chagrin of the Countess Clermont whose most enviable honour it had always been until today; but one cannot question a king's decision.

Philip waited with the Duque del Infantado. They turned to greet her. This time Isabel dared not look at her husband remembering the earlier harsh rebuke and chanced only the briefest of glances. He was in white satin and velvet with some gold edging and embroidery. A short crimson cloak lay across one shoulder, and on his head he wore a black hat with a white heron feather.

She raised her skirt in the French manner, with one hand not two, allowing her to move with such breathtaking grace. Her silver dress, spangled with scattered pearls and diamonds, glistened like frosted snow. The ruff at her slender neck frothed and curled dripping droplets of gold as if to nourish the diamond necklace beneath. Her scarlet gown had the widest sleeves ever seen in Spain falling open from the shoulders to be caught by sparkling diamond clips at the elbows. A French bonnet, which was half cap half tiara, combined black velvet with diamonds and rubies, and included the pendent pearl, *La Perla Peregrina*. The chapel began to fill with her heady perfumes of musk, myrrh and cinnamon.

Philip gazed long and hard at this enchanting child. This was the third marriage contract he had rushed into. In fact this was the only type of decision he could make quickly; normally it took weeks of vacillation with the accompanying headaches and bilious attacks for him to make any decision. The first two marriages had been complete failures. This one had to prove successful. There was one piece of good fortune, there would be no hardship involved in the required visits to this wife's bed.

103

Before that, however, there was the travail of surviving a few hours in the public eye. No doubt Isabel would be intent upon wringing every ounce of pleasure from each minute and still be greedy for more, as children so often do.

ରେ   ଯ

In the banqueting hall hundreds of candles, their flames nodding and dancing, threw shadows up and across walls rich with heavy tapestries all depicting stories of betrothals and marriages.

Isabel thought it all very jolly, but it simply wasn't good enough! Spanish interior decoration in general, she lamented, was in need of some French influence. As soon as she could she would direct changes, certainly to her own apartments in the palace at, where was it; Toledo? These were as yet unknown to her, but judging by every palace she had lodged in on her journey here, they would undoubtedly be unacceptable. Where were the rich velvet curtains she was used to, the silk wall hangings glittering with gold and silver threads, the chairs of gilded wood with stuffed velvet cushions, the candle holders of crystal, the marble fireplaces with the delicious smell of burning apple wood; and where were the capricious fantasies? They were nowhere to be seen. Indeed, where was the elegance? There was none. Another disturbing question was how was she ever to overcome the miserable smallness of most of the rooms? It appeared that the Spanish preferred to allocate most of the available space to galleries and corridors leaving the rooms no larger than store cupboards. It was all going to be so very difficult. And what if Philip refused to give his permission for any changes?

The menu was to Philip's liking: fried chicken, partridge, and pheasant; rabbit, duck, capon, and woodcock pies; venison, beef and pork roasts; fudges, flavoured biscuits and cakes. There were some fruits although they held little interest for him. Isabel on the other hand was most disappointed with the fare and she searched in vain for the vegetables. Alas she would never find vegetables, certainly not at Philip's table. A sigh escaped her. Everything was so, so foreign. Oh, to be back in France.

'You are tired, or has today brought back sad memories of your father?'

'No, my lord; but I am missing my mother. We were always so very close. I love her dearly.'

104

Philip dismissed this as being totally preposterous. Unlike his own mother who had been the epitome of perfection his bride's mother was double tongued and cunning. *Madame Serpent* he called her. He was also most surprised Isabel wasn't still mourning the loss of her father who had died within days of the proxy wedding. A nasty business, although jousting at Henri's age was courting disaster. But to have a lance shatter against one's visor sending a huge sliver of wood through one's eye and into the brain, well, it set one's bowels churning just thinking of it.

For her part Isabel had only wept for her father as she would for the death of some distant relative. He had been accustomed to living somewhere on his own or with his mistress of many years, *La Poitiers*. If and when he had visited his family he had been cold and aloof, especially towards her mother the most loving and caring person in the whole world and hadn't deserved such treatment.

With great solemnity the various dishes for each course of the meal were brought to the table, the leftovers cleared away. A small army of servants worked in unison to remove soiled table cloths replacing them with fresh ones before the next course was presented. Subdued conversation never threatened the delicate music of the vihuela and lute. This was what Philip demanded; not for him the bedlam in which the English indulged, nor the wild extravagances of the French.

Isabel was finding it all too different; rather dull and not at all what she expected of a banquet.

Once the meal was over the dancing began. This was much more to Isabel's liking. She moved easily and lightly. Philip was pleased to note that she knew the Spanish dances; her dancing master was to be congratulated. One criticism remained however, she was far too lively with the half turns and jumps. There must be more control, more restraint; these were not, after all, frivolous French frolics.

'My lord, that lady with the eye patch; Ana, I believe,' whispered Isabel. 'I think she dances well but I see she is a coquette.'

Philip was taken aback, 'What would make you say such a thing?'

'My lord, I saw these things so many times in the French court. To many it is a normal way of behaving and is acceptable. For me, I know it to be wrong. It breaks the heart of the injured.'

This was outrageous. To suggest that Gómez's wife was a flirt stung him deeply, it worried him. He had slept with her recently and had naturally assumed that without question he would be her only lover. Let Ana beware his wrath should she dare encourage another. And as for Isabel, she must realise that her observations on such matters were not required, and in any case she was far too young to hold any opinions whatsoever; all that was required of her was to provide her husband with heirs. But it was growing late, it had been a long and busy day, his patience was at an end, and he was irritated. It was time to retire.

The bishop was summoned to bless the nuptial bed. A servant returned with the startling news that he could not be found anywhere. It was of no consequence to Philip.

15

Isabel emerged from the neck of her nightshift, from amongst the gathered Holland and lace, and could with some effort hear the whisperings in the adjoining chamber.

'Take a look at these drawers. You could catch your death of cold wearing these.'

'I know, and another thing, what do you think about washing your feet in perfumed water?'

'I heard one of the Frenchies say that the perfume is supposed to have special powers. The feet are the most important part of the body – you know, like the root of everything.'

'Go on with you, that sounds like witchcraft. Like as not it will be just another of those ridiculous French ideas same as bathing in milk in that enormous bathing tub.'

'Or is it because they think our ways not good enough for them?'

'No, I just think theirs are very strange.'

Juana could hear them gossiping but assumed Isabel would find it difficult to understand their muffled words. She would deal with those women later. At the moment she was supervising the fastening of buttons, helping place a heavy robe over Isabel's shoulders, then watching as the hairbrush passed through tumbling dark locks. A variety of pots of creams were then dipped into, their perfumed contents smoothed over cheeks, chin and neck.

Isabel smiled at Juana's amazement, 'You must try some. They have brought me great comfort. When we crossed over the mountains the days and nights were so cold, the winds and snows so brutal, I would have looked all shrivelled like a piece of dried fruit without these.'

Juana shook her head, laughing at the young girl speaking of wrinkles, 'I doubt that. But it must have been terrifying. They say that this has been the worst winter for years with blizzard upon blizzard making the mountains virtually impassable. And you have come through all that, and survived. It is too frightening to even dare think about it. You are very brave, ma'am.'

'Or my advisers extremely stupid.' She handed a small jar to Juana inviting her to try some of the cream on her hands while she strained to hear the continued murmurings from the other room.

'And see all these dolls,' the voices continued, 'I never thought for one moment that girls of fourteen still played with dolls, not even French girls; only babies play with dolls!'

'All the same they are lovely. A lot of work has gone into making those tiny dresses. And just look at the necklaces, the brooches.'

'Take a peek under a skirt, you might find they have French drawers on too.'

'Amazing, but true.'

Giggles followed each fresh discovery.

Isabel thought that had those people not been so forward in their ways, she would have told them that her dolls' clothes were haute couture, the very best in French fashion, and an excellent way for her to design new dresses for herself. Instead she wanted rid of them and their unkind tongues.

'Juana, no one has mentioned Prince Carlos. I think it strange for him not to be here and no one explaining why.'

'A sudden fever; he suffers them from time to time.' And she privately thanked God for it. The risk of a dreadful scene had been conveniently dealt with. The timely illness had prevented a more than probable violent argument between Carlos and Philip; a now fairly regular occurrence. Today he would have come face to face with his once intended bride now his father's wife, and there was no telling what might have happened.

'I hope it is nothing serious.'

'He is on the mend already, and will be completely well by the time we reach Toledo.' She changed the subject, 'This cream, by the way, is wonderful.'

'Then you must keep it. I can soon have more made, and I can always rely on my mother to keep me well supplied. So, I must wait until Toledo to meet Carlos. It was interesting meeting Juan; there were so many tales about him circulating in the French court. How strange it must be to have a half-brother of whom you know so little.'

'It is quite easy these days to accept him as my brother.' Juana laughed, 'But you should have seen him a few years ago. One day I shall tell you the whole story but for now I shall only say that he was discovered living in a village and I can tell you he was no better than a village urchin. A good bath and some decent clothes set him on his way towards becoming a prince. Philip met him for the first time only a few months ago and took to him immediately. All credit must go to Juan's guardian and his wife for the years spent educating him, grooming him into the ways of gentlefolk.'

Isabel and Juana fell silent, each lost in their own thoughts about the two young men, one handsome and healthy, while the other ...

Their reveries were abruptly brought to a halt, the ladies in the other room were still finding much to criticise.

'What of that room full of, well, everything. Like an apothecary's it is. Maybe her highness and her ladies are afraid we might think they smell. Someone told me that French folk usually do smell.'

They had gone too far, Isabel didn't know whether to be indignant or cry. 'Those girls, Juana, they must be dismissed.'

Juana was embarrassed. 'Without question my lady, tomorrow without fail.' They would go, but unfortunately so too would many of Isabel's French servants. Philip was determined to rid Isabel of as much French influence as possible, and quickly. His queen was to be Spanish.

'That is good. I think it is because they are overexcited, that is all, but it simply will not do to show such little respect. I must ask you one more favour. I want us to call each other sister; it will make us seem closer, it will make me feel less ... feel more ...'

'Whatever you wish my lady; my sister. I would dearly love you to think us close enough to be like sisters, I am honoured.'

'And the bed, has it been blessed?' She had remembered just in time. It had to be blessed, it was vital to have the wedding bed blessed; her mother had insisted.

'Someone will be found I am sure. But it is not necessary for today. Do not be alarmed, Philip will explain. If you please, it is time for you to retire.'

Juana opened the door to the bedchamber. Ana and the lady of the bedchamber curtsied. Isabel studied Ana, the coquette with the black eye patch. Was this the Spanish equivalent of *La Poitiers*, her father's whore? Was this woman already, or would she become, her husband's mistress. Would this Ana cause her to suffer in the same way as *La Poitiers* had made her mother suffer? She couldn't, wouldn't allow it.

109

But what did Juana mean when she said it wasn't necessary to have the bridal bed blessed?

Isabel was helped into bed and the sheets arranged about her. Juana, Ana, and the lady of the bedchamber retired from the room, to wait at the door until Philip arrived.

Philip locked the door behind him.

She had been waiting: heart pounding, temples pulsing, throat constricting; terrified. Isabel was so unspeakably lonely for the first time since leaving her mother. Unlike other royal families, hers had stayed together. They lived in the same palace, brothers and sisters, growing up in the warmth and security of their mother's love. Now she was on her own to face the real reason for her presence in Spain. Philip, a stranger, was her husband and had the right to her bedchamber, her bed. He would come to lie beside her.

She heard the key click in the lock, heard him walk to the bed.

He was by her side, fully dressed and not partly disrobed as Alba had been for the proxy wedding. Why was Philip still dressed? Was it because he was still angry with her? Had he decided he didn't want her as his wife? The shame of it all! What would her mother say?

Philip sat on the bed, took her hands in his and spoke gently, smiling into her huge dark eyes. 'Look at me, Isabel. I promise not to be a beast. Believe me I will neither snarl nor bite.' He watched as those two dark pools filled with tears.

'I have offended you,' she sobbed, 'and now you will not come to my bed. I have shamed my mother. What will she think of me? The dishonour.'

Yes, she was a child, he realised, a naïve child. 'Not true, not true,' he stroked away the tears. 'I have come to explain why I am not sharing your bed.' He moved closer to take her in his arms in a tender embrace, surprising himself with this sudden wave of affection. The last time he had felt like this was years ago with another Isabel, his mistress, Isabel de Osorio.

'I cannot come to your bed because you are a child. Your ladies tell me that your menses have not yet begun.'

Isabel was astounded. Philip, yes, it was Philip and not a doctor, who was speaking to her about the unmentionable, about blood appearing from that part of her body where she peed, the sign that meant womanhood. How could he bring himself to … was he not embarrassed? She was; and worse, she could feel her cheeks burning at her inadequacy.

'My lord,' she stammered. 'Forgive me. I have done my best; I wash my feet every day in herbs and perfumed salts.'

He burst into laughter, hugging her, 'Let us hope they are effective then!' And, he fervently hoped, that it would be soon. This girl excited him. He was already lusting for her, drawn against his will to take her. 'Nevertheless, we must wait until that happy day when your first and magic bleeding appears.'

'Magic?'

'Almost. The doctors can tell so much from it. They can see how your temperament will be governed, how well you will nourish a child within you.'

He sounded exactly like a doctor, the same as all those who had attended her whenever she had been ill, and she had been ill so many times, sometimes seriously. They too had bewildered her with talk of parts of her body and their functions.

Raised voices from the other side of the door thankfully put an end to further discussion.

'But I must be in, I tell you!' It was a frustrated and angry man's shout. 'Who has the key? The bed must be blessed. What will his majesty say?'

Another man's voice replied, 'He'll say, "You are too late, priest".'

'There cannot be a consummation of a marriage without the blessing. It is a sin against God!'

Philip gave Isabel another big hug then hurried to the door, resting his cheek against one of the panels 'Father, if a blessing is to be made then you must perform it from where you stand. We are not to be disturbed.'

'Your majesty, I pray to God I did not arrive too late,' the priest's words found their way through the keyhole squeezing past the key.

Isabel pulled the sheet over her head to muffle her giggles.

Philip turned, 'Isabel?'

Her head reappeared, 'It is all so silly. I was picturing the priest calling to you through the lock, and then I imagined us going into the corridor to paddle in the holy water and returning to stand all wet-footed on my bed.'

Philip smiled at her foolishness, but in truth had been more than thankful for the priests interruption or the devil would have lead him to have carnal knowledge of a child, from which no amount of bed blessing would save him from damnation or from ruining the chances of any subsequent union and Isabel producing a normal child. He must leave immediately, he must find satisfaction elsewhere. Since Ana was not available he would go to Eufrasia, she was almost as good.

'I am pleased that your tears are now of laughter. I can leave knowing you are no longer sad. Goodnight, my queen.' He allowed his lips the briefest of touches to her forehead, taking care not to breathe in too much of her perfume or for certain his resolve would weaken.

'Goodnight, my lord.'

Isabel lay back amongst her pillows. Her husband had cuddled and kissed her, he had spoken so tenderly, he had laughed with her. It could not be denied; he did love her. They would be happy together. Tomorrow she would write her mother a long letter about her wonderful husband Philip.

16

Isabel strolled about her apartments for the last time. The nightmare of Toledo was finally over, all fifteen wretched months of it.

'I would like to think that I need never again set foot inside these palace walls,' she confided to her French ladies, the Duchesses Clermont and Montpensier.

The rooms they passed through were virtually bare, many of the tapestries and furnishings already removed to be installed in her new home, the palace in Madrid, leaving only a few items to lend an air of occupancy.

'Even when these rooms were filled with their chairs and tables,' Isabel continued, 'they were still inhospitable.'

'The long, bitterly cold winters were of no help,' suggested Clermont.

'It is futile for you to try to make excuses for this place. Everything has been a misery since the day we arrived.'

'Not so, my lady,' Montpensier insisted, 'certainly not the first day when your entry into the town was nothing short of triumphal: you on your white horse, your escort of hundreds in their brightly coloured liveries. I remember every glorious moment of it.'

'Then there was the reception at the castle, and the fireworks,' continued Clermont.

'Ah, yes, the three princes were waiting to receive me.'

In fairness that had indeed been a wonderful day; the first and the last as far as she was concerned. The young men had come to greet her at the entrance to the castle. They were all so different: Don Juan, fair haired, elegant, and strong; Don Alessandro Farnese, Philip's nephew, with his Italian complexion, dark hair and merry dark eyes, so robust and jovial; Prince Carlos, so much smaller than his companions, his skin pallid, his hair lank, and looking quite ill. Her heart had almost burst for him; this tragic boy, his face long and twisted, his body crooked with one side almost useless. He had stuttered and stammered his welcome. From then on the festivities of the day were of no importance; all she had wanted to do was hug this boy as if he were an ailing brother, wanted to weep at the unfairness of life. They spent quite some time together, talking of this and that, talking about nothing at all, really; just talking

The Duchess Clermont, finding that memories of that day had done nothing to lift Isabel's spirits, tried something else, 'And what of your secret outings with the Princess Juana?'

'Not the most daring of excursions, only along narrow cobbled streets and down to the river. But you are right; it was good to escape even if for only a little while.'

'And your growing friendship with the princess?'

This had been the one bright light to punctuate a long, dark, and bleak time of stifling protocol, suffocating multitudes of hangers-on in every room of the palace and in every conceivable part of the little town clinging to the hilltop. It was truly amazing that Juana had so quickly become as much a sister as anyone could be. And, oh, how she had needed that love and friendship; her husband could be so unkind at times, so cold, so cruel. This move to Madrid would change all that; she could feel it, instinctively.

'And we are still with you, my lady,' Montpensier ventured.

Isabel pouted. 'That had very little to do with me.' She was, nevertheless relieved that she had been able to retain some of her French ladies, half of them having been sent packing because of disputes between them and her Spanish ladies. But she would go no further in openly criticising Philip although she was finding it very difficult to adjust to his domineering ways, his dismissive attitude, his cutting words, his anger.

A huge crucifix on the wall reminded her of the auto-da-fé. She crossed herself promising that never again would she attend such a disgusting event. She hadn't wanted to go in the first place, having only recently recovered from an illness. Philip had insisted, perhaps doubting the depth or sincerity of her convictions – he had already replaced her French confessor with a Spanish one – so she had gone. The fanatical crowd baying for the death penalty, a seething mass of hate; the venom in the judges' speeches; it was all so terrifying. And when Philip had deemed it fitting that even men of the cloth should be sent to the stake, albeit on the flimsiest of evidence, and she had begged for compassion all she got was his anger at her lack of religious conviction.

She looked again at the figure of Christ wondering if and when He would rid Philip of the coldness in his heart. She would never forget that dreadful day when they had received the news of her brother's death. She had wept for him and her widowed sister-in-law, Mary queen of Scotland, but Philip had dismissed her emotions as utterly childish, insisting she stopped blubbering; reminding her that she did have three more brothers. And as for weeping for Mary? She could save her tears. Mary would return to Scotland and start meddling in the affairs of England. He then announced to all the courtiers gathered in the room that if his wife had even a modicum of intelligence she would realise that all her sympathies should be concentrated on him; after all he had made a lasting peace with Elizabeth which now could so easily be wrecked; but obviously this was too much for her simple brain to comprehend. Isabel had retired to her bedchamber with an appalling headache, distraught by her inconsolable loss, and reeling from hurt and embarrassment.

But she had remained loyal to her husband, not one word of that terrible scene had escaped her in any of her many letters to her mother, whose large and comforting bosom she often longed for.

'No,' she sighed, 'I shall not miss this place, nor one single day spent here.'

They wandered further down corridors once populated by strolling meditating priests, by the dozen, and into her bedchamber.

Isabel clapped her hands, 'And I will never have to sleep in here again.'

She pictured Philip on his many visits, standing by the side of the bed, full of reproach because she had not had her first menstruation, reminding her she was becoming too old to be still a child. He told her, repeatedly told her, that it was not a good sign and that the sooner she menstruated the sooner she would start to rid her body of sin, seeking redemption through the loss of the unclean blood. For months she had agonised, consumed with guilt; seeking advice, cures, from her mother, but her under linens remained obstinately unstained, not one sign of *the works* as the French called it.

Then there were those weeks when she had suffered pains in her side and chest; but at least those were thankfully long gone.

Duchess Clermont burst out laughing, 'The one thing I will always remember about this room is seeing you lying in bed with your face looking like a huge cream pie.'

'I would have laughed too, if you had allowed me a mirror.'

'Face masks of whipped egg whites, with layers of abundantly thick frothed up asses' cream mixed with orange blossom water and only tiny dark holes for your eyes and mouth. It was just as well few people saw you.'

'But it worked, my lady, as you said it would.' Montpensier shook her head still not believing, 'There is not one scar, not one mark, from the dreaded smallpox. I think even her majesty, your mother, had never dared hope for such a miracle.'

It was Isabel's turn to laugh, not laugh exactly, more a cascade of tinkling teenage giggles, 'You omitted the two little holes for my nostrils; and how good the cream tasted when I allowed my tongue to wander about my lips.

'We know; we licked our fingers clean; look, the smoothest hands in Toledo. But it is such a joy to hear your laughter. I am convinced that once in Madrid smiles and laughter will never be far from those pretty lips. Imagine the freedom just waiting for you in the enormous palace gardens and the parks beyond; imagine the newly completed wings and refurbished apartments and all in the Italian style.'

'Oh, yes; hurrah, hurrah, a thousand hurrahs.' Isabel pointed an accusing finger at the walls, 'I will not have to suffer you infernal wall tiles any longer; cool you might be, cold you most certainly are, and with what one would hardly call subtle designs.' She turned to her ladies and trying to imitate her mother's voice whenever she bitterly complained about something offensive, 'My dears, we simply could do absolutely nothing with them, all the wrong colours and all positively shouting at one!'

They held hands enjoying the fun of a special private moment,

It was time to go and Isabel led the way, 'Come, let us find *La Eboli*, or should I call her Ana, and the ancient Duquesa de Alba. They will be somewhere nearby, probably eavesdropping; but what do I care. Goodbye Toledo, Madrid here we come!'

17

Juana, Juan, and Alessandro were waiting for her. Early morning sunshine crept along the flagstones and the palace walls drawing a warm golden veil over their sleepy greyness.

Isabel lifted her skirts and ran to them calling, 'You are here already! Have I kept you waiting long?' She eyed them up and down, laughing her approval, 'Yes, I think we are quite perfect.'

And they were; all the stiff and courtly attire had been replaced by the simplest of clothes. Isabel and Juana were in serge skirts with black lace-up bodices over plain chemises. Scarves were tied about their heads and they had heavy shawls over their shoulders to protect them from any lingering chill in the air.

The two young men's clothing was just as rustic, Juan's thick woollen breeches and jerkin along with his wide-brimmed hat reminding Juana of when he was that little country child who had been brought to her to be dressed in a style more fitting to his birthright.

'Tell me gentlemen are we not the best looking farm folk in Madrid?'

Juan bowed, 'Ladies, you are certainly the most delightful that one could wish to meet. My Lady Isabel you look radiant.' It was impossible for him to hide his admiration, nor did he wish to. He was so proud of her; she had overcome illnesses, had withstood so many injustices over the last year.

'It is the Madrid air. You cannot even begin to understand how happy I feel to be freed from that suffocating Toledo. Dear Lord, how I hated the place; how I love Madrid!'

And this morning Isabel and her friends were going to escape into the country; to be country folk. They were free for hours to do whatever they wished because Philip would not be leaving his ever-present and ever-growing mountains of paperwork until midday.

Isabel glanced about her, 'No Carlos? He is not joining us after all? Have you heard anything? A message?'

'Nothing, but he often changes his mind without letting others know,' was all Alessandro could offer.

'Ah, well, perhaps another time.'

The three set off, followed at a discreet distance by one or two servants, across the terrace towards the gardens and out and away into the waiting dew drenched fields and meadows.

Montagne, who had been concealed in the shadows, not a difficult task for one so small, made his way back into the palace to offer his thanks to Magdalena Ruiz. A few months ago the two dwarves had made a formal declaration swearing to maintain a truce, to keep rigidly within their mutually agreed territories; they had sealed a bargain that whatever they did would always be mutually beneficial. It had cost him rather more than her, but so far it had been worth it.

'Yes,' he mused, 'my mistress Isabel may well feel that it was because of her pleading that Philip decided to leave Toledo and come to Madrid, but it matters not, just as long as she is here and she is happy.' She need never know how he had reported her desperate sadness to Magdalena. It was Magdalena's ensuing angry words with Philip – as only she was allowed – and her fierce warnings of dire consequences if he chose not to follow her advice; and this included the death of his beautiful young wife who at some time was to become the mother of his so desired heir. That had brought the king to his senses and a more than content queen to a happier home.

'Yes,' Montagne threw back his shoulders congratulating himself, 'Ours is a good partnership. A small cask of wine is in order I think.'

The countryside had been awake for some time and was busily occupied with sheep and shepherds, cows and cowherds, and bent over peasants husbanding crops.

Juan gathered small posies of dainty wild flowers to give his two ladies which they proudly tucked into their bodices.

'Isabel, over there, the man on the donkey, do you see what he is carrying? That, my lady is a huge empanada, a pastry filled with savouries.'

Isabel dared him, 'Go ask if he will sell it, then we can have breakfast on our way.'

He returned bearing a flat pie as big and as round as the brim of his hat. 'We have more than enough for us and your gallant little troop of trailing attendants.'

'Shall I like it, do you suppose?' Isabel couldn't bear the thought of feigning enjoyment over yet another example of Spanish cooking, but she strongly suspected she would have to.

Juana shook her head, 'I cannot understand why you do not find most of our dishes to your liking.'

Isabel merely smiled; there was no point to her reiterating her argument since they always fell on deaf ears. Flesh, fowl, and fish (when it was allowed on the menu) were always so heavily spiced they turned her stomach. Most dishes arrived at the table in the form of either stews or pies. Without fail desserts were pastries or biscuits. And as for vegetables, they were forbidden; she was not allowed to eat them! The reason, Philip insisted, was that only the poor or animals ate vegetables.

Juan tore away a piece of pie and offered it in his handkerchief. He waited. 'Your verdict?'

'Splendid! Delicious!' She dabbed at scarlet juices running down her chin. 'Fish, onions, peppers, tomatoes; I can taste them all! We must thank the man.'

'My money was thanks enough, more than any he might get in town. He can now go straight home to share his fortune with his wife. How glad I am to see how you are enjoying it.' Sharing in her joy made him happy beyond words.

'If only we could eat like this all the time.' She dabbed at the scarlet dribbles on her chin. 'What do you think, sister?'

'The fish is perhaps a little strong, I confess I am not used to ...' Juana turned to the servants to see if they agreed, and indeed they did, for they had thrown theirs away in disgust. Peasant food was for peasants.

'Now for some of God's perfect wine; I shall race you to the stream.' Isabel raised the wet hem of her skirts to run, and was shocked to see her fine leather boots looking so dew stained. 'Too late to worry about that,' she giggled. She threw herself down by the water's side to cup handfuls into her mouth, allowing it to run down her bodice and the sleeves of her chemise. Juana judged it wiser to lie on her front and suck at the crystal stream. She gulped and choked, water going everywhere except where it should; it made her eyelashes wet-heavy, it rushed up her nose, it found its way inside her bodice.

'I cannot believe I am doing this, I am a grown woman!' she spluttered.

They set off again, their wanderings taking them to a small stone building, a house perhaps, with an old woman nearby milking a cow.

'Shall we?' Juana was the one who asked, surprising herself once more with this newly discovered spirit of adventure.

'We must,' Isabel insisted, giggling.

The old lady stood aside shuffling the coins Juan had pressed into her hand. Isabel's efforts brought forth not a single drop, 'I concede defeat. Your turn.'

Juana, perilously perched on the rickety stool, her head against the animal's side, as though she had done this every day of her life, squeezed and pulled on two teats and had the pleasure of hearing milk hissing and squirting into the bucket. 'I win, I win; and I still cannot believe I am doing these things.'

They took turns at drinking the warm, bubbly, creamy milk, laughing at each other's white moustaches and beards not caring that some ran down their fronts.

Later on Juan paid a farmer to allow them to ride on his cart laden with sweet smelling hay. They sat at the back with their legs dangling and swinging in time with their singing; they threw themselves onto their backs amongst the welcoming soft and perfumed dried grasses.

There was a final halt at a cottage to buy cheese and honey. Unfortunately for Isabel there were no creamy cheeses like those of France only sour and strong Spanish ones. Then, merrily laden with their gifts they set off for home, this time riding mules that Alessandro had so cleverly organised for them.

The sun was already quite high in the sky when they got back to the palace. Philip was on the terrace, pacing. He was furious. Isabel and Juana jumped down and rushed to him like returning errant children to an angry father.

'Where have you been, and looking no better than village hirelings?'

'We have been having such fun,' Isabel answered, echoes of laughter from the morning's adventure still lingering in her voice. She was wise enough to look only at his left shoulder.

He stared at the grease and the tomato stains on her chemise, at the crumpled heads of buttercups, daisies, and clover lying limply in her bodice. He glowered at the stray pieces of hay, at the wet hem of her skirt, at the trail of wet footprints left on the flagstones. His eyes returned to her wet bodice.

Juana also came under his scrutiny. She cringed at her damp and muddied skirts that declared her guilty participation in the morning's events; and she a grown woman.

'You, Juana, are supposed to be my lady's mentor. You must have taken leave of your senses. I cannot believe you would betray my trust in you. If I am unable to place my faith in you then what am I to do? As for you, Juan and Alessandro, whatever possessed you? Are you not to be trusted either?'

A few months ago Isabel had begun to wonder if there was, in fact, anyone in this world whom her husband felt he could trust.

'My lord,' Juan offered, 'the ladies were safe at all times, and it was wonderful to see her majesty returned to health, able to enjoy ...'

'Be quiet!'

'My lord husband,' Isabel kept her voice light and cheerful, she would not have her morning spoiled, 'I think if you continue to be so cross, you will not be allowed any gifts.'

His tempers no longer made her afraid; it was true they were upsetting, but they came and went. She accepted his many moments of coldness, knowing that sooner or later they, too, would go away. Yes, she was learning to ride the storms of anger usually by seeking refuge from them, and from his iciness. She would tuck herself away in the warm world of her books, her dolls, or dancing practice. There were those who mocked her for doing so and on occasions she had to retreat even further into her private little world. Nevertheless she was surviving, and was finding her own ways to fill her free time with fun and laughter, and she was determined to keep it that way.

Philip was suddenly overcome with a passion to possess her, to ravish this peasant girl standing there in her wet skirts, her damp chemise clinging to those tiny breasts. He wanted to place his hand where the crumpled posy nestled. He prevented his thoughts carrying him further; better by far to enter into her childish game.

'Do, please, allow me my gifts.'

'You will love them; they are your favourites, manchego cheese and honey.'

'W-w-where the h-h-hell have you b-been and w-w-without m-me!' Prince Carlos limped along the terrace dragging his crippled leg, screeching his ill temper, his long and misshapen face livid with rage.

'Dearest Carlos,' Isabel ran to him, 'you know we made a bargain that if you wished to go with me you had to be on time. I am the disappointed one for being so badly let down. Did you not ask your servant to wake you?'

'I was awake, and would have come, but,' his high pitched screams changed to hysterical laughter; 'but, I had to attend to another matter first. I had to punish my shoemaker.'

Philip took a deep breath, what would he have to put to rights this time? 'What had he done or failed to do to warrant your punishment?'

'The b-boots he had m-made for this morning were too tight. So I made him eat them,' he laughed his strangled laugh. 'I had them cut into strips and then fried. You should have seen him. God but it was funny.'

Isabel took his hand to lead him some distance away from the others. 'Carlos, that was horribly wrong of you, and you know it. You owe the man an apology at the very least.'

'An apology? Princes never apologise to servants.'

'They must if they are in the wrong; and you have been most unkind. You must make amends.'

'If you say so.'

'Oh, but I do. I shall come with you if you wish.'

'Would you come? That will be perfect. You are what I call a really true friend. But I will still have to add his name to my list of the people I hate.'

Juan marvelled at Isabel's calming influence on two very difficult people; first Philip and now Carlos. There was no one quite like her in the whole world.

Philip looked from Isabel to Carlos. At one time he had even thought to have them marry, this sweet girl and this stupid, crazy son of his who was capable of any and all kinds of outrageous behaviour. He thanked God he had changed his mind. He must, however, continue his search for a suitable bride for Carlos for that was the way of things; one of his nieces perhaps, or even Juana? Carlos might not object too strongly to marrying his Aunt Juana, after all he had known her a long time, had been virtually raised by her, and he seemed to like her.

The day had become too tiresome, he turned on his heel. 'I am going for my lunch. I expect to see everyone this evening for dinner.'

18

The door slammed shut behind the tiny Magdalena Ruiz. That had not been intended and she apologised. 'Sorry about that; why do they put the door handles too high for the likes of me? Such inconsideration.' She tethered her two pet marmosets to a chair, straightened her skirts, folded and tied a handkerchief across one eye then turned to face Philip who had barely glanced up from his reading.

Moving in what she felt to be a provocative manner, hands seductively on swaying hips that measured almost the same as her height she crooned, 'Here I am, my love.'

Philip ignored her.

'Put your book down, dammit; hic.' She paused for him to comply with her order. 'Here I am, my love; Ana, *La Eboli*, the squinty-eyed one, come to accommodate you.'

Philip noticed the slur in her voice, perhaps supposed to be sensual, part of this act, but more than likely the result of some midday drinking, and her face had a decided flush.

He returned to his book, 'If you are referring to Doña Ana, the wife of Gómez, Doña Ana, one of the queen's ladies, let me remind you that her title is Princess of Eboli. May I also point out that she wears a patch to cover a blindness in that eye. Show some respect and for goodness' sake rid yourself of that foolish handkerchief.'

'Some folk have no sense of humour; hic.' She struggled with the knot in the handkerchief, 'But I still say I shall give respect when and where it is due. And another thing I say is, she is cross-eyed and that if the gentlemen saw it they would laugh and the ladies would have no fears; hic, never be jealous again.'

'You have been drinking.'

'Most observant. Only a little, the result of an understanding between Montagne and me. We dwarves have to stick together even if he is a damned Frenchie.'

'I am amazed that you would ever have an understanding with a Frenchman.'

'I had to put him in his place first. But what I was saying was we do one another favours from time to time. Recently I did him a favour and he thanked me with some wine.'

'Dear God; that is all you needed.'

'Hush. However I must inform him that having given it a fair sampling I find it somewhat bitter.'

'Perhaps he chose it for that very reason.' Philip's eyes had never left his book.

'He would not dare! Now, look at me; Montagne saw *La Eboli* crossing the patio coming in this direction so I came to warn you.'

The book was finally set aside. Ana was coming at last. She had made him wait long enough; too long.

'Ah! I have your attention at last, hic.' She wagged a crooked finger at him, 'That lady is dangerous, will lead to trouble, mark my words. That other lady you bed is a far safer bet.'

Ana was on her way; he was desperate for her body.

'Are you listening to me or not? Nothing to say?'

'Yes, I do have something to say; I say go away, you are annoying me.'

'Suit yourself; if my advice is not required I shall go and try a little more of that wine, perhaps I was mistaken earlier.' She retrieved her pet monkeys, petting them, 'It certainly wasn't as sour as our master here. Come along my little darlings, we are, apparently, not wanted.'

It wasn't long before the door opened again.

Two ladies entered and curtsied, 'Your majesty.'

For the second time Philip put down his book on architecture. It was a subject dear to his heart, a subject requiring his full concentration. It had been the very thing to keep his mind focussed while he waited for Ana until Magdalena's words had unsettled him sending his thoughts flying in every direction.

'Dear God in Heaven, Ana, but you certainly took your time getting here. Do you know how long I have been waiting?'

'I have no idea whatsoever, but I can assure you, if you were not already aware, my lord, that I am worth every minute of anticipation.' Ana de Mendoza threw him a seductive sideways smile, dropping her cloak into the arms of her faithful attendant. 'I came as soon as I could. We have rushed hither and thither since receiving your note; is that not so, Bernardina?'

Philip continued, 'A royal command requires an immediate response and finds delays unacceptable.'

'I shall ignore that; you are being unreasonable. We made our way here as quickly as possible, walking, since to arrive here in a litter would attract attention. And, let me hasten to add, the streets of Madrid are far from pleasant: they are dusty, dirty, and stinking of rubbish; it is almost impossible to thread one's way between goods spilling from shop windows and the wares of the street vendors spread across the ground; and then there is the crush and noise. It is also very hot and with very little shade to be found.'

'You are here; I suppose that is all that matters,' Philip pouted.

'Not the most friendly of welcomes; I have known better.'

The two ladies made their way, as was the custom by now, to Philip's dressing room. The buxom Bernardina shuffled along behind her mistress, struggling with a large bag and the abandoned cloak.

'I must tell you I was surprised to hear from you,' Ana called. 'It was my understanding that your fancies had flown to another nest.'

He chose not to answer. He had sent for Ana because, quite simply, she was the best when it came to satisfying his needs; and today he was consumed with frustrated desires. Since this morning on the terrace he had been obsessed with visions of Isabel standing naked, that young peasant girl stripped of those woollen skirts, the damp and clinging chemise. He could not rid himself of a picture of her waiting for him; her tiny firm breasts entreating him to touch, to kiss; the triangle of hair at the top of milky white thighs begging him to explore. It was absurd, it was ridiculous; moreover it was obscene. Isabel was his wife not his mistress, and she was still a child. But he was aroused and in his moment of desperate need he had sent for Ana.

Bernardina set about preparing her mistress; undressing her, washing her, dabbing perfume here and there in sufficient quantities to overcome any remaining body odours that may not be pleasant to Philip. She let down Ana's curls ensuring the strap for her black eye patch remained securely pinned in its place.

Ana used the time to make her accustomed inventory of the items on Philip's dressing table: a toothbrush and tooth powder, a stick to remove earwax, a tongue scraper, combs and cleaning brush, thimbles. There were mouth washes, perfumes, various medications and cups to drink them from.

'Goodness me, these are new,' she whispered, holding up one of the medications to show Bernardina. 'He must be suffering twinges of gout; that is probably why these are here too.' She leafed through two or three medical books presumably borrowed from his doctors.

'Do you think we will meet the required standard today, Bernardina?' Ana put her wrists to her nose and inhaled the delicious perfume Bernardina had sprinkled there.

'We'll do our best, madam. It's disappointing, all the same. Personally I like the idea of unrestrained passion, spontaneity, spur of the moment stuff, not all this preparation. Kills it all dead, it does.'

'You, Bernardina? Since when did you ... ?'

'Me and my husband? But, no, I'll say no more. There you are. You're ready, off you go,' she helped Ana slip into a silk gown.

Ana returned to Philip's bedchamber where she found him waiting, wearing only a loose robe. He pulled her close his hands racing to search beneath the silk of her gown for the silk of her skin. As he found her shoulders then her breasts she eased herself free of her gown and stood before him proud, delighting in her own nakedness.

'You wanton hussy,' Philip kissed her breasts.

'I know, and how we love every moment of my wantonness.' She took his hands, guiding them down over her belly, while pushing him ever so gently towards the bed.

'Dear God, my Ana, my *tuerta*, my one-eyed one, I had almost forgotten.'

'Sh, sh.'

He was drowning in seas of ecstasy, Ana's fingernails digging into his back, his buttocks, urging him on until he cried out his exquisite surrender.

Ana's voice floated from the dressing room across his bedchamber and into his bed ruining his peace and tranquillity. 'It will be most interesting to see if my next child looks like my husband, or like you, my lord. I swear my son Rodrigo is the very image of you. As each day passes he grows more like you. Oh, but he is a sweet reminder of that first time I came to you.

126

Gómez never says anything; but with beautiful blue eyes, and blond curls, Rodrigo is obviously not his.'

If, as she said, it was so obvious then everyone would be gossiping. Normally that would have been of no consequence, gossip kept courtiers happy, and the existence of another bastard of the king would be of no surprise. But perhaps Ana was hinting at a veiled threat of disclosure if he did not grant Gómez … What was it she wanted for Gómez? Or was this all fantasy and she was lying? Had Gómez questioned her about Rodrigo? What had she replied? Was Gómez content with her answer, and if so, why? Magdalena's earlier warning niggled.

Gómez was at his side virtually every day, his constant companion. Best to move him to a new situation, somewhere where he didn't have to be face to face with him on a daily basis. Philip was beginning to regret Ana's visit this afternoon, forgetting the urgency of his need and the far from expected delights of the remedy. His passions now catered for he must set himself to think about dealing with a potential problem, and God knows how he hated dealing with problems.

Also, there were the stories of her parties to be considered; the balls, the soirees. If they were true then she was no better than a procuress lending her home to help young men and ladies to further their relationships. This behaviour, while regularly occurring in drama or poetry or even in Brussels where he had taken advantage of such assistance from that type of hostess, could not be tolerated here under his nose and certainly not with Ana playing the role of a Celestine. Obviously he needed to distance himself from both Ana and Gómez.

'You are entertaining this evening?' He would steer the conversation away from any further mention of the child Rodrigo. He leaned casually against the door to the dressing room while he considered several options for her and her husband's futures.

'Yes, you ought to come. Tonight it is a masked ball and there will be many a young lady there eager to discover which of the young gentlemen is your half-brother. Speaking of Juan, I have the feeling that he is disappointed with the title of your excellency and not your royal highness. Could I be right?'

Philip caught himself just in time before giving way to his anger at Ana's meddling, before divulging any personal feelings regarding Juan and his aspirations to be a crown prince. 'He has no business discussing private family affairs with you, and he is far too young to be attending your evenings. I can see him being too easily influenced by you and your friends.'

'Ah! I see it all now; that is why you refused him permission to stay with us when his home was badly damaged by fire. You consider me a bad influence.'

'I might not go as far as that.' He was being cautious, choosing his words with care; Magdalena's warning might be justified. 'Hopefully, however, it will not be too long before he leaves Madrid.'

Philip was of the opinion that Juan was getting ideas above his station. It was something to worry about. The young upstart could well have his sights on the throne; and with only the pathetic Carlos standing in his way who could say what might happen? He wondered why his father had not foreseen the problems when he publicly recognised his bastard son Juan. When was Isabel going to become a woman? He needed more heirs, desperately.

'Yes,' he continued, 'I am sending him to university.' And after that he hoped to be able to offer him a bishopric somewhere.

'Queen Isabel will miss him sorely. He is such a wonderful companion for her. The change in her is quite remarkable.'

'I think she spends too much time with him and in pastimes unbefitting a Spanish queen.'

Ana turned her head quickly, ruining Bernardina's efforts to fasten her ruff. She laughed, 'You are jealous.'

'Guard your stupid tongue.' Who did she think she was to dare to use that word. But she had, and the word, indelible, would remain imprinted on his memory forever, and he would neither forgive nor forget that she had said it.

'It was a joke, nothing more. You are too sensitive today. You must admit that the boy has done wonders for her, and he has been good for Princess Juana. She was spending too much time in church or on her knees to her confessor. Juan has made her look and act more her true age and not like a dried up widow, old before her time. Good Lord, she is only in her twenties.'

This woman Ana brought more aggravation than she was worth. This had to be the last time, she was too outspoken and that could be dangerous. He watched as Bernardina pinned up the final curls, helped her mistress with her pendant earrings. He studied Ana, that velvet eye patch hiding some disfigurement, either accident or defect. Or was it a conceit, an affectation? That wouldn't be surprising. The problem with this woman was she was unfortunately too damned sure of herself, too wealthy, too well connected, and too beautiful.

Gómez would definitely have to go, while she as from today would never be allowed into this end of the palace. There would be no further opportunities for meddling. Neither of them would be party to any information unless he deemed it absolutely necessary. It was true, it never paid to trust people, or let them get too close. His father had been right about that.

Ana was dressed, Bernardina's bag was packed, a diamond brooch was presented for services rendered, Philip bowed and the ladies curtsied and left.

As he waited for servants to arrive with hot water and towels, he pulled his robe about him and wondered if, as Magdalena had suggested, Eufrasia was after all a much better choice of mistress. All he needed was a jolly good romp in bed followed by one or two farewell kisses, the offering of a gift, and with conversation kept to a minimum.

19

A few weeks later Philip, on the spur of the moment, decided to have what he regarded as a celebratory family dinner. He was in buoyant mood, sitting at the head of the long oak table with Isabel and Juana on either side; Carlos, with Juan and Alessandro sat opposite.

This evening Philip was in a magnanimous frame of mind so Isabel and Juana, contrary to his rigid rules of etiquette, were allowed to laugh and giggle as they recounted their day's adventures. Anything, absolutely anything was admissible today.

It was more than a week since he'd been informed of the miraculous event. It hadn't been long before the news had travelled the length of the palace percolating down to the lowliest of servants. The few French ladies who had been allowed to remain had delightedly sent letters to France telling Isabel's mother that her beloved daughter finally had *the works*. Isabel, at last, at the age of fifteen years and three months had started her menses. She was now a woman. She was at last about to play her part in the destiny of the Hapsburgs.

Tonight he would go to her bedchamber. Tonight.

'S-s-side s-s-saddle?' Carlos stuttered and stammered, his mouth stuffed to overflowing with venison pie. 'My darling aunt sitting side saddle?'

'Yes, Carlos, me, your aunt, riding side saddle; and it is much more ladylike than straddling a horse I would have you know.'

Isabel spluttered, her table napkin to her lips, 'Unless you fall off.'

'Unless you fall off,' Juana echoed, laughing.

'And did you?' the young men wanted to know.

'The way I recall it, it was more a question of losing my balance.'

Tonight Philip would go to his wife's bedchamber. The doctors were pleased with Isabel's menstruation. It was of a reasonable quantity, quality, and duration. These augured a good pregnancy. Tonight he would go to her bed.

'I had finally got that mastered when Isabel thought I should try shooting with a bow and arrow.'

'Perhaps from now on we should call you Diana the Huntress,' Juan teased with the others only too eager to develop the theme of Juana turned hunter goddess. Laughter and quips were exchanged from both sides of the table.

Tonight Philip would go to Isabel's bed. The frequent nosebleeds she'd suffered over the last two years or so were a good sign too. They had been from the left nostril, so that while they had delayed her menses, they did indicate that she would have a son.

Tonight after two years of waiting he would go to her bed. He would send word to her lady of the bedchamber informing her that tonight he would be coming to Isabel's bed.

'But every time I let the arrow fly, I took off with it as if attached, leaving the saddle and horse as if pulled away from them by an invisible cord. So then I had to be helped to mount again.'

Philip leaned towards Isabel taking her hand, 'You must tell me when Juana is ready to give a demonstration of these new talents. I promise to be a most supportive observer. The young men, however, will have to forego the excitement for some time.'

He smiled at the three young men, 'Do not look so shocked. I offer you something which will appeal much more. You are going to live in Alcalá. You are to go to university. I am reasonably sure that as well as your studies you will find plenty there to entertain you. Of course you will be under the watchful eye of Juan's guardian, Quijada.'

'Hurrah, did you hear that, Juan? Alessandro, you will soon see that there is no one better than good old Quijada. And will Gómez be going? I hope not, that would really spoil everything.' Carlos prayed his father would say no; Gómez was high on his list of people he hated.

'No, his duties will keep him here in Madrid.'

'This gets better and better. I believe I am going to thank you, yes I am; you have done one thing right for a change.' He tugged at Juan's sleeve and leaning close whispered, 'Do you suppose your aunt, the saintly wife of Quijada will be joining us? God, I hope not, she really is far too stern, would ruin any ideas of fun.'

It was Philip who answered, 'Her presence would do you no harm whatsoever.'

Carlos slammed down his knife, 'You were not supposed to be listening to my private conversation.'

Philip would not be drawn into an argument, would not allow his mood to be broken.

Isabel steered the group away from disaster turning in mock horror to Juana, 'And what of us? It seems we ladies are to be abandoned. That means no more outings except in the gardens or the parks.'

'My lady, I am sure you will find other ways to occupy yourselves.' Philip feigned sympathy; it truly was time she set aside her frivolous antics. This was Spain, not France, she was a Hapsburg, no longer a Valois, and she was now fifteen years old. After tonight it might not be too long before she found it impossible to sport and play. He rose from the table. 'I shall join you in a little while, for a game of cards perhaps. I have a small matter to attend to first.'

It was time to send the message. Tonight he was going to her bed.

Philip rejoined them in a small salon furnished with chairs and tables for games of cards and dice.

'Did you decide against cards?'

'No, my lord, but it was the shortest of games,' Isabel's beautiful dark eyes apologised, 'because Carlos ran out of money so quickly, and no one would lend him any more. I told him that I would not allow him to go to university until he had repaid me every *reale* and every gold button that he already owes me.'

'So instead of cards what have we here?'

'Miniatures of princesses; we want to know whom Carlos will choose to marry when he has completed his years of study,' Juana explained, taking the prince's hand wondering how he could possibly cope with university education, the poor lamb could barely read or write. 'I have told him not to consider me; I refuse to compete with these astonishingly young and beautiful maidens.'

'I want him to choose my sister because French princesses are the best.' Isabel knew they were playing a game and nothing more. She knew of the discussions Juana had had with Philip; she knew that it was Philip's intention to have Carlos and Juana marry; and who could tell, it may be the only realistic marriage prospect for Carlos. It was all so very sad. But back to the game, 'You must admit that my sister is very pretty.'

132

'A-A-And so is Queen Mary of Scotland, b-but I have decided which one, and will not be swayed. I want Anne. I want Cousin Anne from Austria.'

Philip wondered how his sister Maria, the empress, and his niece Anne would respond to that idea. They might not be the happiest of souls to receive the news that Prince Carlos wished for the marriage, on the other hand they might be eager enough for a union with the heir to the Spanish throne. If Carlos were to marry Anne it would certainly strengthen the bonds between the Austrian and Spanish Hapsburgs and would provide him with guaranteed support against the restless Protestants in the Low Countries. On the other hand his sister Juana might yet be the best proposition.

Alessandro laughed, clapping Juan on the back, 'Juan, you are jealous! You want to be her husband.'

'You too!' Juan countered.

'They are both jealous,' Carlos joined in the laughter. 'But I will have her, she is mine.'

Philip had already decided that Alessandro would definitely not marry a Hapsburg, he was considering a match for him with a Portuguese princess of the Braganza family. He suspected that Juan was already entertaining the idea of having an Austrian Hapsburg wife because it would strengthen his challenge for the Spanish throne. But all this would be of no consequence if Isabel gave him an heir.

'So that is all settled.' Carlos pushed the miniatures aside, 'I want to tell you about last night. I was walking down a street and somebody emptied a pisspot over my head. I ran into the house to kill whoever it was and guess what, I came face to face with a priest. What was I to do?'

Philip decided that no one need hear more. 'Not for the ladies' ears, thank you. Juana I would be pleased if you were to withdraw with Isabel. Isabel I shall come to see you in a little while.'

In the choking silence of the room it would be impossible to say whose heart was pounding the hardest. So, the time had come; Isabel was finally to discover the husband's rights of the nuptial bed, was to discover the urgency of a king to sire an heir.

133

20

Juana carried the goblet with the same care and devotion as a priest would a chalice. She brought it into the retiring room and offered it to Isabel sitting in her huge tub full of warm aromatic water.

'Isabel, take a sip it will be good for you.'

Dark, plaintive eyes looked up at her, 'Is it some kind of medicine?' She earnestly willed it to be something of that nature, it might help. Why did she feel this way? There had been no such fears on her wedding night, some apprehension about the unknown, perhaps, but nothing like this.

'The best in the world, believe me,' Juana watched Isabel's shaking hands as the goblet was raised to quivering lips. 'There is nothing like mulled wine for calming the spirit.'

'Will you have some yourself? I would find it more comforting if you were to join me.'

Juana smiled her sympathy for her dear, and oh so young, Isabel about to face her first ordeal of the bridal bed. 'Why not? I shall pour myself just a little.'

When she returned she found Isabel standing, swathed in towels held tight against her throat by white knuckles, the goblet of wine set aside. Throughout the process of drying, perfuming and dressing of Isabel, hindered at each step by everyone's nervous, fluttering fingers, the nightshift of the finest lawn and French lace quivering and twisting and not keeping still, Juana continued to urge her to take further sips. Finally Isabel was helped into a gown of dark blue velvet, its volume hiding her trembling. Only her dark curls tumbling over her shoulders seemed free of care.

Isabel dismissed everyone except Juana; she only wanted her sister at her side, no one else. Together they made their way to her bedchamber and to the welcoming fire; although it was summer she felt it would comfort.

She took another tentative sip of wine then set it down, 'I think I have had enough, we drank several glasses at dinner.'

'A little extra will do you no harm. You look lovely, Isabel. My brother is a most fortunate husband.'

'Juana, I am terrified. What is going to happen? What must I do?'

'There is nothing to be afraid of. Do have some more wine. Careful or you will spill it,' she helped guide the wine cup to and from Isabel's lips. Those encouraging words just uttered of there being nothing to be afraid of burned ever deeper into her heart; admonishing her for the lie she told.

'What must I do, Juana?'

'You simply lie on your back, as you do whenever you go to bed. Then when Philip comes to you, you open your legs wide. Imagine yourself as the fertile soil and Philip as the gardener who will come to plant his seed in you.'

Despite all her fears she laughed, 'I've never considered myself to be a plot of ground. But what is it like? Tell me.'

Juana could not reveal how awful it had been for her. It had been a cold, callous molestation; so much for the soil and seeds! How different from the love she now shared with her confessor Brother Francisco; it was like comparing war with a mystical experience. The palm of Francisco's hand cupping her chin, drawing her face to his was unbearably wonderful.

'It is a wife's duty, dear sister, something to be neither liked nor disliked, and it will not take long. You will see how it is over in no time at all.' Of course were Isabel that other Isabel, Isabel de Osorio, Philip's mistress and not his wife, the queen, then it would be entirely different. It would be pleasurable, with both parties seeking to give satisfaction. But that was the difference between wives and mistresses. 'Do finish your drink then we can have a little more.' Juana waited until the cup was drained then refilled it from the jug standing on the hearth, its silver belly reflecting the dancing firelight's reds and golds.

'I shall be intoxicated.'

Juana thought that that wouldn't be such a bad idea, after all. She shook her head at the grim reality of the situation. Under normal circumstances a wife was always encouraged to drink plenty of wine in preparation for this event; but in this instance the wife was a delicate child and the husband a lusty, robust lover in his early thirties.

'His majesty is on his way, ma'am.'

The lady of the bedchamber's announcement was like a summons to the scaffold. Isabel was led to her bed, the gown and slippers were removed, the bed covers arranged and straightened over her.

Juana's kiss to her forehead almost unnerved Isabel completely. It was one of her mother's tender "be brave" kisses after she'd fallen and hurt herself.

Philip came to her bed; she made a huge effort to smile her welcome. She parted her legs. She would be the garden, and she waited for her gardener. Philip raised her nightshift and began to touch her, right there, in her most private of places. Juana had not mentioned this unknown and delicious pleasure. A warm and tingling sensation began to spread.

But then Philip moved onto her, and ... She cried out. That moment of pleasure was gone an agonising pain now replaced it. She shouted, struggled, pummelling him with her fists, wanting him gone.

It was over. 'You hurt me, you hurt me,' was all she could sob.

'Only because it was your first time.'

She didn't want there to be a second time, ever. She prayed silently. 'Dear God, tell Philip to go away. I want to be on my own, to comfort myself. I want my mother here to cuddle me. I want Philip out of my bed.'

But Philip didn't go. He lay at her side doing nothing, saying nothing, while she lay quietly sobbing. Then he attacked her again, with redoubled force. He gave no quarter, he was brutal, he was deaf to her cries, her pleading, and he ignored her attempts to push him away. His behaviour was unforgivable; he even shouted out his pleasure.

After an eternity and his third assault he was, at last, gone. They had exchanged formal kisses. Hers was one of gratitude that he was finally going and the whole painful business over and done with. His was one of self-congratulation and satisfaction; not only was this was going to be easy, it was going to be downright enjoyable!

Isabel curled into a tight little ball, nursing her wounded body, crying. Her mother, who had ideas and cures for everything must surely be able to help. She would write to her in the morning, giving her the details of what her husband had done to her, asking for something much, much stronger than mulled wine

She whimpered, 'Will someone prepare me a bath?' The water's warmth might help sooth the pain, but it could not wash away the image of the wild animal that had just left her bed.

21

Don Quijada, Juan's guardian, was consumed with guilt. For the first time in sixty-five years his shoulders stooped in shame.

'Your majesty I have let you down. I made a dreadful decision; never thinking.'

They were in the archbishop's study. Yesterday, within hours of receiving the news, King Philip had ridden the twenty or so miles from Madrid to the university town of Alcalá de Henares. He sat in the great carved throne-like chair with Quijada facing him from the far side of the desk.

'Quijada I insist you are entirely blameless. There is no doubting that your actions were for the best.'

Philip studied Quijada; he was the most trustworthy and faithful servant one could wish for. For decades his service to the emperor had been exemplary, right up to the moment of his death. Since coming into the prince's household he had continued with the selfsame unfailing dedication to duty; in fact Quijada was now Knight Commander of the military order of Calatrava, a position of high honour as well as of great financial benefit, in recognition of so many years of faultless duty.

'Nonetheless if I had not locked the door Prince Carlos would never have gone down the servants' staircase.'

'I repeat, under the circumstances you did the right thing, acting as any responsible guardian would. Think no more of it. Remind me instead of what you know.'

'With regard to the accident I have little to tell, the young men can give you the details. I heard screaming followed by Don Juan's voice calling for me. I was there in next to no time and found the prince lying in a pool of blood with Don Juan and Don Alessandro on their knees at his side. I shooed away the gawping servants. The doctor arrived and staunched the bleeding; then the prince was carried to his bedchamber. Other doctors were called in, the trepan used to cut out a circle in the skull, the blood clot released and the wound covered with wax.'

Philip got up, rubbing at his temples, eyes shut tight, deep in thought. 'You have Don Juan and Don Alessandro outside? Good, then bring them in.'

The two friends entered somewhat shamefaced, made three deep bows before going down on bended knee.

'You may stand. Who is to begin the account?'

'My lord,' Alessandro blurted out, 'it was my fault. If only I had minded my own business and not gone to spy on my Cousin Carlos, but I did. I followed their voices and I found them together.

'I am much more to blame than Alessandro,' Juan insisted. 'Sire, when Alessandro came back upstairs to our apartments to tell me what he had witnessed I was only too eager to see for myself and I went down to the patio.'

'To spy?' Philip asked.

'Yes, and I am not proud of my actions.'

'To watch unobserved is not necessarily wrong,' it was something he himself favoured for many reasons. 'And what did you discover? Was your spying worthwhile?'

'No, I discovered nothing; they were simply chatting and laughing.'

'But the point is sire they had been meeting for days, weeks, and we had no idea what their relationship was and how many might know of it.'

'And I thought it best to tell my guardian, Quijada. He said it was probably nothing but that in any case he would put a stop to it. Then two days ago Prince Carlos threw down some playing cards and dice on the table and left, laughing, telling us to enjoy ourselves, that he would be away for an hour or more.'

Alessandro took up the tale, 'Juan and I winked and smiled at each other knowing he would be back in no time at all because Quijada had locked the patio door.'

There was a painful pause as they both remembered.

Juan swallowed hard, 'At first we sniggered when we heard him shouting his anger, heard him raging as he came back up the stairs. We waited for him to burst into the room.' His voice broke for a moment and he had to clear his throat before continuing, 'But instead of coming in he went straight past, along the corridor and through the door to the servants' staircase. Neither of us dreamed for a moment that he knew of its existence.'

'That was when we heard the scream. Juan and I ran as fast as we could, and we found him at the foot of the stairs with a pool of blood about his head. Dear God, it was awful. We sent servants to get a doctor, to let Quijada know. We rested the prince's head on our chemises; put our jerkins over him ...'

Juan finished their story, 'When Quijada arrived we told him what had happened. Sire, we beg you to forgive us for our stupidity in not being more honest with Prince Carlos. If we had not sought to deceive, to play such a childish trick, this would never have happened. We are praying fervently for his full recovery.'

Philip looked from his half-brother Juan to his nephew Alessandro; two handsome, virile, and strong young men, successful students at their studies, in music, and sport; then he pictured his son, lying at death's door, his son who was undersized, a hump in his spine, his left leg longer than the right, in fact the whole of his right side barely functioning, a pallid face and dark, lank hair (what was left of it since the surgeon shaved his head) barely able to speak in full sentences with that squeaky, stammering voice, useless at everything, useless in every way. That Carlos was the one to be heir to the throne was hard to bear, and while he too would pray for his delivery from death he would pray more earnestly that Isabel would provide him with a son worthy of the name.

'You may go. Continue your prayers; and you have my permission to visit the prince whenever you wish.'

'What a mess, Quijada.' Philip moved towards the window. He loathed being confronted by even one problem demanding immediate attention, and at this moment he was forced into facing more than one.

'If only I had not had that door locked,' Quijada could not come to terms with his error of judgement.

'That is of no importance. Where do we go from here? I have to assume that the prince will live; he has the best of doctors, the prayers of the entire country, and the skeleton of San Diego placed at his side. So, the prince will recover. How do I get him to marry my sister? He flew into such a rage the last time I mentioned it; yet she is the only one to offer him any salvation.'

'Perhaps if the princess were to speak to him directly; or perhaps Queen Isabel?'

But Philip wasn't prepared to allow any woman involve herself in marriage negotiations: not his sister, not Isabel's mother, and most certainly not Isabel; already each one had dared to offer him their opinions.

'Let us deal with this other matter. Bring in the porter and his family.'

Quijada led them in, the porter in his brown porter's uniform of some coarsely woven wool, the women in equally coarse grey woollen dresses. And they all stank. Philip retreated to the desk to retrieve his well-perfumed handkerchief. Manly smells of stale sweat he could almost stomach, he had, after all, been a soldier for a short time and had had some experience, but women's bodily odours were quite simply too disgusting.

The porter fell to his knees, his cap gripped in trembling hands. His wife and daughter curtsied and also fell to their knees to stare at the floor, the wife bewildered by the recent events, the daughter terrified.

'I need to ask your daughter some questions and I expect truthful answers.'

'Your majesty,' the porter addressed the tiles in front of his knees, 'I swear to God my daughter Mariana is an honest girl, through and through.' It was a fact but he couldn't be sure if the king would believe him, and so much would depend on that.

'Look up, girl,' Philip commanded.

Mariana raised her head slightly seeing nothing more than the desk top with its papers and ink stand, Philip's hands, and a huge handkerchief.

Philip guessed her to be about seventeen, the same age as Prince Carlos, with not a bad figure and a pleasant enough face, somewhat on the common side; but then she was a servant; and she reeked. It amazed him that even Carlos could bear to be anywhere near anything so nauseating.

'Recently you have been in the habit of meeting His Royal Highness, Prince Carlos.' His voice was an ice-cold reprimand.

Mariana looked at her father who urged, 'Speak girl.'

'Your majesty, we've met a few times. Prince Carlos used to come to the patio most evenings.'

'And what did you do?'

'Sire, we talked and laughed and sometimes played games.' Suddenly those carefree times were being spoiled, laden with guilt.

Philip wondered what, in God's name, did she mean by that? Was she speaking of the games of innocent children, or was it rather that these two simpletons were involved in something ... ?

'Tell me about these games.'

'We were doing no harm.' Mariana didn't like the way the king was managing to make her feel she had done something wrong, that he was probably not going to believe anything she said, or even twist her words. She turned to speak to her father, 'One time he picked a couple of those flowers with long stems, irises I think. He was trying to teach me how to sword fight, he said, so that at least he could say he had beaten somebody.'

'And what else?' It was yet another cold question.

'Usually nothing much really, except there was that one time when he rode in on a strange animal. What was it, father?'

'An elephant.'

'That's right, an elephant. There he was sat on this elephant, almost sitting on its head with its two great big ears. It was so funny, this lumbering beast and the prince riding it like it was a post horse, pretending it was going so fast.'

This was all so trivial and of no interest to Philip. 'Did Prince Carlos ever kiss you or touch you?'

Mariana gasped looking first to her father, then to her mother. 'I swear to you there was never anything like that. We only met because he knew what time I would be returning across the patio; just chance really. He said it was nice to have a chat about nothing in particular. I think he was lonely.'

The porter took his daughter's hand, 'Your majesty, our Mariana is a good girl, an honest girl. I beg you to believe her.'

Philip had tired of the question and answer game. 'Well, whatever she did or did not do is no longer of any consequence as she is to enter a convent immediately.'

A cry of anguish from Mariana filled the room, 'You cannot lock me away. I won't go. I've done no harm. Father, please beg his majesty not to do this to me.'

'If your father wishes to remain here as porter, he will say nothing at all either now or in the future. You are to enter the convent of San Juan de la Penitencia. Your father will tell anyone making enquiries that you have been fortunate enough to be offered a position with a wealthy family in Seville. A settlement of one thousand *ducados* will pay for a small private cell for the rest of your life.' Philip had to restrict her socialising even with nuns.

The porter was overcome with relief, amazed at the king's benevolence; not only was his job safe and he was not to be punished, but there was no longer any need to find money for a dowry since his daughter was not going to marry, and because of this astonishing sum she was to live a life of idle luxury in the local convent.

'Your majesty, we cannot thank you enough for your generosity. Thank his majesty, Mariana,' the porter nudged his daughter.

Instead Mariana gave Philip a defiant glare. The penalty for this might be death but she didn't care, she would rather die than be imprisoned. Yes, she hated him because he was condemning her for having done no wrong whatsoever. She was innocent and could do nothing about it. She was to be isolated from the world, forced into wearing a nun's habit, cloistered amongst all those dried-up women for the rest of her life. This man was the cruelest person she had ever met.

Philip had given her the merest of glances waiting to hear her repeat her father's gratitude, but as he looked away he could feel her searing accusing eyes.

'Thank his majesty,' her father hissed, this could still go wrong and he might yet be punished. His fingers stabbed at Mariana's back.

'Thank you.'

'You say your majesty; thank you your majesty. That is what you say,' the porter grabbed at her elbow.

'Mariana winced, 'Your majesty.' She turned to her mother, her last hope, 'Mother can't you say something to stop all this?'

'No, she can't,' her father fumed, 'and that's an end to it. We'd best leave his majesty before he changes his mind and we all get punished for your waywardness.'

The family left the room: the father highly delighted with the outcome; the wife, a mute witness throughout, incredulous; the daughter in despair.

Philip watched them slowly backing towards the door, Mariana still daring to glower. He threw her his final words, 'I will allow you a few moments to assemble any personal items you may wish to take with you.'

22

It was a beautiful summer's evening. The seemingly unrelenting heat of the day had at last given way to a welcome zephyr from the hills beyond Madrid. It drifted into the town, into the palace courtyard and in through the open windows of the upper gallery.

Philip, Isabel and Juana were standing by one of them enjoying the comforting coolness and looking down at the guests as they arrived for the banquet and following ball.

Isabel had chosen light blue satin brocade studded with sapphires and silver trimmed lace ruffs at her throat and wrists. Juana continued to wear her widow's black but dark green sleeves were revealed beneath the slit hanging sleeves. Philip felt suitably elegant in his maroon doublet and padded hose, with the golden chain and insignia of the Golden Fleece lying perfectly over his shoulders having no other decoration to contend with save cream coloured ruffs.

'I think you two ladies are enjoying this secret preview.' Philip flicked and brushed at his velvet sleeves. He was not comfortable to have his wife and sister join him in an activity he preferred to keep either private or shared only with gentlemen, but there had been no alternative; his apartments, although the best in the palace did not offer a similar vantage point.

'It is as well we have something to enjoy,' Isabel retorted, 'for there is very little else these days, except watch as I grow fatter by the day.'

Outdoor pleasures had been drastically reduced to walking in the garden since the young men had left for university and, once Philip had learned of Isabel's pregnancy, curtailed even further to nothing but a gentle amble along the terrace. Isabel felt little better than a prisoner.

'I know what is best.' Philip patted the hand of his wife, his far too plump wife only four months pregnant. Yet he was inclined to forgive Isabel her size as the doctors had given him such a positive prediction. The child she carried would most definitely be a boy. This had been determined using several criteria: it had been conceived in the spring months - more or less; he, the father was old –not exactly old but decidedly older than his wife; Isabel was young – seventeen was young; and she had continued to have those all-important nose bleeds.

Isabel scowled at him, cross and disgruntled about everything. He had refused to allow her to follow the regimen her mother had suggested: a radical change in her diet, which she insisted should include fruit and the notoriously banned vegetables; and lots of daily physical exercise. Her mother had borne and successfully raised ten children so her counsel must be sound. Isabel hoped and prayed that the second piece of information she had sought which addressed the continued problem of painful sexual intercourse, might also prove sound. Her mother had written assuring her that following childbirth all discomfort would cease. Her first suggestion, that Isabel's insides would become more and more accommodating with each subsequent visit of Philip to her bed, had proved not to be the case, every minute being almost beyond endurance.

Approaching laughter broke the uneasy silence. Juan and Alessandro appeared at the head of the stairs where they waited for the third person to catch up; Prince Carlos. They bowed before approaching the king, Carlos falling behind once more dragging his lame leg which since his accident was more useless than ever.

'But this is so exciting, to have you among us again.' Isabel clapped her hands, the frown on her brow and about her eyes rapidly disappearing, a happy smile lighting up her face.

After the kissing of hands Isabel reached out to Carlos, 'Tell me, are you truly well again?'

His long, grey, and tragic face was more twisted than ever. She had watched him drag his leg like some useless and intolerable burden. The youthful vigour of the other two young men only emphasised his many deficiencies and she was almost overwhelmed with love and pity for him.

'I-I-I am fantastically restored to full health,' Carlos stammered. 'Look, see here where the surgeon made a big hole in my skull to allow all the evil to escape.' He was about to remove his bonnet that she might inspect the wound but she declined the invitation. He giggled, 'It gave these two a scare. They were the ones who found me lying in a huge pool of blood.'

Isabel quickly changed the subject, 'And you have Juan and Alessandro to thank for walking as barefoot penitents praying for you, and the Duque de Alba for bringing the miraculous mortal remains of a saint for you to touch.'

144

'Yes, yes, Alba d-d-did help,' he moved closer to whisper, 'but you know I hate him, so his name will remain in my book of enemies.'

'That is dreadful. What are we to do with you? I will forgive you just this once because you have been so very ill, but never again.'

'Then let me tell you something that will help me regain your favour. You will probably know that my dear friend Mariana was cruelly forced to enter a convent by him,' he tilted his head in the direction of Philip. 'Well, I have given her one thousand *ducados* to buy property that would bring in annual rents good enough to keep her in comfort, and if ever she is allowed to marry I have promised her three thousand *ducados*. Poor Mariana, none of it was her fault, if only I ...'

Philip cut him short, 'Dear God, but you are tiresome. You should have thought of that before involving her. And as for these payments, they are not acts of generosity they are to salve your conscience.'

Carlos sneered, 'How like you to denigrate anything I do. And who are you to talk of conscience?' He turned to Isabel with what he thought was an earnest expression, 'My queen, I will show you, I promise, that I am a reformed character.'

Isabel took his hands once more, giving him an encouraging smile; how she hated these scenes. 'Then here comes your first test, the Duque de Alba.'

'Not him,' Carlos curled his lip.

A tall, thin, and elderly gentleman looking most statesmanlike in his floor length velvet robe of crimson velvet and matching chaperone bonnet with its trailing tippet falling from the rolled brim advanced making three deep bows. 'Your majesties.'

'Welcome back,' was all Philip could bring himself to say.

'You are more than welcome,' Isabel pressed his hand. 'How I wish you need not stay away at your estates so often, your wife and I both miss you.'

'Forgive me, my lady, if I have been the cause of any discomfort.'

Carlos groaned, narrowed his eyes and bit hard on his lips loathing the man's obsequious manner towards his Isabel, his marvellous Isabel. 'I will have to underline your name with red ink next time I open my book' he threatened.

Juan hushed him.

'It was foolishness to leave,' Philip decided he would speak on the matter after all, although he would just as happily let the old fool suffer a while longer. 'You took umbrage simply because the door to my office was locked.'

'That was reason enough. That door has never been closed, let alone locked. Not only was it locked, but you left the key in the lock preventing me from using mine. I was made to wait for over an hour in the presence of courtiers, an embarrassment I would dearly like to wipe from my memory. My lord, my key is a symbol of my unquestionable loyalty and service; therefore this more than suggested I was not to be trusted. I have my pride, your majesty, in myself and in the family honour.'

Philip had realised his error at the time and had rued it instantly. On the other hand it had perhaps helped to put the arrogant man in his place; Alba was incurably jealous of all the other ministers and counsellors who might enjoy equal authority, Ruy Gómez to name but one. He smiled wryly, 'You are right. I should never have done it and I apologise. I was discussing a personal matter with one of my secretaries, it was a trivial matter, but personal. As you know I value your advice too much to allow you to stay away from the Court.'

Carlos squealed with delight, 'Bravo, Alba, you got him to admit he was in the wrong!'

'So there we are then,' Isabel hurriedly interrupted. 'Everything has been set to rights and you won't have to leave us again.'

'My lady, if I may be allowed to admit it, it has been a cloud over my heart being absent these last few months.'

Carlos had the greatest desire to strike him but remembering his promise to Isabel he restricted himself to holding the hilt of his sword and hissing, 'You make me sick, you disgusting old man.'

Isabel shook her head. 'Carlos, please.'

Alba just stroked at his sparse silvery beard quite used to the young man's chronic ill behaviour. Nothing could be done about it; after all he was the king's son.

Carlos bowed his apology muttering something about a determination to draw even more red lines under Alba's name.

Increased noises from the courtyard drew them all to the window to view the commotion of carriages and sedans, of loud greetings and laughter. Isabel and Juana decided they should determine who they considered to be the best dressed lady, and there were some splendid dresses to choose from. There was only one winner, the lady in emerald green. They looked at each other in disbelief.

'Who invited her? How dare she?' Isabel demanded, her eyes blazing. She shot an accusing glance at Philip before turning away from him, the window, and the whole world.

Philip remained unmoved by her outburst, 'It is of no concern of yours.'

'Oh but it is, because that woman is your whore, and she is pregnant with your child. How dare she insult me in this way, coming to flaunt her fat belly!'

Everyone froze.

Tears tumbled over Isabel's cheeks, her nose dripped, wouldn't stop dripping.

Philip began to speak but she pressed on, her back a rigid wall between them. 'You know how I feel about such women. Heaven knows I watched my mother suffer so many humiliations at the hands of the Poitier bitch, and I tell you,' her nose had to be continually dabbed at, her tears blotted, 'I will not suffer the same indignities.'

'Look at me Isabel, I am speaking to you. Very well, if you care not to. I will remind you once more that a mistress is none of your business. The subject is closed. Although it may be of interest for you to know that she is soon to be married.'

'No doubt that will give you more time to brood over Cousin Christina's letters.'

'She is an ambassador. I do not need to go on.'

'And what about the love letters you send to the Osorio woman?' The floodgates of her unhappiness were open and the torrent was not to be stopped.

'Turn round to face me!' He demanded, but he hurriedly mastered his anger for it probably wasn't wise to have her so upset when she was pregnant. 'Isabel, that affair was long before your time.' He was annoyed that he had to discuss any of this, especially in the presence of others.

'So now you are merely making polite enquiries regarding the lady's health, and of the progress of the bastard boys?'

Juana could take no more and rushed to her side. It was the way of things, husbands did take mistresses, so how could she criticise her brother? But when it affected her dear sister Isabel her heart cried out in sympathy. How could her brother do this to such a wonderful wife? She offered her handkerchief trying to reach out across the painful gulf of Isabel's hurt.

'Oh, dear God; Isabel!'

Isabel now turned to face Philip, 'And I know about Ana and about the daughter of the lady of my bedchamber. I suppose you never considered how much servants revel in court whisperings and note passing.'

They moved as one towards her before Philip brushed them aside. He held his handkerchief to her nose, lips, and chin to clear them of blood, but the haemorrhaging defeated all his attempts. Alba called out for a doctor while Juan and Alessandro raced off searching for one. Carlos put his hand on the hilt of his sword ready to draw it on his father if his precious Isabel should die.

Isabel was desperate not to be defeated by the untimely nose bleed. 'Get that woman out of here. If she attends the ball then I will not.'

But the fire and fight were gone and she crumpled to the floor.

Carlos screamed at Philip, 'You stole this precious being from me and this is how you treat her. You bastard, you will die for this.'

'Go away, you irksome retch.'

23

Juana was in Isabel's bedchamber sitting some distance from the bed, watching, straining to hear what the doctors were saying.

What little air there was smelled stale and sour, and she flapped at it with her fan; if only she could open a window just for a moment, or if the merest of draughts could find its way through the closed doors then the room would be rid of this vomit and excrement-filled foulness.

She was in sombre mood. Several days had passed since her dear sister had been forced to take to her bed following that disastrous evening. The nose bleeds had continued although mercifully they had become less frequent and of shorter duration. Hopefully, when those men in their black robes completed today's examination, there would be more positive news for this couldn't possibly go on for much longer or Isabel would … Juana refused to think the unthinkable.

Isabel peered through migraine dimmed eyes at the four doctors, three Spanish and one French, gathered like huge black birds about her bed. First they shuffled up and down one side then moved around to the other side to repeat the process, quite similar in fact to crows peering, poking, and arguing, for all the world as if they squabbled over carrion.

It was not unusual for her to be surrounded by physicians. It had been this way throughout her life because she was so often ill; but what she now hated and feared was the Spanish doctors' insistence on bloodletting. They had pestered her, even threatened her with the inevitability of death, should she not consent to it. She had finally succumbed, with the proviso they explained their reasons to her French doctor who would then hopefully reassure her that this was the best way to restore her health.

But it had not made her feel any better; no, in fact after a few days and several bowls filled with her blood she felt worse than ever. Her nose still bled unexpectedly and without any provocation, she suffered chronic headaches and had pains in her chest and down her side. She prayed for an end to it all.

The bedchamber was stifling in the heat of Madrid's summer and she felt more nauseous than ever. Thankfully today all the bed curtains were drawn back, courtesy of the doctors' visit, and she lay spread-eagled, her arms and legs uncovered. It might offend her modesty but she was finding some welcome coolness in the slightest movement of air across her skin.

'So, Docteur Montguyon, do you agree that the body has been disturbed by forceful influences, changing it from healthy to sick?'

'Yes, of course, but why all this bloodletting?'

'Quite simply, sir, it is the only way to return the body to its former state. The unwanted humours flow out in the blood. It is all quite logical.'

'My lady queen has surely lost sufficient blood with her nose bleeds.'

'Nose bleeds have nothing to do with it,' snapped another of the Spanish doctors irritated by the presence of this interfering foreigner. 'The blood must be taken from specific points close to the source of the hot humours which are located in the nose. By taking the required quantity of blood from the forehead near the left eye close to the nose the nose bleeds will cease.'

'And from the right temple too?'

'We always take a similar amount from an area on the opposite side, but more slowly, drop by drop. One must be alert to the devious nature of these humours that seek at times to hide themselves in another location. The more time we take over this the greater our chances of success. It does surprise me that in France you do not follow this practice.'

Montguyon ignored the taunt. 'The arms, too, and so frequently?' It seemed to him that they had taken enough blood to make an ox weak.

The third Spanish doctor replied making no effort to conceal his disdain for the ignorance of Montguyon. 'There is obviously an excessive irritation of the internal humours. Its cause, a predominance of sanguine humours, must be expelled.'

'But this is making her weaker; surely you can see that.' Montguyon shook his head in total disbelief at what he was hearing.

'That is the whole point, Monsieur le docteur, we must weaken the resistance of her body. It has been stimulated by strange influxes making the body sick yet still indomitable. We must take this aggressive action against them.'

'It is the only cure,' said another deciding to put an end to such ill-informed questioning, 'The demons will flow out of the body in the blood.'

Montguyon refused to be drawn into discussing devils and demons, Isabel's illness was physical not spiritual. 'And yet the nose bleeds continue, she continues to run a fever, is plagued by headaches and various other pains. It would seem that your treatments have proved ineffective. In my opinion, a purge was and is all that is necessary.'

Isabel offered her thanks to God and the Duque de Alba that permission had finally been granted for her French physician to visit. If only his advice would be heeded.

After much mumbling and grumbling the Spanish doctors removed the mustard plasters from the incisions on her arms and face, lifted the bloated leeches from her groin and armpits, and freed the cups from her chest.

'The patient is all yours, sir. On your head be it if you fail.'

They stood aside to witness the naïve practices of uneducated foreign medicine.

'A simple, straightforward elixir of rhubarb root in honey, gentlemen. I assure you that within hours there will be an improvement.'

Isabel sucked on the spout of the feeding cup, greedily swallowing the bittersweet drink, even though she knew that in a few hours she would have appalling cramps in her bowels and dreadful diarrhoea before she felt any of its benefits.

Juana fanned herself more rigorously, impatient for the doctors to retire allowing her at last to sit beside Isabel. Then Philip's sudden arrival prompted a further delay.

'Brother,' she whispered, 'the French doctor has advised no more bloodletting, and has administered a purge. The others had no objection.' She hoped the Frenchman's action wouldn't anger him.

'At this stage any avenue is worthwhile.' He was angry; he had been so for days, but with the infuriating Isabel and not the doctors. After the briefest of exchanges with them he approached her.

Isabel's beautiful face was now scarred and bruised and it made his fury soar to a new level. She had refused to learn, and this after five years, never to involve herself in matters which were none of her business. It should have been of no consequence whether or not he had mistresses. Her sole duty was to provide him with heirs, and now because of her stupid, childish tantrums, she was ill and she was putting his unborn son's life at risk.

'My lord, to have you here by my side makes me feel much better.'

'Sh. Sh. Do not exhaust yourself by talking, save all your energy for getting well, for protecting our child. Everyone in Spain is praying for you, from the oldest to the youngest, from the richest to the poorest. There are special church services and processions in every city seeking the intercession of Our Lady.'

He was amazed and not a little envious at Isabel's ability to touch the hearts of so many in so short a time, and she a French woman at that.

Of course most felt they knew her because she went out into the city unveiled. He had railed repeatedly against the unseemliness of her actions, but still she walked among the people, her face uncovered, instead of travelling in a litter shielded from prying eyes. She had remained aggravatingly stubborn and would not desist from this the most outrageous of her many unwelcome French customs. He promised himself he would be magnanimous and forgive her as soon as he held his newborn son in his arms; a son so unlike Carlos, a son to give him and Spain some hope for the future.

'My lord, the window, may I not have some air?'

'Soon; as yet it would be too dangerous.' He soothed her brow, his fingers lightly touching the edges of the discoloured wounds.

Two more visitors slipped into the room. Carlos and Juan had not been expected in fact they had been forbidden on the express orders of Philip yet here they were and looking obviously dismayed to find Philip at the bedside.

'Damn. I was certain the bastard would have been gone by now,' Carlos cursed his bad luck. 'He should be buried under a mountain of his beloved paperwork at this time of the day.'

Juana put her fingers to her lips, urging caution. No doubt the young men would be dismissed before long but in the meantime she prayed there would not be a terrible scene.

Carlos limped towards Isabel. He stopped short, staring in horror at the results of the doctors' work. His beautiful Isabel had been subjected to unspeakable atrocities and mutilations. That beautiful face had been marred by the surgeon's knife. There were bruises on her arms where the tourniquets had been bound tight and accompanying scalpel wounds nearby. Her breast was covered in red welts.

'Y-y-y-you bastard. L-l-look what you have done to her! So help me I will kill you! I want everyone to know I'm going to ...'

Juan took him by the shoulders to prevent him moving closer, urging him to be quiet. 'Carlos,' he whispered, 'those are words of treason. And think; such outbursts could make the queen worse. I will make your excuses, but we must leave, immediately.' Still holding him he turned to Philip, 'Sire, Prince Carlos is upset, he never intended those rash words.'

Philip waved the excuses to one side. 'Who gave you permission to come here?'

Carlos hissed, 'I did.'

'It was my express command that you should never be given access to this room.'

'I took it upon myself to ignore you. I say that if the French ambassador is allowed to visit whenever he wishes then so am I.'

'Get him out of here, Juan, before I lose my patience. I will not have my wife upset.'

'Carlos we should never have come. Hopefully his majesty is so concerned about the queen he will forgive us.'

Carlos was unrelenting, 'I have no fear of him,' and as Juan led him away he called over his shoulder, 'My dearest lady I am going to pray for you in every church in Madrid. I promise to see you soon.'

In a few moments Philip also took his leave.

Isabel beckoned Juana to her side, 'Juana, what is to be done with Carlos? His intentions were of the best. It seems he can never be in the same room as his father without one or the other of them losing their temper. I do believe they hate each other. I worry about them both, but especially Carlos. There are so few who care for him. He knows I am his friend that is why he wants to be with me.'

'I am sure Philip will allow him to visit once you are recovered.' This was neither the time nor the place to concern themselves with the growing rupture between father and son that could never be mended.

'And I will recover, won't I?'

'Without question; what with your confidence in your compatriot doctor, and Carlos visiting every church in Madrid, there is no possible alternative.'

Juana held Isabel's hand and chatted, recalling their outings, the picnics and the adventurous escapades, then spoke of her ideas for future excursions once Isabel was well and the baby born.

Isabel's fingers curled and tightened their grip, 'Tell the doctors, the purge has begun its work.' She clutched at her belly as if to hold back the gripes, the burning and tearing inside. The pains grew hotter, a boiling turmoil coursing through her. Sweat beaded her forehead. She bit hard on her lip.

'Juana, don't go, hold my hand again. It was never like this before.'

The Spanish doctors scowled their anger at French medical incompetence.

Montguyon shook his head, 'It is too soon for the purge to take effect, it is something else.'

Isabel had gasped short whimpers at first, now she cried out, pulling Juana close. She screamed out her agony, writhing, thrashing, pushing to free herself of the pain. Then the convulsions took over with their relentless attacks.

Juana watched her flailing limbs and saw what she hadn't wanted to see, and prayed earnestly that she was deceived and that there was no bloodied mess on the sheets.

'My poor sweet Isabel, not this.'

The Spanish doctors were in agreement, a return to the bloodletting was more important than ever, it was either that or leave God to do His will.

Montguyon was furious, 'Over my dead body!'

154

France

1565

24

Almost a year had passed since the miscarriage, since the loss of twin girls, since Montguyon had miraculously cured Isabel's ensuing fevers with a purge of agaric. She was in jubilant mood, those dark days of grief and desolation a thing of the past. Behind her was Irun, in northernmost Spain; ahead of her was France. The royal barge was carrying her across the narrow estuary to see her young brother, now king, and, unbelievably, to be with her beloved mother.

In her growing excitement she had to keep reminding herself of the true nature of this visit. It was to discuss the growing problem of Protestantism in France and in the Netherlands. Isabel was resolved to prove herself a successful diplomat for Spain with nothing being beyond her capabilities.

In truth it was Alba who had been charged with leading the negotiations. She was to be no more than a witness to the proceedings. She was here purely and simply because it suited Philip to be free of her for a while, and he had not come because he refused to give Catalina, the *Medici Serpent,* the satisfaction of the most powerful king in Europe's presence. That would give her more status than she deserved.

The banks of oarsmen in scarlet livery dipped and lifted glistening blades in unison thrusting the royal barge on its way. As the prow gobbled up the remaining stretch of water, Isabel dispensed with all thoughts of Lutherans, Calvinists, and the warring Huguenots of France to focus entirely on family, her family.

And there they were, with a massive entourage, an immense jewelled ribbon that ran along the length of the shore; it seemed all France had come to welcome her.

No sooner had they touched land and before the barge could be secured her brother leapt onto the deck and came running to her. He bowed and kissed her hand with great ceremony. Isabel delighted in this mixture of daring boy and courtly young king in his purple robes. Here was a youthful knight stepped directly from one of her favourite romances.

He escorted her to their mother, waiting on the shore, statuesque in her widow's black. They kissed hands in formal greeting then they hugged and kissed as any loving mother and daughter would.

Alba stood slightly apart, maintaining a discreet presence; the negotiations would not begin for at least a week.

As he watched he recalled Isabel's joy that day when she was told that the first week would be set aside for her to spend with her family. There would be lots of time to share memories of their childhood; brothers and sisters growing up together under the watchful eye of their doting mother, remembering courtiers, ladies-in-waiting, pageboys.

He shook his head admiring his beautiful queen in her tawny brocades and satins decorated with scattered pearls and diamonds. Eighty thousand *ducados* had been spent on jewels and dresses instead of covering the expenses of the journey; these had still to be found. Alba hoped that Philip would forgive any, all extravagances, would even pardon that tragic miscarriage if he could see the returned enchanting vivacity or hear the renewed sparkle in her voice and the music of her laughter. But the king had taken it badly; had seen it as a personal affront.

The cortege, all on horseback, set off for Bayonne. Every horse was magnificently caparisoned yet none could compare with Isabel's. Her mount was draped in lace and pearls, a family heirloom worth thousands of *ducados*, a leaving present from Philip.

The young King Charles IX accompanied by the Duque de Alba led the cavalcade followed by Catalina and Isabel.

Catalina had been impatient to begin, she wanted to know everything. 'You are truly well again, my darling child?'

'Completely; Montguyon was a marvel at overruling the other doctors. You cannot imagine how cross he was that they should suggest further bloodletting after … after… after what happened with my babies. He had me well again in next to no time. The Spanish people were wonderful, too, all praying for me. Once I was out of danger there were fireworks and fiestas, and when I visited the churches to offer my own thanks to God, I was greeted by such cheering!'

'It is gratifying to know that the Spaniards are capable of such discernment, recognising true worth. And what of Philip's behaviour, has he decided to be a faithful husband at last?'

Isabel sighed a tragic sigh, a sigh bereft of hope, a sigh of one resigned to betrayal. 'He is especially kind these days.'

'Kindnesses do not interest me; what of mistresses?'

157

'The Eufrasia woman is married and has left the court.'

'Was she the one who caused the loss of your babies? You are well rid of her.'

'Yes, but Philip says it was not her fault. He insists it was mine, says I should not get involved in what is his private business. His favourite mistress fortunately lives more than a hundred miles away.'

'But you suffer still, I know, for there is another. There is that person, Ana de Mendoza, the Princess of Eboli.'

'Ah, yes, *La Eboli*. However there are changes being made there, too. The Duquesa de Alba has been appointed as head of my ladies-in-waiting, the position *La Eboli* had designs on, and she is not best pleased. I must admit I find the duquesa somewhat old but then ...' she brightened, 'and you will have noticed that Alba is here alone, without Gómez, the husband of *La Eboli*. Gómez has been made head of the household of Prince Carlos. In future neither will be spending much time in the king's presence. Gómez was so put out by his removal from Philip's court, and then his being passed over for Alba to accompany me here, that he actually went to bed for a few days in a fit of pique.' She laughed, 'It seems to be a Spanish custom, retiring to one's bed when peeved, to nurse one's wounds. Philip does it all the time.'

'That comes as no shock, men are such spoiled children. *La Eboli*, this Ana, will in future be what?'

'One of my attendants, nothing more; that is as much as I can hope for at the moment.'

'I think I shall send her a gift; a ring, a bracelet, or a brooch. It would be the first of several inducements to place her sexual favours elsewhere.'

'If only it were as easy as that.'

'We shall see. And what of Philip's visits to your bed? Does he still hurt you, cause you pain?'

'Mother! Please, not here, not now!' Isabel looked about her, anxious to know if anyone could possibly have overheard. 'Those things,' she whispered, 'should never be voiced aloud.'

'Later, then; but allow me to tell you what I intend to do. I will need your help with some of the details. I am going to write to your husband insisting you have a second honeymoon. You are a beautiful bride and he should need no one else. Also, if he thinks of it as a second honeymoon, he might be different, take more care in the bridal bed. This will provide him with the child he desires. And something else; you will stop worrying your pretty little head about Prince Carlos. Somehow or other I will persuade Philip that your sister Margot is the very wife for him. I think Carlos is simply at a loss as to how to spend his time. His father gives him nothing to occupy his mind. A wife like Margot certainly would change that.'

Margot, the precocious and wayward daughter; only twelve years old but with an energy and zest for life like no other, with a total lack of sexual restraint where neither age nor social status presented a barrier. There was no doubting she would be ideal for Carlos.

'He has set his heart on marrying his cousin, the quiet and retiring Anne of Austria. I doubt he would countenance any other. But listen,' Isabel leaned towards her mother, 'I'll tell you a secret. I know it can never come to anything, but Juana has been urging Philip to choose her as bride for Carlos. The Cortes took up her cause and Carlos was furious when he found out. He stormed into the council chamber, interrupting an important meeting, blazing with fury. He informed them in no uncertain terms that he was not going to be told by anyone, and certainly not them, that he had to marry his aunt.'

Mother and daughter laughed but Isabel's laughter died as suddenly as it had started. She suddenly missed Carlos, missed that pathetic, unloved, crippled creature who had wept the day they had said their farewells. He was convinced he would never see her again, making her promise repeatedly that she would return soon, not wanting to let go of her hand. 'Poor Carlos, I cannot help but feel a great sadness for him. There are so few people he likes, and fewer still with any fondness for him. I worry, too, about the affect Gómez will have on him; you see Carlos already suspects him of being Philip's spy. And as for Philip, he doesn't trust Carlos for one moment.'

Catalina raised her eyebrows, 'Tell me, who does Philip trust? Not his son. Not his half-brother. Not his friend Gómez.'

'Me, mother, I know he trusts me. But I want to hear about you and my brother the king, and the rest of my family.'

25

The talks, as Philip had so rightly predicted, were not going well. Catalina, regent for her son for the last five years, was aggressively robust in her arguments; determined to lay all fault, blame, and lack of resolve firmly on Spain.

Alba, a wily old negotiator, was finding it increasingly difficult to maintain his composure. It was vexing that his understanding of French having always served him so well was today stretched to its limits with Catalina's still heavy Italian accent. Nor did it help being aware from the outset that there was no future in these discussions, no possibility whatsoever of signing an accord between the two countries, knowing it to be a complete waste of time and effort.

He looked across the table at the fourteen year-old king of France, who from time to time renewed his efforts to simulate interest, to appear knowledgeable about the religious problems of his country, but who at this moment was engaged in studying the rings on his fingers.

Catalina suddenly threw her fan into her lap, glaring at Alba. 'I say again, that if King Philip had any desire to work with France he would be at this table.'

'With respect, and Queen Isabel will vouch for this, my master has every confidence in me to negotiate on this matter for it is quite straightforward. Also, my coming here has allowed him to travel immediately to the Cortes of Aragón to attend to pressing business which cannot be postponed. It is vital that they grant him sufficient funding to support our struggles against the Reformers in the Netherlands.' He glanced only briefly in Isabel's direction because he more than suspected that Philip would also be taking the opportunity to stop off at the small palace at Saldañuela, to be with Isabel de Osorio.

'I am not convinced, but, very well, back to business; we had got to where you were telling us, that we made a grave mistake signing a peace treaty with the Protestant Huguenots. I say, *au contraire,* it has afforded us some breathing space.'

'We see it in an entirely different light. Indeed, it has weakened your position. The depraved Huguenots must be rooted out, ma'am, nothing less will suffice.'

'And Spanish troops, will they be sent in to assist us or will King Philip use the opportunity to attack us?'

'Neither is our intention.' He picked up a sheaf of papers from the table, inwardly fuming at the accusation. 'Here is our advice, the basis for a treaty of trust and support in a concerted effort to rid ourselves of the heretic. Strength of purpose by our two Catholic nations is required if we are to succeed. First, your chancellor must be replaced immediately by one less tolerant of reformers. You must apprehend all Protestants using France as a point of emigration threatening to poison the New World. We insist you stop aid reaching the dissidents in the Netherlands.'

'These are orders, not advice. I think Philip threatens us. I can no longer sit at the same table.'

Alba merely lowered his head.

Catalina was angry, angry enough to turn on her daughter, 'Your husband, *madame,* evidently does not trust us. Alba's words together with other information already in our possession strongly suggest war. That is why Philip is not here, he has already determined his plan of action!'

Isabel could not allow her mother's words to go without challenge. 'Your majesty, my husband would not entertain such thoughts, would never set our country at odds with yours, would never renege on the peace treaty signed with my father, and well you know it! I would venture that everything you have heard that is attributed to my lord, the king of Spain, is no more than the evil machinations of your own ministers, many of them Huguenots.'

Her firmness surprised everyone. Her brother was wrenched from the detailed inspection of his jewels. Her mother found herself speechless. Alba looked up raising his eyebrows. Isabel hoped that once Philip heard of her bold speech he could not fail to recognise that she was much more than a frivolous young woman.

Catalina rose from her chair, her huge bosom heaving in fury, her eyes blazing. 'How Spanish we have become!'

Isabel would not be bettered, 'Madame, with due respect, it was your wish I become queen of Spain. However that does not mean that I am no longer your daughter in whom you may have implicit faith and trust. The two are not mutually exclusive.'

Catalina moved round the redundant conference table and kissed her, 'You are right, of course. Alba, see what a clever queen you have. I will agree in principle to your suggestions; verbally of course, nothing written; you understand?'

Alba was relieved that there was to be no further waste of time. 'You echo my sentiments exactly. A tacit agreement, your majesty, this is what King Philip expected.'

'Then my daughter and I intend to spend the next few days together. We must have new dresses made, a trousseau. My goodness, when Philip discovers how it was you, my child, who brought about the success of our negotiations, he will fall in love with you. He will take you in his arms to kiss you.'

Alba closed his eyes, rubbing at his knitted brow with his bony fingers, thinking that it could only be the Italians, or the French, who would entertain such foolish romantic notions about a man's feelings for his wife.

Spain

1565

26

'Never in my wildest dreams did I expect to enjoy moments like these. Pinch me; tell me I am not in a land of fantasy.' Isabel de Osorio nuzzled her head on his naked chest then reached up to stroke his trimmed beard, to run a finger along his full and sensual lower lip.

Philip looked down at the blond waves of hair as beautiful today as they were ten years ago when they had said what they thought to be their final farewells before he left for England. 'Nor did I believe we would ever be together again. It was a weakness on my part, and I thank God for such a weakness, to alter my plans that I might spend some time with you. Sometimes it is unwise to revisit the past, times and people change, but you are as precious to me now as you ever were.'

They lay comfortably in each others arms; content. Late afternoon birdsong heralding the approaching coolness of evening lent further enchantment.

For the moment the world beyond this little palace with its olive groves and orchards had ceased to exist. There were no foreign policies for him to fret over, no financial concerns to burden him, no preoccupation with a son unfit to inherit, no immature wife with her demands for total and unwavering fidelity to consider, nor her tardiness in providing him with an heir.

Distant voices joined with the birds' chorus to drift through the open window, floating on the same breeze that lazily nudged the gossamer curtains deep into the bedchamber. Saldañuela was returning to life after a few hours of indolence and siesta.

'My adorable Venus.'

'My Adonis returned. I had almost forgotten the joys of our lovemaking.'

'But not the art.'

'You are dreadful.' Isabel de Osorio rolled onto her front. 'But it was as good as all the other times, wasn't it?' She lay studying the face of this man she had not seen for more than eleven years. She drank in every aspect, slowly moving her head thrilling to his soft touches about the nape of her neck.

As in the days of old, they bathed together, still enjoying the other's body: hers still silky smooth, his perhaps not quite so athletic as she remembered.

'Your hand, so swollen; is it painful?' Isabel tenderly dried the puffed and reddened knuckles.

'I am to suffer the dreaded gout just as my father did.'

She kissed each burning finger, 'My medicine, reserved just for you.'

They dressed, saying adieu to their nakedness, laughing as they struggled with unruly laces, buttons and brooches. Then they moved out onto the shaded terrace where bowls of grapes and a jug of cool white wine awaited them.

'You have attended to every detail. I drink to you, my darling Isabel, and to my fortune in finding you. Now tell me of our sons. Is everything well?'

'Perfect. Both are enjoying the soldiers' life. You would be very proud of them they are everything sons should be, everything gentlemen must be. And although I speak as a mother besotted with love for them, they are incredibly handsome.'

'If only you would have allowed me to find them a position in my court.'

'No, it was best for my family to take a different path. In this way we cannot be an embarrassment to you.'

'Hah! My God, Isabel, the worst embarrassment is stuck to me like my shadow. My conscience revolts when I consider what I will be doing in a few days time. Can you believe that I am going to ask Aragón to swear its allegiance to Carlos as my heir? Dear God; what is to become of Spain with him as its king? I despair.'

It broke her heart that Philip should be tormented by this tragedy of having but the one heir and he a maniac according to the gossip. What could she say? Remind him that he did have a half-brother? Juan apparently was healthy, robust, astute, ambitious and incredibly popular; and being the bastard child of a monarch was no barrier to wearing a crown. Elizabeth of England had proved that.

But perhaps this was not the moment to mention Juan; Philip would accuse her of meddling in matters forbidden her.

'How can anyone possibly measure up to your standards? You're intelligent and handsome, a valiant soldier, expert horseman, hunter, and dancer. There, I have done, I shall spare your blushes.'

165

Although she had hoped to keep the real world at bay with her words of flattery and accompanying kisses it had simply been biding its time like a cruel snake poised to strike.

'And the queen was pregnant with girls! I don't need girls, I need boys!'

'Carlos is your heir. It is unfortunate that he suffers such constant ill health,' she touched his arm.

'And if something should happen to him?' It had often crossed his mind that it would be such a blessing if Carlos died.

'If the queen can only provide you with female heirs and, just supposing, Carlos should die, I see no problem in women inheriting the throne.' She had been presented with an ideal opportunity to lightheartedly fight the female cause. It would move them both to safer ground.

She laughed, 'Women can be every bit as competent as men when it comes to leadership. We'll begin with your great-grandmother. She has already become a legend as a great queen. Her efforts to build this nation were tireless, even to the point of never finding time to change her chemise. A new shade of off-white was even named after her; "Isabeline". I wonder what name they secretly gave to the smell. Then what about Columbus? She pawned her jewels to support his ventures, her feminine intuition bringing a fortune to our shores. Then we come to those female relatives who have served as governors in the Netherlands; unfortunate that some should have developed deep voices and hairy chins, something they should have considered before accepting the position? I tease. Your mother acted as regent during your father's absence for many a year. Then there's your sister Juana, regent when you went to England. Oh, and how can you ignore your Cousin Christine, who although not a monarch is an exceptionally able ambassador as well as possessing other sterling attributes?' She threw him a smile of mock censure.

'Always the same, you never miss an opportunity to lecture me.' He held her face in his hands, 'But why have you carefully omitted Mary Tudor, a failure if ever there was one. As for the present queen of England, Elizabeth, she of the heart and stomach of a man in the body of a woman, I doubt she can do anything with that unruly little country. I give you another you sought not to mention, Catalina de Medici, my dear mother-in-law, whose only defined policy is one of greed and envy. That reminds me I received a letter from her the other day and haven't read it yet.'

166

He set his glass down, brushed aside the white billows of gossamerlike curtains across the doorway and disappeared, to return immediately with the small package, breaking the royal seal as he walked.

'Now what do you suppose my dear mother-in-law feels compelled to write to me about? Not about the negotiations, to be sure, Alba will be doing an excellent job. Could it be regarding my wife? I can imagine how much gossiping has been going on, although considering they write such lengthy missives to each other, I would be surprised if they could find anything new to discuss. I hope she has told her mother that I give in to her every whim.'

'And do you?'

'Only when it suits me, it is for wives to yield to their husbands. However I have been most accommodating of late, even keeping my temper when she spent the whole of the generous travel allowance on herself.'

'A lady must always look her best.'

'I want her to, but within reason. I have only managed once or twice to persuade her to wear the same dress again if I particularly liked it. She gives no thought to how much she spends.'

'So, what is in the letter?' Isabel was not disposed to discuss the queen, neither her beauty nor her profligacy.

Philip scanned the words. It was written in Spanish, 'Just as I thought, this is a combined effort, my wife responsible for the translation, and presumably the source of information for much of its contents. Well I never; such a dressing down for an erring and thoughtless husband. My lady wife has indeed told all: about Eufrasia, Ana de Mendoza, and about you my dear. Catalina demands that I desist from all extramarital relationships.'

'Thank goodness you chose not to read it earlier it might have ruined a perfect afternoon.'

'I am told that from now on I must show my wife affection when I visit her bedchamber. What kind of betrayal is this, what intimate secrets has my lady been revealing? Listen to this ... *a rethink is required. You are fortunate in having a beautiful, charming and intelligent wife. You must make more effort; apply yourself to wooing her instead of considering only your masculine urges'*. Were this not so outrageous I would be furious.'

Isabel de Osorio handed him his glass, 'It is my turn to propose a toast. *Bonne chance, pour la seconde lune de miel,* and for good measure another toast; to *le petit mort.*' She became serious, 'I have told you often enough that there is nothing to compare with a lover's wooing. The thought of being no more than a passive receptacle is too awful to contemplate. But, my love, I am sure you could never be accused of such coldness, I know you too well. Your wife must be exaggerating.'

27

It was the hottest June that Isabel's dwarf, Montagne, could remember; but despite the almost intolerable heat he was feeling most comfortable, at ease with the world. He shuffled his small body all the way back amongst the cushions of his chair so that every part of him could be accommodated, everything except his feet in their buckled shoes, then he let his eyes roam over the other furnishings of Magdalena Ruiz's reception room, trying to ignore the marmosets chained to their climbing rails.

Although it was sparsely furnished, true to Spanish style, the pieces were all exquisite examples of craftsmanship in carved dark oak; the tapestry was most certainly from Flanders; the silver plate on the chest was also of superior quality. There was no doubting that Magdalena ran a lucrative business; when not entertaining the king she was granting favours for those prepared to pay the price. He looked down at the wine glass in his hands, it was no less splendid than the rest of her possessions; Venetian glass at its best with silver filigree decorating its base and stem.

'Let us hope that sixty-six is a better year,' Magdalena leaned forward in her chair raising her glass in his direction.

'Come now, last year wasn't all bad; our lady queen was restored to full health.'

'Granted.'

'And she was allowed to travel to France to be with her family.'

'Granted; and you benefited too, you old devil, visiting your homeland.'

'Ah, yes, indeed. Such banquets and festivities, the like of which you would never see here. There was one evening in particular; we were on an island set out with rows of tables radiating from the centre where the royal family were seated. Nymphs and goddesses appeared from nowhere, making almost magical music, dancing, their robes shimmering with silver and gold ...'

'Yes, yes, I've heard it all before. In any case your so-called incomparable festivities invariably got rained off sending everyone stampeding for shelter. You were almost trampled underfoot at one time as I recall.'

'True, but I still have many wonderful memories.'

'And all the while I was here on my own with no one to share my gossip; and the king forever in an ill temper with anyone who got near. I had to tell him I was not prepared to tolerate his miserable face. The only time there was any peace was when Philip went off to Aragón. Yes, many were the times I could only find solace in a glass of wine.'

'Or two or three or more ...'

'I'll have no criticism of that nature.'

'As if I would. Any news from Brussels, from Don Alessandro? That was a thunderbolt; had all of us gasping.'

'Still annoyed, Montagne, bitter; never took kindly to being suddenly commanded to marry the Portuguese lady, even if she is a princess. I think he had ideas about a Hapsburg match. He's such a pompous individual anyway, and I imagine finding himself no better than any other pawn in his majesty's power game won't suit at all.'

'And the bride?'

Magdalena reached forward to slap the toe of Montagne's shoe and laughed. 'Lord, what a shock she must have got on her wedding night!' She took a sip of wine. 'Bless me, before she wed she wouldn't even suffer a gentleman to offer her his arm, thought it was a contamination of her pure self. I tell you I can't wait to meet this wife-cum-nun. Apparently the happy couple are on their way back to Madrid before going to Parma to live.'

'And Don Juan,' Montagne set down his glass, 'has he been returned to the king's favour? I remember how very chastened he looked when he came to greet the queen at the Spanish border.'

'Well, if he will indulge himself in schoolboy's tricks, running away to sea. Yes, it's about time he and Alessandro grew up and stopped considering themselves to be the centre of the universe.'

'Be fair now, both are desperate to prove themselves as military men instead of idly wasting their days at Court. All Juan wanted to do was go to the defence of Malta. So, has he been forgiven?'

'I suppose you might say he has been forgiven, although the king isn't one to forgive or forget. Anyway, after being made to eat humble pie he was allowed to kiss the king's hand. To my mind Don Juan is damned lucky that his majesty hasn't had him made a cardinal already.'

'That wouldn't suit;' Montagne shook his head, 'he's far more interested in the ladies than the church. I understand he's dallying with a pretty young thing, using the home of the Eboli's as a meeting place.'

'Not dallying, my friend, this is much more serious. The girl is of *La Eboli's* family. Good stock; but Juan can never marry.'

'Why ever not?'

'You're not thinking. Juan is the king's half-brother, so Philip will never give his permission. How can Juan be allowed to marry and have children when the only other heir to the throne is Carlos. Things are bad enough as they are without further complications.'

'Speaking of *La Eboli*, I see she still haunts the king's apartments, I thought you said he was no longer interested.'

'That is correct, the king has no wish to bed the woman. But let me tell you this, he would be interested to know why she is paying a great deal of attention to Antonio Pérez, the secretary's son. I could tell him, in fact I might do just that, tell him that the Princess High and Mighty is determined to seek out the sort of information she was once privy to when her husband was closer to the king.'

'So it not just a question of trying to rouse the king's jealousy?'

'That would be playing a far too dangerous game, Montagne. In any case, rumour has it that Antonio is Ruy Gómez's love child – no proof of course – and that Gonzalo Pérez is passing him off as his own.'

'This Antonio, is he the young man who pours such quantities of perfume on his clothes and person that he leaves behind him a reeking trail worse than any Parisian whore?'

Magdalena's screeching, cackling laughter brought an end to the quiet tête-à-tête. 'What a delightful picture you paint; a toast to the Parisian whore.'

Montagne lifted his glass then paused, 'Let us drink to something far more interesting, something worth raising our glasses to, something that will bring happiness to all of us.'

'How right you are; and regarding that there is something we must discuss. But that calls for more wine.'

Was there a serious note that he detected in her voice or was it his growing awareness of those damnable marmosets that was beginning to erode his feeling of wellbeing?

'Only if you get rid of the monkeys.'

Magdalena pulled herself forward, placed one foot on the footstool, and lowered herself to the floor. She rearranged the skirts of her black dress and checked that the miniature portrait of King Philip hanging from its golden chain rested carefully on her bosom.

'Lord, but I will never master the art of getting off a chair in a ladylike manner.' She unclipped the monkeys' leashes from their perch, 'Come along my little darlings, the gentleman doesn't care for your company. But you can have a special treat for being such good babies.'

Montagne glanced about him once again enjoying the luxury of it all before turning his attention to the row of beautiful pearl buttons running down the front of his jerkin, disappearing over the mound of his pigeon chest. His fingers delighted in the fine lace at his wrists, his jewelled rings sparkling as they moved about the folds.

While it was true that his favours didn't attract the same rewards as Magdalena's he would be eternally grateful for her assistance in suggesting many an unexpected source. The recently acquired silver buckles that gleamed at him from his shoes were a gift from the puppeteer for helping him secure another performance for the queen and her ladies.

ᘓ   ᘔ

Magdalena returned carrying a silver dish holding a small mountain of marzipan sweets of every shape and size. 'These go well with wine; help yourself.' She clambered up into her chair, 'Now, to serious business. You know I always give sound advice, go no further than that of the holy relics of San Eugenio.'

'You mean persuading my lady queen to be false to her conscience.'

'How you exaggerate, Montagne, it was no more than dissimulation, all in a good cause, and with excellent results; and she looked so lovely prostrating herself before the saint's leathery remains begging him to intervene on her behalf. There's no denying it, the saint asked God to grant the queen a child thereby sparing her the dishonour of failing in her duty to her husband and sovereign lord.'

'It still makes me feel uneasy. We French do not share your kind of religious fervour, it's not natural, not ...'

'You French, I might point out, are highly suspect when it comes to the depth and conviction of your faith. But ignoring that I need not remind you that I told you his majesty would be greatly impressed with Queen Isabel if, of her own accord, she were to send to Paris for the relics and then make public her petition. Far better that than her having to suffer his temper tantrums, sulks, and whatever else until he got his way. And, despite what you think of our ways, it worked; the queen is with child and the king is head over heels in love with her. I tell you he's behaving worse than a common village youth; he's like a puppy dog at her beck and call.'

'The outcome is a marvel, although I would suggest there is some degree of play acting on his part. But the most wondrous part is that throughout the queen's seven months of being with child she has suffered little illness, denying those ignorant doctors their cherished bloodletting.'

'Our doctors, Montagne, know what is for the best and we'll have no further argument on that. We agree that my advice was most beneficial for Queen Isabel, now I am going to advise something equally important because you French might find it just as unacceptable.'

'I wondered when this euphoria would come to an end,' he studied the blood-red contents of his glass wishing to delay some dreadful, unavoidable demand. He had been too optimistic, caught up like the rest, enjoying the queen's health; too happy as he watched her merrily preparing to leave the stinking summer of Madrid for Valsaín and its cool, shady woods and crystal streams, to ever consider that the Spanish might yet conjure up something totally unexpected. He took a sip of the wine and closed his eyes.

Magdalena felt a moment's sympathy for him before downing her drink and refilling her glass. 'As you know the queen is in good health; that is not what I want to talk about. When we get to Valsaín a team of lawyers will be waiting in the palace; ready and prepared.

'Lawyers?'

'Hush now, no need for alarm. I am referring to custom and protocol, nothing more. Her majesty must draw up her last will and testament.'

'Good God; if that doesn't put the fear of death into her nothing will.'

'That is why I'm telling you now, that you might explain, reassure her.'

'Twenty years old, blooming with health and you want her to think about her mortality. We can't do this to her.'

'We can and we must.'

'Hopefully this can be done quickly.'

'I am afraid not, it could take several days.'

'Good God.'

'Everything must be attended to with great care.'

'My lady queen, to be frightened like this, it's intolerable; you people ...'

Magdalena stopped him, 'I'm not about to argue with you. If you will hush for a moment I will explain. The queen will have the right to bequeath small items of jewellery; so have her make a list in readiness. Also she can request that Philip arranges small pensions for her servants. The rest, a lengthy rigmarole will already have been outlined by Philip and set down by the lawyers.'

'Then why don't they just get on with the whole thing and not terrify my lady,' Montagne shook his head in despair.

'To continue; reassure her majesty that these are nothing but words on papers and mustn't bother her pretty head about them. I give you my full permission to be as derogatory and sarcastic as you wish about us strange Spaniards and our weird ways. Just one more thing; the queen has already pleased Philip by showing the earnestness of her faith in sending for San Eugenio; now she can gain his everlasting favour by requesting she be dressed in a Franciscan habit for her burial. To please her husband in death as well as in life is, after all, her duty.'

'You people are ...'

Magdalena looked at Montagne, never had she known him be so angry. 'Dear Lord, let's have some more wine.' She topped up their glasses and settled back in her chair. 'We're not all bad, his majesty has sent to France for Doctor Montguyon. Queen Isabel will have her favourite doctor at her side before, during, and after the birthing. Now, what do you have to say about that?'

28

Two months had passed by so quickly, so easily, so happily. If the days became too hot there was the welcoming shade in the woods encircling the small palace, and the nights were always deliciously cool.

All had been well until this evening.

'How do you feel?' Philip returned the napkin to soak in the small bowl of iced lavender water. From the moment they had carried his wife to her bed he had not left her side, soothing her forehead or taking her hand in his. The pools of candlelight made the scene of husband comforting his delicate wife all the more touching.

'I fainted again, didn't I? You must find all this so tiresome. Is everything alright? The baby? What did Doctor Montguyon say?'

'Everything is fine he assures me. And so it should be we have followed each and every one of his or, should I say your mother's, instructions to the letter; and God knows the list was as long as my arm. I have to congratulate my Spanish doctors for holding their tongues throughout Montguyon's lecture as he poured scorn on their practices, rebuked them for their refusal to seek better remedies, their intolerance of innovation.'

'My mother had ten children, all safely delivered. We must take her vast experience into account.'

'Why do you take me so seriously? I have found some of your mother's advice to be exceptionally valuable, especially that regarding the second honeymoon. Have I not been the most loving and attentive husband?'

'You have. It has been a wonderful year. I never thought to be so happy. If it pleases God to take me from this world, I will be more than content to go having been loved so much.'

'My lady, we will have no talk of death.'

'It happens, we must be prepared. We all know of the dangers. I am no longer afraid, unlike when I had to make out my will.'

Despite all her dwarf's efforts to prepare her, to set her at her ease, it had still been an ordeal. Gone were his jokes, his sarcastic jibes at the stupid foreignness of the situation. All she could picture was her imminent death as she listened to a complete inventory of her belongings and how they were to be distributed; the futures of her ladies. Then when they got to the part detailing the directions for her funeral including her being robed in a Franciscan habit she was sick with fear. It was a death knell. She was so upset she had written to her mother about it who had taken no time at all in replying, unleashing her Medici wrath on Philip for daring to make his young wife read and sign such a document.

Philip brushed her cheek with his hand, 'You must stop concerning yourself with something that is no more than an age-old Spanish custom, simply a matter of form.' That was a complete lie and they both knew it; his masculine authority would have been undermined had she not conformed to something so crucial. 'What is far more important is that you are soon to be delivered of a healthy child; a boy. There are no complications; those one or two fainting spells are of no account; so no more pessimistic thoughts. We shall talk only of the days we have spent together.'

He had followed Catalina de Medici's instructions to the letter. He had devoted himself to ensuring his wife's happiness from the moment she returned to Spain. The several months of separation along with the directives from his mother-in-law and the even more important reproaches of Isabel de Osorio were all instrumental in the reforming of Philip. When at last he saw his wife step from her carriage he could have sworn he was in love. His new self saw her as a woman to be wooed, a beautiful lady whose heart he must conquer. From that day and for almost a year he had courted her, sought to please and delight her with gifts, excursions, banquets and balls. Even now he marvelled at his success in clinging so tenaciously and for so long to a role completely out of character. But he was tired of it all, it was too much of an effort and he doubted that he had the will to continue the charade.

'I wonder if your ambassador's reports to your mother will convince her to look favourably on this imperfect Spanish husband, who could never measure up to the high standards of the French.'

'You are unfair. My mother thinks of you as her dear son, whatever you may say.' She sought his eyes, a cherished favour allowed her these days, 'Philip do you remember that day in Aranjuez, the lazy ride along the river, then that quiet little

176

spot under the trees? It was so different, so special, just the two of us.'

'And about two dozen others.'

'They were all some distance away. You played with the curls at the nape of my neck, you cupped my face in your hands to kiss me. I still tremble remembering how you whispered in my ear, calling me your Helen of Troy and how you could imagine me in diaphanous robes tinted orange-gold by the sun setting behind me as I waited for you.'

For his part that vulgar episode was now closed. That kind of indulgence was unacceptable behaviour for a man and wife. The Church was emphatic in its condemnation.

He changed the subject. 'And then we danced. You are quite the best partner I have ever had.' It was just one more lie, for she could never equal Isabel de Osorio.

'Juana taught me.'

'I know; I used to watch you from the patio as you practised.'

'How wicked of you! Aah.' She pulled her hand from his to hold herself. 'It must be time. Oh, Philip, I am scared.'

'There is no need. San Eugenio has kept watch over you all these months and he will continue to intercede for you.'

Philip had complete faith in Holy relics. He was convinced that it was the bones of Fray Diego that had saved his son Carlos's life. Since the arrival of Eugenio's remains in Spain he had had Isabel on her knees for many an hour by the casket praying for the safe delivery of a boy, promising to name the child Eugenio.

And yet for all that Philip was anxious. Isabel had almost died two years ago with that unforgivable miscarriage. Not only did he need this son, he needed Isabel to survive to have other children, more sons. The useless Carlos and the arrogant Juan were ever present to add to his fears.

The room had filled with doctors, all come to deliberate anew their entrenched and incontrovertible opinions on procedure; still angered by Philip's insistence that the midwives and the interfering French doctor had precedence on this occasion simply to oblige the queen. It was a ridiculous state of affairs.

A priest entered bearing a cushion with an embroidered girdle laid over it.

'Your majesty, the girdle of the Holy Virgin Mary, as you requested.'

'Excellent; if you wear this, my dearest, there will be no problems with the birthing of our son.'

Isabel cried out her pain, her fears. Doctor Montguyon approached the bedside, 'My lady; your mother Queen Catalina has sent this elixir for the pains.'

'I knew she wouldn't be too far away; allow me.' Philip took the feeding cup and held it to Isabel's lips.

Two midwives behind their towers of folded white linens bustled over to a huge chest setting down their burdens before organising their territory ushering away any encroaching physician, directing a small army of servants with their pitchers of hot water and numerous bowls.

One of them eventually asked, 'Which method is it to be, your majesty?'

It was Isabel who had been asked but it was Philip who replied, 'In bed, it is by far the safest way according to everything I have read.'

'That is up to you, of course, but many prefer the chair,' the other midwife answered, shrugging her shoulders.

Philip's first wife had used the birthing chair. Carlos had not left his mother's womb until forcibly removed. He dared not allow Isabel to endure that ordeal nor suffer the same consequences; a damaged son and her death. He was convinced that it would be less dangerous for the child to be delivered in bed.

'Time for you to go.' The midwives, their sleeves rolled up, their formidable bare forearms folded, took up their positions by the bed.

'I leave you in safe hands.' Philip took a last look about the room. There lay the linens, there the swathing bands, and nearby the bowls of steaming water. Close to the fire stood the newly made crib with its hood of crimson brocade and golden fringe looking like a miniature tent, a safe haven following the battle which was soon to begin. And what if, at the end of the travails, there was no child to place on the feather mattress in the crib and no mother to stand watch over it?

He must be off to pray without delay. 'The doctors will keep me informed.' He patted her hand and was gone.

Isabel smiled submissively at her two midwives. They were now her mistresses; she the dutiful servant. Her mother had told her to have every confidence in midwives because they knew everything there was to be known about babies. She surrendered, willingly tolerating their embarrassing touching and examination of those most private parts of her body. She followed their series of orders as they guided her through the increasing contractions. She thanked them profusely as they massaged away the cramps in her thighs and calves.

'Doctor Montguyon, may I have more syrup?'

He guided the spout to her lips.

'A stick to bite on is all that is required in this country,' the impatient women muttered before unceremoniously pushing him back into the jumble of crowded black caps and gowns. 'Some strange ways you French have, my lady, but if it works, I suppose that's all that matters.'

If they only knew, Isabel thought, that in her mother's opinion it was the Spanish who had peculiar ways. Catalina de Medici also thought that Spanish doctors were no better than ignorant, uncouth beasts swollen with presumption and arrogance.

She heard herself giggling.

'It's good to have you so cheery, my lady.'

'It must be the syrup.' She blinked hard to refocus, 'I find it really funny watching you order these doctors about. My goodness, they intimidate me and I am the queen.'

'Well, you see, they don't have any part in this. Oh, they know what has to be done, sure enough, but they don't know how to do it,' answered one.

'Once the child is born, that is different, that's when they can bring all their vast learning to bear,' said the second woman winking at her colleague. 'They have to note down the sex, the weight, then judging by its colour and the strength of its wailing whether or not it's going to be healthy.'

Isabel was seized by an indescribable pain, she was being torn asunder. The midwives calmed her with heartening words and advice. There were further screams, hers, as she did her utmost to obey their every instruction. Then there was a moment of emptiness, of exhaustion, of silence, followed by the sound of a smack and a tiny but hearty wail. The infant was announcing its arrival. It was alive! Isabel in her lightheaded weariness congratulated herself; she had given Philip the longed-for heir. San Eugenio had answered her prayers after all. She was impatient to hold the baby.

The doctors surrounded it; weighing, measuring, conferring earnestly and learnedly.

At last the precious bundle was brought to her side.

179

'A healthy babe, and perfect in every way, my lady.' Doctor Montguyon presented the child lying naked in its little white sheet. Tiny arms and legs were flailing with anger, howls of fury vigorously demanding better from the world than an undignified slap on the backside.

'Here is your beautiful baby girl.'

Isabel gazed at this miracle of God's creation, and she wept.

29

'My lady, may I come in?'

At the far end of the room the Duquesa de Alba and her small company of ladies hearing the dwarf's voice looked up for a moment before returning to their needlework.

Isabel closed her book and put it down on the bed, 'Montagne, of course, do come in and please leave the door open. I would enjoy a change of air.'

'I thought you might care for some company while everyone is in the chapel. Here we are, the two outsiders; me, because I am too small and would only get in everyone's way as I struggled to find a place where I could see what was going on, you, well, you because you are not yet recovered from the childbed fever.' He studied the beautiful Isabel; her nightshift and gown of white silk and lace, the paleness of her face making her large brown eyes larger than ever, the waves of her dark hair carefully trained back and away from her face even more luxuriant.

'You know well enough that only a few days have passed since the birth of Clara and many more must pass before I am pure enough to enter a house of God.'

'You are as pure as the driven snow, as pure as those virgin drifts that lay in wait for us in the Pyrenees.'

Isabel smiled at the memory, 'I do believe you are still cross because I insisted we continued that journey. Imagine, that was seven years ago. Come sit beside me; tell me what is happening beyond my bedchamber.'

Montagne couldn't resist rocking the empty crib with its scarlet canopy and gold trimmings as he passed on his way to Isabel's bed. Then, with one foot on the rung of the bedside chair, he pushed himself onto the bed to sink into the deep down-filled cover. He sat with his legs crossed, observing the bed hangings and shaking his head. 'This is like a huge log fire with gold flames darting this way and that across all these red velvets. You must feel that you are being roasted alive.'

'Have no fear I have enough lavender water to dowse the fires if needed. So, Montagne, they are all gone?'

'Gone suggests a far greater distance than it actually is; from these apartments down to the chapel does not fall into the category of an expedition requiring intrepid travellers.'

'You mock; but oh, it would have been a different story if my baby was a boy. The baptism would have been in the Cathedral of Segovia at the very least, not a small private chapel. But I was delivered of a girl. Not for her the cheering crowds, the ambassadors, the papal legates, the grandees, the cities' representatives ...'

Montagne clapped his hands with their beringed stubby fingers, 'Just one moment my Lady Down-in-the-Mouth, I would have you know that his majesty has determined that nothing less than a papal nuncio shall perform the christening of Princess Isabel Clara Eugenia. Let me also remind you that there are princes, princesses, archdukes and two archbishops. When they return you will see how magnificently they have all dressed for the occasion.'

'It is still not the same.'

'You are right, of course. It was ever thus whether queen or dairymaid you will come second to king or cowherd, ladies always take second place. I might venture to suggest, were it not for my economy of height, that you are all of inferior quality.'

'Your lack of height is certainly compensated for by the liberality of your tongue.'

'The best way for me to get myself noticed; but where was I?'

'Speaking of all those at the ceremony. Who did his majesty choose to carry the princess?'

'Don Juan, although Prince Carlos is still to be the godfather.'

'And rightly so; the insult would be too great; poor Carlos. Philip was right, my baby would not have been safe; Carlos could so easily stumble. And there is the more serious question of his being left handed.'

Montagne snorted his disgust, 'Are you telling me that, with all the problems Carlos has, someone is going to be concerned at this deficiency?'

For a while there was nothing to say, and then Montagne burst into laughter, slapping his knees.

'Montagne this is no laughing matter.'

'No, but something else is. His Majesty King Philip of Spain at one time considered carrying the baby; in fact he was doing some serious practising.'

'Practising?'

'Yes, with one of your precious dolls. Magdalena Ruiz came upon him by accident, surprised him, leaving him spluttering and stammering, trying to excuse himself. Lord, but I would have loved to have been there to see the all-powerful master of half the world strolling up and down the room cradling a doll.'

Isabel giggled, 'Really, this is disrespectful, it is no laughing matter.' But it was, and she giggled and laughed until she was exhausted.

The ladies dropped their sewing, hands cupped over their mouths to stifle their giggles. Even the Duquesa de Alba, so arch, so correct, had to hide her face in her embroidery.

'Sadly, it was the gout in his majesty's hands that finally prevented him from performing the duty.'

'He does suffer so; it is very painful I am told.'

Montagne folded his arms across his chest. 'We shall, therefore, talk of something else. Don Juan has received a letter from Don Alessandro. Apparently he has singularly failed despite all his charms, of which he has many, to thaw the ice surrounding his wife who still prefers to spend her time memorising the scriptures or solving mathematical problems.'

'Never reading romances?'

'Perish the thought.'

'No games of chance with cards or dice?'

'Heaven forefend that such an evil would dare intrude into the life of one so upright.'

'Then our Alessandro, prince of Parma will sorely miss the company of Juan, and perhaps ourselves.'

'I am sure Don Juan will tell you more. But here is more news for your delectation – such a big word for so small a person – *La Eboli's* father is about to remarry. That will fair ruffle her fine feathers.'

Isabel wagged a warning finger, 'I know what it is like to see one's mother cruelly betrayed and scorned by one's father.'

Montagne brushed that aside. 'You will like this part. She is so damnably conceited strutting her superiority as a Mendoza y Cerda; but, if her father sires a son her inheritance, all those fortunes, will go flying out of the window to a cradle far away. I can only repeat, you ladies are ...'

'Yes, quite; but my goodness Ana would not take kindly to that.'

'Nor will she be best pleased with another lady who is about to knock her off her perch of importance, this time in her beloved home of Pastrana,'

'Gómez is not about to leave her for another? You know my feelings on infidelity, and her spirits must already be very low having just lost her baby in childbirth.'

'I would never jest on such serious matters; no, the lady in question is of the Church.'

'A Jesuit like Princess Juana?'

'A nun, a Carmelite nun, a barefooted nun, a fanatical reformer. Ah, but here comes the christening party.' Montagne slid from the bed.

King Philip led the small but glittering party into the bedchamber. He was followed by Carlos and Juana, then Juan carrying the child in its frothy layers of lace, then the papal nuncio, and finally Ruy Gómez.

'You have been entertained in our absence.'

'Yes, my lord, Montagne never fails. Juan, bring Clara here for a moment before she is returned to her cradle.' Isabel kissed the plump little cheeks, caressed the tiny pouting lower lip so like her father's. 'Sleep on my little darling, no doubt you will let us know when you are hungry. Juana, will you take her?'

Juana placed Clara in the cradle and the wet nurse positioned herself close by in readiness.

Isabel was impatient to hear more news of Parma, 'Juan, Montagne tells me you have heard from Alessandro.'

'My lady, he sends you his warmest regards and congratulations. He prays that God will look as favourably on his wife when she is brought to her childbed.' He chuckled, 'I hope he lives long enough to see a child of his own.'

King Philip was quick to question, 'I hope there is nothing serious hidden behind your laughter?'

'Alessandro says that he is so bored by his far too cosy hearth with nothing more than a ticking clock for company that he has taken to going out at night with hat pulled down over his ears the collar of his cloak pulled up to meet it and his sword at the ready.'

The ladies gasped.

'This is reckless behaviour.'

'I think not, my lord, I doubt if anyone could better him. In truth I think his words are a plea to be returned to the court here and thence on to some real fighting, for you and Spain. The idle life is not for him.'

Carlos stammered, 'M-m-my feelings exactly; just like me, twenty years old and with nothing to do. I say he must return immediately, we need him, I need him.'

'I will order his return as and when it is necessary. The matter is closed.'

'It is always the same; you refuse to listen to anybody's requests for something to do; Juan's, Alessandro's, and especially mine.'

Isabel hurriedly moved on to her next piece of gossip. 'What is this story about a nun going to Pastrana?'

The papal nuncio's ears pricked up.

Juana smiled and shook her head, 'I have met her; a most odd person, not one to be deterred by anyone no matter how great or powerful. Isabel; she sees it as God's express wish that she reform the Carmelite order, that they return to the old ways of solitude and abstinence. She will not suffer anyone to stand in her way.'

The nuncio raised his hand to interrupt, 'That gadabout woman; Teresa of Avila she calls herself. Your majesty she is a nuisance, causing consternation wherever she goes.'

'With respect,' now it was Gómez who interrupted, 'I found her to be a most sincere and obviously devout lady; and yes I have offered her a building in Pastrana for her small group of nuns. The bishop has given his permission for this new order of barefooted Carmelites.'

The nuncio grasped at his pectoral cross to help control his frustration, 'Permission? He would be only too eager to see the back of her!'

'If it were up to me,' Juana continued, 'I would give her my unreserved support. To return to a life free of all luxuries, temptations, to concentrate wholeheartedly on contemplation, the desire to follow in Christ's footsteps ...'

'Aunt Juana!' Carlos tried to sound shocked, 'You sound like you want to join them. But then what would you do without your jewels? You could give them all to me, I suppose. Does this mean you finally have given up the idea of wanting to be my wife? You would go with my blessing.'

Isabel laughed a loud nervous laugh, 'But this is becoming all too serious. I had only a passing interest. Obviously there are some who consider her as something quite out of the ordinary and I mean more than her not wearing shoes.'

185

Philip who had kept his own counsel throughout silently agreed that Teresa of Avila was indeed someone quite extraordinary. In the first instance, when she met his sister Juana she had dared to say that she could not spare the time to come to see him, and he the most powerful sovereign in Christendom and she unable to afford anything more than a worn and patched habit! When Juana had told him of their meeting she had then handed him a letter from the nun. The handwriting was a disgrace, worse than his and he at least had an excuse with his gout. But the contents had unsettled him; in her misspelled scrawl she had let him know that God had revealed all his darkest secrets.

He didn't like being reminded of that, it scared him.

30

Alba decided that the open door to Philip's office provided the frame to a portrait with the seated King Philip behind his littered desk its subject. The late morning sun stole over his shoulders, throwing the shadow of his quill over the minute annotations scratched in the margins of reports.

It was a gentle Madrid springtime sunshine spreading its friendly warmth, and with no hint that very soon it would begin its aggressive summer onslaught on the city.

Alba announced his presence with a polite cough.

'Come in Alba, just the person I wanted to see.' The delivery was flat, suiting Alba's earlier image perfectly. 'I needed to have a word with you. After long and careful deliberation, I have decided to send you to the Low Countries.'

'My lord? I understood you were planning on going there yourself, taking Prince Carlos with you.'

'Not exactly planning, more of a passing thought, and just as well considering his growing determination to remain there as governor; and he is also insisting we meet his Cousin Anne thinking it a forgone conclusion that they will marry. He has sent her a diamond ring as some kind of pledge.'

'Would that be such a bad thing, their marriage?'

'If Carlos marries anyone it will be my sister. I have also decided that Anne should marry my nephew Sebastian. A union with Portugal is desirable.'

'And if you were to go alone?'

'Exactly what the Cortes suggested, leaving Carlos here as regent. That would be irresponsible. Fortunately Carlos played into my hands; he convened a secret meeting with them. He reminded the members of their earlier interference in suggesting he marry Juana and let them know in no uncertain terms that he would not tolerate any further intrusions on his plans. He had every intention of going to the Low Countries and would be obliged if they minded their own business. So there you are, I cannot take him with me and dare not leave him here. There you have it; you are the one to go.'

'With respect, a man in his sixtieth year may not be the best to be entrusted with this mission.'

'It is not your age that is of significance, it is your conviction, your dedication to protecting the faith.'

'To serve God and yourself are my greatest honours, but would it still not be better if you, the monarch were there to put the rebels in their place?'

'Who would I leave here as regent?' There was still no emotion.

'Her Majesty, Queen Isabel, without question.'

'Indeed, Alba, without question?'

'Queen Isabel was most impressive in Bayonne, a damned good match for her mother.'

'Was she now? Or was that, shall we say a performance? You see, I have been thinking a lot lately about Isabel, and her mother, and France. The peace we have with that country is very tenuous. Catalina and Isabel write lengthy epistles to each other; many in code; and I worry.'

'My lord, my ears must be deceiving me. You are not seriously suggesting some form of conspiracy; that they might be in league against Spain?'

'Surely not too much of a surprise; it cannot have passed your notice that she was raised in a French environment of distrust and belligerence towards our nation.'

'You must pardon me if I come to her majesty's defence. Leaving to one side the peace treaty you signed with France when you married, my Lady Isabel is your devoted and obedient wife.'

Philip threw down his pen in disgust leaving an ugly black splattered trail over someone's carefully prepared report. All he had had from this devoted wife was a daughter. He was still burdened with the inept Carlos, and only recently he had had to sever relations with the Vatican because the Pope continued with his refusal to make Juan a cardinal.

He had so desperately needed to have Juan distanced from the admiring hearts and minds of his countrymen, and this would have been the first move in his overall plan to rid himself of the man and the threat he posed.

Alba continued his defence of Isabel. 'She has given you a beautiful and healthy daughter and is again with child. I repeat that for seven years she has been your dutiful consort, attending banquets, balls, giving alms and comfort to the poor; fulfilling all her duties perfectly. Is she to stand accused and condemned because of her lasting close and loving relationship with her mother who happens to be the regent of France?'

188

'I do not say that she definitely is a spy,' Philip shocked himself as much as Alba by voicing the allegation, but continued, 'however this closeness must pose a risk. There could be a conflict of loyalties. And something else I want you to consider; she is forever urging a marriage contract between her sister Margot and Carlos. I believe that Catalina de Medici hopes that with this marriage she will become the power behind our Spanish throne. Isabel, knowingly or not, is her accomplice.'

'I think not. Catalina seeks nothing more than to make the best provision for her children; family pride.'

'She thirsts for power!'

'Do you have any grounds for suspicion? Dear God but it pains me to be talking like this about the queen.'

'At present I have no proof, but then that could be because I never allow her into the council chamber. At the moment all she hears is inconsequential gossip. Now, if I were to go to the Netherlands leaving her here on her own as regent, she would be privy to all state matters. Now do you appreciate my problem?'

'I cannot, will not, believe her capable of any disloyalty. This is a grave injustice.'

Philip was beginning to feel unwell; his bowels were objecting to the world of problems. 'Enough, the discussion is closed. You will go to Brussels. I have written to the governor to send for German troops to assist you. On another matter, one which should please you, I have appointed your friend as secretary to work alongside Pérez.'

'At least that is pleasing news. God knows that young Pérez disturbs me. If he is not being obsequious he is the reverse, arrogant and ill-mannered, even insolent. He has far too much money and he spends it like water. He is neither averse to using bribery nor being bribed. And what about the rumours of his not doing the honourable thing by the mother of his child? And there are those disgusting orgies involving young boys.'

Philip laughed; how he relished the overt hatred between the Alba and Gómez factions. 'I had gathered you held little affection for Gómez's man which is why I am employing your friend. At the same time I hope that Pérez will measure up to the high standards set by his father. That is all for now, you may go. You will have much to organise for your departure.'

'Your majesty,' Alba bowed. As he walked down the corridor he growled to himself, 'I would much rather stay here to protect my Lady Isabel. And as for that damned Pérez; a

Gómez man through and through. Unfortunately I will not be here to prevent his politicking. Hopefully the disreputable young pup will be held in check by my man. I pray Philip will not be made to regret this decision ... Ah! Good day Gómez. Not looking too happy this beautiful morning.'

'Might I suggest you look far from pleased; my discontent stems from my charge and never knowing what he is going to do next, and yours?'

'It would seem we each have a cross to bear, no doubt you will soon discover mine. Adieu.'

'Good morning, your majesty. I just passed Alba; I must say he was looking rather miserable.' Gómez was feeling much happier having noted Alba's disgruntled mood.

'I am sending troops into the Netherlands and he is to lead them,' Philip's voice had resumed its expressionless tone.

'I beg to suggest that that will cause more difficulties than you already have. Allow me to go there to negotiate. I have never disappointed you.' He desperately wanted to be away from the violent young prince in his care, wanted to play a role far more suited to his talents.

'Out of the question.'

'Feria could take over the responsibilities of the household.'

'No, Feria needs to visit to his home whenever he wishes. I promised him that when he returned to court. In any case I need your watchful eye on Carlos.' Philip studied the man he had successfully cut down to size. Long gone were the days when he was nicknamed King Gómez because of his power and influence.

'There must be someone else who could carry out these duties equally as well.'

'You are the best, the only one in whom I have complete confidence. I cannot possibly replace you.'

'Prince Carlos has sworn that I will live to regret being his governor or, more exactly, being your spy.'

'My spy? I suppose you are. Let me assure you that eventually you will be well rewarded.' Philip had an important role for him, the plans were taking shape, but it would not be for a while yet. 'Your weekly report?'

'The prince threatened to kill the president of the council; he was discovered holding a dagger to the man's throat and had to be forcibly restrained.'

'Dear God,' he swallowed hard, he could feel a bilious attack brewing to add to his already disturbed bowels. 'What was his reason?'

'The president refused to allow a lewd actor to perform.'

'I shall apologise to the president; anything else?'

'There have been complaints from several distraught ladies-in-waiting. I insisted the prince meant no dishonour and that I would make every effort to see that it would not happen again.'

'What this time?'

Gómez had to fight to keep a straight face; if it were not so serious a matter it would be comedy straight from a playhouse. 'He grabbed them forcibly kissed them then shouted, *kiss me, you whore!*'

'I despair. On another topic, I have appointed young Antonio Pérez as my secretary.'

'An excellent choice.'

'I think so, too. Let us hope he will be as good as his father,' he gave Gómez the briefest of quizzical looks. 'Well then, you may go. I hope Carlos has not caused further problems in your absence.'

'We all do. It is very difficult for his servants to know how much force they may use to protect either themselves or others from the actions of someone who is the heir to the throne.'

'That is precisely why you are the head of his household. You have full authority to make whatever decisions are necessary. Good day, Gómez.'

'My lord.' He bowed. He was furious. He wanted to go to Brussels, to be rid of all this nursemaid business. In Brussels he could have proved himself indispensable to his king. On a more positive note Alba might be killed while fighting in the Low Countries thereby opening a door for his own re-entry into court. The appointment of Antonio Pérez as secretary was excellent news and brought cheer and consolation. Pérez was to be Philip's right hand man. Pérez was his supporter. He was much, much more; Pérez was family. His cross, as Alba would have it, had suddenly become lighter.

King Philip returned to the papers on his desk. He picked up his quill, dipped it in the ink then paused to congratulate himself, 'I gave both Alba and Gómez a bitter pill, but I gilded them nicely. Yes, I think I have handled a difficult situation rather well.' His inner churnings had all but abated.

31

Juana strolled up and down the queen's private salon unable to sit idle a moment longer. Her frustration was increasing by the minute; the green wall hangings were beginning to annoy, to say nothing of the paintings which were all well and good in a chapel but not here. Isabel, she observed, was obviously content to sit forever, enthralled by yet another French Romance where no doubt some chivalrous hero rode through the pages on one or other extravagant adventure never failing to stir the heart of a young maid or goddess.

There had been little conversation this morning, the atmosphere was as quiet and strained as so many were these days, as they had been for the last six, seven, perhaps eight months. Winter had come and gone and so had much of spring without Isabel seeming to notice. It was only when Juan or Carlos came to visit that she brightened.

Juana knew some of the reasons for Isabel's low spirits and guessed at others. She looked at her sister, still so young, only twenty-one, and yet weighed down by melancholy, any love and joy in her life being found only in the written word. The sparkle seemed to have gone from her soul as well as from those huge dark eyes. At least today she had not returned to her bed which was something to be thankful for.

Retracing her steps for the third or fourth time a small portrait on a side table caught her attention, 'May I?'

Isabel raised her head and put down her book. She came to join her, moving slowly as though hindered by her black velvet dress with its heavily embroidered blue sleeves, weighed down by the loops of her broad gold chains encrusted with pearls and amethysts.

'My mother is as beautiful as ever; you can see that, although I think the artist has not done her justice.' Isabel handed her the portrait, 'Please, do take a closer look.'

'At last; here we have a smile. This is the first I have seen in a long time.' Juana studied the likeness of Catalina de Medici. 'I see you have inherited your mother's good looks. This is the same shaped face, nose, lips and eyebrows. It is uncanny, it is you but much older. It is only in the colour of hair and the eyes where there is a difference.' She turned to Isabel, 'Let me see you smile that I might compare.'

It was impossible. Instead Isabel took the miniature portrait of her mother pressing it to her lips, crying.

'Oh, Isabel no more weeping; you have no reason for tears. I should be the one to cry. You have a mother I do not for mine died when I was a little girl. My husband died within weeks of our son's birth, your husband still lives. I had to leave my young baby in Portugal when I was recalled to Spain; you have your enchanting daughter Clara Eugenia at your side whenever you wish. My child is thirteen years old and I haven't seen him since he was a babe in arms. Now be honest with me, which of us has the right to shed tears?'

Isabel dabbed at her reddened eyes with the finest of linen handkerchiefs, toyed with its lace border then took a deep breath, sighing. 'Perhaps you are right. Perhaps I am indulging myself; one of the luxuries of being with child.' She ran her hands down over the bulge that told of her fifth month of pregnancy. 'Perhaps if I had been given more time to recover my health after Clara's birth I would feel stronger and not weep so readily. Yet that isn't the problem. If I could only be sure that Philip cared for me, has pardoned me for giving him a daughter instead of a son.'

'Of course he cares, he loves you!' Juana gave it every ounce of conviction she could muster, knowing this to be untrue. He probably never had loved her even during those strange days almost two years ago at Aranjuez and Segovia when he had behaved no better than a plebeian showering Isabel with his attentions, playing the gallant, the lover. In any case it was not one of the prerequisites for marriage. The world was not ideal like those found in the books Isabel chose to read filling her head with impossible notions and foolish ideas regarding the ideal gentleman.

'I have caused him shame. Girls are inferior; they are a weakness in a family.'

'I refuse to allow you to say that! Where would the world be without us?'

'I cannot argue with such logic,' she smiled a little smile, returning the portrait to the table then turning over a piece of paper to hide its scribbles and crossings out. 'So, what shall we do today? I refuse to play any more card games, watch puppet plays or comedies. I believe Philip sends the entertainers here to ensure that I am kept out of his way.'

'Nonsense, it is because he knows you enjoy them, and the games of chance.' Another untruth had escaped her. She knew, in fact everyone in the court knew that her brother grew colder by the day. Isabel was right, she had failed her husband, had failed the king, by not providing an heir.

'Shall we walk along the gallery?' The words had come surprisingly from Isabel.

'Hurrah! I thought we were never to set foot outside this room.'

They walked along the wide corridor, giving only the merest of glances at the paintings, tapestries and statues; all chosen by Philip.

The doors were opened for them to pass through and Isabel led the way along the gallery and down the steps into a sunny morning. They breathed in the warmth and freshness of early June.

Her thoughts flew back to those days in Aranjuez before they could be stopped. They still continued to torment her with remembered scenes of blissful times when Philip would enfold her in his arms, or charm her with his laughter, and be so gentle in their lovemaking.

Following the birth of Clara everything had changed. She now saw Philip only on timetabled occasions. She submitted to his sexual demands as if by royal command. These were scheduled for either late in the evening or in the early hours of the morning. The painful businesslike process was quietly endured.

Oh yes, he had made a great public show of his delight when he was told that she was once more carrying his child, but since then he had been formally polite, nothing more.

'Shall we go to the gardens, Isabel? We could search out some arbours to provide refuge during the summer, for it appears we are to remain in Madrid this year.'

'Is that so? Why have I not been told?'

'Surely an oversight.'

'It seems that while Philip has every confidence in you he has little or none in me. But look, we have visitors. Juana, after so long, we have visitors!' She stretched out her arms to welcome Carlos, 'You have been neglecting us. Juan we are cross with you too, imagine your wanting to desert us for some unknown beauty. We expect apologies from you both. I tease you Carlos; I know you have been ill again. Oh, but it is so good to see you!'

She took his hands; his cold, wet, shaking hands. She smiled into eyes set sad and deep in an unhealthy, pallid face.

'I-I-I bring more than apologies, I bring gifts, so you will have to forgive me.'

'You are far too generous. Indoors, everyone; Carlos you must accompany me.' She was worried. Carlos was exhausted from doing no more than walk from his apartments. 'Cool drinks,' she ordered in the general direction of several attendants.

Isabel's step had lightened and quickened and she had to pause from time to time for Carlos to keep pace with her. His back was more twisted and stooped than ever, his leg more loath to do his bidding, and he had lost so much weight. She couldn't help but compare him with the handsome gallant who escorted Juana. He had grown taller and sturdier.

It was a strange world she thought; while it blessed Juan with every favourable attribute Carlos had been denied everything, except the throne of the most powerful country in Europe.

32

Refreshing drinks of lemon and lime were served.

'Everyone must sit down.' Isabel was conscious of her own energy disappearing fast, her burst of enthusiasm on seeing her friends and all the excitement of surprise gifts had drained her.

The impatient Carlos unable to delay a moment longer unceremoniously thrust a red velvet box into her hands. 'T-t-tell me you like it.'

Nestled inside on a satin cushion was a ruby ring, charming in its simplicity, 'You spoil me. This is beautiful. See, Juana, how lovely it is. Carlos, I cannot thank you enough.'

'But there is more. Where are the damned – forgive me – where are the wretched men? Go look, Juan.' He would have preferred to have gone himself to make sure they were suitably punished but it would have taken too long. 'Blasted leg,' he cursed, 'blasted servants.'

Isabel forced a giggle. 'We are so alike. You remind me of myself at Christmas time, always so desperate to open my gifts, frustrated at having to wait for others.'

'Really Isabel? You know you are the only person I know who admits to having faults, even little ones like yours. That is why you are my best friend. You are a friend, too, Aunt Juana, but Isabel is really quite special.'

Juana groaned inwardly at this man in his mid twenties sounding not unlike a seven-year-old.

Eventually a line of servants brought coarse linen bundles into the room.

'Set them down, quickly. Unwrap them. Why is it taking you so long? You're all useless. A good beating would speed you up.'

'Carlos.' Isabel took his hand to calm him.

'I can't wait to see your face.'

Bolts of silk were finally rolled free of the linen. There was her gift; yards and yards of it in exquisite shimmering blue and white. 'Blue skies and milk-white clouds, and here are even better clouds. Hurry, you dolts,' he clapped his hands in exasperation, furious at having to wait for servants to bring in six very large and very plump white floor cushions. You can sit on your clouds in your own little heaven.'

'Why, everything is quite exquisite!' Isabel was touched. Here was another demonstration of his affection, of his determination to please, and from a tragic prince more disposed to dispensing violence and hatred.

She was delighted to think that the green wall hangings might soon be gone for good, and what an ideal opportunity to be rid of those portraits of saints, their self-righteous eyes raised heavenwards, their martyrs' palms held with such overbearing arrogance across their breasts. But would Philip give his permission? Sadly, despite all her plans and schemes she had never been allowed any opinion regarding the decoration of her apartments.

There were shrieks of laughter as Isabel tried unsuccessfully to direct her friends to the best places to drape the shining lengths. Carlos stood precariously first on chairs then on chests and tables setting free blue waterfalls of silk. Juan and Juana wrapped themselves in togas of white silk to deliver addresses of homage to imagined gods and goddesses of these wondrous cascades.

They finally collapsed into chairs, Juana gasping, 'How is it that I am so easily persuaded against my better judgement to do such outrageous things?'

Juan was first to recover, 'I have brought a gift, but mine is quite ordinary. I bring flowers for the two most charming ladies in Spain.' Summoned by his call, servants entered with small tubs of pink rose plants.

'But they are lovely! We shall find somewhere special for them then Juana and I can visit them every day. Actually, Philip will know where best to plant them, he is an expert when it comes to gardens.'

'Oh God, he thinks he is expert at everything,' Carlos sneered. 'But let me tell you this, I am an expert too. I got the money for these gifts by tricking a merchant into lending me lots and lots which he couldn't afford, and which I shall never be able to pay back. Rather clever, eh?'

Isabel quietly reminded him that what he had done was deceitful, insisting he sought the man's forgiveness, and to do his utmost to repay him.

'I know, I know, but I could not resist asking for so much when he bragged that he was so rich I could borrow any amount I required. Anyway he ran off whimpering to Gómez who will have told the king by now, no doubt taking delight in giving every little detail just like that other swine did.'

'Who was that, not more trouble?' Isabel dreaded further confrontations, a deepening animosity, between father and son. 'You must try not to cause problems for yourself.'

'I do, believe me. Anyway on that occasion it was his fault, not mine. He tried to stop me listening through the keyhole to what was being said in the council chamber. In the first place I should have been in there taking part, because it was about the Netherlands and I shall be going there soon. Secondly, it was none of his damned business what I happened to be doing. The insolent beggar told me it was bad manners and a terrible example to the servants. I mean to say, I just had to punish him for daring to speak to me in such a way, so I punched him in the face. Well, he told the king and you can imagine the rest. No matter; now I want to see my godchild, my Clara Eugenia.'

'She is in the next room. Let us go together.'

Isabel watched him grab his thigh to urge the virtually useless leg forward to take him to Clara, the leg that had prevented him from carrying her to the christening. Philip had denied him the honour, justifiably, but it had been yet another public humiliation for Carlos.

Where was it all going to end? Would Philip listen to her if she were to raise the issue of a marriage between Carlos and her sister Margot? If Carlos did have a wife they were bound to see a big change for the better.

High pitched giggling and an infant's babbling released Juana and Juan from a silence that both were uncertain they dared break.

Juana took the lead, challenging, 'You told a little white lie when you called us the two most charming ladies in Spain.'

'Why? What have you heard?' He reddened.

'That there is another most charming lady, a beauty who has stolen your heart.'

'Who told you?'

'Ana, the Princess of Eboli.'

'Dear God in Heaven. Do many others know?' He looked towards the door, dreading he might discover a witness standing there.

'Fortunately only a few, and they know how to keep their counsel, and I told Ana that she must on no account speak of it to anyone else. So, what is she like, this *petite amour*?' Juana barely disguised her anger.

'She is far from that. I love her dearly. She is a distant relative of Ana's; distant and poor.'

While Juana might abhor Ana and anyone connected with that lady, it was a relief to hear about this relationship, whatever its nature. She had been plagued for months by the fact that Juan and Isabel were far too friendly, fearful that she might uncover some unthinkable intimacy, that they were lovers.

'I see. I expect her family hoped that by placing her in Ana's court she would find a rich husband. My goodness, imagine their delight when they discover just how marvellous a catch she has made.'

Juan found her insinuations and sarcasm offensive, 'That is unfair. It's not like that at all. As I said, I love her dearly. Nor did it take long for me to discover her true beauty,' he threw back at her, 'something which many ladies lack; honesty. I tell you I wish for nothing more than to be able to make her my wife, but as you know that would be impossible. His Majesty would not countenance such a contract. In fact I believe he will never allow me to marry. If he should hear of this; well, God knows what the consequences might be. He has never truly forgiven me for my efforts to be involved against the Turk.'

'You cannot blame the king's wrath when you positively invited it through your own wilful behaviour; you had been forbidden.'

'Perhaps, but I have never sought to conceal my desire to be a soldier; I have always longed to fight for Spain. King Philip knew that before he ever met me. A part of me still insists that he was being unreasonable in not giving his permission. Nor am I the first to run away to join the army; and I am twenty-two! However, I returned and apologised. I was forgiven, or so he said, but not before suffering the shame of having all my defects made public, and with Eboli and Alba sitting there so virtuous.'

The image would never be erased. When Juan had entered the audience chamber Philip had turned aside ignoring his formal bow, refusing to offer the royal hand for the obligatory kiss. Remaining seated and as still and cold as the statues arranged along the sides of the room he had icily delivered a detailed list of all Juan's failings, and all from memory.

'Something you should have considered before taking the decision to dash off? The king was more than likely angered by your selfishness.'

'Do you think I am selfish?'

'No more than any of us, but you never stopped to concern yourself about those who love you. It was right that you should be reminded.'

'It was far more than a reminder.' He could well sympathise with Carlos and the many times he had been subjected to such humiliation, could understand in some way his desire to retaliate. 'King Philip dragged up my continued refusal to be a priest, citing every instance from when I was eight years old to the present. Juana, I am not made to be a priest. He said I had shown little regard for everything he had done for me, gravely disappointed that I must have forgotten that he had been generous to a fault; grieved that I had no sense of obligation that I was not anxious to do anything he desired and without question. He said I wanted to be a soldier because I was nothing more than a glory seeker!' He threw out his arms inviting her sympathy, her support, but she would not be drawn.

'That is all history. I am more interested in the present. What are your plans for the lady you would so dearly like to marry?'

'Maria and I have made our vows to one another, and that is enough to make us man and wife in the eyes of God; and we have made arrangements for the birth of our child.'

'Child? Dear God, I had no idea things had gone so far.'

'Maria will soon be going to live with her family until the child is born then she will return, alone, to her cousin. It is imperative that all this is kept secret, the king must never know. Blast Ana for being so loose tongued!'

'How little you know the lady. She took great delight in informing me of your liaison. However, my lips are sealed.'

This was a secret that must never be divulged beyond the very few. The ramifications of the situation made her head spin. This handsome, intelligent and most popular prince, half-brother to herself and the king, had sired a bastard child, but a child nonetheless. Unless something miraculous was to happen with Carlos, Juan could become an even stronger challenger for the throne. He would, more than like, make a fine monarch; one with an heir. There was also the possibility that Carlos may not have many years to live, his fevers were becoming more frequent and increasingly debilitating. Isabel had so far only produced girls, the aborted twins and Clara, the little chatterbox next door. She prayed that God would grant Isabel a son and that Juan's child was a girl. She stopped;

shocked that she was so easily and readily turning Juan from cherished relative to scheming usurper.

Carlos appeared in the doorway with Clara following, now on all fours, now shuffling along on her bottom. She stopped to clap her hands, happy to see her Aunt Juana and Uncle Juan.

Juan laughed at the small bundle of white speckled with numerous black brooches. 'She looks like some kind of pudding thought up by a cook with thoughts of winter. What on earth is that all about?'

'You will discover soon enough when you have children of your own,' Isabel was most serious, 'that there is nothing quite so effective as jet for warding off the evil eye. That explains the brooches and buttons on her pinafore.'

'Don't embarrass the poor man; he is too young and innocent. See how he blushes.'

Juan squatted beside the little bundle that dribbled from a wet mouth with four of the smallest teeth he had ever seen. He looked up at Carlos, 'Carlos, here are pearls far superior to any gift we could offer.'

Clara, in recognition of the compliment beamed wider and wetter than ever setting them all laughing.

'A most charming scene,' Philip announced closing the door behind him and going directly to his precious daughter to lift her and plant a kiss on each cheek.

A loud and liquid response of, 'Pa - Pa - Pa,' was enough to set them all laughing again.

Philip turned to Isabel. 'You are in better spirits today. That pleases me.' He handed Clara to her nurse then strode to the table and the portrait of Catalina de Medici without acknowledging the others' presence. 'Is this a good likeness of your mother? It is very like you; the nose, the lips.' He shuffled the papers lying in disarray about the portrait.

Carlos had limped his way to look at the miniature. 'Isabel she is almost as beautiful as you.' Suddenly he grabbed Philip's wrist, 'Sir, those are my lady's papers you are reading. Put them down, they are private.'

Philip freed his wrist without effort, 'Nothing is kept from a king's eyes. Ah, Isabel, I see you have been writing poems again. How very dreary these are. Perhaps after today's visitors you may find a more cheery topic for your verse.'

'M-my Lady Isabel is made to spend too much time on her own, and that causes her to be sad. That is why Juan and I come as often as we can. Today I have brought her gifts to make her happy. See, beautiful silks for the walls.'

'I was unaware that new wall hangings were necessary. The green is entirely adequate.'

'My lord husband, we thought that the blue and white would be like the welcoming morning sky. It would bring me great pleasure,' her voice trembled.

'We, as in just the two of us, will discuss that later. And as for you, young sir, I can imagine where the money came from for so extravagant a gift.'

'You know exactly where the money came from because that bastard Gómez, your spy, told you.'

'Either moderate your language or leave the room.'

'Believe me I was planning on leaving the moment you entered. But before I go I want to suggest that you visit your stable soon, to look in on your favourite horse. A little surprise awaits you. It might persuade you not to grant Gómez so much power over me for I am beginning to find it tiresome.' He bowed. 'Juan, are you coming?'

'I must first give Clara this tambourine. This comes from your adoring Uncle Juan with all his love. I wish I could have stayed longer to appreciate the music.'

Clara took the tiny tambourine, and was about to deliver it to her waiting mouth until interrupted by the jingling of the rings.

Carlos and Juan left the room played out by the little musician.

'I, too, cannot stay. I came only to say that we will lunch together.' He could have added that he had also come to see what Carlos was doing, having been informed of his presence here and not trusting him for a moment.

The two ladies were alone once more.

Isabel picked up the paper where she had laid her heart bare in a few brief lines, and which Philip had so cruelly criticised. 'Juana, what have I done to be treated this way, as if I were no more than a stranger, an unwanted visitor?'

'You are being too sensitive; your pregnancy is making you think this way. It is not Philip's intention to be unkind. May I see your poems?'

Isabel handed her the lines that declared her unhappiness, the words now cruelly tarnished by Philip's criticism.

Juana read:
My eyes fill with tears of sorrow and laughter,
My very last tears will be those of a martyr.
Tears harm the heart that is happiness led,
But to the unhappy they are almost as bread.

Clara in her nurse's arms burbled, delighting in her new toy. Juana drew the weeping Isabel close to hug and comfort her.

33

'My lord and brother,' Juana curtsied before moving across the room to kiss the royal hand. Magdalena Ruiz made sure the door to the king's private salon was firmly closed then she and her marmosets stood guard. For her this was a most satisfactory arrangement; she would deter any visitors who might interrupt the proceedings whilst undoubtedly enjoying some useful gossip.

'Sweet sister, what have you discovered?' From the moment Juana had told him of their brother's sordid affair Philip had visited the nearby church almost daily to pray to San Isidro. He had every faith in the saint who years ago had delivered him and his mother from the jaws of death and was quietly confident that Isidro would guide him safely through this mess. For good measure he had also prayed to a selection of the hundreds of holy relics he was steadily amassing in the castle. His collection boasted numerous fragments of the True Cross; several thorns from Christ's crown; a variety of bones, strands of hair, and hearts of holy men; several entire bodies waiting to be finally raised to the ranks of the Blessed.

'It is true; the person in question is with child.'

'Dear God in Heaven!' He was furious, he was jealous, he was afraid. 'So, there may well be an additional challenge to the throne. Why did our father not leave Juan in Germany, consigned to obscurity along with his tavern singer mother?'

'Quite probably because our father was old, unable to resist a sentimental urge; many of his decisions at that time were highly suspect. Or was it because the child was a boy? Be that as it may, Juan has got this woman pregnant.'

'Why, in God's name, did Ana not put a stop to the relationship?'

Magdalena was moved to voice her opinions on Ana, the Princess of Eboli, on her desperate need to be returned to the inner circles of power. If the young couple were to marry she would then be related to the king's half brother and with her innate aptitude for scheming the political world would be at her feet.

Philip raised his hand to ward off any interruption and continued, 'Juan is such a young fool; whatever made him frequent the house of the *Celestina?*'

Juana was swift to reply, 'For the same reason you visited the Madame's house in Brussels, and from where at least one young lady was obliged to leave rather hurriedly and secretly.'

Philip began to feel twinges of something resembling guilt; had God told that nun about those nights when he and Gómez went out into the streets of Brussels to seek their pleasure? But there was no guilt, he could justify his actions. 'The difference, dear sister, is that kings have a special license for affairs. Nor was I setting a precedent within the family.'

'Weak and lame excuses; but let us turn to some better news I have for you. There is no possibility of their marrying. This is a certainty; the girl is of *infected blood*.'

'You know this to be a fact? I thought she was a Mendoza, of the same family as Ana. I understood her to be a cousin.'

'My informers have been very busy and finally they unearthed the truth of the matter. It dates back several generations. It is an undeniable fact that this Maria's side of the family tried, by taking only the name of the Old Christian parent and ignoring the tainted parent, to obliterate all traces of Israel.'

A cough escaped Magdalena at her post at the door, followed by muttered names of others whose families had sought to hide their origins including a certain Eufrasia, one of his recent mistresses.

Philip ignored her and was about to make some critical racial remarks of his own regarding this deceitful practice when he was checked by an image of his beautiful Isabel de Osorio. Her forbears had done exactly the same, had sought to conceal their Jewish blood. And did the nun know of these transgressions too? He was becoming increasingly angry with Juan who was forcing him to face his own transgressions. 'You must congratulate your researchers. It is a great comfort knowing that Juan and Maria cannot marry, at least that is one less threat to contend with; now to the child.'

'Hardly a threat; you exaggerate. As to the child, Juan said that Maria was returning to her home for the birth. I have a suggestion for the next action to be taken. Supposing the child to be a girl, then she should be taken by Juan's foster mother to her home; the castle and village are fairly remote and ...'

Philip laughed, releasing all the tensions of his recent fears, 'Quijada's wife; excellent, God's Personal Almsgiver! She is the very one to rear the child through early infancy then donate her like so many of her other donations to the local convent. She would be giving them a baby abbess, and the child would be lost to the world. An annual gift of a hundred or so *ducados* should keep the present mother abbess happy.'

'And should it be a boy? You cannot look to the church for an answer, both you and father failed miserably with Juan.'

'Father weakened when he saw the young knight-to-be. My lack of success is due to the stubborn Pope's refusal to cooperate.'

'Which still leaves us with the problem; what did Isabel de Osorio do?'

'Raised the boys on her own; she still refuses to allow them to come to court,' he presumed the nun from Avila would know of their existence, 'instead they are off to the army, a military career.'

'Isabel was always fiercely independent; but you did find her somewhere to live, somewhere out of the way.'

'You are right, that is probably the best answer, although an expensive one. But can we find a place far enough away from Ana that her interest will eventually wane? I must also seek out some suitable occupation for Juan.'

Magdalena Ruiz put her hands on her hips before calling her observations across the room, 'You know; if you had allowed Juan to join the army or run away to sea none of this would have happened. He would have been married to the military almost day and night and with whatever energies were left he might bed some willing wench.'

'Oh how easily one can sound so wise after the event.'

'My lord, had I told you sooner you would probably not have taken any notice. But the pair of you apparently have the matter in hand,' she gathered up her monkeys, 'so I shall retire to my apartments for some light refreshment.'

No sooner had she left than Juana whispered, 'My informers gave me a spectacular piece of information; astonishing in fact. The nun, Teresa of Avila, also has ties to the Israelites, and not so very far removed. Her grandfather was hauled before the Inquisition at Toledo.' She laughed, 'I find it all rather amusing, really; until today all those ladies with Jewish blood that you have known have thrown themselves body and soul into your bed. Teresa has thrown herself into the bosom of the Christian Church.'

What amused Philip rather more was that the person to whom God had chosen to divulge his imperfections was burdened by a far more serious secret.

206

34

Madrid in August was as hot as predicted, if not hotter. Isabel had moved to her ground floor apartments and the doors and windows to her salon had been flung wide bidding welcome to the cooler air of the late afternoon.

The Princess of Eboli and the Duquesas of Alba and Feria, were languidly occupied with their books, leafing through some pages, or putting them to more immediate use as fans.

Isabel sat close to a window writing to her mother. Ordinarily a pleasant task, today it was a painful duty, one forced on her by her husband. Her fingers traced down columns of letters and numbers seeking out the required characters. She hated refusing her mother's help knowing how everything she did was done with the best of intentions; but this was what she must do, what she had been commanded to do. Lest anyone should suspect her disloyalty to Philip in any of her words (and she knew of one only too eager to do just that) it was best that the letter was in code.

A few weeks ago Doctor Montguyon, her favourite and trusted doctor had died. Catalina had offered to send her another eminent physician from France. Philip had been adamant in his refusal. There would be no further French interference; Spanish doctors and their methods were good enough.

Every lie she wrote extolling the competency of her ignorant Spanish doctors filled Isabel with a growing fear. She was committing herself, her life, to physicians who could see little beyond the knife and bowl and who had a long-held prejudice against water, fresh air, and clean clothes.

She moved on to the next subject, Prince Carlos. Her mother, she knew full well, would never be short of despatches from the French ambassador but her own observations on Philip's thinking regarding the prince would be equally valuable. She was increasingly disturbed to see how he no longer sought to disguise his disgust, his shame, at his son's disabilities and inadequacies. Everyone knew. Recently she had even heard rumours that were it not for the fear of the people's disapproval Philip would lock him up.

A rattling of small wooden wheels on floor tiles brought blessed relief. Princess Clara, plump fingers dug deep into the red velvet rail of her baby walker, proudly approached calling to everyone she passed for due recognition of her prowess.

Isabel set down her pen, folded and tucked the paper with the cipher key inside her bodice, then threw out her arms to the tiny adventuress making her way as strong and sturdy as any heroic voyager. A girl she may be, but she was a healthy girl.

The miniature barque jerked steadily onward, its captain bouncing against the heavily padded sides and giggling as she righted herself

'Here is my clever girl come to greet her Mama. She shall have a big kiss to let her know how proud her Mama is.' She leaned sideways accommodating her seventh month of pregnancy, inviting her ladies to praise this child wonder before them. 'Is she not a marvel?'

The ladies had left their chairs to follow the young explorer clapping their hands in admiration, for Clara at only twelve months was quite remarkable.

Ana freely admitted, 'She is exceptional in everything she does, and much more advanced than any of mine at this age.'

'And she looks more like the king every day,' added the Duquesa de Alba, stroking the golden curls and raising the plump cheeks and chin of the chubby infant from where they nestled in the frilled lace collar of her white brocade dress decorated with a profusion of red bows to keep its wearer safe from any danger lying in wait.

Jane Dormer, Duquesa de Feria, thought of her two boys so far away in Zafra, growing up without her love, care, and guidance. 'But perhaps she should not spend too long a time on her feet at such a tender age, it may be detrimental? May I suggest that while it is good to ensure the Princess Clara has an abundance of amulets to ward off dangers, it would surely be foolhardy to court disaster by making unnecessary demands on her tiny limbs?'

'How sensible you are Jane.'

The decision was made for them with the announcement of the arrival of the carefully vetted (there was not a hint of Jewish blood in her family) and recently appointed wet nurse. It was time for Clara's next feed.

'The nurse is aware that the princess is the proud owner of several strong teeth?'

'Yes ma'am.'

'Let us pray that my child remembers her manners, and will not rush to the well too greedily.'

'Amen to that.' They had all witnessed or heard of many an untimely death resulting from the chewed and infected nipples of wet nurses.

Clara was lifted from her walker and offered to her Mama for a farewell kiss, but the papers on Mama's desk proved more interesting and she chose one with lots of black markings transferring it to her mouth for further inspection.

Ana, never missing an opportunity to discover something private was quick to retrieve it. She returned it to the table smoothing out the crinkles, unfortunately smudging some of the dribble-wet ink. It would have made no difference since she could not make out one single word. She looked across at Isabel, quite unashamed that she had been observed. She was merely following instructions.

Isabel savoured her enemy's failure before turning to enquire of the Duquesa de Alba, 'When does your husband leave for the Netherlands?'

'Quite soon; I earnestly hope he will not have to stay there long. I know he wishes for nothing better than to serve his king but we are not getting any younger.'

Ana swallowed her anger for the second time within as many minutes. This time it was on her husband's behalf, he was the one who should have been chosen and not Alba. That family along with all their relatives were becoming too powerful. Hopefully Gómez and Pérez, who was almost a family member and the king's new secretary, would profit by his absence.

Isabel noted her anger and discomfort.

'M-my lady queen,' Carlos waited in the open doorway.

'Come in, come in.'

'I-I have such news for you,' he stammered, impatient to tell. 'But they are not allowed to listen.' He ushered her ladies away, 'For the life of me I cannot understand how you tolerate those women. They are all spies, just like their husbands; despicable, the lot of them.'

'Carlos, no more of that, if you please.'

'Isabel, my future is all arranged. I am to be in charge of my own destiny,' he stumbled over his excited words.

'What perfect news! At last! I am so happy for you. When did his majesty discuss this with you? I have heard nothing. Oh, Carlos, this is wonderful. So, you are to marry Anne.' She held his shaking, moist hands in congratulation. It was strange that she should have heard nothing, even from *La Eboli* who appeared to know everything.

Carlos put a finger to his lips urging secrecy, 'I did not make myself plain. This has nothing to do with the king. I am talking about making my own decisions.'

'I urge you to be cautious; think before you say anything more.' She whispered and turned to walk to the window hoping the ladies had not heard.

Carlos limped along keeping close to her determined she should know his plans. 'Remember when I told you about my eavesdropping at that meeting the Cortes had with the envoy from the Netherlands, and how that uncivil fellow said I should be ashamed so I punched him? Well, the envoy has been to see me on several occasions. He says that all the Netherlanders want me to be their governor. So, when the king and I are in Brussels I shall announce my intention to stay there. Then I will send for my Cousin Anne of Austria to be my wife. I know for certain that my uncle Emperor Maximilian is impatient for his daughter to marry me. Now, tell me, what do you think of my plans?'

Isabel feared for this poor fool and his harebrained schemes. It hadn't occurred to him that he was speaking treason. He was siding with the rebels, encouraging the emperor's involvement. Fortunately it was Alba who was going to the Netherlands and not Philip and Carlos. No doubt when Carlos discovered he was to remain in Spain he would be infuriated beyond measure, but at least he would be saved from an unmitigated disaster, would be saved from himself. It was a blessing in disguise. Meanwhile she must turn his thoughts away from all dangerous intrigues.

'Were there not some plans for you to wed Mary of Scotland?'

'Thank God she has married, too impatient to wait for my father to arrive at a decision. Anyway, who would want to live in that dreary little country?'

'Then what of my sister Margot? She is young and beautiful, and so lively.'

'You jest; she is a nymphomaniac.'

'Hush, Carlos, do not say such a thing!'

'I must, because I know it to be true. And do you know she lifts her skirts for any man at all, young or old, nobleman or scullion.'

'Carlos, you forget yourself!' Isabel put her hands over her ears refusing to hear more.

'Forgive me, for a moment I forgot she was your sister. In any case I want Anne, and I shall have my Anne of Austria.'

Isabel, casting about to forget Carlos's monstrous allegations against her sister, offered a last suggestion. Some years ago Juana had proposed herself as the ideal bride for Carlos. She had possibly done so to protect him, and not to get her hands on the Spanish crown as many vicious tongues would have it. 'Your Aunt Juana would make a perfect wife.'

Carlos spluttered his laughter, 'Ridiculous! Can you imagine me marrying anyone who for years threatened to cut off my left hand if I continued to write with it? And, I would have you know, I have no intention whatsoever of having a second-hand wife. I want a virgin. I am surprised you would even mention a used woman.'

'Oh, Carlos, you must not have such unkind thoughts. I think you forget how much love and affection Juana has always given you.'

'You could well be right, but that is all in the past. I want Anne.'

Alba's deep voice preceded him into the room, 'Your majesty, if I may, I have come to bid goodbye.'

'Do come in. So we are to say adieu. I shall miss you dear friend.' Isabel had to fight back the tears. He had always been there at her side to be her champion; his stern demands winning through where her timid commands were ignored. Alba had always been there to support and encourage, she couldn't imagine the future without him somewhere nearby. She also hoped they could say their farewells without mentioning his destination. She put her hand to her pounding heart, if only she could return to those precious minutes with Clara.

Carlos was jealous and incensed as usual by Isabel's continued show of favour for this man, one of his worst enemies. But he would show tolerance for her sake, and because he was elated with his own plans. He forced himself to show interest, 'So, where are you going?'

'To the Netherlands, your majesty.'

'No, you're not,' Carlos shouted, 'because the king and I are going!'

'Not until I have ensured that there will be no rebellion, and that you will be safe.'

'You are not to go. If you do, I shall kill you.'

211

Isabel took him by the arm. 'Carlos this is neither the time nor the place. We shall go together to the king to seek an explanation. That would be far wiser. We both realise that the Duque de Alba cannot make his own decisions; he must follow the king's orders.'

Carlos was not to be deterred. 'Alba, say you promise not to go, or else ...'

'His majesty is sending me to the Netherlands.'

'Then I have to kill you.' He shrugged off Isabel's hand and drew his dagger.

The ladies screamed, running to Isabel's side to protect her, to draw her away from Carlos even as she continued to reach out to restrain him.

Alba grabbed the prince's left wrist, squeezing it until the dagger was released clattering to the floor. He pinioned his arms behind his back ignoring the squeals and whimpers, hissing in his ear, 'I apologise, sire, but I advise you not to attempt such a foolish move ever again, do you hear?'

'Yes. Let me go, bastard.'

Alba released him, watched him pick up the weapon and begin to put it in its sheath. But he was a seasoned soldier and well prepared for the sudden lunge that came from a still determined Carlos.

Philip entered to find his son on his knees and being held in an arm lock, 'Alba?'

Carlos screamed up at him, 'You promised me! You said I was going to Brussels!' His plans were falling into disarray.

'You will remain in Spain,' Philip couldn't bring himself to look down at the pathetic wretch.

'Alba is a soldier! They'll know that means war. In any case they hate him, they hate you. They want me, they like me!'

'You know that for a fact?'

Isabel prayed in vain that Carlos would have more sense than to answer.

'Yes, because their envoy told me. We have met often and he has told me lots of things.'

'Precisely! That is the reason why Alba is going to the Netherlands, why you will stay here, and why the envoy is now my prisoner under lock and key. I will have the Netherlanders brought to heel. There will be no undermining of my authority by you or anyone else. I suggest you return to your apartments and consider yourself fortunate that as yet I have not put a name to your actions.'

Carlos dragged himself to his feet and hobbled away yelling all his hurts and disappointments finishing with, 'And you have made Juan the Commander of the Mediterranean fleet. I am nothing, have nothing!'

Philip came to Isabel's side. 'I thank God you are unharmed. But you are shaking, my dear. Let us visit Clara she will help you forget what you have witnessed. Rest assured I shall see to it that as from now Carlos is denied access to your apartments.'

'My lord, may I beg you not to do this. I am glad to offer him companionship, there are so few who care.' She wanted to plead the case for the unfortunate man lost in a bewildering world; the sad and unloved prince so desperate to find his way and never knowing how, making mistake after mistake.

'The prince is no longer a subject for discussion.'

At this stage all he wanted was for Isabel's pregnancy to go full term without any major problems and to be delivered of a healthy son. He was also formulating a plan to rid himself of Carlos. It would require steadfastness, but it was his duty, God expected it of him.

35

Montagne grabbed at the silver pomander that swung lazily from the Princess of Eboli's waist. 'If you get much closer you will be treading on her majesty's gown.' He inhaled the sweet scents of lavender and rosemary, so delightful a change to the rather more brutal body smells at his nose level.

Ana gave him a withering stare, tugging free the chain and its filigree ball.

The small company of mostly ladies were strolling along the upper gallery making a complete circuit of the patio. Heading the group were Isabel and the French ambassador with Ana and Montagne close behind followed by half a dozen or more attendants.

Isabel had done her utmost to persuade Philip to allow her to take her walk outdoors. It was such a beautiful September afternoon and the patio offered shade from the sun and protection from any breeze, it would be perfect. But he had been adamant in his refusal, to the point of being hysterical, insisting she content herself with a walk indoors, he would not have his unborn son put at risk.

This suited Ana since it kept their group tightknit, she could remain close to Isabel whose words would not get lost into the air. She chided herself on not being an attentive student in her youth. Had she been then her understanding of French would be so much better.

'And what is it that you hope to hear?

'What business is it of yours, little man?'

'I might ask exactly the same of you, my lady. Of what concern is it to you what her majesty and the ambassador are saying.'

'Perhaps I am only seeking to improve my French.'

'Then I should say you take me for a bigger fool than I am. But I should not be distracting you. If, after you have listened long and hard there is anything that still remains unexplained, you have only to ask and I would be most happy to oblige. I know everything there is to know about my lady queen.'

'Ha! So it is vanity that swells that little chest of yours.'

'No, my lady, anyone as diminutive as myself cannot afford to be vain; what you see is a breast swollen with pride.' He bowed and retired to join the Duquesa de Alba.

'*Monsieur ambassador, vraiment je serais trop marrie*, truly I would be too upset if I were left behind in Spain. As soon as I can after the birth of my child I must go to join my husband. Please help me to convince my mother, that this is what I desire most.'

'She is only trying to point out that as the daughter of a king and now the wife of a king it is your duty that you should consider yourself as the natural regent of Spain in your husband's absence.'

'Ambassador, I have no objection to Princess Juana acting as regent, permitting me to be in my proper place at my lord's side. Besides I could be of some assistance with Carlos if as suggested by recent events the king intends to take Carlos with him after all.'

'I would read nothing into the king's command that the prince prepare himself and his household for the journey; I would suggest rather it is all a means to keep him occupied. It would be too much of a liability to take the prince anywhere. In fact if God delays much longer in sending a remedy for Carlos's behaviour some terrible mishap may occur here in Spain.' He crossed himself vigorously.

Isabel smiled a sad smile, shaking her head. 'Carlos needs friendship, affection; both have been seriously denied throughout his life. Never once has he demonstrated any of the unkind actions and words towards me he is so often guilty of towards others. The reason is quite obvious; I show him warmth and companionship. Don Juan is another who has never been the object of the prince's wild ways and why, because he shows infinite patience.'

'The prince is a man not a child. He needs a wife; which reminds me I have yet to see the several portraits of the Princess Margot your mother sent recently.'

'I hate to disappoint my mother yet again but a marriage between Carlos and my sister Margot is quite out of the question. The prince is determined to marry his Austrian Cousin Anne. There is nothing more to be done.'

'But what if your mother is desirous of a marriage between Anne and your brother, King Charles?'

'Then my mother will be disappointed once more. The emperor wants nothing other than for his daughter to marry into the Spanish house.' She took the ambassador's hand, 'I do have a great deal of sympathy for you, it must be most discouraging to have nothing positive to report to France, but that is the way things are and will remain.'

'Do you suppose the king will leave for the Low Countries?'

'He says he still intends to but he has not been well since the sacking of the churches in Flanders. The unacceptable sacrilege would make any true Christian ill, and how can a sovereign in good conscience govern heretics? I seem to recall my mother and I discussing this very subject years ago, and would remind France that the problems with the Huguenots will not go away of their own accord. But, returning to his majesty he is showing signs of a full recovery since he was last bled.' She paused for a moment, 'To be perfectly honest with you I seriously doubt if any of us are to go. The situation is still most difficult. We must pray that Alba is successful with the pacification of the rebels.'

They turned the last corner of the gallery stepping into the slanting golden beams of sunlight that cast themselves across their paths.

Montagne drew alongside Ana, 'Anything to report? Are you just a little out of sorts unable to discover nothing other than my lady queen is indeed a faithful and loving wife and not the scheming confidante of Her Majesty Queen Catalina, regent of France, or a spy for her brother King Charles? As I said earlier I could have told you all this without you running the risk of suffering a stiff neck. I suspect it will sadden you having nothing to report to the king.'

'I have no idea what you are talking about.'

'For some time I have known there has been mischief afoot. I was disturbed to think that King Philip could actually doubt Queen Isabel's innocence but now I see it all; you are the guilty one. Tell me, does it stem from your jealousy of the queen or is it a desperate hunger for power this seeking to poison the king's mind?'

'I have no idea what you are talking about, you offensive little Frenchman!' Ana stormed away from him her whirling skirts and the swinging pomander knocking him off balance.

36

The ride from Guadalajara on this brisk October morning had been invigorating. A creaking of leather, a jingling of harnesses and a thudding of hooves were the only sounds to accompany the barrage of thoughts of one of the four horsemen, King Philip.

He had desperately sought the country air to free a mind sorely plagued with an ever increasing number of problems, not the least of which was his latest child; another girl.

He bitterly regretted this French marriage. Why had he been so hasty? Why had he ignored his policy of long and careful deliberation? Why had he not honoured the contract between Carlos and Isabel? He had made a huge mistake, committed a grave error of judgement, and because of it God was punishing him. There would be no male heirs from his union with a French heretic. A heretic? She had to be, she was French!

The galloping was reined back to a saunter as they made their way up the hill to the small town of Pastrana.

Then there was the question of Carlos. Dear God, what had he done to deserve such a son? The prince was ugly, misshapen, continually ill, given to frequent outbursts of violent temper, an idiot with a history of sadism. Philip would never forgive him for mutilating his favourite horse. He patted the neck of his present mount that had replaced the victim of Carlos's latest hideous crime. Then there was the recent attempted treachery, yes it was nothing short of treason, which had taken his behaviour to a different level altogether; a step too far. Investigations, observations, would now be redoubled to determine whether or not there had been any collusion between him, Isabel, and Juan, and indeed if this collusion continued.

Juan; this was another subject demanding his attention. That young man was too arrogant, too handsome, too intelligent, and too damned popular. A recent rumour would have it that Juan was not, after all, the son of a liaison between his father and the daughter of a tavern singer, but was, in fact, the love child of Aunt Maria, the result of an affair with one of her ministers. The question was did that alter anything? No, because he remained a royal bastard of noble and royal lineage.

In any case his father had recognised him as his son, so that was that. However, there remained the fact that too many people were showing far too much interest in him.

They were passing the last of the mulberry farms and the busy weavers' sheds.

'Gómez has achieved wonders, and in so short a time,' observed the Duque del Infantado resettling his velvet bonnet and smoothing his thick, silky beard. 'He has turned this into a prosperous community.'

'Too bad he had to bring in Moors from Aragón to do it.' Philip was of the opinion that even the most mediocre Christian workers, despite the evidence to the contrary, would have been distinctly more desirable. This thought moved him on to congratulating himself for having finally put into effect a range of laws imposing radical changes to Moorish lifestyle. It was now law that they must never speak, read, or write in Arabic. They could no longer wear Arabic dress, and women must leave their faces uncovered. All Moors must have Christian names, get married in church, and so on. And still he wasn't satisfied, there was much more to be done.

'The silks and velvets are second to none,' the other continued. 'It is interesting that his father-in-law had such little success with a local workforce. It must be a different attitude to work.'

Philip glowered and the subject was dropped.

The four horses clattered under an archway emerging into a square heaving with all the animation of market day. It was a riot of colour and noise. There were stalls with every manner of merchandise, pens of squealing pigs or squawking hens; tradesmen were bellowing their wares, buyers shouting good naturedly to drive a bargain; excited children were chasing here there and everywhere getting under folks' feet and attracting many an oath and a cuff around the ears. On three sides of the square washing fluttered in and out of the upper galleries of houses.

'Difficult to imagine that in a few hours the square will be completely deserted, all back to normal for another week.' The duque prattled on, trying to bridge the tension he had caused with his blundering faux pas about hard working Moors.

'And mercifully quiet,' added Philip wheeling his horse about to turn into the huge entrance to the palace which formed the fourth side of the square. They made their way into the courtyard, the noise of the market soon becoming but a faint echo of itself.

Philip and his companion dismounted throwing the reins to the two servants who had ridden with them and began their climb up the wide interior staircase. Philip fully approved of this marble staircase; the banister richly carved with intertwined vines barely hiding tiny creatures of field and forest was most impressive. The stairs climbed gently on shallow rises to the reception rooms above.

'Boo!'

Philip looked up, startled. A fair haired boy perhaps six years old jumped out to stand at the head of the stairs. There could be no doubting it, this was his son. Ana had not exaggerated when she had said the child looked like him. Why had Isabel not given him a boy like this? Could God really wish to punish him in this way? He swallowed hard, turned to laugh with the duque while he regained his composure.

'And who might you be, young fellow?' He called up the stairs.

'I am Rodrigo, son of Ruy Gómez, Prince of Eboli and Duque de Pastrana.

And he was every bit as proud and bumptious as his mother had said; the voice, the arrogant chin, the red velvet jerkin and breeches all proclaimed hauteur.

The boy put his hands on his hips. 'Who are you, sir?'

'I am Philip, king of Spain.'

Rodrigo sank to one knee, head bowed, not daring to face the monarch to whom he had been so disrespectful, nor to look towards the nearby doorway where, he now realised, his mother had been all the while. He had gone too far with his boldness this time and he felt sick with fear.

Ana whispered, 'You had best be quick with your apology, or his majesty may have you sent to prison.'

'Mama, no one told me the king was coming. Nor did I know what he looked like. Your majesty I humbly seek your pardon, although it was through no fault of mine, I had no idea it was you.'

Philip liked the boy's nerve, his confidence; he was incredibly self-assured for one so young. He smiled up at Ana, 'I think he shall be pardoned this time. Rodrigo can practise his manners on the Duque del Infantado, by taking him on a guided tour of the palace.' He wanted him gone before the desire to hug and kiss the child, his child, became too great.

Ana made a deep curtsey, 'Welcome to my home. It has been a long time.'

Behind her the faithful Bernardina curtsied before waddling away down the corridor and into the shadows.

The reception room was large but still managed to maintain an air of intimacy. On a day like today it was especially warm and inviting. Gnarled olive logs crackled in the fireplace sending out an extraordinary heat, and two welcoming chairs waited at either side of the hearth. Other chairs stood by walls covered with tapestries and family portraits. Here and there were tables with bowls of late autumn fruits and flowers. A window on the far wall overlooked the square.

'You are well? We have missed you at court.'

'Very well my lord; and with child once again.'

Philip struggled to keep his envy under control. 'Nor would it surprise me if it is with another boy. How many is that?' He knew that she had given birth to five sons. Two had died in early infancy the others were as robust as the young Rodrigo he had met at the top of the stairs. Isabel de Osorio had two sons. His own sister had given her husband six heirs. The fault lay with the infuriating de Valois family; too many damned girls.

Ana had no intention of speaking of her boys. 'I heard the news of Queen Isabel's safe delivery of a child, and that you have a daughter; Catalina Micaela.'

'She is to be known as Micaela. I refuse to hear that other name and could never bring myself ever to utter it, I am heartily sick of the Medici woman.'

'I assume by your presence here you are not at the christening celebrations.'

'No; I did attend Clara's, in that I watched it from a gallery in the chapel; but I refuse to attend yet another girl's christening.'

'You are too hard. Fortunately Isabel is young and fertile, so there is plenty of time for a boy. But we are in danger of treading over old ground. Where are you staying, in Guadalajara?'

'Yes, I have come to do some hunting. I find it one of the best ways to overcome disappointments and worries. May I enquire how your hunting went?'

'Ah, so that is the true reason for your visit. This is not a social call after all.'

He had never wavered in his determination to keep Ana at a distance but he had retained her services as one of Isabel's ladies, and for good reason too. She would have no qualms about prying into her mistress's affairs, no guilt about searching or rummaging through personal and private belongings.

'My search was fruitless. I have no idea where Isabel keeps her code. The only information I had was regarding her conversation with her ambassador, and you know of that.'

'If only you could have found the code and made a copy.'

Ana knitted her eyebrows, 'What makes you think she is a spy?'

That nettled. 'Take care. I forbid you to use that word; I see where your son gets his boldness from. So, I am left disappointed. I want you back in Madrid before Christmas.'

'That is an order if ever I heard one. I was rather hoping to stay here in Pastrana, Madrid has become such a bore. The life and soul of my soirees disappeared along with Juan when he went away,' she sighed, 'even if he was becoming too full of his own importance. I suppose Pérez is gradually filling the void. There is nothing like a bit of harmless gossip, and he makes it sound quite fun.'

Philip remembered Isabel's words when she first saw Ana, "the coquette" she had called her, and he was grabbed once again by an all-consuming jealousy. He rose and moved about the room to clear his mind insisting it was of no consequence whether she flirted with Pérez or not.

'I see you have made some changes in here; the tapestries are different.'

'Oh, those, Gómez wanted those. I would rather have picnics and weddings than a Christian king fighting the Turk. But there one is, at times one must give way to a husband's preferences.'

'There will be important work for you to do. Gómez will soon have the details,' he thought of some letters he had written, all carefully worded, and all locked away in a casket only awaiting a date and his signature. 'And in the meantime I do need you to be my eyes and ears in the queen's apartments.'

His eyes were drawn to her dress, the skirts bulging with Gómez's child, and his thoughts returned to the times when he had enjoyed Ana's body, its silky smoothness. It was as well she was pregnant for he was now such a confusion of feelings. He must be strong, it was time to say farewell to the world of mistresses, they caused more trouble than they were worth.

He strolled to the window. Below in the square trading was over for the day and unsold goods were being stacked on carts

221

or thrown across the backs of donkeys. Above and beyond the housetops opposite was a magnificent landscape of sweeping green hills broken here and there by orchards and long parallel rows of olive trees.

'I think it would be a far better life to be a nobleman with no other cares than his estates, his labourers and his crops.'

Ana had joined him, 'God would not have made you a king if He thought you hadn't the strength to carry the burden, and friends about you to understand.' She pressed herself up against him, just for a moment, to remind him of the past and to suggest promises for the future.

'Thank you, Ana.' He stood back to kiss her elegant fingers then caressed her cheek and eye patch with the back of his hand. She was still the most beautiful woman he had ever met; *the envy of all women, the desire of all men*. But he would never weaken his resolve; there would be no more infidelities, only business and politics in future.

A polite knock at the door was followed by the appearance of the head of Bernardina. 'With permission your majesty, a courier has arrived from Villagarcía. He says the letter is important.'

'Bring it here, Bernardina.' Philip paced back and forth by the window then strode out of the room too impatient to wait.

Ana heard his exclamations growing louder as he returned, 'Excellent! Such excellent news!' Then a burst of laughter ushered him back into the room. He waved the letter.

'Something has obviously brought you great cheer, my lord.'

'Indeed it has; this is perfect. Quijada's wife has written of two safe deliveries. Juan's mistress has been safely delivered of a girl, and the child has been delivered, also quite safely, to Quijada's home in Villagarcía. In due time she will enter a convent and the world will never have known of her existence.'

'Was that always your intention? You are depriving Juana and Maria of their child.'

'There was no alternative. Let this caution you never to encourage them again.'

'They will be deeply hurt.'

'Hurt?' Philip enjoyed more laughter as he tore the letter into tiny pieces and dropped them into the flames. It was exquisite, 'Apparently Juan has already overcome any sadness; a bowl of his stepmother's chicken soup with an egg beaten into it worked wonders. Chicken soup is such a panacea!'

'What will become of Maria?'

Philip shrugged, 'She is at liberty to return to Madrid. Juan, of course, will be away much of the time. Of greater importance is young Rodrigo, I must speak to Gómez about him. I must arrange for his education and removal to court. I want him as my pageboy.'

He had to have one of his sons nearby. Isabel de Osorio had refused whereas Ana would relish the idea. It also pleased him to offer some palliative for her dashed hopes for Maria's marriage to Juan.

37

It was not the happiest of evenings; it was a cheerless group that sat around the card table.

The Duquesa de Alba was preoccupied with fears for her husband in the Low Countries; if only the whole sorry business could be over and done with and he was home safe and sound.

By royal command the Duquesa de Feria, Mary Dormer, had had to leave her family home to be at the side of her husband. Her thoughts were constantly in Zaffra; with her little family, with the estates that were finally yielding a good return after the many years of neglect when Feria was in England, but mostly with her little family.

Ana, the Princess of Eboli, continued to be in a sour mood. She was still angry, embittered by Philip's decision to place Juan's child in a convent to be conveniently forgotten, and by his refusal to readmit Gómez to his position of king's favourite. And then, as if to add insult to injury, he had ordered her return to Madrid that she might witness her husband's embarrassment at having to play the role of nursemaid to Prince Carlos.

Isabel could not be more miserable. She longed for those halcyon days, days of fun and frivolity with her dear friends. Alas they were lost and gone forever. Juana was no longer the constant companion, her duties at the nearby convent having taken precedence. Juan and Carlos she rarely saw and Alessandro was far away in Parma.

If only they were here with her to help rid her of thoughts of the other night when Philip had come to her bed and forced himself on her. She was suffering indescribable shame. She had been abused and soiled. Philip was to blame. He knew full well he had no conjugal rights before her menses recommenced, but that was of little consolation. Nor could she excuse him because he was so desperate to sire another child. He had ignored all social mores and church rulings and had brutalised her like some ignorant animal and she felt unclean.

Carlos almost fell into the room. The four ladies rose as one dropping their playing cards in disarray onto the table.

'Oh no, Carlos, you should not be here!' Isabel rushed to where he stood leaning against the door struggling to regain his breath. Should she push him away or bring him in quickly? 'My lord Philip said on no account must you come here. If only Juana were here, she would know what to do.'

Showing no emotion whatsoever, without anger or sorrow, Philip had issued the order prohibiting Carlos visiting Isabel and warning him to beware the consequences should he go against his will. And she had been cautioned, to heed well, that on no account would receiving Carlos be tolerated. She had been instructed to summon the guards the moment he set foot over the threshold. But how could she do such a thing? Friends did not behave in such a way.

The chill of December was banished by suffocating waves of panic. Conflicting thoughts ran amok: accusations of fraternising with the enemy; visions of her ladies, spies and betrayers only too ready to rush to Philip with half heard tales; her continuing belief that Carlos was no more than an innocent child frustrated by a life holding no role for him; memories of her several failures to plead his cause only to exacerbate the situation; the threat of Philip resorting to extreme action were it not for public opinion.

But Carlos was here and surely the finger of guilt would point directly at her. She was trapped. If only he hadn't come; but who else was there for him to turn to? She tried to think; what would Juana do?

'Ladies,' she surprised herself at her control, 'would you retire to the anteroom.' Not that their removal would make much difference, they would continue to listen. 'Carlos,' she repeated, 'why are you here? You know you should not have come. Those are his majesty's orders.'

He beamed, 'B-b-because his majesty is not here. He is visiting the new palace, that huge and hideous tomb at Escorial.' He laughed. 'And that's exactly what it is Isabel; *escorial,* a shit heap! May he enjoy it, along with all his dead relatives, and with goodness knows how many next-to-dead monks filling the place with their miserable chants. Who else but King Philip could have thought up such a place?' He giggled helplessly, 'An expensive heap of shit!'

'Carlos, no more of that.'

But she had to agree. It was so far removed from the beautiful palaces of France, it couldn't even begin to compare with the palace in Toledo and that fell short of most aesthetic criteria. Escorial was an ugly and cold building both in concept and design. It was a palace, a monastery, but also a final resting place for Philip's family whose remains would be brought from various parts of Spain. There would be a place for her, too. Provided she gave Philip a male heir she would be offered the privilege of lying opposite her husband in the Pantheon of Kings, if she didn't she would be relegated to lie amongst lesser mortals in the Pantheon of Princes and Princesses; another idea of Philip's. What awaited her, reward or disgrace?

'You have still to tell me why you are here.'

'Because I knew that Don Juan was coming to see you and I thought this would be the safest place to finish off some private business.' Carlos rubbed his hands together with delight, 'Isabel, my plans are almost complete.'

'Shall we sit near the fire?' It would take them further from the door and the listeners on the other side.

'Yes, yes, but no more interruptions. You know that extra allowance I got from my deceitful, hateful, lying father, a form of compensation for my not going to the Netherlands? Well, little did he know I would put it to good use and not squander it as usual; it will pay for my journey.'

'Journey; where are you going?' And she could have asked him how far he supposed he was capable of travelling as barely a week went by without him suffering a dreadful fever confining him to his bed.

'That money together with rents from my properties will finance horses, overnight stays and a sea crossing to Italy.'

'I doubt it would be sufficient to meet such expenses.'

Carlos brushed that aside. 'I am sure to get more on my way, probably in Burgos or somewhere like that. Not everyone is as stingy as the money lenders in these parts. I cannot begin to tell you how angry some of those have made me. But I have no wish to talk about them. I am going to be free of my father at last. All I need now is to finalise the arrangements for having a ship ready and waiting in Cartagena. That is where Juan is an important part in my plans. He has promised to meet me here. Yes, Juan is my best friend in the world.'

Isabel had never known him to be so excited as he continued, detailing his plans for travelling to Italy and then on to Vienna and his beloved Anne, and the more animated he became the more terrified she grew.

'Wait, wait a moment. We must give ourselves time to consider what it is you are saying.'

A way must be found to dissuade him, to stop his proceeding with such a dangerous scheme. This was treason.

The poor fool had learned nothing from the last time when he had been boasting about his meetings with the Netherlands' envoy and Philip had made it abundantly clear that he was no better than a traitor. This time Carlos was involving her and Juan, and if Philip's head was already filled with doubts and suspicions, where would this leave her?

'Carlos, you are not strong enough to contemplate such a long journey. You might travel no more than a few miles before you are overcome by one of your fevers, and what then; what about doctors, special nursing?'

'The point is I won't get sick. I only get ill here because of him, I cannot stomach the man.'

'How many are going with you? Can they be trusted to keep your secret?' How she wished she had left those words unsaid. There would be concerns on the other side of the door at their conspiratorial implications.

'That is a good question. The answer is I have invited several grandees to go with me.'

'Such foolishness! Did you not stop to think they would inform the king?'

'You are mistaken. Anyway, so far three have already agreed to accompany me and I have complete faith in them. Ah, here comes Juan.' Carlos rose to greet him. 'In a moment or two everything will be finalised. You cannot imagine my happiness.'

Juan bowed to Isabel then kissed her hand. 'My lady, you are fully recovered, and the tiny Micaela is well?'

'We are both quite well.'

Carlos shuffled from one foot to the other, impatient. 'W-w-we are not here to discuss people's health. We are here to discuss my plans.' He repeated his arranged escape, how the first horses would be ready and waiting on the eighteenth of January, how all posting stations had been informed.

Juan urged him to keep his voice low for though this was stupid child's talk he would be overheard by Isabel's ladies whom he knew had to be on the other side of the half open door. He kept pointing out that his ideas were no more than impossible dreams.

Carlos began to storm and rage. First Isabel had been negative and now it was Juan's turn to pour cold water on his grand scheme. His arguments became more heated, insisting the plan would work.

227

Juan decided to put an end to this infantile nonsense, enough was enough, Carlos must face reality.

'For God's sake, this will be seen as treason!'

'Never, it's an escape from tyranny.' He waved away any further objections. 'Hush now,' his enthusiasm was rekindled. He rushed on, 'All I want you to do is have a ship made ready. I will make it worth your while. As your prince I am offering you a kingdom in return for a ship and embarkation papers. It will be easy for you to do as Admiral of the Mediterranean Fleet.'

'You refuse to listen. This is treason and I will not be party to it.'

Carlos drew his sword. He shuffled towards Juan dragging his useless leg, 'Die, you damned coward!'

Isabel leaned forward in her chair and covered her face with her hands, 'Dear God, not again.'

The queen's three ladies stood in the doorway.

'Stand back Carlos.' Juan's sword was out and threatening.

'Some friend you have turned out to be,' Carlos sobbed, tears rolling down his cheeks. With consummate ease his sword was flicked from his hand and sent spinning. Juan went to pick it up unsure what he should do with it.

The moment he saw Juan bend over Carlos flung himself at his back, arms wrapped tight about his neck.

'You have to do this for me, Juan, it's my last chance. I'll make you king of Milan, or Naples, I promise.'

'Carlos, if this wasn't such a damned serious matter, so help me I would fall about laughing at the thought of you riding me piggy back while offering me a choice of kingdoms.'

'You must help, you bastard!'

'I may be a bastard, but my father was a much greater man than yours!'

Carlos burst into giggles, 'I like that, you are so right. The Holy Roman Emperor Charles V has no competition when it comes to Philip. So, will you help?'

The only thing to be done was to stall for time. Carlos was determined, and Carlos had involved him. His own life was at risk as well as that of the prince.

'Sire, I shall see what can be done, it will take time. I will need to see what ship or ships are available, what provisions are necessary, and of course the writing of a permit. At the same time will you give this matter and its consequences some serious thought?' Meanwhile Carlos would hopefully either be made to see sense or, even better, whoever had made the arrangements so far would decide to cancel them, putting an end to the whole madcap scheme.

Carlos loosened his grip and climbed down from his back. 'See, you are my good friend after all.'

Isabel took her hands from her face and looked sorrowfully at the cheery smile and sparkling eyes of an idiot – how she hated that word – who continued to cherish hopes of success and without the faintest notion that he was putting all their lives in peril.

Juan made his farewells, 'Isabel, I must go to attend to these matters.' He whispered as he bowed, 'My lady, I promise you all will be well, trust me.' Then he turned to Carlos. 'I shall see you at Mass on Sunday.'

No sooner had Juan left than Carlos swore, 'Damn, I'll have to wait outside the church, I can't go to Mass, I haven't confessed.'

Having put their lives in jeopardy, Isabel felt that such an omission was singularly immaterial, 'Then you must confess,' she replied her voice flat and weary.

'What if I cannot trust my confessor?'

She was exhausted, her head was aching, she was suffering palpitations her heart fluttering wildly; all she wanted to do was weep. 'Confessors never divulge the secrets of the confessional.'

'That would be alright then, because I have to confess to him that I intend to kill someone.'

How much longer, Isabel wondered, must she listen to crackbrained obsessions? 'Who are you going to kill this time?' She asked in despair.

'The person we hate the most, the person who is cruel and hurtful to you. I am going to kill my father.'

'You must confess,' she muttered holding her hands to her ears; she couldn't bear to listen to any more. She was completely out of her depth and didn't know what to do or say. After a moment or two she looked at him and quietly begged, 'Do it, Carlos, just do it for me, and do it soon.'

'Do what for you, Isabel, kill the king or confess? I could do both I suppose.'

Tears fell uncontrollably down her cheeks, 'Carlos, please leave, I am very tired.'

1568

38

The Escorial had been bitterly cold, the ride through the January winds and snow even colder, and Philip back in his apartments eagerly sought the warmth of the fire to comfort his painful hands and feet.

Pérez knocked and entered carrying a large package, 'The courier brought this shortly before your return. I thought it best to have it in my safekeeping since it comes from the doctors of law in Barcelona. I knew you had arrived earlier and came looking for you but you didn't come to your apartments.'

'Correct, I had urgent business to attend to first. Leave that on the table I will deal with it later. It is of no great import.'

Pérez raised his eyebrows, surprised; the package had been delivered by Philip's elite team of express riders, those entrusted with the most secret despatches.

'Would it be best for me to lock it away in the chest until tomorrow?' Pérez sought the necessary key from among the bunch that hung at his side, keys that informed the world of his position as private secretary.

'That will not be necessary. I may even decide to look at it later once I have melted the ice from my bones. You may go Pérez, but I want you in my office very early tomorrow morning. I have in mind a number of letters and I will need your help with the diplomatic wording of some of them.'

'As you wish, my lord; I shall say goodnight, then.'

Philip could barely wait until Pérez was gone before picking up the all-important communication.

The seal snapped open under his impatient thumb. At last he had the information from Barcelona after anxiously waiting for weeks.

He held it close to the candle to read the title *The case of the Prince Viana*. He already knew in essence the sequence of events of the case which took place about a hundred years ago, but it was good to see it all set down. For the present it would be locked away. As and when necessary he would have it translated from Catalan into Castilian.

231

It was now time to seek God's advice, guidance and understanding. He carried the important document to his bedchamber, to the chest near the altar.

On his knees before the crucifix and the triptych, both at one time belonging to his beloved mother, he began outlining his proposed actions. He wanted God to know that whatever he did would be done for the safety of the realm and out of his obligation as a dutiful son of the Church.

He rose from his prayers his heart lightened in the certainty that he now had God's support in what was to be, as he called it, *a momentous affair.*

A servant, patiently waiting for the king to leave his bedchamber, stepped forward. 'Your majesty, His Excellency Don Juan seeks an audience. He says that he realises the lateness of the hour but must speak with you as a matter of some urgency.'

'Of course, good; send him to me. I shall be in my office.'

Looking from the doorway into the office the room appeared to be dominated by the expansive desk with its never diminishing mountain of papers. It was destined to remain this way; how could he delegate any of the administration to others when he could trust no one?

Juan joined him and bowed. They took a few steps then stood in awkward silence.

Philip was first to speak, 'I wondered how long it would take before you came to tell me. I think you should close the door before answering.'

Juan closed the door then paused, his hand lingering on the handle. 'Your majesty I find this very difficult, but I have no choice.' He threw himself into a prepared speech, 'I am your most loyal and devoted subject. I hold you and my country too dear not to speak. I have a great affection for my nephew Carlos, and do not wish to cause him any hurt, and I am utterly convinced that he is completely unaware of the seriousness of his proposed actions. However there is only yourself who can prevent him from trying to carry them through. I am ashamed to be betraying Carlos like this.'

'Out with it Juan; he has sought your help. He wants you to arrange his passage across the Mediterranean.'

'Sire, it is the adventurous mind of a child, nothing more. But you knew?'

'There are very few things I don't know. For example, I also know about the readiness of the horses and the posting stations. I have also been informed of my son's intention to kill me.'

'Dear God, I swear I knew nothing of this, believe me.'

'So tell me what it is that you do know.' Perhaps he had misunderstood Ana and Juan hadn't been with Isabel and Carlos, after all, when Carlos had spoken of it. Could it be that Juan didn't know that Isabel had encouraged Carlos? He must ask Ana once more to clarify what had transpired that night.

'Carlos told me of the post horses, and he requested a ship and the required travel papers. But these are all part of ill-considered, childish whims. I hoped to discourage him by delaying the date of his departure. I made excuses about the travel permit, explained the difficulties of finding ships' provisions at this time of year, emphasised the risks of sea travel in winter months. But I have only succeeded in angering him, making him more determined than ever. And then today he sent for me; I didn't go, I cannot go; what is there that I could possibly tell him? I sent him a note saying I was ill.'

Philip's laughter interrupted him, 'You too? I sent for Carlos but he wrote a note saying he is too ill to leave his bed and that it would be unwise for me to visit since his illness might be infectious. We certainly seem to have a minor epidemic of falsehoods in the palace. So what is to be done?'

'I beg you to stop him before he makes himself look a fool; that is why I am here.'

'He is a traitor, not a fool.'

'With respect I believe he does not see it that way, I am sure that treachery was never intended. He is obsessed with the desires and frustrations of an immature boy.'

'I appreciate the difficulty my son has placed you in, but rest assured I see no blame attached to you. In actual fact because you have come to me so promptly my confidence in you has grown considerably. Would that the queen had shown the same allegiance; instead she has chosen to say nothing.'

'My lady loves the prince dearly, as a mother loves her son, and wishes to protect him from a world which is often beyond his comprehension.'

With dismissive contempt Philip shrugged his shoulders and pursed his lips. He picked up a quill and began idly playing with the vane, first separating then endeavouring to rejoin the barbs.

233

Juan insisted, 'My lord there cannot be any who would doubt the queen. All she has ever done is to continue her ceaseless efforts to understand Carlos when everyone else has given him up as a lost cause.'

There was no response whatsoever from Philip.

Juan was furious, 'Which of her ladies has stooped to falsehoods, for I know them to be nothing more. Oh, how I would dearly like to take Carlos by the shoulders and shake him until he could be made to understand all the trouble he is causing the sweetest lady in the land.'

Philip still wasn't listening, was still engrossed with the quill.

'My lord, this whole business is outrageous!'

Philip threw the quill onto the piles of papers. 'If you will assist me with my armour,' he pointed to his breastplate and helmet on a table in the shadows, noticing as he did so that his hand was shaking.

'Armour, my lord?'

'A precaution,' he answered, taking deep breaths to control his fears, hoping to still his turbulent bowels, as Juan fastened the buckles at the side of the breastplate. He reached for the helmet, 'It pays to be prudent. We shall now proceed to the anteroom to join the others.'

Gómez, Feria, and Quijada, all members of the prince's household, were waiting. They had been waiting for some time. Now they rose to greet the king. All were armed. With a swift shake of his head Quijada warned Juan to say nothing.

39

It was almost midnight and the stone stairs and dark corridors usually silent at this late hour now rang with the footfalls of several men, the sound heightened by the stillness of the sleeping palace.

It was the strangest of torch lit processions headed by Feria along with the king and his fellow gentlemen of the prince's household. They were followed by eight of the king's bodyguard. Bringing up the rear were several workmen some with leather aprons bulging with hammers and nails, others with lengths of wood.

Juan walked a few paces behind but when he saw them turn to follow a corridor to the right he stopped, not wanting to believe. He was overcome with misgivings about his part in the drama that was unfolding and his eyes filled with tears of guilt and remorse.

The group halted by the doorway guarded by two servants.

'You know what to do Feria. Gentlemen, your swords.'

With his sword Feria motioned the servants to stand aside. The doors were then flung wide. Three men were playing cards at a small table.

Philip allowed himself the briefest of glances at one of them, the one he considered to be an insane cripple, his son, before stepping to one side to allow Gómez to pass.

'Holy Mary, Mother of God,' Prince Carlos's two companions begged, dropping to their knees.

'Take them out and hold them,' Philip ordered.

They began pleading for their lives. 'Mercy, my lord, mercy; what have we done? We don't deserve to die, let us go, and we'll never be seen again in Madrid. We'll do anything you want, just let us go free.'

Two soldiers hauled them up onto their feet dragging them past Juan the silent witness. Once in the corridor they were pushed roughly up against the wall and held there with halberds.

Gómez's sword point was inches from Carlos's breast. Carlos began shrieking in his thin and high-pitched voice, 'Has your majesty come to take me to prison or to kill me?'

Philip stepped forward. 'You are under arrest. It is for your own good.'

'Why? What? I don't understand!' Carlos was terrified, he was shaking, sweating, retching.

'There is just cause to suspect treason. The case against you is being prepared.'

'As God is my witness I haven't, I wouldn't. All I wanted was a life of my own, and you wouldn't allow it,' he spluttered his panic. 'You can't imprison me. Let me kill myself instead to save you the shame.'

'That would be madness.'

'You think I'm mad anyway. Let me end it all. I would be free at last from your cruelty. You are the worst father in the world!' he screamed through tears.

Gómez pushed Carlos into his chair his sword point now at his throat.

Philip's words could have been those of a stranger, 'I am not your father, I am your king. You have lost all rights to consider me your father. As your king I have begun legal proceedings to determine whether you are guilty of treason.' Those were not the sentiments he had expressed in his letter to the Pope; what had he said? *I am a father first and foremost, and the honour, reputation and good of my son touch me directly. Unfortunately he is not competent for the duties required by God and my realms and so, with all the pain your holiness can imagine, I have had to make certain changes with regard to his person.*

Carlos twisted and turned, eyes searching everywhere, hoping to find a knife. Instead he watched the removal of all his weapons. Quijada and Feria had been ordered to conduct a thorough search.

The room was a veritable arsenal: swords, daggers, pistols, arquebuses were mounted on walls, tucked behind curtains, in chests; bullets and gunpowder were under cushions and pillows.

Gómez called to Feria, 'Take the fire irons, too, they are weapons. Try to explain the presence of so many weapons to his majesty.'

Carlos sobbed, 'I have them because I knew that one day you would come for me and I wanted to protect myself.' He appealed to Quijada, 'Tell them, speak for me, help me against all these people who hate me, tell them I wouldn't ...' He made as if to stand but the sword's point pressed hard against his jerkin.

Quijada stepped towards him. He wanted no part of this, he would rather console the lad, offer him counsel, even if it was to no avail. There were too many wrongs on both sides, and he could see no happy end to it all.

'Leave him,' ordered Philip.

A sigh escaped Quijada as he forced himself reluctantly back to his duties. The sooner it was over the better.

Feria held two books, 'I found these, my lord.'

'Those are private! They are none of your business,' Carlos squealed.

Philip took them and read one or two pages of the first. It was written in a childlike, unformed hand. *Journeys of His Majesty. King Philip thinks he is such a wonder at travelling: April; Madrid to Aranjuez, Aranjuez to Madrid. May; Madrid to Segovia, Segovia to Madrid.* It was a catalogue of sneering comments and comparisons with Philip's father, the emperor, who had travelled through most of Europe and North Africa.

Philip tossed it onto the table then opened the second one. 'Now this is interesting, *My Friends and Enemies*. Ah, Quijada, I see you are included amongst the friends along with Isabel, Juana, and Juan. It says here that you are of the few who have shown kindness. Sadly, Gómez, you and your good lady wife are both enemies as are Alba and myself, and I read that we are to be pursued to the death. It is plain to see how we all stand; and quite a condemning piece of evidence of planned regicide.'

Carlos whimpered his dismay; 'That was my only way to retaliate against the hurtful things anyone does against me. You bastards have all the power, I have none. Who can I complain to? Only my book.'

Philip ignored him. 'As from now you will not be allowed out of this room. Gómez will be in charge, arranging supervision and meals.'

'You may as well kill me now, that swine and his wife will see to it that I'm poisoned.'

'Feria you will see that the prince's food is cut up and ready to eat with either fingers or a spoon.'

Carlos shut his eyes tight as they began to carry away his clothes and jewellery; all those precious belongings which if anyone in the past had even dared touch would have stirred such violence within him.

Philip called across to Quijada who was supervising the removal of a small casket brimming with *ducados*, 'The horses will be transferred to Juan's stables.'

237

Relief spread across Carlos's face and he giggled nervously, 'I see it all now; this is just spite, farcical spite to scare me. All of you dressed in armour, the stupid talk of treason, then taking my things away, it is all to frighten me. Well, you have succeeded, you have terrified me. Now it's time to stop the silly game.'

'We are finished here. The workmen may begin.'

Bars were fixed across a window, others were boarded up. Doors were nailed shut.

Carlos screamed into the noise of banging and sawing, 'Don't do this! You know I can't bear small spaces. I need room to move, to breathe. You mustn't do this, I beg you not to!'

Philip turned for one last look at Carlos, that twenty-three year old creature warped in body and mind, then turned on his heel and walked out of the room.

Carlos threw himself onto the floor, begging.

'As from now, I want a twenty-four hour guard on this room,' Philip ordered.

40

Philip was standing by the fire in his office dictating to Pérez. His whole system was in turmoil; his bowels were tied in knots, a massive migraine was beginning to blind him, then there was the gout in his fingers and toes. He held his painful hands towards the warmth gazing at the swollen knuckles.

'Where was I?'

'*He had to be set apart*, my lord.'

'Just so ... *set apart, not as a punishment, but to avoid inevitable problems.* Get that written before you do anything else; Alba must be informed as soon as possible.'

He limped over to his desk to sit down. Several letters were awaiting his final approval. Pérez had done well adopting the right tone with each one. The letter to Aragón stated ... *Because of his disorderly conduct and despite my fatherly love and pity I have had to have him restricted to apartments in the interior part of the palace. I can give no further details at present.*

The next was to his aunt in Portugal, he quickly scanned its contents ... *as a monarch you will understand that one is sometimes called upon to sacrifice one's own blood ... I cannot say more, it would upset us both.*

The letter to his brother-in-law, the emperor, was read next, Philip nodding his approval; Maximilian will be sympathetic. ... *it was to save the dignity and honour of the prince; if we had come to Vienna you would have seen for yourself my difficulties. What had to be done was done without anger; nor have I sought his punishment. I am greatly pained.*

He had also written to his sister, the empress. ... *I would like to explain how I intend to change my son's conduct but it would take too long.*

'Precisely!'

'You spoke my lord?' Pérez looked up from his writing.

'Nothing in particular. These are quite perfect and are ready to send.' They were signed, dated then sanded. 'You are a very clever man. I made a wise choice when I made you my private secretary.' He thought not only was the man intelligent but he was also cunning; Alba had some justification in being suspicious. 'Make sure that all the accompanying letters to the ambassadors have a footnote insisting they discourage any suggestion of the monarchs or the Pope sending emissaries to discover more.'

There was another letter that he had written that Pérez had not seen; that Pérez would never see. It lay in the small locked ivory casket amongst the remaining sheaves of paper. Philip looked at the piles of documents still awaiting his attention; if only he could make himself hand some of them to Pérez to deal with and somehow resist interfering. There was no doubting that Pérez was an excellent secretary; his diplomacy, acumen, intellect, judgement could not be faulted. The penmanship of Pérez was perfect, unlike his own barely legible scrawl; and yet he insisted on every letter or document, no matter how trivial, being amended lest there be any hint of innuendo hidden amongst the words. Pérez could then rewrite them, unless after further scrutiny something else was discovered not quite to his liking.

He studied Pérez as he worked. It was true, he was like a peacock; handsome and proud in his expensive and elegant clothes and jewels. And Alba also said money passed through his fingers like water. Nor could the question of a growing relationship between Pérez and Ana be readily dismissed from his mind.

Quite simply, Philip did not trust Pérez.

There was a knock at the open door and he jumped, snatched from his thoughts. He was annoyed; Isabel, Juana, and Juan had no business to be here. He was also offended by the two ladies appearing all red eyed, handkerchiefs to noses, and Juan had dared to dress entirely in black.

He ushered them into the adjoining room.

'My lord,' Isabel made a hurried curtsey. 'Juan told me that when he went to the prince's apartments this morning there were guards posted at his door and they would not allow him to see Carlos. Not wanting to believe him I returned there with him. I, too, was denied access. I sent for Juana and we have come as one to discover what is happening and to seek your permission to visit Carlos.'

Philip had sat down. Not a muscle moved in his face, he stared straight ahead stroking his short, greying beard, running his fingers over his dry and cracked lips.

Juana took up Isabel's plea, then Juan.

An interminable silence followed before Philip took his hand from his face. 'There will be no visitors, ever.'

240

'Brother, what can he have done to deserve this? I know he has many problems, but there must be other ways to help him rather than lock him up. I am more than willing to do whatever I can, and if I were his wife I could be of even greater assistance.'

'Too late; he has gone too far this time. You would agree with me Juan?'

Juan was silent; mortified to be reminded of the role he had played.

'Do tell the ladies.'

'Juana you will not know that Carlos asked me to have a vessel prepared and ready to take him to Italy. We all know that he couldn't possibly undertake such a journey but, all the same, I felt duty bound to inform the king. There was too much at stake.'

'And you were right to do so,' Isabel was eager to show her support. 'Philip it was no more than another of his impossible dreams.'

'You knew of it?' Philip had no need to ask, Ana had reported every word.

'Yes, and Juan and I did try to discourage him. Given time and understanding he will see reason, he always does.'

Juana was not interested in the whys and wherefores of his incarceration; the fact remained that Carlos was imprisoned and she wanted to see him, wanted him freed. 'Philip, I practically raised Carlos, was virtually a mother to him; it would be too cruel of you not to allow me to be with him in his hour of need. You cannot leave him without family. I worry about his reactions to being confined; I know he will be terrified.'

The request was ignored but she continued, 'His problems could be resolved if I were to spend some time with him, somewhere far from Madrid, perhaps, and then ...'

'You haven't understood. He will *never* be released.'

'Never? You cannot mean it; poor Carlos.'

Both ladies wept; pleading, appealing to the generosity of Philip's heart. But it was all in vain.

Juana dispensed with her useless tears, was resolved to be strong. 'Imprisoning the heir to the throne is a bold step to take. The world will be an unforgiving judge.'

Philip was unmoved, 'That has been dealt with. I might also add that the situation is not unprecedented. Many years ago the king of Aragón imposed the same punishment on his son, the prince of Viana, when his treachery was discovered. I have all the case details.'

Isabel cried out in horror, 'My lord, it is unimaginable that you could believe Carlos is a traitor because of his stupid plans!'

'Madam, be quiet!' he hissed at her. He took time to calm himself before resuming, 'Dry your eyes and listen to me carefully. A man who threatens to kill the king should be what, imprisoned or beheaded?' His raised eyebrows invited an answer.

'Dear God, who told you such a thing?' Isabel was dismayed but not surprised at what she knew to be Ana's betrayal.

'You were party to the conspiracy.'

Isabel clutched at Juana's hand, she felt faint. 'My lord, there was no conspiracy. I suspect it was Ana told you the lie. We all know Carlos says ridiculous things at times. That particular evening I was unwell and too tired to humour him by seeking his supposed reasons for such thoughts. Instead I said he should tell his confessor. In fact I begged him to for my sake if not his own; to tell his confessor. As God is my witness that is the truth.'

'Ah, the truth; everyone speaks the truth. Have you noticed how we are all awash with the truth, drowning in it?'

Juana returned to her arguments, 'You run the risk of angering the people. That happened in the Viana case. The people of Aragón turned against the king. There are many malcontents who would find this an ideal opportunity to create unrest.'

'I think not, this will be kept out of the public domain and, unlike the king of Aragón, I will play no part in the enquiry. I have set up a commission to study the evidence. When the people are eventually informed, they will see that I am unbiased.' Those chosen to conduct the enquiry were no friends of Carlos; the chairman was none other than Gómez. Philip knew they would find the prince guilty.

Isabel, not knowing anything of the Viana case searched for something to say, something to keep the discussion alive, 'Will he at least be allowed his doctors?'

'This is becoming tiresome. These are my final words; I will have no more questions, no more tears. You may not visit, nor will you be permitted to write or try to communicate with him in any way.'

'For pity's sake, my lord husband, do not do this.'

'Return to your apartments. You and Juana will find other topics for discussion. There will be no further meddling. Juan you will send home for a change of clothing, I will not have you travelling the city streets dressed like that.'

Philip was determined that Juan should not draw attention to himself in order to invite questions, lending an opportunity to advertise his sympathy for Carlos and possibly rallying the people to his side. 'From now on I will not have the prince mentioned or referred to by name or title nor will he be mentioned in any prayers. Those are my orders. Isabel, one more thing before you go, you are to tell the French ambassador not to meddle. Any news sent to the French court will go via my Spanish ambassador in Paris. You can also use the opportunity to show your unwavering support for your husband. Here are pens and paper.'

Isabel was deeply hurt by his undisguised accusations and she began to cry fresh tears. Juana wept too, not wanting to believe that she had just heard her brother speak so cruelly of Isabel's disloyalty. Juan wanted to throw his arms about Isabel to comfort her, to protect her from such a vicious and unwarranted injustice.

Between painful sobs Isabel wrote her letter. *Monsieur, although I would like to talk to you about the misfortunes of the prince I find I cannot because my lord the king suffers such great sadness for what God has asked him to do. I assure you that I feel the prince's misfortune as if he was my own child and I will do whatever I can to help him. This is all I can say until such time as my lord the king directs otherwise. The king has also ordered that no couriers either on foot or on horseback shall carry any information to the French court, be it by letter or word of mouth. As for me, you can imagine how I feel. I cannot find the words to describe my feelings so I shall finish here.*

She put down the pen and joined Juana and Juan. Philip followed them out before returning to the fire and its welcoming warmth. Suddenly he felt old, tired and ill; every bit of his forty-one years. At least he had the comfort of knowing that should he die suddenly the findings of the commission, which would soon be in his hands, would prevent Carlos from inheriting. Spain and the Faith would be safe. He thanked God for bringing about a swift conclusion to this whole business, *this momentous affair*; Carlos was safely removed, everyone had been informed and the treason enquiry in process.

A log shot explosive sparks up the chimney, stirring his thoughts to the letter in his casket, and he wondered how long it would be before he was obliged to send it to Vienna.

41

In one of the several rooms forming the apartments once belonging to Prince Carlos and now occupied by the Prince and Princess of Eboli, Ruy Gómez and Ana, were sitting by a cheery fire. They had drawn their chairs close to the hearth, March continuing to cling to the harsh winter weather. Ruy sipped on his wine reading a letter while Ana busied herself with embroidery.

Their quiet was broken when the door was thrust open and Philip rushed in. They hurried towards him; even in the soft and gentle candlelight he looked unwell.

'You are ill, sire?' Gómez offered him his chair.

'Some wine, perhaps?' Ana's voice reminded Philip briefly of the past when they had enjoyed their wine together in more intimate circumstances, but that was the past.

'That would be most acceptable.' He whispered to Gómez, 'It is nothing; I have had another shock; quite infuriating really. This has gone on for weeks now, it has reached the point where each time I hear crowds outside the palace I imagine the worst; revolts, unruly crowds storming their way in here to rescue Carlos. Tonight it happened again. You know how these things start, indefinable noises of disquiet, and then raised voices; tonight it ended with the sound of breaking glass. I was caught off-guard.'

'Have no fear; my security arrangements are too good to allow access to any intruder.'

Philip might allow Gómez to share some of his thoughts but he would not permit him to accuse him of being afraid. 'Nothing to do with fear; it is simply that I do not want extra demands on my precious time of having to deal with unruly and ignorant people.'

He wondered if Juana had been right in warning him of unrest; but no, he countered, there was no need to justify his actions and everyone would soon see that by arresting his son he had adopted the only possible course. More than likely the commotion was no more than the result of a rapidly growing Madrid, the streets seething with ne'er-do-wells, the cutpurses and cutthroats, attracted from the now less lucrative cities. Yes that was a far more logical reason.

'Your majesty; the people know nothing, at most only scraps of hearsay, and in any case they will soon focus their attention on some other gossip.'

'I would hope so. For at least two months the grandees have been pestering me to provide them with doctor's evidence to prove that Carlos would be unfit to rule. Delegates, from God knows how many cities, are badgering me for information. Now Aragón has sent a deputation demanding a written statement. Demanding a statement! And because I have refused they have dared to suggest that because Carlos was never sworn in as heir if necessary they would determine for themselves who should inherit the crown of Aragón. I avoid the public rooms as much as possible so as not to be pestered by ambassadors and emissaries. Now I dare not leave the palace fearing some madcap tries to assassinate me. I ask you, who is the prisoner, the prince or the king?'

Ana handed them their wine, returned to her chair and picked up her sewing.

Gómez pursed his lips, 'These last few months have been difficult for quite a few. I have to tell you that the lords chosen to guard the prince, having initially sworn to obey without question, have become disgruntled with their duties. I can appreciate their dissatisfaction. They are required to spend eight hours at a time at the prince's side in a small room with only two other companions and with very little to do. The hours between midnight and eight o'clock in the morning are the worst. They question why lords instead of guards are being used as gaolers. However, I have told them there will be substantial rewards resulting from this delicate undertaking. That appears to have cheered them.'

Philip gazed into his wine. He was only too aware that the situation couldn't continue.

Gómez was pensive too, musing on his dread that Carlos might outlive Philip. It didn't take an intelligent man to see that if Carlos became king, not only would there be no future for him in a new government, like as not there would be little or no future for him at all. His fingers traced along the lace collar at his throat where the evil garrotte could one day be tightened.

'You must tell his majesty about the prince's confessor,' Ana had stopped her sewing to smile at her husband.

'Ah, yes, this will gladden your heart. I persuaded him to write the prince a letter of stern rebuke. It reinforces all your arguments and puts paid to any criticisms mouthed by would-be supporters of Carlos.'

Philip took the folded paper and eagerly read its contents. Thankfully there were no references to the prince's so-called great virtues, nothing about his behaviour being just the result of childish obstinacy gone uncorrected, nor was there any reference to mere youthful folly, and all the other reasons put forward by those who had high hopes for Carlos as king and for themselves as his beneficiaries.

The words he did read were as music to his ears. The priest accused Carlos of contemplating such serious crimes that were he not a prince his life would be at stake. He asserted that with such an iniquitous record he could never be considered a worthy candidate to be God's representative in Spain. He concluded by pointing out that Carlos had made no attempt at contrition, another grave character defect.

'This is good. If this were to be shown to the people they would be left in no doubt as to how deeply concerned I am with his behaviour.'

'And there is this, my lord,' Gómez tapped the top of a sheaf of papers carefully tied with red ribbon and sealed with the State Seal, 'our completed report.'

This would be the best solution by far. Philip had set up a commission of three men: Gómez, the Cardinal Espinosa, and the lawyer Briviesca as judicial expert. Their mandate had been to provide the proof supporting the accusations levelled against Carlos. It was unfortunate that this way of denying the prince's rights ran counter to the laws of Castile and would take some defending, but there was little doubt that with good lawyers it could be done. In the meantime that sheaf of papers with its seal detailed the investigations and conclusions. Carlos had been tried without calling him or any other witness; and he had been judged.

Philip sipped slowly on his wine, 'Your findings?'

'Prince Carlos is guilty of treason on two counts: first, seeking the death of the king; second, usurping the monarch's sovereignty in the Netherlands. The punishment is death. As his father you will naturally wish to mitigate the penalty.'

The wine glass was set down. Philip stroked his beard then rested his chin on his swollen knuckles. 'My conscience as king would never allow a reduced sentence on personal grounds.

However painful for me I must allow the law to take its proper course. But,' he hesitated, watching Ana once more plying her needle with its green thread, seeking the precise spot to pierce the silk, the fine trail of green gradually disappearing only to reappear a moment later and drawn taught, 'but, Carlos may yet be saved that humiliation. There is the possibility that he might die.'

Philip had taken the words out of Gómez's mouth. 'Every possibility, my lord. In fact I have told the prince's doctor to remain in the palace this evening in case you would want to speak to him. He can give you some up-to-date information on the prince's health and also has information for you regarding the treatment of fevers.

'Have him called.'

Gómez went to the door to have a servant seek out the doctor.

Ana put down her sewing. 'While we are waiting I simply must tell you about the nun Teresa of Avila.'

Gómez, on his way back, interrupted her, 'Sire, you must understand that there are two words unknown to Ana's vocabulary: shame and embarrassment.'

'What nonsense,' she chided. 'Be that as it may I want to tell you about her diary. No interruptions Ruy or I shall get everything mixed up.'

Philip sat forward, his elbows on the chair arms, 'The mysterious Carmelite whom I have yet to meet.' He swallowed hard, Ana knew of her diary, and by now possibly knew of his dark secrets.

'I asked if I might be allowed to read her diary; she carries it everywhere with her to write down her mystical experiences. She refused, but I got Ruy to persuade her. I think she was afraid my husband would withdraw his offer of buildings in Pastrana for her small communities of monks and nuns.'

Gómez insisted, 'I assure you, my lord, I never put any such pressure on the nun.'

Ana was cross at yet another interruption. 'I promised never to reveal its contents to anyone so she gave me a few pages.'

'I believe you are about to do just that.'

'You are not the first, my lord, her promise was quickly broken.'

'Hush now, both of you. It was all about raptures. One was about her soul being struck by some word of God, inflaming its interior, setting it on fire, renewing it and pardoning her sins.

Another said that when God concluded his betrothal to her he so enraptured her soul that she was left unconscious. Then there were the visions: Jesus speaking to her from the crucifix in the chapel and always on her right hand side, the devil throwing her up against the wall for not following his orders because she had recognised him for what he was. But I have saved the best till last; she is no longer Teresa of Avila, but Teresa of Jesus! Apparently she was coming down some stairs and there at the bottom was a young boy, the Christ child. She asked him who he was and he said he was Teresa's Jesus. Then he asked her who she was so she replied she was Teresa of Jesus!' Ana clapped her hands in delight at her story.

Ruy Gómez was beginning to feel uncomfortable.

Philip was intrigued. There was surely enough evidence here to have the nun brought before the Inquisition. There were a disturbing number of weird heretical sects these days and they had to be stamped out. Her imprisonment would also rid him of any possible future irritation.

'Teresa discovered Ana reading the diaries to the servants and she was most upset, demanding their return.'

'I made amends by giving her a special gift. A small statue of the Virgin had been discovered in my family's castle many years ago, in a crypt or cellar. They called it The Virgin of the Underground. Apparently it had been put there to protect it from the Moors during the Conquest. Teresa was most grateful. So what do you think about my story?'

'I think you never change, Ana.'

There was a knock at the door and a somewhat stooped and grey-bearded gentleman in black doctor's robe and hat hobbled towards them, a stout stick helping his progress.

'So, doctor, the wounds on the prince's forehead,' Philip had barely given the old man time to get into the room, 'have they healed?'

'Only a few scars remain, my lord. It is some days since he realised the futility of banging his head against the iron grill at the window. Instead he has now resorted to a sullen silence. Ah, but time must weigh heavy on him, he does little else than play cards; he still refuses to read the books you sent.' The doctor paused allowing himself a little smile. 'The prince has successfully passed the diamond ring he had swallowed.'

'Diamond ring?'

'He had heard that a diamond in the stomach would lead to death by poisoning; but it has been safely retrieved.

'And the fevers?'

'Sadly there is no improvement; indeed they are becoming worse, more severe and more frequent. I have to report that his health is very poor. He grows weaker, has lost a lot of weight; but then he is refusing to eat. I am concerned.'

Philip was indifferent, 'He will eat when he is hungry. A glutton cannot resist food for long. But you came to discuss specific remedies for the fevers.'

The doctor dared not look directly at the king. This was a very delicate area, extreme caution was required. He addressed Gómez, with whom he had already discussed his suggestions in depth.

'There is nothing better for reducing fevers than buckets of snow water poured over the flagstones and for the patient to walk over them barefoot for hours. At night a warming pan filled with ice and placed in the bed beside the patient as he sleeps is also highly recommended. These may sound severe at this time of year when it is still so cold but I can assure you that they have been proven most effective.'

The doctor expected a reaction, a comment, but there was none. Gómez nodded for the doctor to continue.

'Now I come to my purges whose composition is known only to me and will always remain so. These are to be mixed into his meals. I have been told that these are prepared here so it will be an easy matter for me to add the required dosage. There will be a marked change in the prince within days; that is a certainty.'

An awkward silence greeted his words.

'My lord would you care to know more?'

Philip had been twisting and sliding some rings on his swollen fingers. 'I think I may safely leave everything in your expert hands. You may proceed. Goodnight.'

The doctor bowed and hobbled out leaving the three sitting in a silence of complete satisfaction.

Philip got up from his chair stretching his legs that had grown stiff as he sat. 'Before I leave I shall take a brief look at the room.'

He and Gómez walked in a pool of candlelight through an unfurnished room at the far side of which they stopped before a locked and bolted door.

Gómez whispered, 'It is here where the priest comes to say Mass and listen to the prince's confession. It is better that we watch from here than have the guards open the other door.' He raised the candle close to a smaller bolt set in the centre. Philip drew it back and opened the cover to a small latticed viewing window. It looked directly into the prince's chamber.

He peered into the little room, dreary and airless, filled with the odours of all manner of unpleasant things. Carlos lay on his truckle bed tossing and turning in fitful sleep. At a small deal table one man dozed, his head cushioned on folded arms, while another two kept vigil. They turned towards the door the moment they heard the rasping of the bolt and raised a hand in salutation.

There was little else in the room save a few breviaries and a candle or two.

42

May was the perfect month for enjoying the formal gardens of the palace; the warmth of the sun was just right, there was such a splendour of colours and the air was sweet with the perfumes of the flowers.

Amongst those taking advantage of the midmorning air were Magdalena Ruiz and Montagne.

'Such difficult times, Doña Magdalena.'

'I grant you, Monsieur Montagne.'

'I'd go so far as to say disturbing.'

'I did not come for a walk in the gardens to be made miserable; and speaking of misery you cannot be of much value to her majesty if that is your permanent countenance you are now wearing. Cheer up my man. You must have had some good days at Aranjuez, far away from Madrid's politics.'

They turned from the terrace to pass along one of the paths through the gardens Philip had designed in the Flanders' style.

'True; the return of my lady's merry laughter was like a song to my heart, and she looked so much stronger too. But then came Princess Juana's accident and we had to return to Madrid, to my lady's churchlike apartments. If they weren't dreary enough already King Philip had to send along that abominable relic.'

'You French will never understand, will you? Naturally he would send the arm of Saint Vincent. The significance is obvious, well perhaps not to you. Juana broke her arm, hence the arm of Saint Vincent noted for mending or repairing divisions.'

'Not that I have much time for Spanish doctors but I would have thought even they would be capable of mending broken bones without having to resort to saints.'

'Saint Vincent did even more than that; he healed the great schism in the church, at the time when there was a French Pope and an Italian Pope. Your ignorance, my friend, appals me.'

'Whatever the reason for having it there it looks disgusting.'

'Princess Juana should consider herself fortunate in being offered just the one relic. King Philip has rooms full of bones and the like, something for every occasion: fingers, legs, hearts, skulls; a veritable anatomical warehouse.'

'And does he have something to cure Carlos? Perhaps he might have an urn of humours, hot or cold, whichever might be required.'

Magdalena laughed, 'You do have a light side after all. But I don't think curing is on the agenda, it is rather a case of being confined.'

'So what have you heard? It's a queer thing but no one even mentions his name these days. At one time Carlos was on everyone's lips.'

'It is difficult to come by information these days; too many locked doors to contend with. Now I don't want to start putting ideas into your head, but I have managed to get some information. Quijada has gone home to his saintly wife.'

'But, Magdalena, he was ...'

'He was too close, too sympathetic to Carlos; at least that's the way I see it. Same thing with Feria I should imagine, otherwise why should he be dismissed as well? He has been a loyal servant to his majesty for goodness knows how many years.'

'If you cannot answer it then I certainly cannot. Do you suppose the king made the decision himself or, in the absence of Alba, *King Gómez* has wheedled his way back into power? That might just be the very answer. I wonder if Feria will stay in Madrid. I know that his wife, Doña Jane Dormer is never happy here. I do hope they may remain a while longer, my lady queen has great trust in her.'

'You are right in thinking Gómez has returned to his position of king's favourite now that there is no Alba constantly demanding Philip's ear.'

'I find it difficult to fathom the man. I have to admit that my heart sees him as a fair-minded man while my head says he is a power seeker, although it would be a rare sort of creature that wasn't.'

'Gómez is in complete charge of the prince's imprisonment, therefore I think one could assume he was the one responsible for the removal of Quijada and Feria; unless of course it is *La Eboli* who holds the real true power.'

'She is certainly making her presence felt everywhere she goes in the palace. She unashamedly flirts with the gentlemen and gives the ladies the sharp edge of her tongue as if she were a queen and not a Jezebel.'

Magdalena tapped her forehead then pulled Montagne close, 'I almost forgot, I do have something to cheer you, I do have some gossip after all. There is a certain rumour being passed around regarding *Eboli La Tuerta* or *My Lady Cinnamon, The Spicy One*. But first let me tell you of the jokes some of the ladies are having at her expense, no doubt because secretly they are jealous. They make mock of her eye patches, whispering behind their hands, saying that on cold days she wears one made from flannel cleaning rags and on hot days something lighter, more airy, something to keep the mosquitoes at bay; a piece of silk serge cut from Pérez's cloak.'

'Foolish women; how childish! Tell me the gossip.'

'You are too impatient,' she looked about her lowering her voice to a whisper, 'I have heard it on good authority that she has neither lost an eye as the result of an accident nor does she have a squint. The eye is as marbled as a blind dog; and all due to syphilis! So that says farewell to all romantic theories.'

'Syphilis; good Lord; who gave her that?'

'Her father; he's been a lecher all his life. The infection only started showing itself when she was twelve or so. I can understand why Gómez has little time for his father-in-law. Such a gift to have given a daughter; a syphilitic eye!'

'If you're not careful you will have me feeling sympathetic towards the lady. Imagine the effect it will have on her when she discovers it is common knowledge; it's all too cruel.'

'Have no fear, it will be a closely guarded secret known only to a few.'

Montagne began picking flowers, 'These should cheer my Lady Isabel. She is not well these days; from what I hear it is not going to be an easy pregnancy this time. And then she is continually tormented by the plight of Prince Carlos. She needs more diversion than we can offer, although we do our best.'

Magdalena helped him in his quest for the best blooms to make a small posy, 'I think you worry too much. I say don't go looking for trouble, let it come to find you.'

'As usual you are right.' Suddenly he burst into laughter. 'I will share a delicious image with you. Close your eyes; now, first you see Pérez, reeking of perfumes like a Parisian whore, wafting his handkerchief to spread the scents all around as he bows and scrapes to *La Eboli*, the only one he finds more beautiful than himself. To him she is the pearl, the most exquisite of all the jewels in Philip's court and who, unknown to him, just happens to be his stepmother. *La Eboli* inclines her

254

head. She smiles, disguising her contempt for Pérez, a little upstart, but one who would do anything for her because of her wealth and beauty. Until now he has been unaware that she is actually a flawed gem. The patch falls off revealing the eye, the famous eye, all marbled and blind. And our Pérez, never at a loss for words, whispers a new endearment in her ear, *my Opal-Eyed One.*'

'That's more like you, Montagne. Now that you are restored to joy shall we savour the sights and sounds of the garden for a little while longer?'

43

Isabel held the posy close to her nose, breathing in its delicate perfumes as she watched Montagne and the twenty-one months old Clara dancing. Princess Juana accompanied the performance on the clavichord playing with her one good hand.

Montagne held Clara's hands as she perched on his feet. He moved one step gently this way then one step that, almost in time to the music, trying to prevent his little partner from losing her balance. But she did slip off, giggling and laughing, for surely that was the point of it all, then she climbed aboard once more.

After that game had palled Montagne took the little princess's false sleeves. She was his pony and when he tugged on her "reins" and clicked his tongue she would gallop about the room, stopping here and there to drink at some pretend pool.

'Have we galloped far enough today?'

'No, no,' replied a little voice full of determination.

'I think I shall be the first to tire of this game,' whispered Montagne as he passed Isabel for the sixth time. 'Shall we have a game with a ball?' he pleaded.

Isabel came to his rescue. 'Of course, a game with a ball; let us have a game with a ball. You deserve a rest Montagne, you and Clara have entertained us magnificently.' She whispered, 'And I did so enjoy your gossip.'

Juana sought out a ball from a basket of toys. 'Clara here is a big blue ball to play with.'

The game of galloping ponies ceased to exist and she ran to take the ball from her aunt. She gave Juana's arm a serious look before running back to Isabel all ready for this new game.

'Throw it to Mama.' Isabel reached out to catch the feather-stuffed ball if and when Clara decided to let go of it and if by remarkable chance it should come in her direction. 'Throw it, dearest,' she coaxed.

The ball was eventually launched, freeing itself from tiny hands, disentangling itself from a ballooning pinafore to land on the floor not far from the thrower's feet. She ran to pick it up only to succeed in kicking it further away at every attempt. Mother and child laughed helplessly as they and the ball chased

256

the full length of the room. Isabel had to stop to catch her breath, Clara continued in pursuit until she and the ball found themselves lost in a forest of table and chair legs.

The French Ambassador came to join in the entertainment leaving the dark eyed, dark haired baby Micaela in the crib to occupy herself with her ivory rattles.

'My lady you have such beautiful children. I have written many times to my queen about her grandchildren; the one so dark and the other so fair and both like angels. I know it is expected of an ambassador to give praise even when not deserved, but these princesses are so charming they leave me almost speechless.'

Isabel sat down glowing with pride at the compliments, and also somewhat flushed with the exertion of the ball game. Her breathing was coming in short gasps but she shrugged away any assistance.

'It will pass.'

She had felt unwell since her return from Aranjuez a week or so ago. It had been good to be away from all the problems of Madrid. Days of riding and country walks with Juana had made her feel so much stronger. Now she was plagued with breathlessness, with migraines, with pains of every sort. However, in a few days time it would be June, her favourite month. She promised herself she would make every effort to take advantage of its perfect weather.

Juan entered to find the ambassador still singing praises, his arms, two monstrous flapping wings, emphasising each superlative.

Juana emerged from behind a curtain with Clara in tow clutching the retrieved ball.

'Juana; your arm, your face, what has happened?' Juan was shocked by what he saw.

'Before I tell you that, I want to tell you of another accident I had. I will have you know that I also nearly drowned.'

Isabel chuckled, 'You couldn't possibly drown in six inches of water; how you exaggerate! Juan, you know the small leisure park well. We had walked through the glade until we reached that stream, the one with the little waterfall. On the other side there were some spring flowers growing in the clearing where we picnic in summer. I thought how lovely it would be to gather some to make chaplets for our hair. I proposed we use that little bridge rather than risk the stepping stones, perhaps in the event not the best of decisions. I reached the other side but Juana did not, she slipped and ended up sitting in shallow but very cold water. That is my story, now it is your turn Juana.'

'Juan, you know what Isabel is like, always persuading me to do things against my better judgement; and, I might add, that plank of wood barely warrants the name bridge.'

'Poor Juana, I should think that at this time of year it will be as treacherous as stepping stones.'

'Exactly; the moss and lichens were too slippery for me, one moment I was walking towards the island, the next I was trying unsuccessfully to keep my balance on slippery stones in freezing water. The rest you know. If only you had been there to help. It's a wonder I didn't come down with a chill the length of time it took Isabel and her ladies to get me back to dry land. Then I had to walk all the way back to the carriage in cold, wet petticoats leaving a wet trail behind me. Remarkably I had suffered no damage whatsoever, not even a scratch; as for the arm and my bruised face, they are the result of my riding side saddle and trying to use a bow and arrow at the same time.'

Juan held her gently by the shoulders inspecting her injuries. 'I cannot believe you still persist with that sport. I thought you had seen sense and given it up long ago. In any case you have had a very poor teacher. Falling off your horse is becoming too much of a habit. I want you to promise never to attempt this again, it is far too dangerous.'

'That would be silly. Everything is on the mend, with no complications, but I do miss playing with Clara.'

Juan picked up Clara holding her high above his head then bringing her down that he might plant two noisy kisses on her little plump cheeks.

'More,' she insisted; and two, three, four more she was given.

He choked back a pang of longing for another little girl, his own little one, baby Ana, the child he had been forbidden to see.

The ball escaped and Clara struggled free to go in search of it; off she ran with two ladies-in-waiting close behind.

Juan knelt before Isabel to kiss her hand. She looked unwell, was too thin, with eyes sunk into dark hollows. He would be away for several months and he was concerned.

'My lady I have come to say farewell. I am off to the naval base at Cartagena to meet my staff, arrange the appointment of others, and to inspect the new ship the king is having built for me. A part of me wishes I could stay to be of comfort to you during these difficult days.'

'And we will all miss you, but this is the opportunity you have been waiting for.'

Juana looked at her tall, handsome half-brother; at his face with its fair skin; at the sparkling and intelligent blue eyes. 'You look every inch a military man and at last you are able to follow in the footsteps of our father. I expect you to show the same qualities of leadership. Listen to me, goodness I sound like an old lady!'

'You will become very famous, Juan. We shall be here waiting for news of you that we might celebrate your victories in style.'

'Dearest Isabel,' he laughed, 'it is only administration that I go to face, not flashing swords and thundering cannon on the high seas.'

'Oh, but if you do hear or see anything exciting you must let us know, your letters will be most important to us. But tell us what you have heard about Carlos.'

'I have heard nothing. The court is as silent as a tomb; fingers pressed to lips at the very mention of his name. No one dare ask the king who continues to go about his duties as if nothing unusual has taken place.'

The ambassador added, 'One would think Prince Carlos had never existed.'

Juana ignored the impertinence of the man; it was too embarrassing to even contemplate the contents of his florid epistles to France, which everyone was certain he was smuggling out of Spain. She spoke instead to Juan, 'You must have visited him to say your goodbyes.'

'No, it was absolutely forbidden. Only Gómez and his chosen few are allowed anywhere near.'

'At least,' continued the ambassador, 'these charming little princesses will benefit. Out of the bad always come the good.'

'Ambassador!' Isabel was shocked. 'Two people that I love most dearly are suffering terrible pain and sorrow. My heart aches for what my husband has had to do; what God has demanded of him. And I feel such anguish for Carlos. He has always been my friend and shown me great love and affection and saved me from many a lonely day. I repeat it is God who has determined upon this course of action, and I regret it beyond words. I hope when you write to France you will convey these sentiments and nothing more.'

Somewhat abashed the ambassador replied, 'I do, my lady, I do. And I insist that, contrary to gossip, the prince is not in prison but in spacious apartments.'

'Well I am truly amazed!' Juana was furious with the man, 'To think that you could know more than us. Where did you get such information?'

'From his majesty; he addressed a meeting of ambassadors, emissaries, delegates, grandees. He said he would speak this one time and never again. He informed us that Prince Carlos would never succeed him because it would mean ruin for Spain and its people. He said that the prince would spend the rest of his life in comfortable apartments but under supervision that he might not attempt to flee to Italy. Those were his very words and the moment the prepared speech was concluded he turned and left the hall.'

Isabel was visibly shaken, 'The rest of his life? That is impossible, it cannot be true. There is some mistake. You must have misunderstood.' She pressed her fingers to her temples to quell the gathering pains. 'I hope and pray for Philip and Carlos to be reconciled. Carlos cannot be kept from us his friends and family. It is unthinkable.'

Juana looked at Isabel, she didn't know what she feared most, nose bleeds or fainting, but was convinced that one or the other was about to happen. One of the ladies attending Micaela was sent to fetch a doctor. This time they would meet the emergency well prepared.

'My ladies, I must take my leave of you. Juana you will take good care of my lady queen. I shall miss you both; and you too Clara. See, I have brought you a little farewell gift.' He whispered towards Isabel, 'She may be disappointed that it is not another ball to chase.'

'A baby, new baby,' Clara unwrapped her present and proudly waved a doll at her mama and aunt before running with it to the crib to show it to her sleeping sister, 'Look, a new baby girl.'

Isabel silently prayed that this was not an omen.

Juana accompanied her soldier brother to the door. 'Do not worry about Isabel, she has never had an easy pregnancy and yet observe the wonderful results. This dreadful business with Carlos is of no help, of course, but I know she will be alright.'

Juan had to have one more look at the beautiful Isabel for whom he had such love and compassion. 'Juana, she looks ill, in body and in spirit; and yes I am worried. What has happened to that lively young lady that we all fell in love with?

'Juan, you must stop right there. Our brother, the king, who demands nothing but the best of medical attention for her will see that she comes to no harm.'

44

Gentlemen's voices announced the approach of Philip and the doctors. Her heart thumped and bumped all rhythm lost. What was she afraid of, if indeed it was fear that was the cause of the pandemonium in her chest? She dabbed at the fine prickly beads gathering on her forehead and about her lips then concentrated on mastering her breathing.

Clara ran to Philip proudly thrusting her new doll into Papa's hands. He gathered her up to kiss and cuddle her as only her beloved Papa knew how.

'Sit Papa, sit; a horse ride for Clara and her baby.'

'A short ride is all we have time for today.' Philip sat down and straddled Clara across his knees her doll in front of her and off she went galloping, up and down, accompanied by Papa's horse noises.

'See me, Mama,' Clara called laughing and giggling as she bounced.

Watching him Isabel was angry with herself for entertaining any doubts whatsoever about her husband and his ability to love. This was yet another scene to be stored in her heart against those coming days when she would be hurt again by his cold words and unfeeling demands on her.

'Prepare Clara for a walk in the gardens. Wait with her in the gallery. I shall be there directly,' he ruffled his daughter's golden curls setting her down. 'Papa will take you to find spring flowers, and Papa will tell you all about them.'

'A letter first.'

He could refuse Clara nothing; she was his delight. He followed her to the table, hurriedly scribbled *my dearest Clara* then held her up to sprinkle the fine silver sand over Papa's letter, over lots of other papers and much of the table.

'Isabel, I can tell you now that one day this young lady will become my secretary; and more than likely she will be better than all the rest.'

Isabel smiled her pleasure. 'It is so good to see you again so soon, and I do so enjoy watching you with Clara. But why are the doctors here?'

Juana rested her hand on Isabel's shoulder, 'I sent for them. You held your forehead and temples so often, I was concerned.'

Philip set Clara down then stared at Isabel in disbelief. 'I understood you to be well after your visit to Aranjuez.'

She felt the full force of his criticism. 'I did too. But I think I know the reasons for my returned illness, and I seek your understanding and forbearance. You see, I worry so about Carlos, about how distressed he must be.'

Philip searched her eyes for signs of guile and cunning; was she seeking to use her pretended illness to procure his freedom?

'I have told you put him out of your thoughts.'

'I cannot. How can I when I have known and loved him for eight years? I cannot dismiss him, and I find I am mourning him as though he were dead. He must be missing us all, must be so lonely and miserable on his own. And he isn't very robust. If only you would tell me something to make me rest more content.' She pressed Juana's hand, hoping.

'We will speak of it now, and that will be the end of it. Carlos is well. He has had a series of fevers but he is now quite recovered. I moved him to spacious and comfortable apartments in the south tower, so there will be plenty of sunlight to cheer his days.'

'Apartments; so he has a suite of rooms?'

'Of course; and why should he not?' The lies would come easily because they were in a good cause. He needed Isabel well again to provide him with a son, so he set about painting a picture of beautifully decorated salons and bedchamber. They bore no relation to that one squalid and stinking room in the tower where Carlos was confined, with the smallest of windows guarded by a grille. Nor did he mention the grille across the fireplace should Carlos consider making his escape up the chimney.

'But he must miss the fresh air, his riding?'

'Strangely enough he doesn't. He has taken up studying at last. Yes, Carlos has discovered the joys of knowledge.' The fact was that not one of his breviaries or books of devotion had been opened, and that was the only reading material Philip had permitted.

Juana was more than a little sceptical, that was not the Carlos she knew. 'And does he have companions? Juan said that he thought not, that only those chosen by Gómez were allowed near, and I know how little affection Carlos has for him.'

263

'Juan should refrain from discussing things he knows nothing about; I am afraid he has fallen into the trap of repeating false information. Carlos does have companions, including his favourite attendant.'

It was a far cry from the truth, Carlos and his young friend had been brusquely pulled apart as they hugged and sobbed their farewells. Carlos did have people near, three of them at a time, twenty-four hours a day, all required to speak in loud voices that every word could be heard from the other side of the door. How Juan had come by his information was disturbing but Juan, conveniently, would soon be on his way to Cartagena.

Juana was delighted to hear about the prince's favourite, 'I know that attendant. Carlos gets on so well with him. That makes me feel much happier knowing he is there.'

To Philip it was of no consequence whether she knew the attendant or not, since he along with the rest had been dismissed, all replaced by enemies, people who Carlos felt had to be *pursued to the death*.

There was nothing more to be said, an insipient headache and grumbling bowels would not permit it. 'Is my lady wife now contented?'

'One last question, my lord, does he have his own doctors?'

'Why should you ask, is it your obsession with Spanish doctors? Let me assure you he has only the very best of doctors. I chose them personally.'

'I thank you for being so patient with me, my lord.' Isabel exchanged smiles with Juana sharing the belief that although it was still a very sorry state of affairs it was good to know that the wellbeing of Carlos was paramount in Philip's thinking.

'Now, dear lady, tell me of any other reason for your illness?' Hopefully this could be despatched with the same speed and relative ease.

'My pregnancy.'

He shook his head, how he would have rejoiced had the news been true. 'Your doctors say that sadly you are not with child.'

'Philip, if you were to ask the midwives, they would confirm that I am.'

He smiled a patient smile. 'The midwives have been dismissed, my dear, the doctors found them to be no better than ignorant fishwives.'

Isabel knew that to be absurd. Had it not been for the midwives she would not have survived the birth of Micaela.

'Then if they do not believe the midwives perhaps they would do me the honour of believing me. It is my body, and I tell them I know when I am with child. After all, this is my fourth pregnancy!' She wiped away icy beads of perspiration forming about her mouth.

'My lady,' the voice of a doctor oozed condescension, 'you must leave these things to those who possess the knowledge.' The same voice directed an appeal in Philip's direction. 'The queen was most reluctant to take the necessary medicines for her headaches, the palpitations of the heart, the pains in the kidneys. We had to insist. And now she is refusing every powder and every elixir we suggest. Naturally, if her majesty had been with child we would have chosen other remedies. My lady,' the doctor took one of her hands to demonstrate his scholarship, 'when we tested the pulses in your fingers, that was to give us the information on the state of every area of your body so that we would know for certain our course of action to restore your health. We also know from these pulses that you are not with child.'

He was about to give her hand a patronising pat but she hurriedly withdrew it.

Isabel paused for her racing heart to calm before trying once more. 'But if I am with child my mother says those potions would be harmful to us both.'

The doctor shook his head, 'If I may make so bold as to suggest that your mother is not a doctor. Dear lady, it saddens me to think that you doubt our wisdom.'

Philip took her hands in his. 'Isabel you must be like me, and have every confidence in these gentlemen. See how quickly Juana's arm is improving.'

She was ill, she knew it, and she would far rather accept her illness than endanger the life of her unborn child with suspect medicines. Could her mother be mistaken, after all, and the doctors did know what they were doing? She doubted it, but would write to her again.

'I will do as you advise, my lord.' She added a weak plea, 'But I beg you to insist they do not bleed me.'

'This is quite ridiculous, my lord,' one of the doctors hissed his exasperation.

45

Philip sat by the open window peering into the dusk, all that was left of a fast fading summer's day. The room behind him, thrown into premature darkness, was gradually being given a new life with the glow from the fire and increasing pools of light from candles as they were lit. The servants had dared questioning looks when ordered to lay and light the fire; it was none of their business, some things were necessary.

A wine jug and goblets were placed on a table. Wine was poured and offered to Philip from a second jug, which was then replaced on the hearth. Everything was now ready and the servants left the room as noiselessly as they had performed their tasks leaving him alone with his thoughts.

'Perhaps mulled wine will be just the thing,' he said to the goblet before taking a sip, savouring the spiced drink, 'and God knows I need something to settle the ceaseless battle in my guts.' But their disorder would soon be a thing of the past; the moment he was convinced that everything had been done that ought to have been done.

Gómez was struck by a wall of heat the moment he set foot inside the room, 'A fire in July my lord?'

'Later, later, help yourself to some wine and sit down over here by the window.'

Gómez slowly poured himself a drink. He was feeling a luxuriant pleasure on several counts: that an enemy and potential author of his ruin was safely disposed of; that he was once again Philip's confidant and close friend; that fortune had indeed smiled on him when Alba had been sent abroad. The music of the wine tumbling into the goblet suited his mood to perfection, a merry song of all being well with the world.

'Your good health, your majesty.'

The toast was acknowledged. 'And to a matter now concluded to everyone's satisfaction; an excellent solution.'

'He is far better in Heaven, sire, and we praise God for taking him to Himself.'

'Amen to that. Tell me how my beloved son died.'

'As you are aware it took longer than I ever supposed. It was frustrating at first; the results of snow water and ice in the bed were quite the opposite of our expectations. The prince positively thrived on walking barefoot over cold wet flags wearing only a light silk robe, and to sleeping next to ice on cold nights. Incredibly instead of his illness worsening the fevers disappeared completely. Then the medicinal soups turned out to be useless so far as any of our plans were concerned; and I must admit that the doctor's daily visits to our kitchen were becoming quite irksome. It wasn't until I suggested he use his extra strong purge that we saw the change we hoped for.'

'One of the doctor's secret compositions, I assume; but why an extra strong purge?'

'Because the prince had gorged himself on pies and pasties upsetting a system already weakened by his fasting.'

'You encouraged him to overeat?'

'My lord, who were we to set ourselves up to deny the prince a favourite indulgence? So, radical measures had to be taken.'

'Logical.'

'It worked within the hour with violent vomiting followed later by uncontrollable diarrhoea.'

Philip clutched his goblet tight to his belly, 'No details.' He sipped the warm drink to control his own insides which were threatening a revolt.

'With your permission I would like to offer some additional compensation to the lords who were guarding the prince at that time.'

'Indeed, it must have been quite an assault on their finer senses.'

Gómez nodded. 'To conclude, from that point on it was quite straightforward. The prince knew he was dying and called for his confessor. He also asked for you to visit. He wanted to see you before he died.' He watched and waited to witness Philip's reaction. There was none.

Philip was picturing the servant who had brought the message standing weeping unashamedly at his office door. He also remembered the man's sorrow turning to dismay hearing the reply, 'Impossible.'

'He cried when you didn't come,' Gómez continued.

'Everyone knows that a Father of the Church is far more important to a departing soul than one of mere flesh and blood.'

'God alone knows how he managed to stay alive until the Eve of Santiago but he had set that as his target and was determined. For someone so weak and debilitated he showed such fortitude. The day arrived and he knew it was time. He begged your forgiveness, asked that you look after his dismissed servants wherever they are, and named various churches as the beneficiaries of any remaining money and jewels.'

Philip waved the requests aside. 'What did Carlos think of the Holy relic I sent to comfort him on his final journey?'

'He thanked you for your generosity. It is quite beautiful, impossible almost to think that it is a part of the true cross. You are a fortunate man to possess such an important relic. The setting of diamonds and pearls is quite perfect.'

'Quite; and the coffin, did you personally attend to its sealing?'

'Yes my lord, once the body was well covered with lime. The doctor was somewhat excessive with the amount used and I had to explain away the unusual weight to the pall bearers as being due to the presence of many of the prince's personal effects that he had asked to have placed beside his body.'

'Ah, Gómez, you think of everything, from beginning to end. I thank God I have had you by my side to rely on. Bring me that,' he pointed to a folded square of linen on his desk.

Inside the cloth was the sheaf of papers tied with a red ribbon and bearing the State Seal, the findings of *The Case Against Prince Carlos* presented by Gómez and his Commission some months ago.

'You will help with these.'

'Now I see the reason for the fire, far better than a candle.'

The sheets were carefully dropped, one by one, into the flames that singed and curled their edges before obliterating the words of evidence of supposed treason, leaving nothing more than shrivelled blackened tissue floating and dancing in the hearth.

'So Gómez, there is very little else to attend to. Secretary Pérez has almost completed the letters informing the royal houses and the Pope. I have ordered nine days of Masses for the repose of the prince's soul. I will retire to the Monastery of St. Jerome for a few weeks; that should demonstrate to the world the suffering of a devoted father devastated by the loss of his son.'

He knew Gómez would view this as nothing more than a move to keep himself as far away as possible from a suspicious public. He walked over to him to grasp his arms and to kiss each cheek, 'I appreciate your loyalty. What will you do now?'

268

'I wish to spend some days in Pastrana; my affairs there have been neglected these last few months.'

'Ana will go with you?'

'She is to follow shortly. Pérez will escort her.'

'I may pass that way myself following my retreat.'

'You would be a most welcome guest. If that is all I would like to make a start with my arrangements; I shall tell Pérez to make preparations too. He is with Ana at the moment. He has been a good friend to her, bringing comfort and diversion during difficult times. Goodnight, my lord.'

Pérez and Ana; he was stung again by those damnable pangs of jealousy. It was aggravating and he must seek a solution; perhaps not at this moment, but soon.

On the desk lay an unfinished letter to Alba. When it was done he would retire to his bedchamber. Tonight, mercifully, sleep would not be such a stranger. He read what he had written so far then took up the pen. *You may appreciate the pain I have suffered since God decided to take away my dear son. I am certain God will help me endure this tragedy with patience and fortitude. I, the King.*

He sat back, stroking his beard convincing himself he had taken the only possible course. It had become demonstrably clear of late that a good proportion of the country were loyal to their Prince Carlos and the type of government he allegedly espoused and promised. Had he lived there would have been civil war. He thanked God for His guidance in saving Spain. He took a final sip of wine.

The next item on the agenda was Isabel. All that was necessary was enlisting God's help once again, this time regarding the poor health of his wife.

269

46

It was cold in the chapel. Philip could feel it creeping into every bone, warning him not to tarry. He was on his way to Isabel's apartments to take a much deserved break from the incessant paperwork. If only Pérez could be entrusted with the more trivial details. If only Pérez could be trusted! Something must be done about him and soon. And yet, he needed him; the man was clever, he could build bridges across rivers of doubt, could guide him safely into appropriate action.

The chapel had beckoned him to enter, to kneel down and bare his soul before God. He prayed aloud, giving thanks for preserving the life of his unborn son. Isabel had taken the death of Carlos very badly and there had been grave fears of a miscarriage. She had insisted all along that she was pregnant; she had been right and no one had believed her until recently.

As he prayed he examined his swollen, red, and painful fingers, probably God's punishment for his marrying a French heretic. He begged forgiveness for his haste to marry Isabel, pleading the importance at the time of a peace treaty between the two countries and the unsuitability of Carlos as a husband. It was important that God understood that it was his responsibility as the king of Spain to *bed a part of France*.

And what had been the result of the marriage? Yet more punishment; two girls, two useless girls! He knew that was completely unfair, for any man would be proud to be their father.

He laughed at the image of his darling Clara when she had been served with her first solid meal two months ago. She had regarded it with bewilderment. Her ladies had tried placing tiny morsels of meat in her mouth while making encouraging noises only to be confronted with stubborn tight lips in a little red face turning violently this way and that. How she had screamed her dismay on discovering that because she was two years old she was now considered to be a big girl and had to eat big girl's food from dishes and that feeding from the breast was no longer allowed. It had taken two days of hunger before the obstinate little miss finally capitulated.

Micaela; dear Micaela was almost too beautiful to be real; those enormous dark brown eyes, unfortunately not Hapsburg blue, were capable of melting stone.

But Clara and Micaela were not boys; and he must have boys. Spain needed an heir.

He completed his prayers for his wife and his unborn son with an earnestness which would not deceive God, for his true feelings had already moved on to another theme. He was by now convinced that there was little likelihood of Isabel giving him a son. No, it was to the Austrian Hapsburgs he would have to look for male heirs to the Spanish throne. His sister, the empress, had given birth to at least seven boys and two girls so far, and they were all healthy.

He pushed himself up from the prie-dieu and waited until he was able to move his stiff and aching knees. In a moment of self-pity mixed with not a small portion of anger he bemoaned the fact that he seemed to have spent his whole life waiting; forever disappointed and frustrated. He was losing patience.

CR   SO

Juana had demanded huge bowls of potpourri, had raided Isabel's shelves of perfume, and insisted on fresh flowers from the garden. She was determined that the bedchamber would not smell like a sickroom.

Isabel sat in a well-cushioned chair watching the ladies following Juana's instructions trying to ignore the aches and shooting pains in every part of her body. Her fingers gently soothing her temples brushed across the bloodletting scars reminding her of yet another lost battle.

She was waiting for the doctors to return from their meeting called to form a consensus of further ill-formed opinions. She might be waiting, but this time she would be ready for them, she had had enough of their ignorant ways and was about to tell them so.

Juana called, 'What do you think of my efforts? If I cannot get you out of doors, we shall have the garden brought in here with all its colours and scents.'

'You are so thoughtful.' Her gaze wandered from table to table each with silver bowls of flowers and crystal bowls of petals. The splashes of colour did their best to cheer the room

271

and her spirits. 'I think you and I will never go to the gardens again.'

'What nonsense; have patience and you will see how once the child is born and my arm fully mended everything will be as it was before. I am already planning some jolly excursions.'

'Those days are gone forever.'

Carlos was dead, Juan had left, and she was either ill or with child. But how precious those former days had been: evening picnics in the gardens, early morning rides in hay carts, walking barefoot in the dew, and so many more, all ringing with laughter. And how wonderfully they had filled the emptiness of hours, of days, when Philip didn't need her to accompany him.

'No, those times will never be repeated.' Isabel closed her eyes, resigned, 'What little enjoyment in life I had is over, is finished.'

'I refuse to hear you speak like this!'

'Look at me, tell me honestly, what do you see?'

'Stop this, Isabel, you will be well again!' Juana was joined in her protests by the French Ambassador, insisting all her problems were to do with her interesting condition.

At last the four doctors arrived and Juana rushed to them, pleading with them to tell Isabel that her illness would pass.

One of them opened his mouth as if to say something, but Isabel stood up, leaning heavily on her walking cane, 'I will speak before I have to listen to any stupidities issuing from your lips.' She looked at the ugly group of men in black; black crows come again to look for carrion, and she hated each and every one of them.

Her lips trembled and she had to fight hard not to weep. 'You are responsible for ruining my health.' Isabel took a shallow, faltering breath, 'I told my mother again of the medicines you were giving me, certain they were making me feel worse. I knew I was right.' She was forced to pause, 'The concoction you gave me for my fainting causes a bleeding from the womb, as does the one for the pains in my right side. I marvel that I am still carrying the child.' Her hand went protectively over her belly.

Struggling for breath and refusing to be distracted by a sudden searing pain in her leg she continued, 'You gave me drinks to make me vomit and to give me diarrhoea because you said they would cure my kidneys, strengthen my heart, and what else? Oh yes, they would rid me of my headaches. Every one of those drinks is harmful to an unborn child, and has done nothing but weaken me. I tell you I will have no more of it!'

Her mother had been her sole champion for no other existed. Montguyon was long dead and Alba was so far away, and her suggestion of help from other French doctors had been vehemently rejected by Philip.

Her confidence soared as she staggered towards them pointing angrily with her cane. 'How dared you ignore my midwives, how dared you ignore me when I said I was with child. You are the cause of my illness, not the cure!'

She and the cane tumbled forward, collapsing into the nearest doctor's arms.

'Juana,' Isabel cried out in terror, 'Juana, my leg, I can't feel my leg!'

The queen's ladies were ordered to put their mistress to bed as the men in black huddled together this time to discuss a new situation.

Juana instructed a servant to make haste to the king's apartments.

The men of medical science knitted their brows, tugged at beards, raised their hands in consternation at this troublesome patient. It had always been difficult determining the correct medication for Isabel; in the first place she was French and had set herself to respond best to French cures, anathema to Spanish educated minds. Secondly she was a Valois, and that family was notorious as a dynasty of consumptives. It was in their humours and it had been agreed there was little a Spanish doctor could do about that. Now they had reached the point where Isabel spewed back anything they gave her, and why? For no other reason than her determination to be downright obstinate, that was why. There was nothing else for them to do except to continue the bloodletting. The knife was the one remaining remedy.

'So, do we advise complete bed rest and bloodletting?' asked one.

'Or perhaps nothing; leaving it in God's hands,' was another suggestion.

The French Ambassador hearing this whispered in Juana's ear, 'If only they would.'

'Would what?'

'Leave everything in God's hands.'

Juana quietly raged, 'I have no doubt that our doctors and the prayers of all those who love her will be sufficient to bring

Isabel safely through this pregnancy. I would like to point out to you Monsieur that while my queen may criticise, a French ambassador may not.'

Philip had walked as quickly as his gout would allow and now stood by the bedside.

'Sire,' Isabel whispered, 'will you tell these charlatans to stay away from me. I suffer more now than I ever did before they started with their quackery.' She sobbed like a frightened child, pressing his hand to her cheek, 'And now my right leg is useless, it has gone numb.'

'Sh, sh, quiet now. I will talk to them.'

There were several moments of mutterings and mumblings before Philip returned to her side smiling. 'The doctors have promised they will do nothing you do not wish. They suggest you get as much rest as you can.'

Isabel thanked him through her sobs and tears, kissing his hands as though they were holy relics. Pains shooting across her back made her cry out and she bit hard on her lip.

'Philip, I am sorry I am leaving you without giving you a son. It would have made my death easier.'

'Hush; I will not listen to this. Put your mind to getting well.'

'It is too late for that.' Her words were losing themselves among sobs, 'I know you love our little girls and will care for them, but it breaks my heart to leave them, they are so young.'

'Isabel, that is enough, you will get well.'

Every part of her was hurting, 'Please honour the accords with my brother and keep our two nations at peace.'

'Isabel, why do you concern yourself with this nonsense? I will have no more of it. You will live, must live, for the sake of the son you carry.'

'I pray you enjoy a long life filled with health and happiness.' She gasped out the words in fragments, her body convulsing.

'Doctors, here; ladies you too, come here to comfort your mistress. Somebody do something to stop this damned shaking.'

Philip was frantic. He fled the room. He hated sickness, couldn't bear to be near it, it made him ill. What had the doctors told him? Was it: leave it to time, time will tell, a matter of time?

47

He sat in his bedchamber holding the small ivory casket for some moments before placing it on the table. Almost as a sacrament he slowly put the key in the lock.

What he was about to do was a crucial for him and for Spain. This had to be the right decision or all was lost.

The justifications presented themselves one by one: a God-fearing family with sound Spanish Catholic principles; a young woman noted for her piety, her quiet and sober disposition; her modest dress; her pastimes including nothing more adventurous than reading her devotional books and sewing. Apparently she made public any enthusiasms she might harbour via timid smiles and a gentle nodding of her head, nothing more outrageous than that.

The union of the two families would be important politically, Spain would strengthen the Austrian house with the addition of the Netherlands and Italy.

This marriage would ensure the purity of the family blood, Spanish Hapsburgs and Austrian Hapsburgs, what could be better?

It augured well that she was from a family numbering at present nine children. There could be no doubts regarding fertility with such parents, and with so many brothers she was bound to give him sons.

He ran his fingers over the casket, tracing the carved figures so busy about their seasonal tasks, tilting it this way and that the better to see the story of autumn: the harvests of corn, the wine making, the pruning of vines, the killing of the fattened pig; everything prepared, everything secure.

But first he must send his favourite relic, the fragment of the Holy Cross, to Isabel. Carlos had appreciated it in his dying hours. He kissed it and handed it to a servant with instructions to deliver it without delay.

The casket beckoned, yet still he toyed with the key, hesitating.

His father had recognised the importance of keeping marriages within the family; it was now time for him to follow his example. Should this first plan prove unsuccessful his daughters would marry Hapsburg cousins.

He turned the key. The box was opened. It was the moment to take out the one remaining document; it had lain there long enough. It required only a date and his signature. This done, it was refolded and sealed. Later he would hand it personally to his courier. His sister and her husband the emperor would be more than delighted to receive this request for Anne's hand in marriage.

Once he was married he could then apply himself to the question of Ana, Pérez, and Gómez. Then he would deal with Juan. There was a new rumour that he was now the proud father of a son.

He congratulated himself on his ability, at last, to organise the world to his liking.

It was also more than gratifying to know that he was at the start of something new, something positive and that this time he would be successful.

∞

'You will soon be well Ma'am,' whispered Jane, casting aside the haunting memories of Queen Mary Tudor and those terrible days before her death; remembering how in Brussels she had prayed that God would forgive Philip for his callous treatment of the English queen.

Her night's vigil was over and she could now retire to take some rest. King Philip, Princess Juana, and the French ambassador arrived as she left and as they passed there was only the briefest moment to drop a curtsey and renew her prayers.

Philip approached the bedside alone. The white face that looked up at him, those huge dark eyes set in deep brown hollows, upset him more than he expected.

'How are you this morning?'

'I have slept a little and that helps.' Isabel tried desperately to ignore the bitter taste of vomit that she was continually forcing down.'

'And the child rests easily in your womb?' It would surely be a miracle if it did after these last few days of interminable vomiting and diarrhoea.

Tears welled up in her eyes, her hands returned once more to her swollen belly, to the cramps that had been growing stronger and fiercer since early morning. And then it happened, a wave of something warm and wet flooded over her thighs, 'Dear God; I have tried so hard to keep my baby. Call the midwives.' What she had hoped would never happen was happening and her death would surely follow; there was much to be said. 'My lord; I seek your forgiveness for only giving you girls. May I beseech you to ensure all my ladies are cared for when I am gone, I know there are some seeking a dowry others preferring to return to France. Most of all I want Montagne to have a good pension. Everything is in my will ...'

'Now is not the time to discuss this.'

The doctors were first to arrive; those very men who had insisted that Isabel's womb was filled not with a child but with blood and treacherous humours; those same men who had spent days disputing which herbs were best for her stomach, her liver, her kidneys, arguing about the significance of the amount of blood and the size and quantity of the bladder stones in her urine.

Juana, as stern and immovable as any bodyguard, stood firm and wouldn't allow them anywhere near until the recently reappointed midwives examined Isabel.

This was a job that no midwife wished for, to assist at the birthing of an infant with but five months in its mother's womb and with no hope of survival.

Philip paced about the room torn by anxiety and anger; he was losing his son.

Isabel went into labour, her efforts and cries eating away at her remaining strength. Juana stood close by prepared to do anything, frustrated that there was in fact nothing for her to do but wait and pray.

Then a midwife closely followed by Philip bustled by her with a bloodied bundle whispering hurriedly, 'A priest?'

'He is here, waiting.' Juana replied, then turned to the ambassador lowering her voice, 'Perhaps without the child, Isabel will have a better chance.'

He shrugged, 'Who can tell? She has been ill for so long. She has been plagued with melancholy; recently with the death of the prince, but mostly because of the years of being nothing more than a jewel in Philip's court, to be worn on occasions when his majesty thought fit. Oh, I know there were excuses that she was often too ill to take on any major responsibilities, but,' he decided to throw caution to the wind, 'I know for a fact that Philip would never share any of his thoughts, plans, or cares for Spain, of which she is queen I might remind you. From the beginning she has been made to feel redundant, superfluous. And because of this there were some close to the king who thought she was denied any knowledge of Spain's affairs because her loyalty was suspect. I wonder if she ever heard the rumours I heard about her loyalty.'

'I warn you to take care what you say, ambassador.'

'I do not seek to offend, I simply present the facts; facts, which if you are honest with yourself, you will readily recognise. So, to answer your question, I think there is more to be remedied than a seriously afflicted body, and I fear it may be too late. His majesty has something to answer for in all this.'

The tiniest of beings now bathed and wrapped in swaddling bands was brought for Juana to carry to the priest for its baptism. She would not, could not, look down at what she held in her arms feeling its frailty, its ever weakening struggle to cling to life. She looked instead into the eyes of her brother, but he turned from her immediately muttering as he left, 'I am going to pray. Perhaps with some rest Isabel will regain her strength. Thank God it is only another girl.'

Isabel fell into an exhausted sleep as those about her watched and waited. After a little while she woke to see her ladies, Ana, and the Duquesa de Alba. She could ask them to help her with her bathing and dressing, but no, there was to be no more getting dressed.

But she had some important things to say.

'Ladies, I wish you better fortune in your future posts. Duquesa, I thank you for your constancy, and Ana I wish you peace and contentment.'

She smiled at the person who had done nothing to prove herself her friend; who, on the contrary, had often deliberately sought to be her enemy.

'Ambassador, are you there?'

The French ambassador came to kneel at her bedside.

'Ambassador; you can see that I will soon be leaving this miserable world to go somewhere far more enjoyable, where I hope to be closer to God, in Heavenly bliss that has no end. I pray you tell my mother to share in my joy in going to meet my Creator where I can be of better service than in this world. I ask my mother to maintain the peace between our two countries. I pray she accepts that I am happy to die.'

'With the grace of God, my lady, I am sure you will live for many years yet.'

'No, ambassador, even if I were to wish it, it cannot be, and I set a higher value on that which I believe in and hope for.'

'You must not think this way. There is still so much waiting for you in this world. We all need you: your husband, your children, your family, your friends, your ...'

'Whatever you say I can only reply that I know my parting will be very soon and I am happy to set aside the world and all that is in it. Tell my mother I shall be waiting for her in Heaven when God calls her. I am tired, farewell my friend.'

The ambassador pulled himself up from his knees and retired keeping stern control of his tears.

'Juana,' Isabel searched for her sister holding out her hand beckoning her to her side, a hand so thin, those once much admired slender fingers little more than skin-covered bones. 'Juana, look after my darling little girls.'

'Better than if they were my own.'

They kissed each other.

Isabel fell into her final sleep clasping her rosary and Philip's favourite holy relic, the piece of the Holy Cross in its diamond setting.

Her ladies dressed her in a Franciscan robe and placed her in a coffin with her little baby girl lying at her side. An aromatic powder of myrrh was sprinkled over the two then Juana brought a bowl of rose petals to scattered over them. In sorrowful procession *Isabel of Peace* was taken to the royal chapel.

It was nearing midnight but inside the chapel the light from a multitude of candles made it as bright as a summer's day.

In one corner two small figures huddled together.

'I never thought we would be saying our farewells here or so soon,' Montagne whispered to Magdalena Ruiz. 'I thank you for coming to keep vigil with me.'

'Aye it's a sad day for us all. Such a pity her highness being so young, no doubt but God has His reasons. So, despite all our good times you are choosing to go back to your Heretic Huguenots. Probably the best place for you, you Frenchies aren't truly Catholics, God knows I have tried to teach you.'

'There may yet be another to take my place. If I know Catalina, the queen regent, she will be sending a letter post-haste to Philip offering her youngest, the Princess Margot, as his next wife. She will undoubtedly bring her own dwarf.'

'Good God, man, and Isabel not cold in her coffin! Such callousness, although I suppose one must expect that from *the Serpent*. However,' she tapped the side of her long bony nose with her long bony finger, 'Philip has his eye on another.'

Montagne raised his eyes in mock horror, 'Good God, woman, and Isabel not cold in her coffin! Philip could never be considering ... but here he comes.'

Three men, King Philip, Ruy Gómez, and Don Juan, with heads bowed stood in silence in the entrance, between the door and the font. They had stepped into a theatre the scene illuminated by golden candlelight. The coffin of plain wood was in central stage before the altar. Complying with the customary importance of the mystical number twelve for these solemn occasions it was surrounded by twelve *Monteros*, the king's personal bodyguard; on either side were twelve page boys from Isabel's court; and twelve monks from the nearby monastery.

Slowly, silently, as if not wishing to disturb the golden buds of fire atop the tall votive candles, the three made their way forward to say their last farewells.

Philip gazed down on Isabel, the young wife of such promise, or so he had thought. He could honestly say he was devastated by her death, the latest calamity in an *annus horribilis*. He wanted the curtain drawn down on this final act. He had no male heir and time was running out; he felt every one of his forty-one years. A new era was beckoning; he prayed that if he promised to always wear black, to be in perpetual mourning, God would be more merciful and beneficent.

Gómez looked for only a moment. Isabel had been queen, yes, but in name only, beyond that to him she had been nothing more than a frivolous young girl with a weak constitution. She had added nothing to the power of Spain. Where were the male heirs necessary for Philip to uphold the nation's worldwide influence? He blamed Alba, he was the favourite at the time when Philip offered himself to bed a part of France; personally, he would have strongly advised against it. Fortunately the sorry affair was now at an end. All the same it was a tragedy that one so young and pretty should die.

It was then Juan's turn to approach that plain wooden box with its coarse linen lining. The sweetest, dearest, kindest, and most beautiful lady in the world lay at peace in her rough Franciscan robes. He would never again see those dark eyes sparkling with delight, nor would those rosebud lips broaden into a smile or open into merry laughter.

His eyes drifted down over the brown habit to the tiny bundle at her side. The dead baby girl was no bigger than the doll he had given Clara a few weeks ago.

He had to fight back the tears as he looked once more at his beloved queen, whose cheeks were a purer white than the finest Carrara marble. 'Dearest Isabel if I only had the gift of a poet I would use such perfectly chosen words to pen the best of verses for you. I would ask why death came like some villainous thief to rob us of your presence ... I would tell you that our one consolation is that you are in Heaven ... Lamenting why you, with the purest of souls the enemy of all evil, should be called away ... How blessed we are that your two little girls, fairer by far than any stars in the firmament, are proof of your enduring love ...'

Philip clasped his shoulder, 'That is enough, Juan, let us go. It is time to look to the future.'

Philip returned to his office to sit alone looking to the day he would take his niece, Anne of Austria, his fourth bride, to the altar.

He studied the miniature which had found its way from Carlos's belongings into his possession. The hair was so blond it was virtually white, the eyes so pale a blue they were almost indefinable, the skin so fair it could be alabaster. She looked as colourless as he understood her personality to be.

He would draw up a written agenda with a copy for her to keep. It would itemise the days of the week when he would visit her bedchamber. It would indicate the two most favourable times for siring a child, according to his medical books, which were late at night or very early in the morning.

She, with the same ease as her mother would provide him with more than enough male heirs.

Perfect!

Anne of Austria

Wives of Philip II

1543	1554	1560	1570
Maria Manuela (cousin)	Mary Tudor (aunt)	Isabel de Valois ___	Anne of Austria (niece)
I		I	I
Carlos		miscarriage Isabel Clara Catalina Micaela Miscarriage	Ferdinand Carlos stillborn Diego **PHILIP III** Maria

Selected Bibliography

Alvarez, Manuel Fernández
    Felipe II y Su Tiempo, Espasa Forum 2004

Kamen, Henry
    Philip of Spain, Yale U.P. 1997

Llamas, Antonio Martínez
    Isabel de Valois, Temas de hoy 1996

Marañon, Gregorio
    Antonio Pérez, Espasa Forum 1998

Nadal, Santiago
    Las Cuatro Mujeres de Felipe II, Ediciones Mercedes
    1944

Petrie, Sir Charles
    Philip II of Spain, Eyre & Spottiswoode 1964

Prescott, H.F.M.
    Spanish Tudor: The Life of Bloody Mary, Constable
    1940

Vaca de Osma, José Antonio
    Don Juan de Austria, Espasa 2004

Walsh, W.T.
    Philip II, Sheed and Ward 1938

Yeo, Margaret
    Don John of Austria, Sheed and Ward 1936

Also by
Linda Carlino

That Other Juana
Queen Juana I of Spain
(Juana la Loca)

*A story of obsessive love, uncontrolled passion
- and cruel, cynical betrayal.*

A Matter of Pride
Charles V, Holy Roman Emperor

*An historical novel that takes a humorous and rather
sceptical view of Charles V (Holy Roman Emperor)
the king, soldier and lover – a story of power, passion
and regrets.*

VeritasPublishing

For **information** about the publisher, future publishing plans, and how to purchase books:

www.VeritasPublishing.co.uk

The Author

For information about the author:

www.LindaCarlino.com

To contact the author, ask questions, or comment:

LindaCarlino@VeritasPublishing.co.uk
or
author@LindaCarlino.com

www.ingramcontent.com/pod-product-compliance
Lightning Source LLC
Chambersburg PA
CBHW051414170626
46809CB00006B/2155